The Books of FAERIE

Bronwyn Carlton
John Ney Rieber ~ *W r i t e r s*

Peter Gross ~ *A r t i s t*

Gloria Vasquez
Stuart Chaifetz ~ *C o l o r i s t s*

Richard Starkings
& Comicraft ~ *L e t t e r e r s*

T i t a n i a   c r e a t e d   b y

N e i l   G a i m a n

a n d

C h a r l e s   V e s s

Welcome...

This volume opens with THE BOOKS OF FAERIE, a story that presents for the first time the history of Titania, Queen of the Faeries -- an important character in the ongoing series THE BOOKS OF MAGIC.

The following story, "Long Walks in Dancing Shoes," was first published as ARCANA ANNUAL #1, and was the precursor to the ongoing BOOKS OF MAGIC series. It was conceived as part of a longer tale called "The Children's Crusade," which told the story of Free Country, the mystical realm that served as a haven for children throughout the ages. Because of the importance of this story to the BOOKS OF MAGIC series, the involvement of Tamlin the Falconer in both BOOKS OF MAGIC and THE BOOKS OF FAERIE, and in response to popular demand, the story is being reprinted here.

Taken together, the stories in this volume form a prehistory for THE BOOKS OF MAGIC ongoing series, and a pair of hopefully entertaining tales from the twin books of Magic and Faerie.

~Stuart Moore

Senior Editor

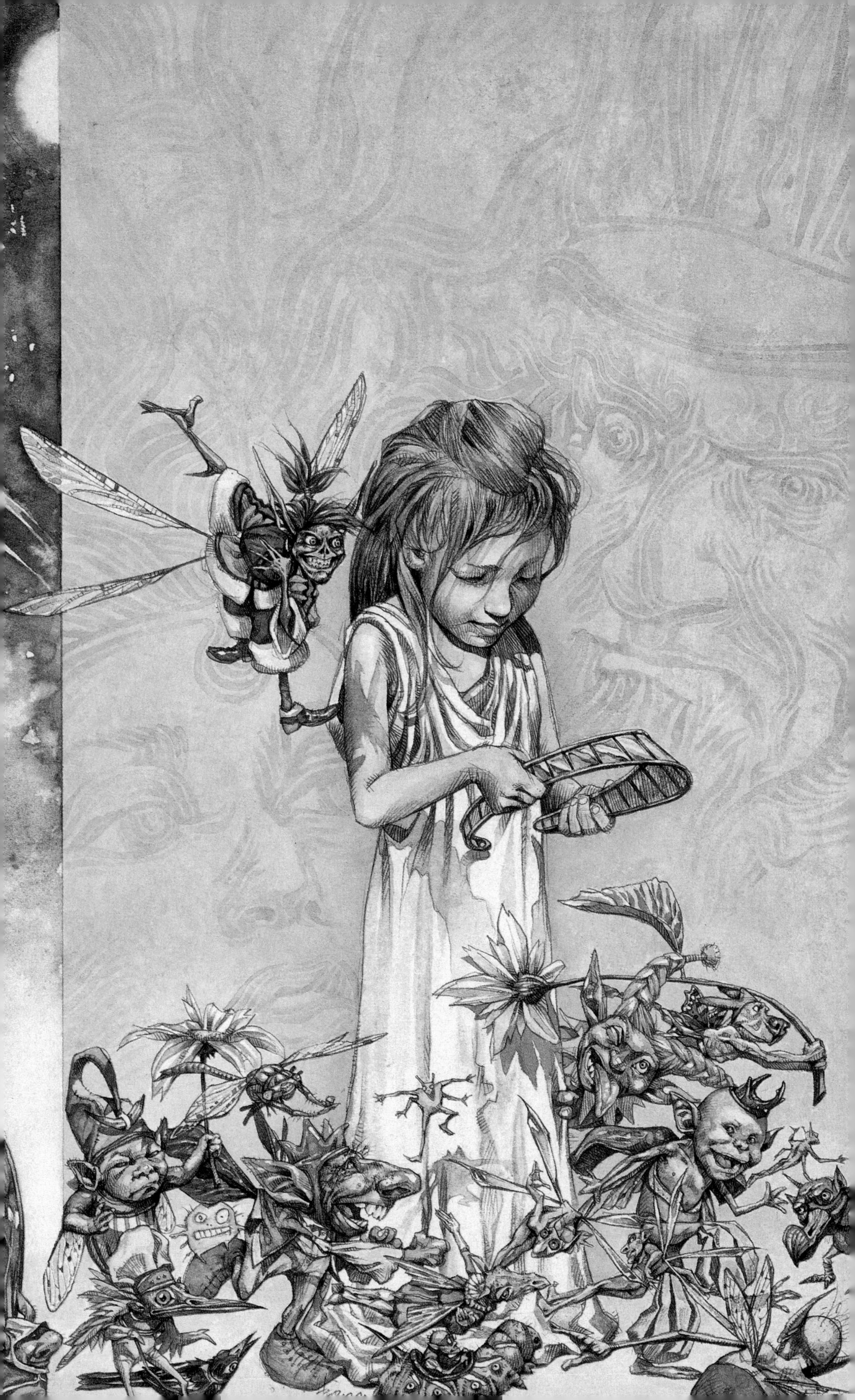

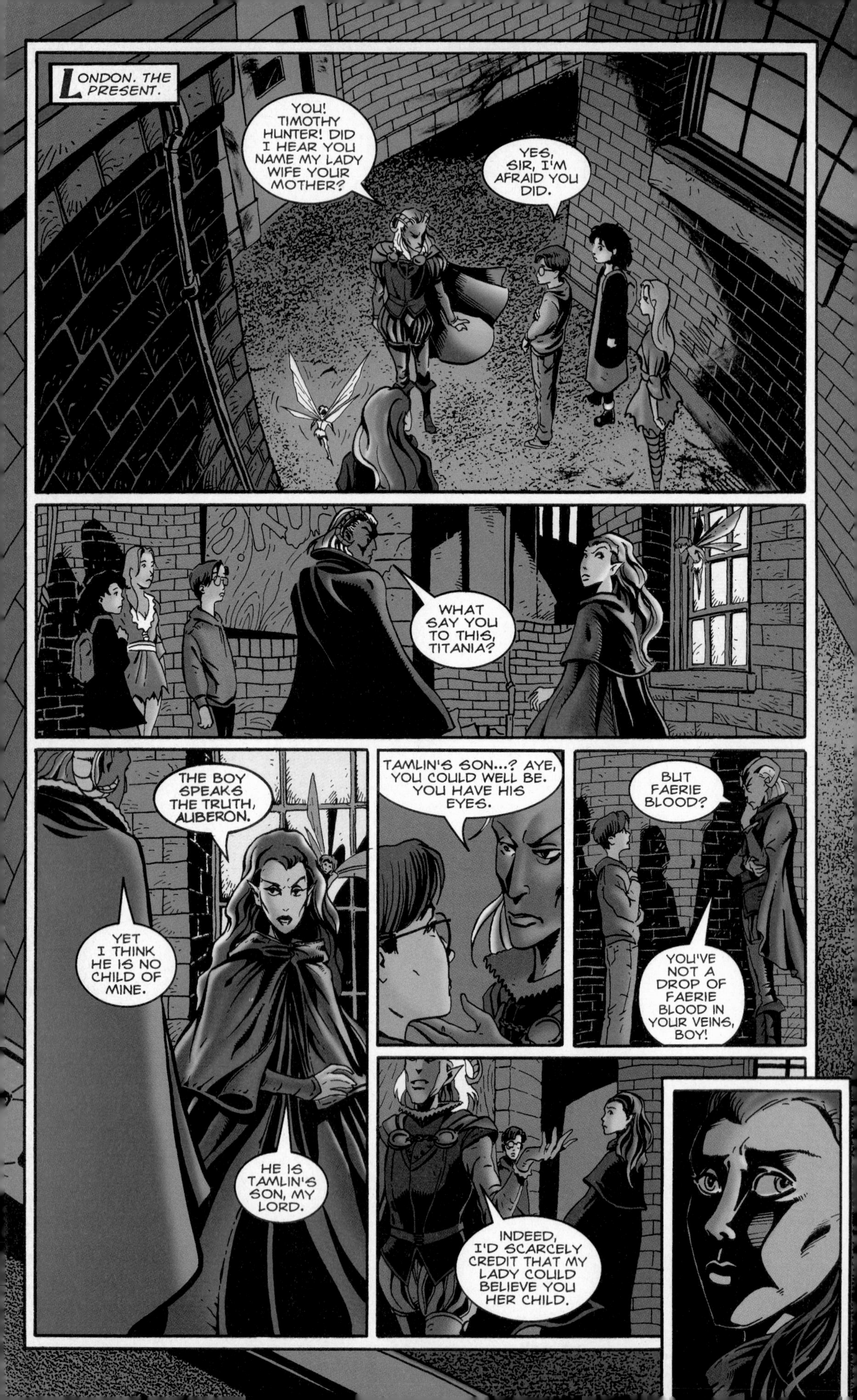
LONDON. THE PRESENT.
YOU! TIMOTHY HUNTER! DID I HEAR YOU NAME MY LADY WIFE YOUR MOTHER?
YES, SIR, I'M AFRAID YOU DID.
WHAT SAY YOU TO THIS, TITANIA?
THE BOY SPEAKS THE TRUTH, AUBERON.
YET I THINK HE IS NO CHILD OF MINE.
HE IS TAMLIN'S SON, MY LORD.
TAMLIN'S SON...? AYE, YOU COULD WELL BE. YOU HAVE HIS EYES.
BUT FAERIE BLOOD?
YOU'VE NOT A DROP OF FAERIE BLOOD IN YOUR VEINS, BOY!
INDEED, I'D SCARCELY CREDIT THAT MY LADY COULD BELIEVE YOU HER CHILD.

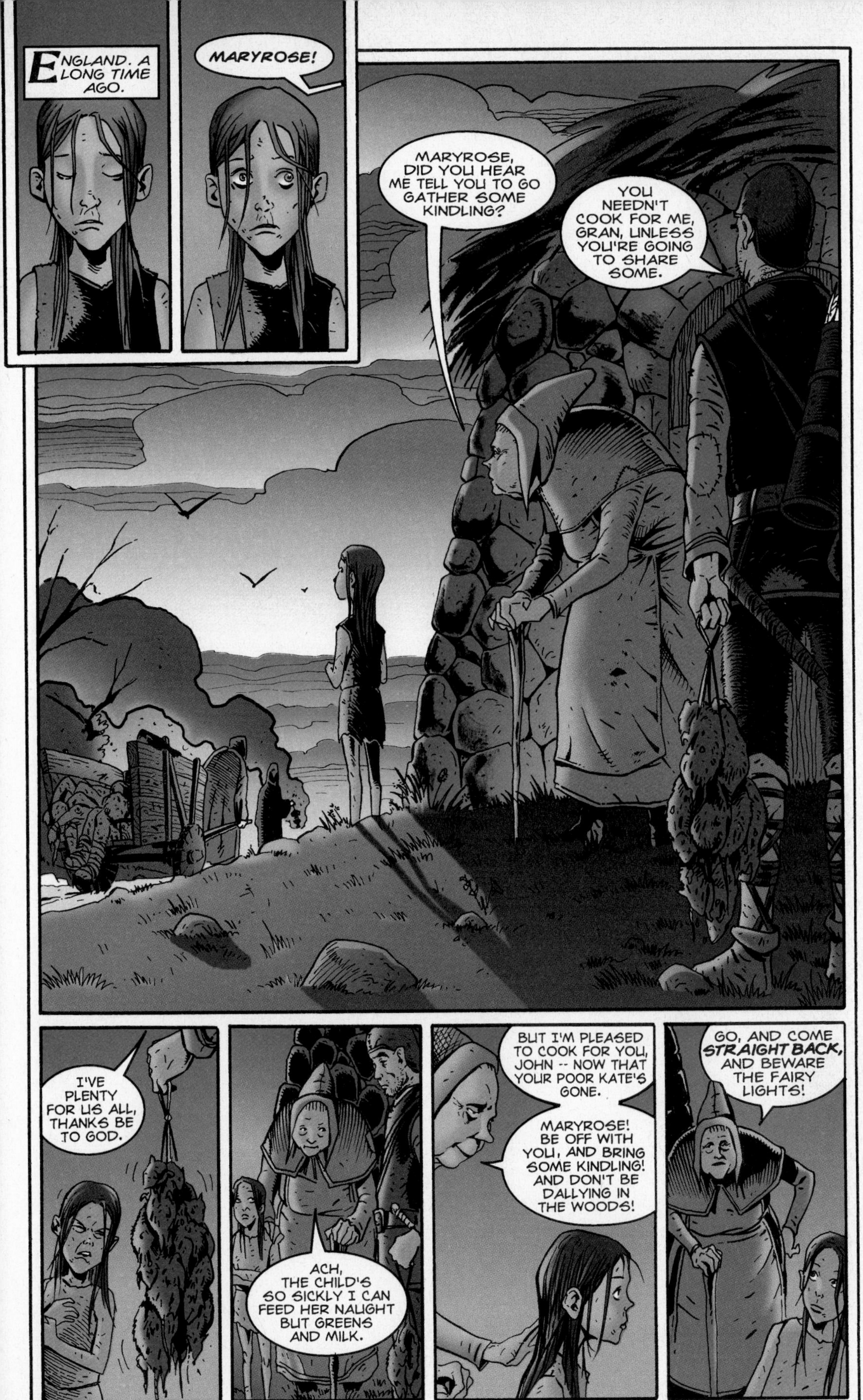
ENGLAND. A LONG TIME AGO.
MARYROSE!
MARYROSE, DID YOU HEAR ME TELL YOU TO GO GATHER SOME KINDLING?
YOU NEEDN'T COOK FOR ME, GRAN, UNLESS YOU'RE GOING TO SHARE SOME.
I'VE PLENTY FOR US ALL, THANKS BE TO GOD.
ACH, THE CHILD'S SO SICKLY I CAN FEED HER NAUGHT BUT GREENS AND MILK.
BUT I'M PLEASED TO COOK FOR YOU, JOHN -- NOW THAT YOUR POOR KATE'S GONE.
MARYROSE! BE OFF WITH YOU, AND BRING SOME KINDLING! AND DON'T BE DALLYING IN THE WOODS!
GO, AND COME STRAIGHT BACK, AND BEWARE THE FAIRY LIGHTS!

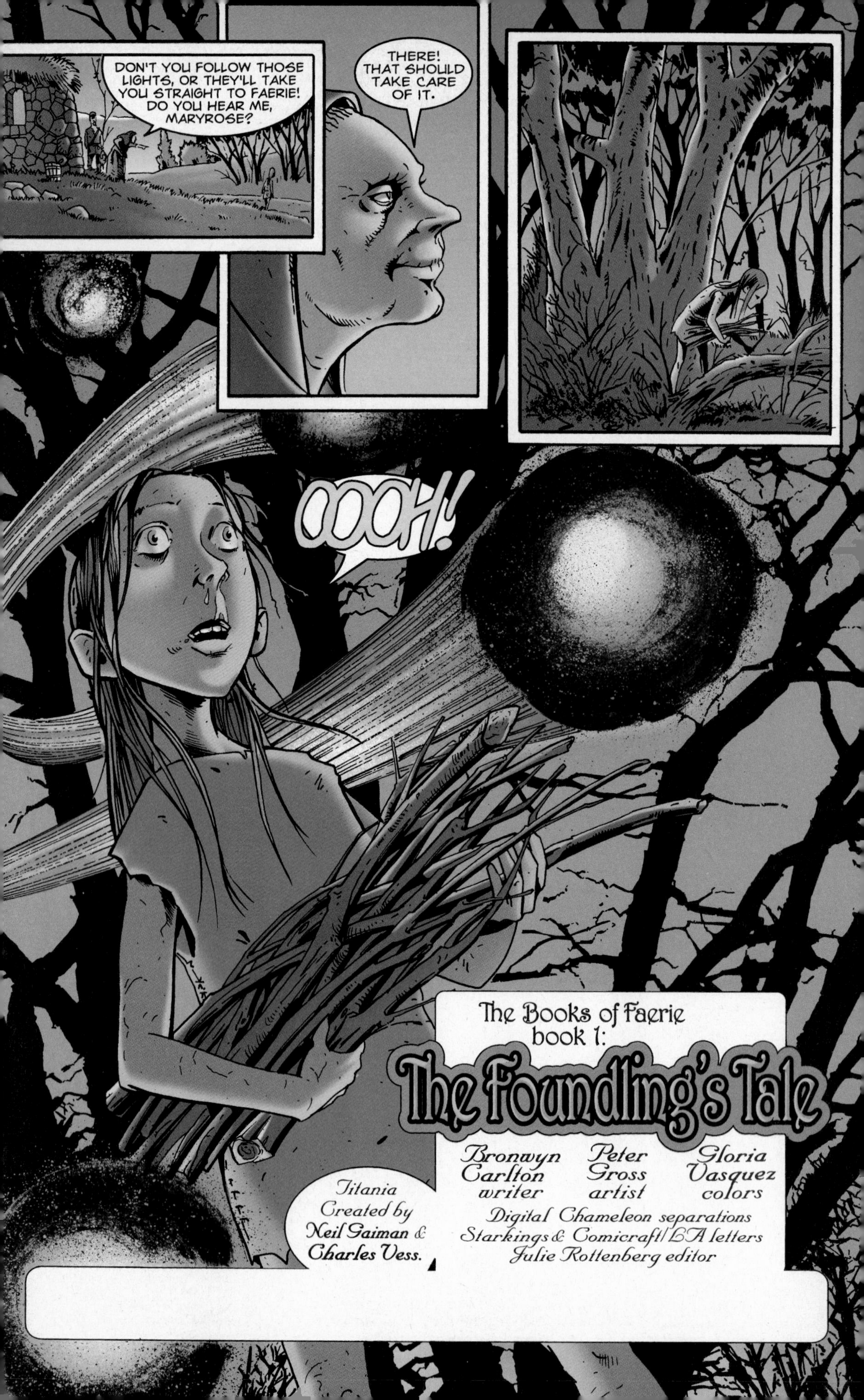
DON'T YOU FOLLOW THOSE LIGHTS, OR THEY'LL TAKE YOU STRAIGHT TO FAERIE! DO YOU HEAR ME, MARYROSE?
THERE! THAT SHOULD TAKE CARE OF IT.
OOOH!
The Books of Faerie book 1:
The Foundling's Tale
Bronwyn Carlton writer
Peter Gross artist
Gloria Vasquez colors
Digital Chameleon separations
Starkings & Comicraft/LA letters
Julie Rottenberg editor
Titania Created by Neil Gaiman & Charles Vess.

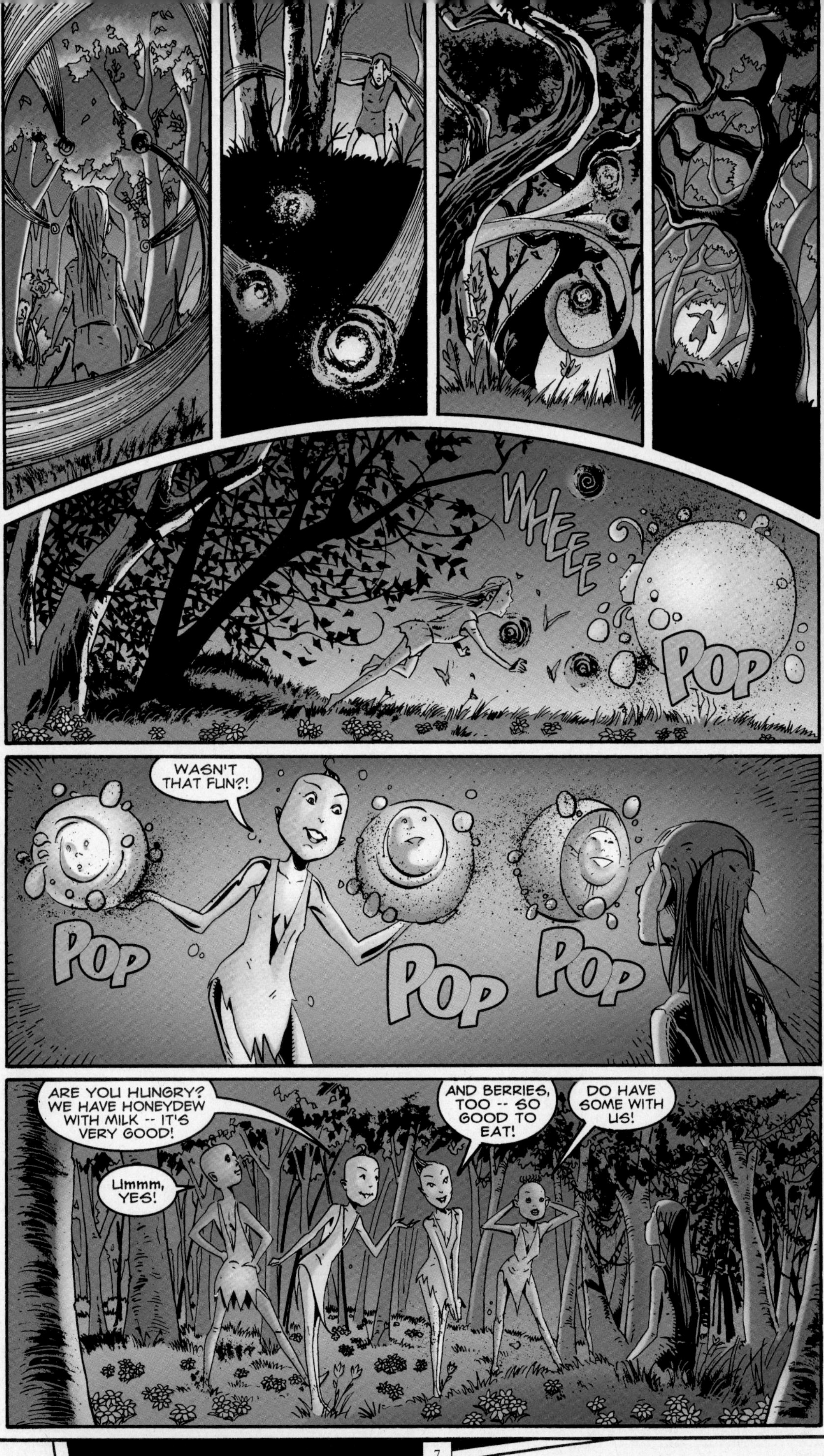
WHEEE
POP
WASN'T THAT FUN?!
POP
POP
POP
ARE YOU HUNGRY? WE HAVE HONEYDEW WITH MILK -- IT'S VERY GOOD!
Ummm, YES!
AND BERRIES, TOO -- SO GOOD TO EAT!
DO HAVE SOME WITH US!

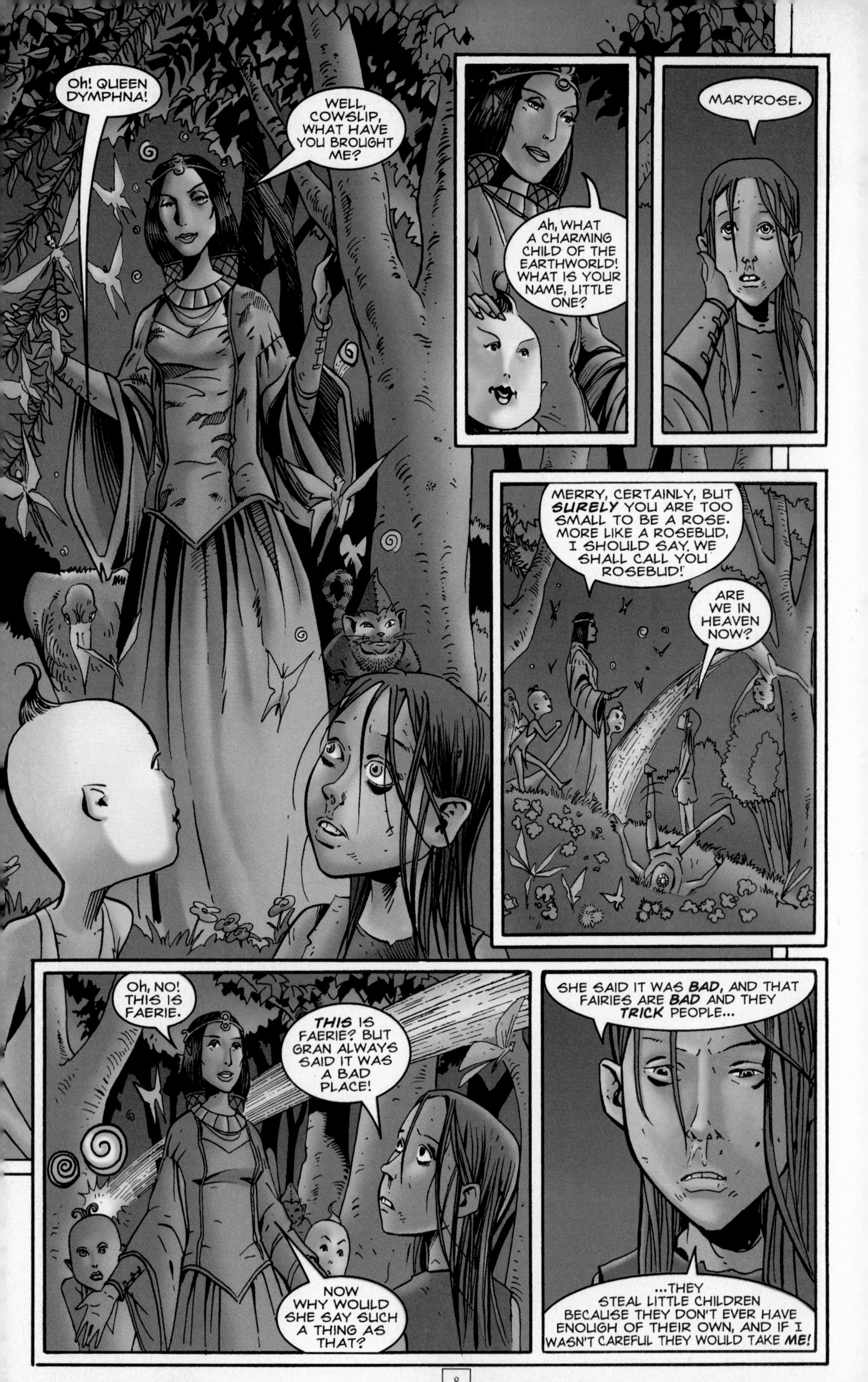

Oh! QUEEN DYMPHNA!
WELL, COWSLIP, WHAT HAVE YOU BROUGHT ME?
Ah, WHAT A CHARMING CHILD OF THE EARTHWORLD! WHAT IS YOUR NAME, LITTLE ONE?
MARYROSE.
MERRY, CERTAINLY, BUT SURELY YOU ARE TOO SMALL TO BE A ROSE. MORE LIKE A ROSEBUD, I SHOULD SAY. WE SHALL CALL YOU ROSEBUD!
ARE WE IN HEAVEN NOW?
Oh, NO! THIS IS FAERIE.
THIS IS FAERIE? BUT GRAN ALWAYS SAID IT WAS A BAD PLACE!
NOW WHY WOULD SHE SAY SUCH A THING AS THAT?
SHE SAID IT WAS BAD, AND THAT FAIRIES ARE BAD AND THEY TRICK PEOPLE...
...THEY STEAL LITTLE CHILDREN BECAUSE THEY DON'T EVER HAVE ENOUGH OF THEIR OWN, AND IF I WASN'T CAREFUL THEY WOULD TAKE ME!

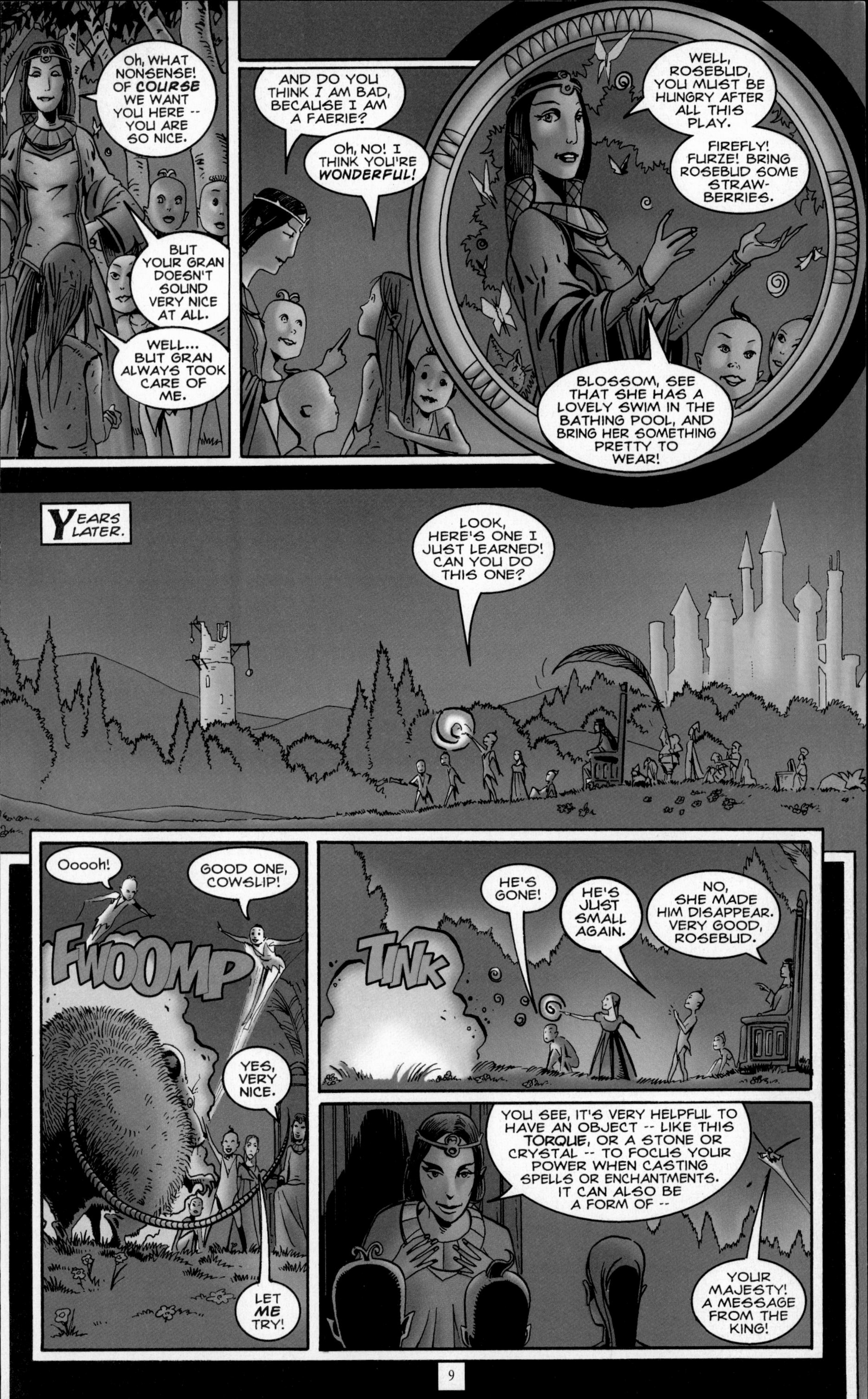
Oh, WHAT NONSENSE! OF COURSE WE WANT YOU HERE -- YOU ARE SO NICE.
BUT YOUR GRAN DOESN'T SOUND VERY NICE AT ALL.
WELL... BUT GRAN ALWAYS TOOK CARE OF ME.
AND DO YOU THINK I AM BAD, BECAUSE I AM A FAERIE?
Oh, NO! I THINK YOU'RE WONDERFUL!
WELL, ROSEBUD, YOU MUST BE HUNGRY AFTER ALL THIS PLAY.
FIREFLY! FURZE! BRING ROSEBUD SOME STRAW-BERRIES.
BLOSSOM, SEE THAT SHE HAS A LOVELY SWIM IN THE BATHING POOL, AND BRING HER SOMETHING PRETTY TO WEAR!
YEARS LATER.
LOOK, HERE'S ONE I JUST LEARNED! CAN YOU DO THIS ONE?
Ooooh!
GOOD ONE, COWSLIP!
FWOOMP
YES, VERY NICE.
LET ME TRY!
TINK
HE'S GONE!
HE'S JUST SMALL AGAIN.
NO, SHE MADE HIM DISAPPEAR. VERY GOOD, ROSEBUD.
YOU SEE, IT'S VERY HELPFUL TO HAVE AN OBJECT -- LIKE THIS TORQUE, OR A STONE OR CRYSTAL -- TO FOCUS YOUR POWER WHEN CASTING SPELLS OR ENCHANTMENTS. IT CAN ALSO BE A FORM OF --
YOUR MAJESTY! A MESSAGE FROM THE KING!

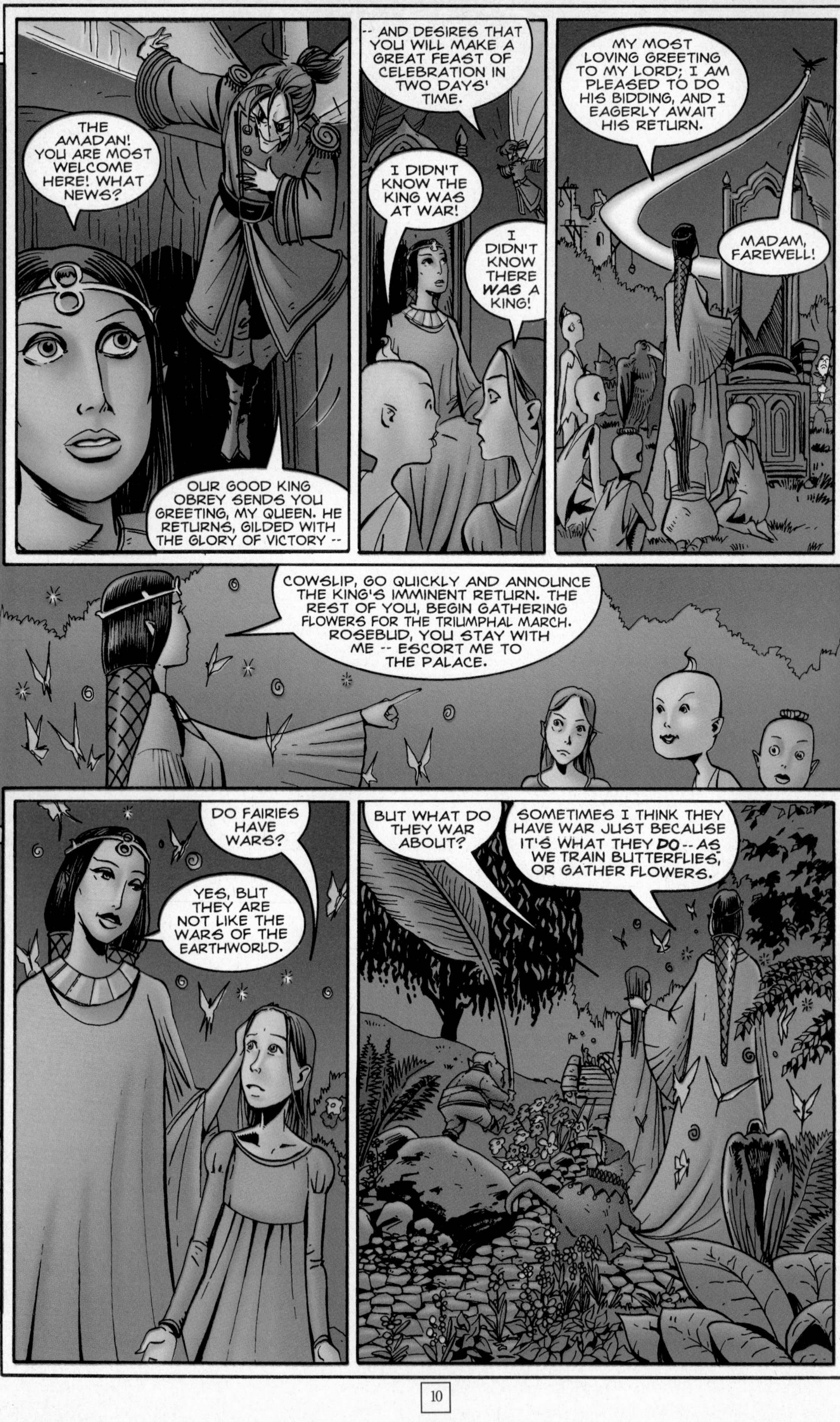
THE AMADAN! YOU ARE MOST WELCOME HERE! WHAT NEWS?
OUR GOOD KING OBREY SENDS YOU GREETING, MY QUEEN. HE RETURNS, GILDED WITH THE GLORY OF VICTORY --
-- AND DESIRES THAT YOU WILL MAKE A GREAT FEAST OF CELEBRATION IN TWO DAYS' TIME.
I DIDN'T KNOW THE KING WAS AT WAR!
I DIDN'T KNOW THERE WAS A KING!
MY MOST LOVING GREETING TO MY LORD; I AM PLEASED TO DO HIS BIDDING, AND I EAGERLY AWAIT HIS RETURN.
MADAM, FAREWELL!
COWSLIP, GO QUICKLY AND ANNOUNCE THE KING'S IMMINENT RETURN. THE REST OF YOU, BEGIN GATHERING FLOWERS FOR THE TRIUMPHAL MARCH. ROSEBUD, YOU STAY WITH ME -- ESCORT ME TO THE PALACE.
DO FAIRIES HAVE WARS?
YES, BUT THEY ARE NOT LIKE THE WARS OF THE EARTHWORLD.
BUT WHAT DO THEY WAR ABOUT?
SOMETIMES I THINK THEY HAVE WAR JUST BECAUSE IT'S WHAT THEY DO -- AS WE TRAIN BUTTERFLIES, OR GATHER FLOWERS.

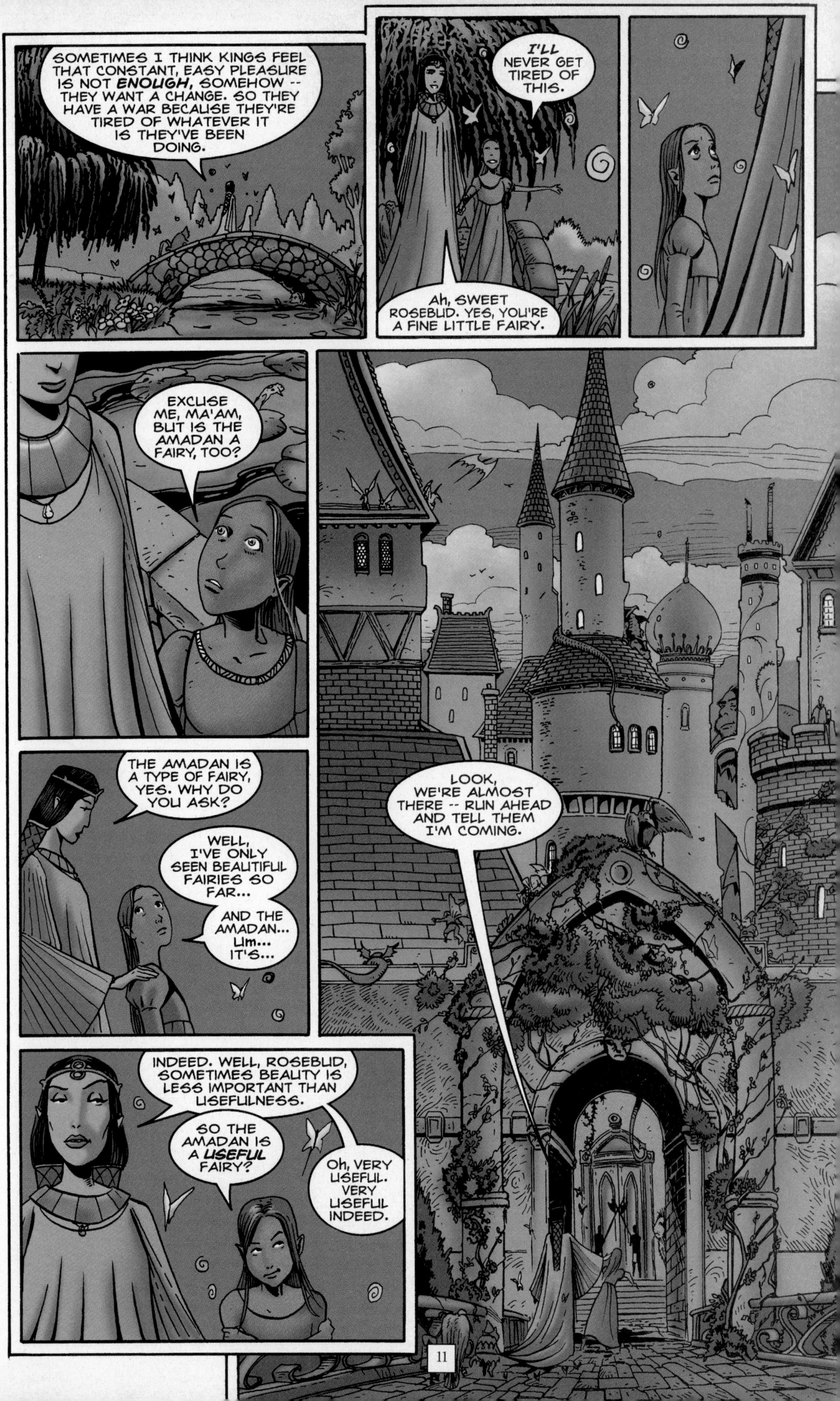

SOMETIMES I THINK KINGS FEEL THAT CONSTANT, EASY PLEASURE IS NOT **ENOUGH**, SOMEHOW -- THEY WANT A CHANGE. SO THEY HAVE A WAR BECAUSE THEY'RE TIRED OF WHATEVER IT IS THEY'VE BEEN DOING.
I'LL NEVER GET TIRED OF THIS.
Ah, SWEET ROSEBUD. YES, YOU'RE A FINE LITTLE FAIRY.
EXCUSE ME, MA'AM, BUT IS THE AMADAN A FAIRY, TOO?
THE AMADAN IS A TYPE OF FAIRY, YES. WHY DO YOU ASK?
WELL, I'VE ONLY SEEN BEAUTIFUL FAIRIES SO FAR...
AND THE AMADAN... UM... IT'S...
INDEED. WELL, ROSEBUD, SOMETIMES BEAUTY IS LESS IMPORTANT THAN USEFULNESS.
SO THE AMADAN IS A ***USEFUL*** FAIRY?
Oh, VERY USEFUL. VERY USEFUL INDEED.
LOOK, WE'RE ALMOST THERE -- RUN AHEAD AND TELL THEM I'M COMING.

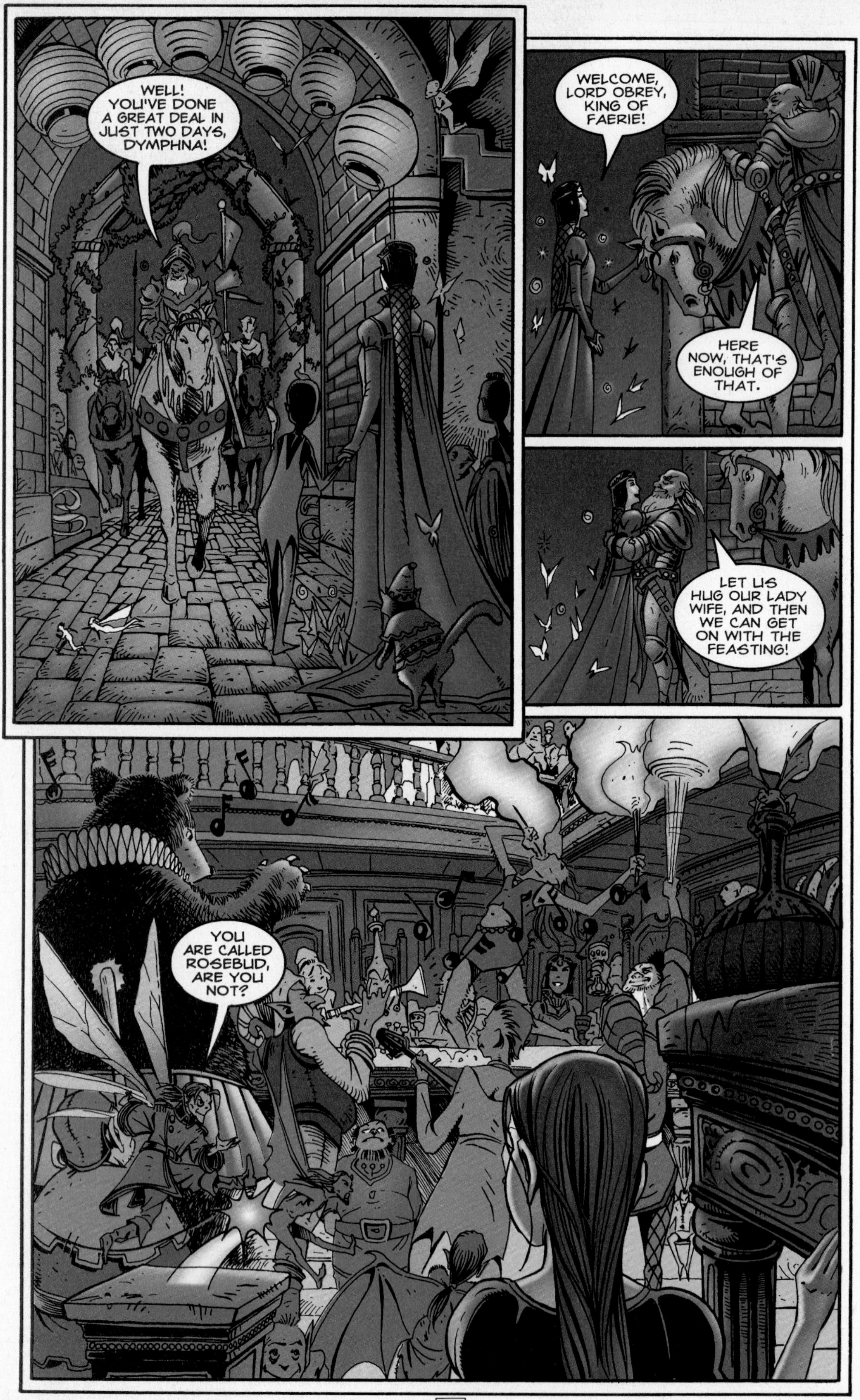
WELL! YOU'VE DONE A GREAT DEAL IN JUST TWO DAYS, DYMPHNA!
WELCOME, LORD OBREY, KING OF FAERIE!
HERE NOW, THAT'S ENOUGH OF THAT.
LET US HUG OUR LADY WIFE, AND THEN WE CAN GET ON WITH THE FEASTING!
YOU ARE CALLED ROSEBUD, ARE YOU NOT?

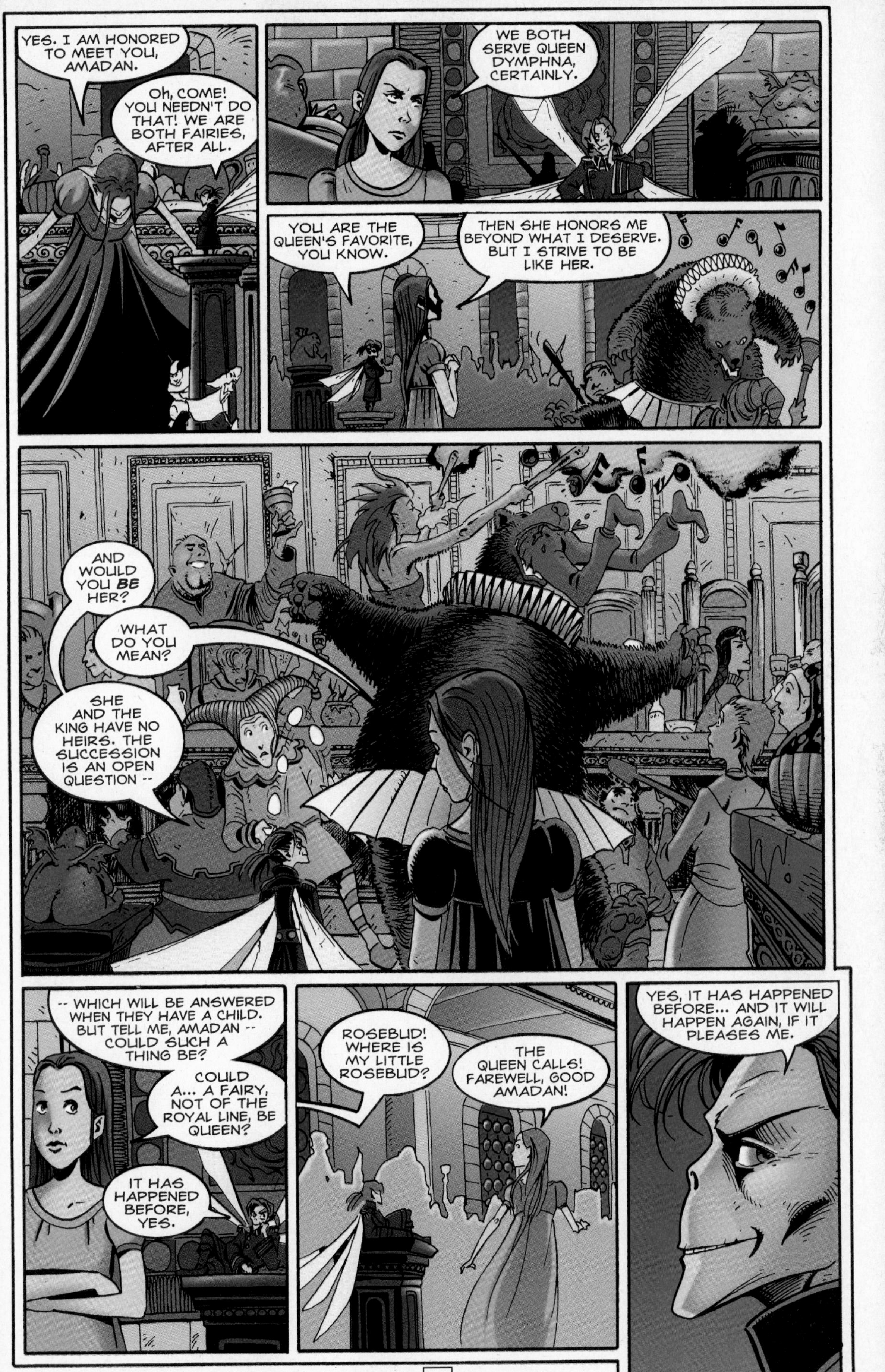
YES. I AM HONORED TO MEET YOU, AMADAN.
Oh, COME! YOU NEEDN'T DO THAT! WE ARE BOTH FAIRIES, AFTER ALL.
WE BOTH SERVE QUEEN DYMPHNA, CERTAINLY.
YOU ARE THE QUEEN'S FAVORITE, YOU KNOW.
THEN SHE HONORS ME BEYOND WHAT I DESERVE. BUT I STRIVE TO BE LIKE HER.
AND WOULD YOU BE HER?
WHAT DO YOU MEAN?
SHE AND THE KING HAVE NO HEIRS. THE SUCCESSION IS AN OPEN QUESTION --
-- WHICH WILL BE ANSWERED WHEN THEY HAVE A CHILD. BUT TELL ME, AMADAN -- COULD SUCH A THING BE?
COULD A... A FAIRY, NOT OF THE ROYAL LINE, BE QUEEN?
IT HAS HAPPENED BEFORE, YES.
ROSEBUD! WHERE IS MY LITTLE ROSEBUD?
THE QUEEN CALLS! FAREWELL, GOOD AMADAN!
YES, IT HAS HAPPENED BEFORE... AND IT WILL HAPPEN AGAIN, IF IT PLEASES ME.

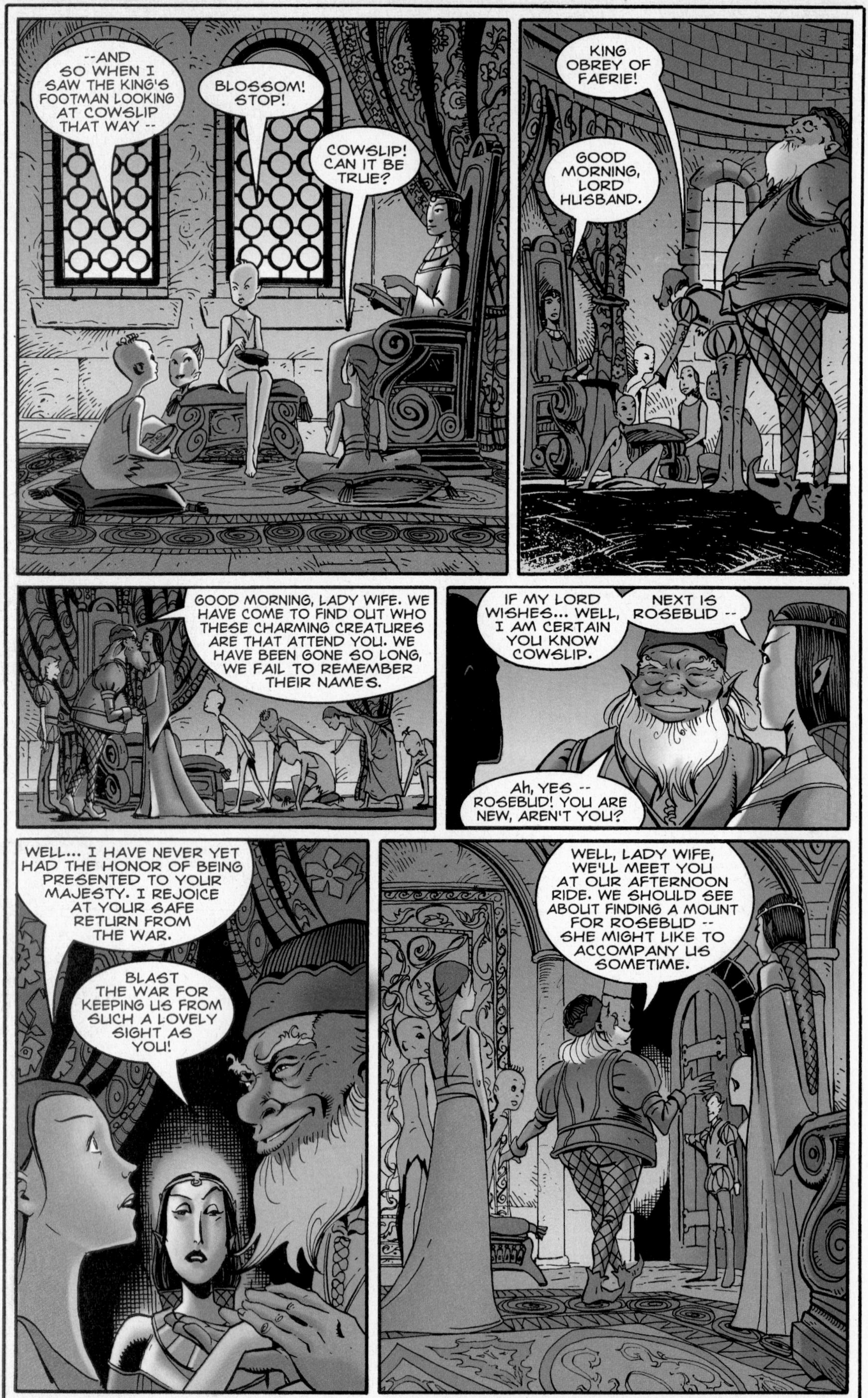
--AND SO WHEN I SAW THE KING'S FOOTMAN LOOKING AT COWSLIP THAT WAY --
BLOSSOM! STOP!
COWSLIP! CAN IT BE TRUE?
KING OBREY OF FAERIE!
GOOD MORNING, LORD HUSBAND.
GOOD MORNING, LADY WIFE. WE HAVE COME TO FIND OUT WHO THESE CHARMING CREATURES ARE THAT ATTEND YOU. WE HAVE BEEN GONE SO LONG, WE FAIL TO REMEMBER THEIR NAMES.
IF MY LORD WISHES... WELL, I AM CERTAIN YOU KNOW COWSLIP.
NEXT IS ROSEBUD --
Ah, YES -- ROSEBUD! YOU ARE NEW, AREN'T YOU?
WELL... I HAVE NEVER YET HAD THE HONOR OF BEING PRESENTED TO YOUR MAJESTY. I REJOICE AT YOUR SAFE RETURN FROM THE WAR.
BLAST THE WAR FOR KEEPING US FROM SUCH A LOVELY SIGHT AS YOU!
WELL, LADY WIFE, WE'LL MEET YOU AT OUR AFTERNOON RIDE. WE SHOULD SEE ABOUT FINDING A MOUNT FOR ROSEBUD -- SHE MIGHT LIKE TO ACCOMPANY US SOMETIME.

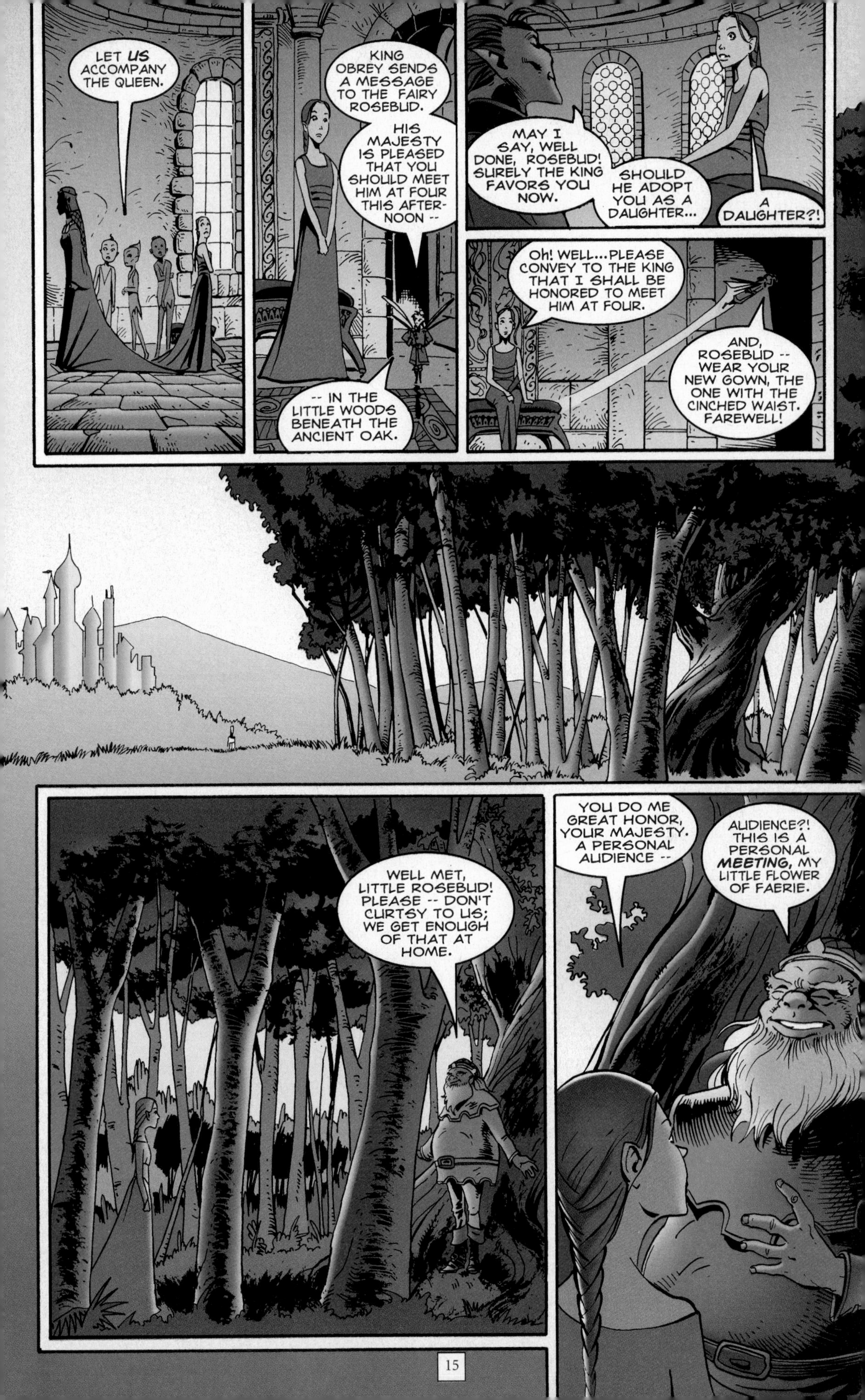
LET US ACCOMPANY THE QUEEN.
KING OBREY SENDS A MESSAGE TO THE FAIRY ROSEBUD.
HIS MAJESTY IS PLEASED THAT YOU SHOULD MEET HIM AT FOUR THIS AFTER-NOON --
-- IN THE LITTLE WOODS BENEATH THE ANCIENT OAK.
MAY I SAY, WELL DONE, ROSEBUD! SURELY THE KING FAVORS YOU NOW.
SHOULD HE ADOPT YOU AS A DAUGHTER...
A DAUGHTER?!
Oh! WELL...PLEASE CONVEY TO THE KING THAT I SHALL BE HONORED TO MEET HIM AT FOUR.
AND, ROSEBUD -- WEAR YOUR NEW GOWN, THE ONE WITH THE CINCHED WAIST. FAREWELL!
WELL MET, LITTLE ROSEBUD! PLEASE -- DON'T CURTSY TO US; WE GET ENOUGH OF THAT AT HOME.
YOU DO ME GREAT HONOR, YOUR MAJESTY. A PERSONAL AUDIENCE --
AUDIENCE?! THIS IS A PERSONAL MEETING, MY LITTLE FLOWER OF FAERIE.

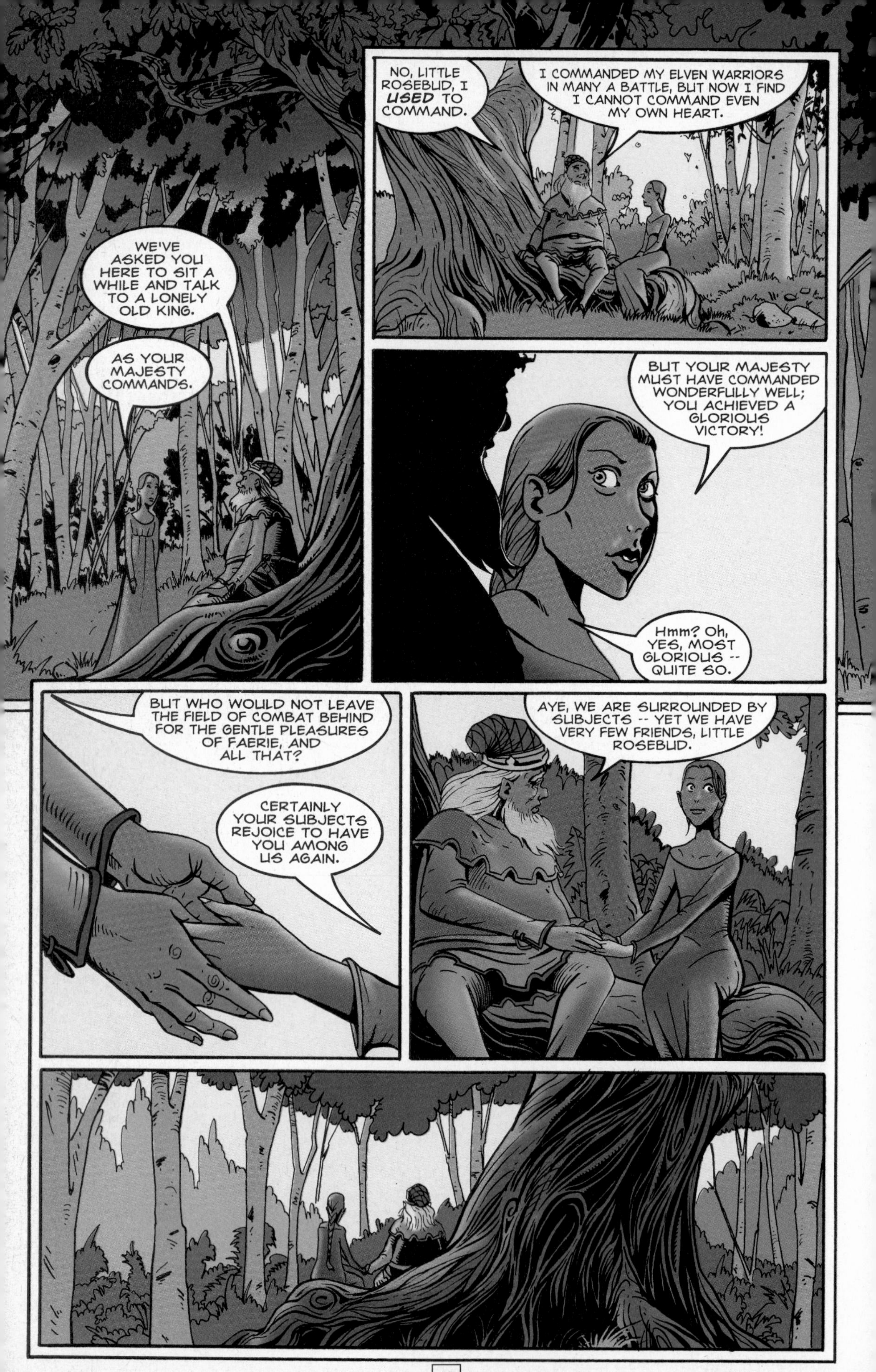
WE'VE ASKED YOU HERE TO SIT A WHILE AND TALK TO A LONELY OLD KING.
AS YOUR MAJESTY COMMANDS.
NO, LITTLE ROSEBUD, I USED TO COMMAND.
I COMMANDED MY ELVEN WARRIORS IN MANY A BATTLE, BUT NOW I FIND I CANNOT COMMAND EVEN MY OWN HEART.
BUT YOUR MAJESTY MUST HAVE COMMANDED WONDERFULLY WELL; YOU ACHIEVED A GLORIOUS VICTORY!
Hmm? Oh, YES, MOST GLORIOUS -- QUITE SO.
BUT WHO WOULD NOT LEAVE THE FIELD OF COMBAT BEHIND FOR THE GENTLE PLEASURES OF FAERIE, AND ALL THAT?
CERTAINLY YOUR SUBJECTS REJOICE TO HAVE YOU AMONG US AGAIN.
AYE, WE ARE SURROUNDED BY SUBJECTS -- YET WE HAVE VERY FEW FRIENDS, LITTLE ROSEBUD.

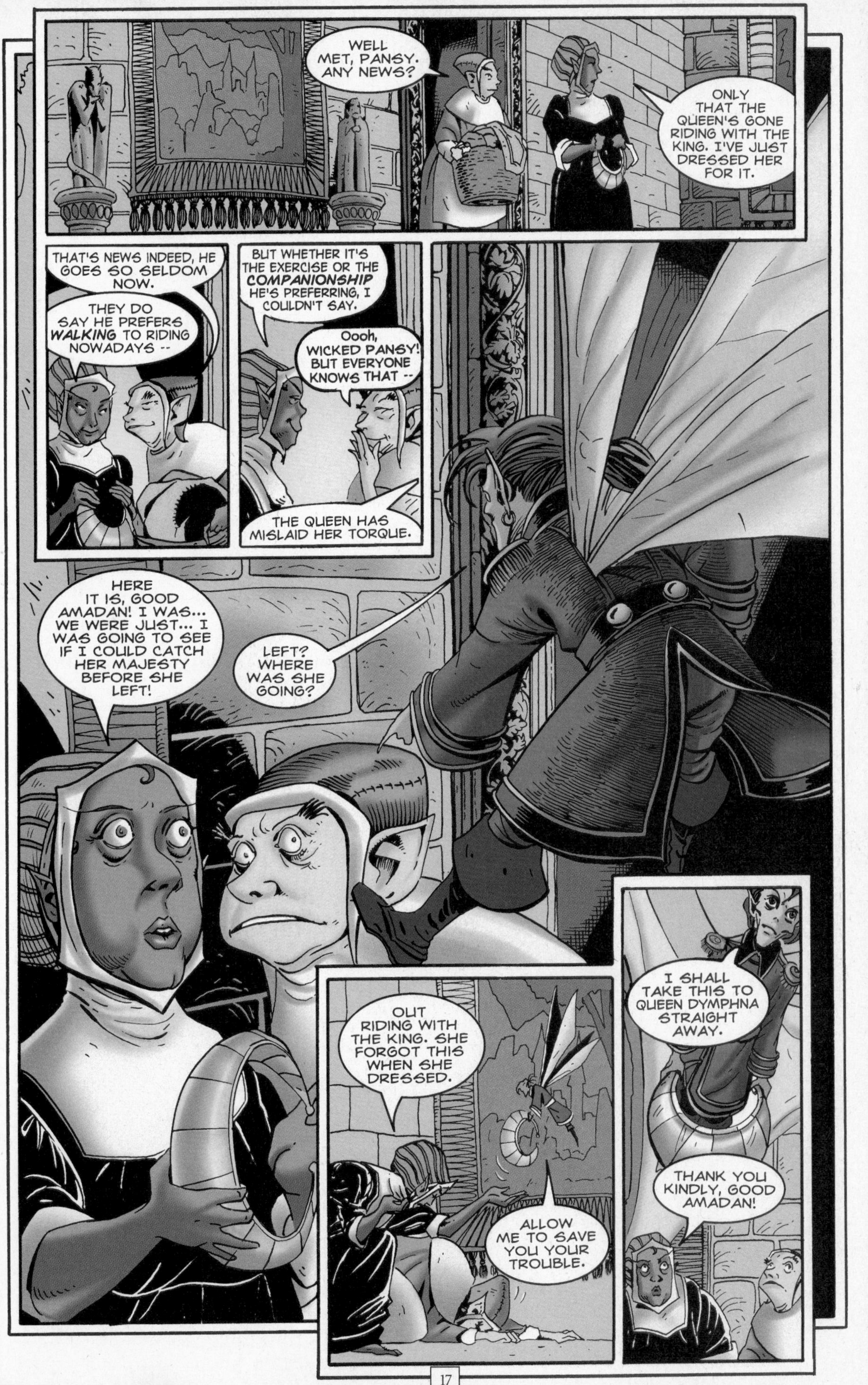
WELL MET, PANSY. ANY NEWS?
ONLY THAT THE QUEEN'S GONE RIDING WITH THE KING. I'VE JUST DRESSED HER FOR IT.
THAT'S NEWS INDEED, HE GOES SO SELDOM NOW.
THEY DO SAY HE PREFERS WALKING TO RIDING NOWADAYS --
BUT WHETHER IT'S THE EXERCISE OR THE COMPANIONSHIP HE'S PREFERRING, I COULDN'T SAY.
Oooh, WICKED PANSY! BUT EVERYONE KNOWS THAT --
THE QUEEN HAS MISLAID HER TORQUE.
HERE IT IS, GOOD AMADAN! I WAS... WE WERE JUST... I WAS GOING TO SEE IF I COULD CATCH HER MAJESTY BEFORE SHE LEFT!
LEFT? WHERE WAS SHE GOING?
OUT RIDING WITH THE KING. SHE FORGOT THIS WHEN SHE DRESSED.
ALLOW ME TO SAVE YOU YOUR TROUBLE.
I SHALL TAKE THIS TO QUEEN DYMPHNA STRAIGHT AWAY.
THANK YOU KINDLY, GOOD AMADAN!

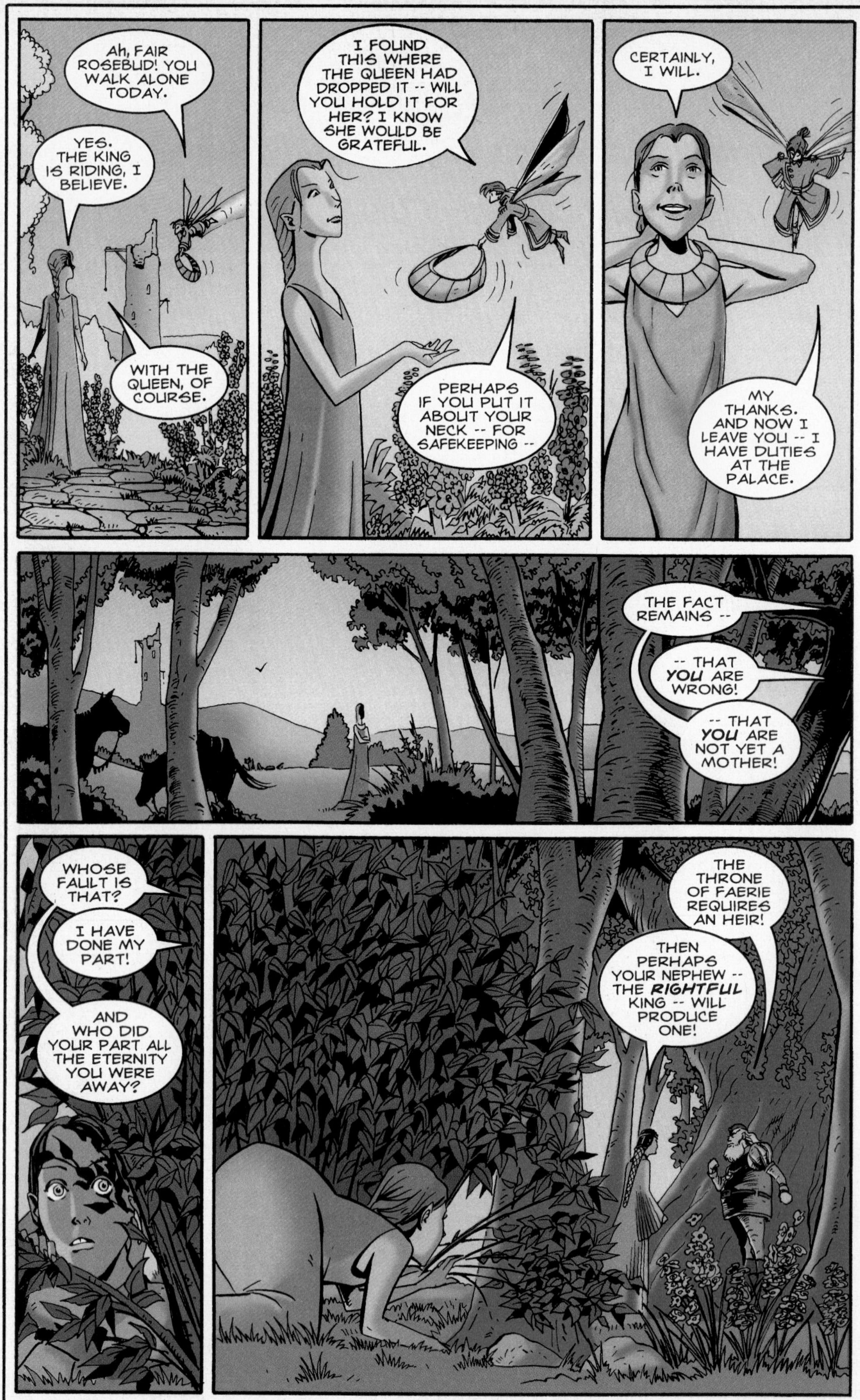
Ah, FAIR ROSEBUD! YOU WALK ALONE TODAY.
YES. THE KING IS RIDING, I BELIEVE.
WITH THE QUEEN, OF COURSE.
I FOUND THIS WHERE THE QUEEN HAD DROPPED IT -- WILL YOU HOLD IT FOR HER? I KNOW SHE WOULD BE GRATEFUL.
PERHAPS IF YOU PUT IT ABOUT YOUR NECK -- FOR SAFEKEEPING --
CERTAINLY, I WILL.
MY THANKS. AND NOW I LEAVE YOU -- I HAVE DUTIES AT THE PALACE.
THE FACT REMAINS --
-- THAT YOU ARE WRONG!
-- THAT YOU ARE NOT YET A MOTHER!
WHOSE FAULT IS THAT?
I HAVE DONE MY PART!
AND WHO DID YOUR PART ALL THE ETERNITY YOU WERE AWAY?
THE THRONE OF FAERIE REQUIRES AN HEIR!
THEN PERHAPS YOUR NEPHEW -- THE RIGHTFUL KING -- WILL PRODUCE ONE!

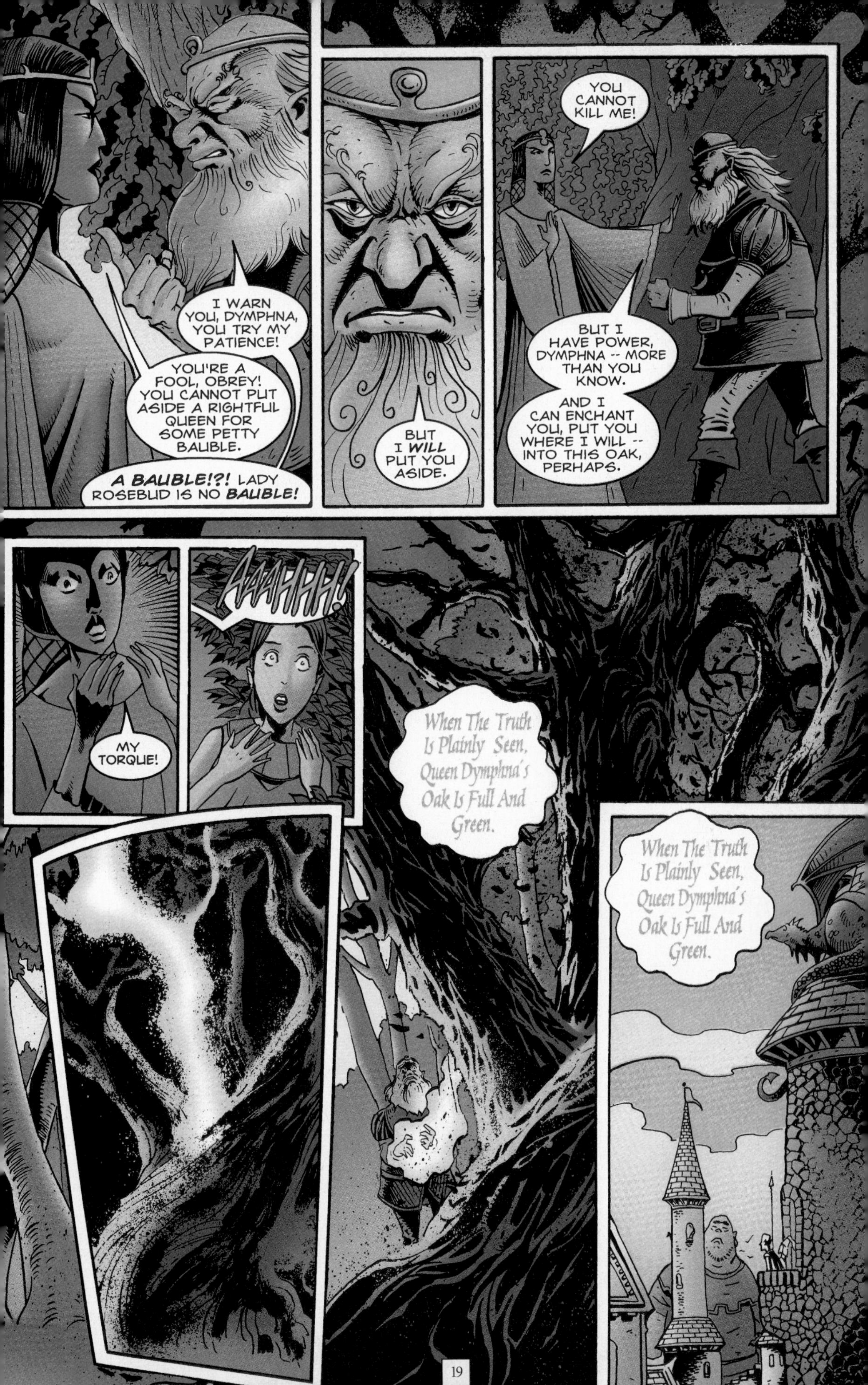
I WARN YOU, DYMPHNA, YOU TRY MY PATIENCE!
YOU'RE A FOOL, OBREY! YOU CANNOT PUT ASIDE A RIGHTFUL QUEEN FOR SOME PETTY BAUBLE.
A BAUBLE!?! LADY ROSEBUD IS NO BAUBLE!
BUT I WILL PUT YOU ASIDE.
YOU CANNOT KILL ME!
BUT I HAVE POWER, DYMPHNA -- MORE THAN YOU KNOW.
AND I CAN ENCHANT YOU, PUT YOU WHERE I WILL -- INTO THIS OAK, PERHAPS.
MY TORQUE!
AAAHHH!
When The Truth Is Plainly Seen, Queen Dymphna's Oak Is Full And Green.
When The Truth Is Plainly Seen, Queen Dymphna's Oak Is Full And Green.

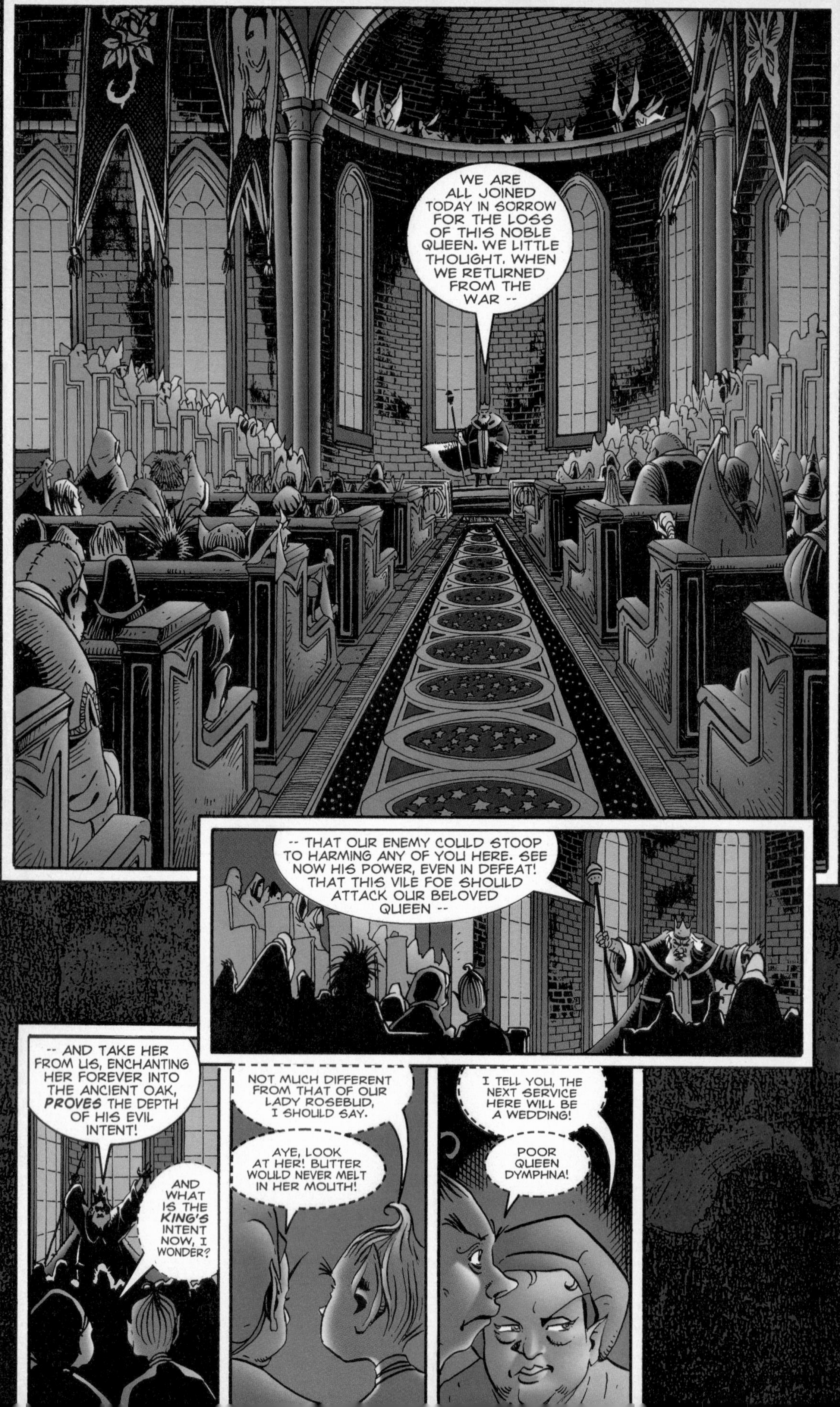
WE ARE ALL JOINED TODAY IN SORROW FOR THE LOSS OF THIS NOBLE QUEEN. WE LITTLE THOUGHT, WHEN WE RETURNED FROM THE WAR --
-- THAT OUR ENEMY COULD STOOP TO HARMING ANY OF YOU HERE. SEE NOW HIS POWER, EVEN IN DEFEAT! THAT THIS VILE FOE SHOULD ATTACK OUR BELOVED QUEEN --
-- AND TAKE HER FROM US, ENCHANTING HER FOREVER INTO THE ANCIENT OAK, **PROVES** THE DEPTH OF HIS EVIL INTENT!
AND WHAT IS THE **KING'S** INTENT NOW, I WONDER?
NOT MUCH DIFFERENT FROM THAT OF OUR LADY ROSEBUD, I SHOULD SAY.
AYE, LOOK AT HER! BUTTER WOULD NEVER MELT IN HER MOUTH!
I TELL YOU, THE NEXT SERVICE HERE WILL BE A WEDDING!
POOR QUEEN DYMPHNA!

ONE MONTH LATER.

SO DID I.

THE KING PREFERS A CINCHED WAIST, I THINK.

WHAT THINK YOU, AMADAN?

I LIKED THE OTHER ONE.

GETTING MARRIED IS HARDER THAN IT SEEMS!

WELL, MY LADY, BY THIS TIME TOMORROW IT WILL ALL BE OVER.

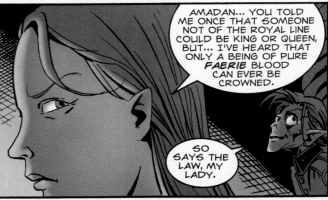

AMADAN... YOU TOLD ME ONCE THAT SOMEONE NOT OF THE ROYAL LINE COULD BE KING OR QUEEN, BUT... I'VE HEARD THAT ONLY A BEING OF PURE *FAERIE* BLOOD CAN EVER BE CROWNED.

SO SAYS THE LAW, MY LADY.

BUT... WHEN I FIRST CAME TO... THE COURT, BLOSSOM AND FIREFLY, AND COWSLIP, THEY SAW ME -- AS I WAS THEN --

IT HAS ALREADY BEEN TAKEN CARE OF. SIMPLE, REPEATED SUGGESTION --

-- THEIR WILLS ARE NOT VERY STRONG.

NOT NEARLY SO STRONG AS YOURS.

THANK YOU, AMADAN. YOU'VE DONE ME GOOD SERVICE.

BE SURE YOU KEEP THAT WITH YOU ALWAYS.

YES.

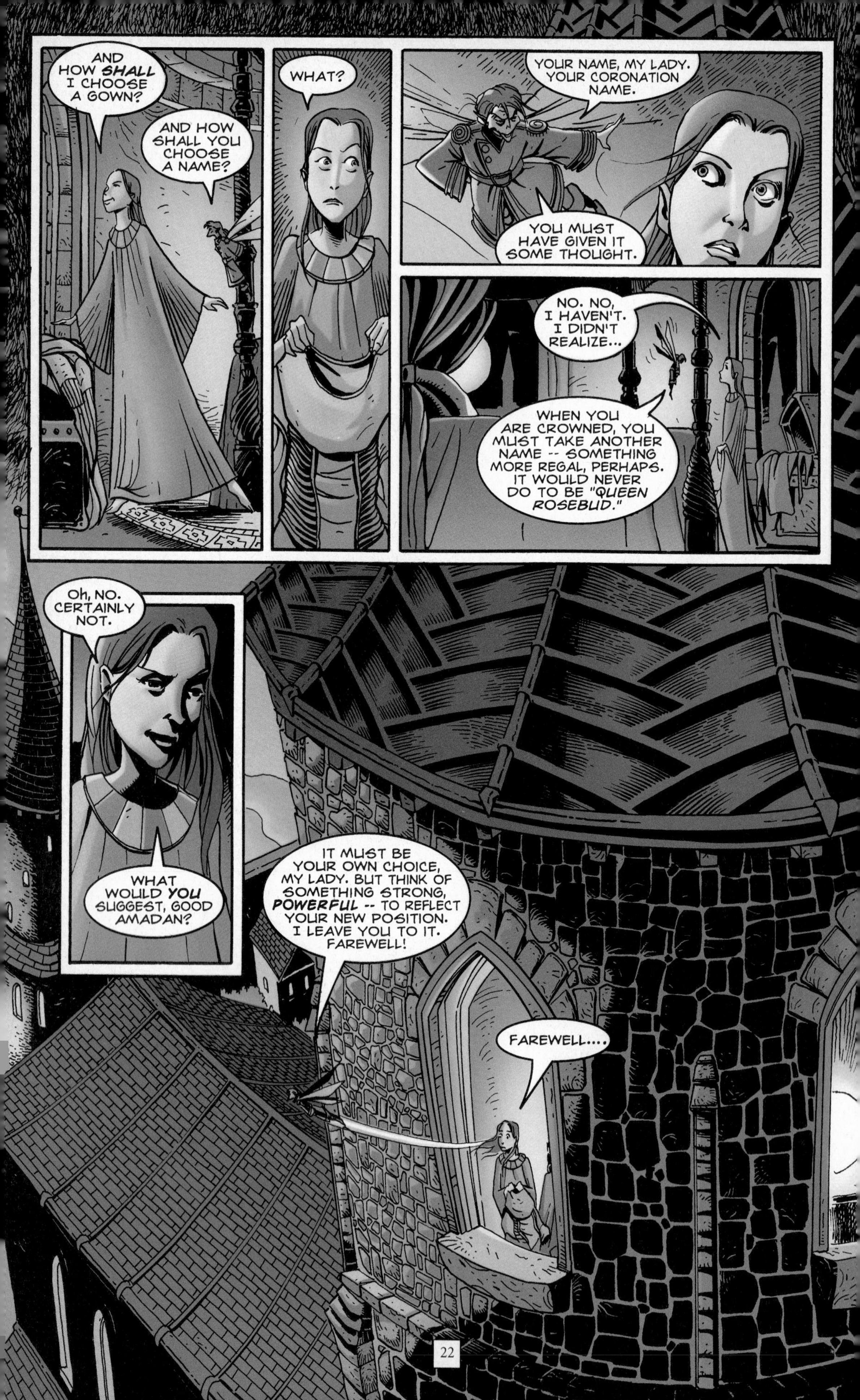

AND HOW SHALL I CHOOSE A GOWN?
AND HOW SHALL YOU CHOOSE A NAME?
WHAT?
YOUR NAME, MY LADY. YOUR CORONATION NAME.
YOU MUST HAVE GIVEN IT SOME THOUGHT.
NO. NO, I HAVEN'T. I DIDN'T REALIZE...
WHEN YOU ARE CROWNED, YOU MUST TAKE ANOTHER NAME -- SOMETHING MORE REGAL, PERHAPS. IT WOULD NEVER DO TO BE "QUEEN ROSEBUD."
Oh, NO. CERTAINLY NOT.
WHAT WOULD YOU SUGGEST, GOOD AMADAN?
IT MUST BE YOUR OWN CHOICE, MY LADY. BUT THINK OF SOMETHING STRONG, POWERFUL -- TO REFLECT YOUR NEW POSITION. I LEAVE YOU TO IT. FAREWELL!
FAREWELL....

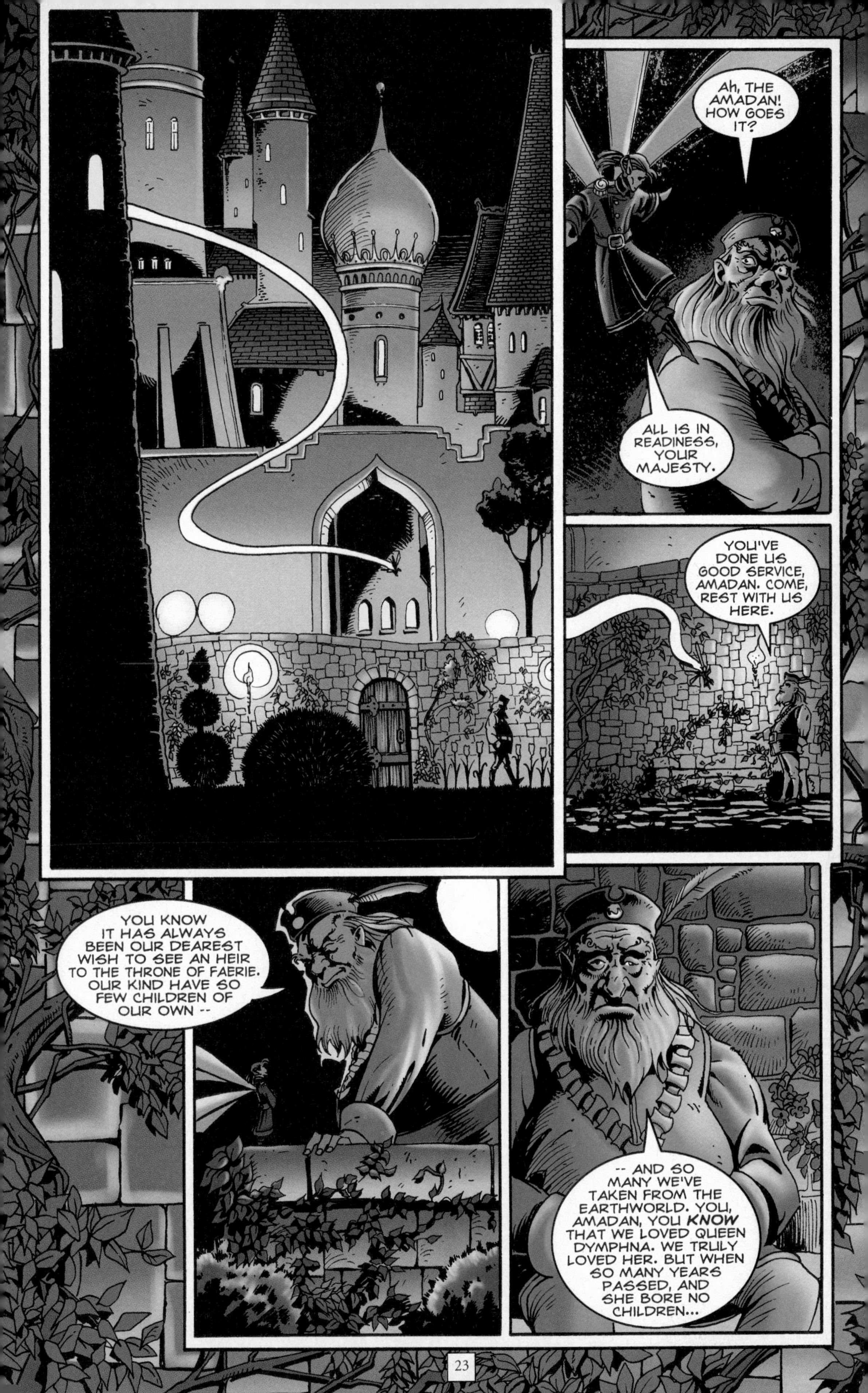

Ah, THE AMADAN! HOW GOES IT?
ALL IS IN READINESS, YOUR MAJESTY.
YOU'VE DONE US GOOD SERVICE, AMADAN. COME, REST WITH US HERE.
YOU KNOW IT HAS ALWAYS BEEN OUR DEAREST WISH TO SEE AN HEIR TO THE THRONE OF FAERIE. OUR KIND HAVE SO FEW CHILDREN OF OUR OWN --
-- AND SO MANY WE'VE TAKEN FROM THE EARTHWORLD. YOU, AMADAN, YOU KNOW THAT WE LOVED QUEEN DYMPHNA. WE TRULY LOVED HER. BUT WHEN SO MANY YEARS PASSED, AND SHE BORE NO CHILDREN...

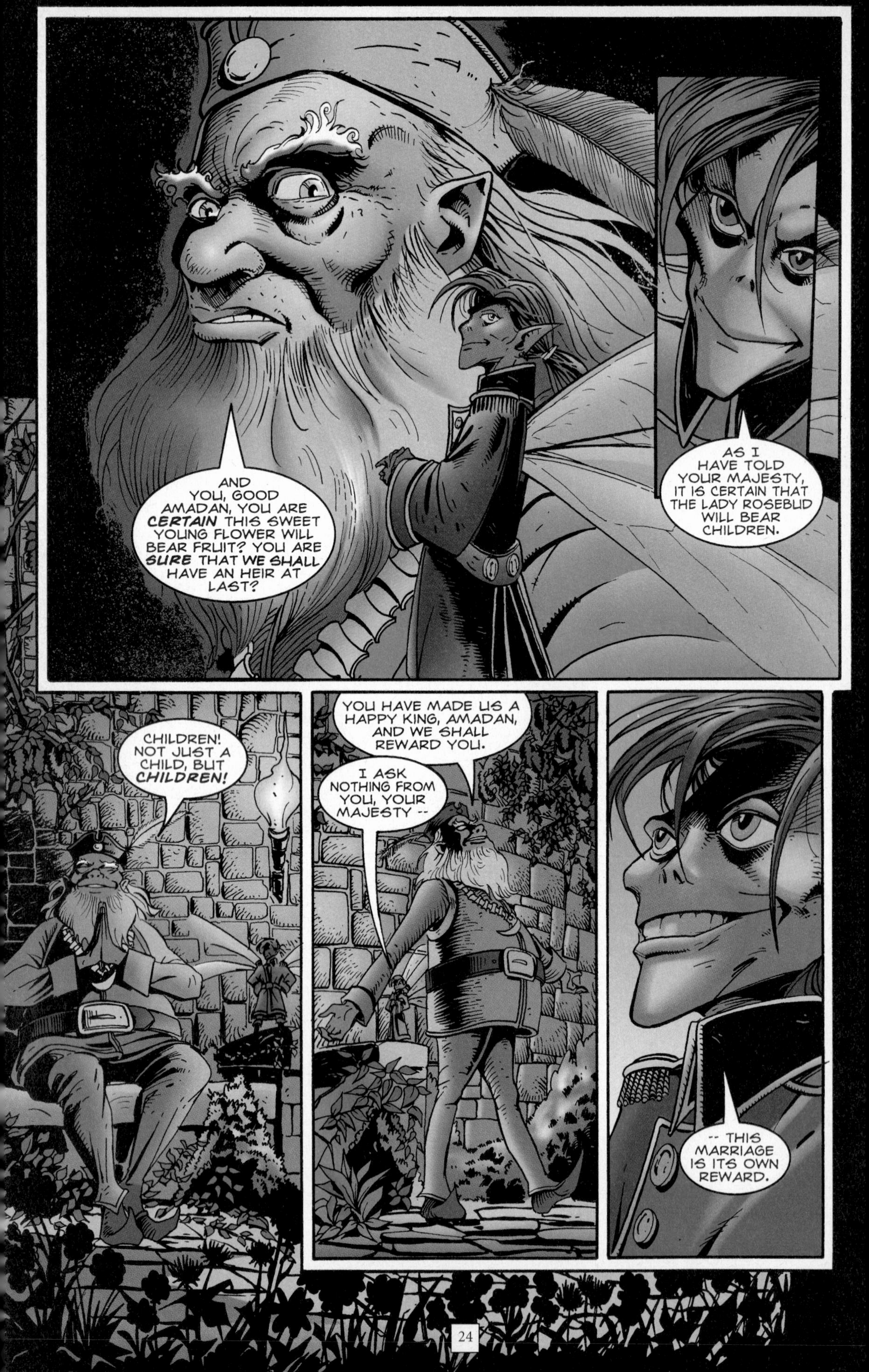
AND YOU, GOOD AMADAN, YOU ARE CERTAIN THIS SWEET YOUNG FLOWER WILL BEAR FRUIT? YOU ARE SURE THAT WE SHALL HAVE AN HEIR AT LAST?
AS I HAVE TOLD YOUR MAJESTY, IT IS CERTAIN THAT THE LADY ROSEBUD WILL BEAR CHILDREN.
CHILDREN! NOT JUST A CHILD, BUT CHILDREN!
YOU HAVE MADE US A HAPPY KING, AMADAN, AND WE SHALL REWARD YOU.
I ASK NOTHING FROM YOU, YOUR MAJESTY --
-- THIS MARRIAGE IS ITS OWN REWARD.

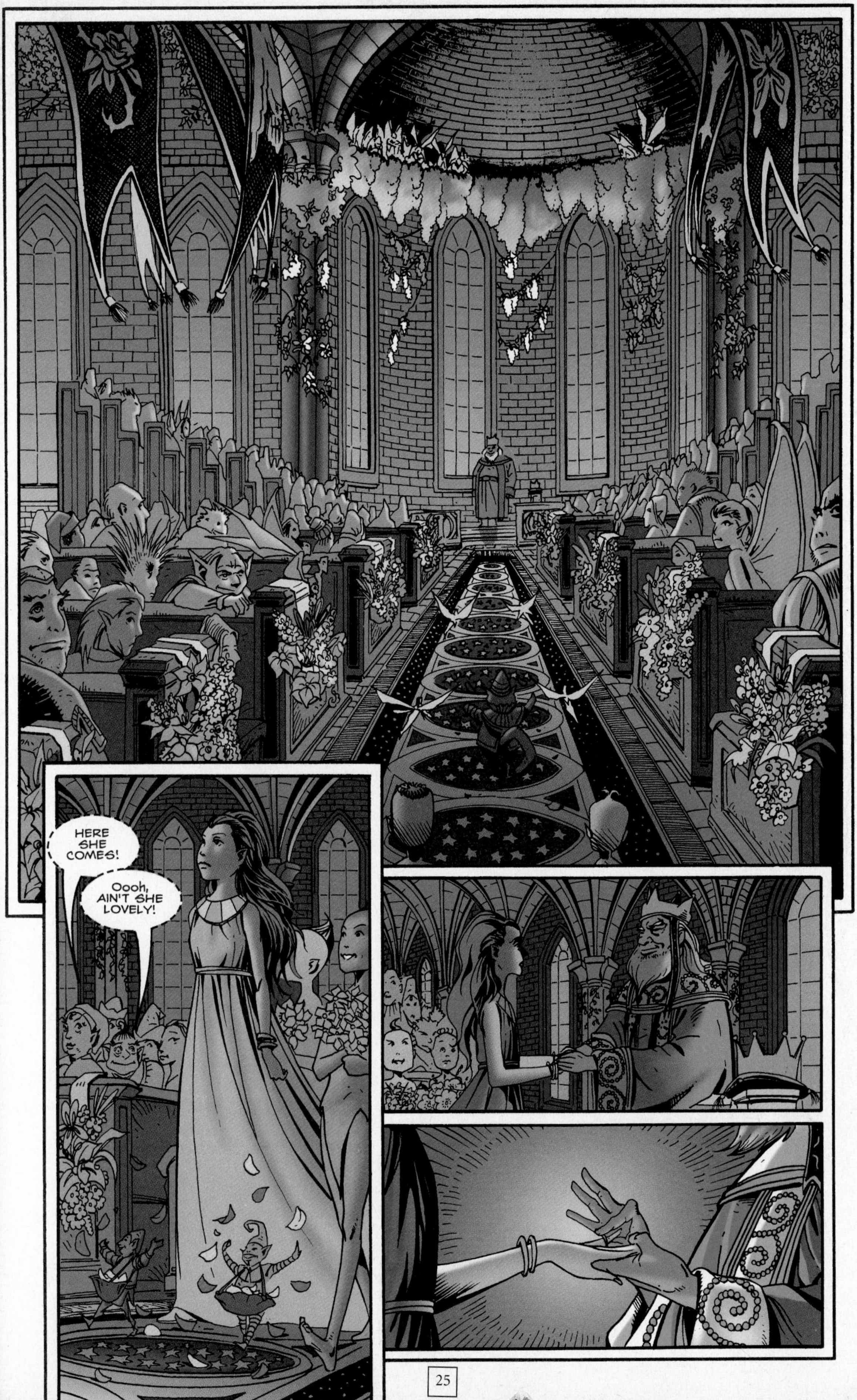
HERE SHE COMES!
Oooh, AIN'T SHE LOVELY!

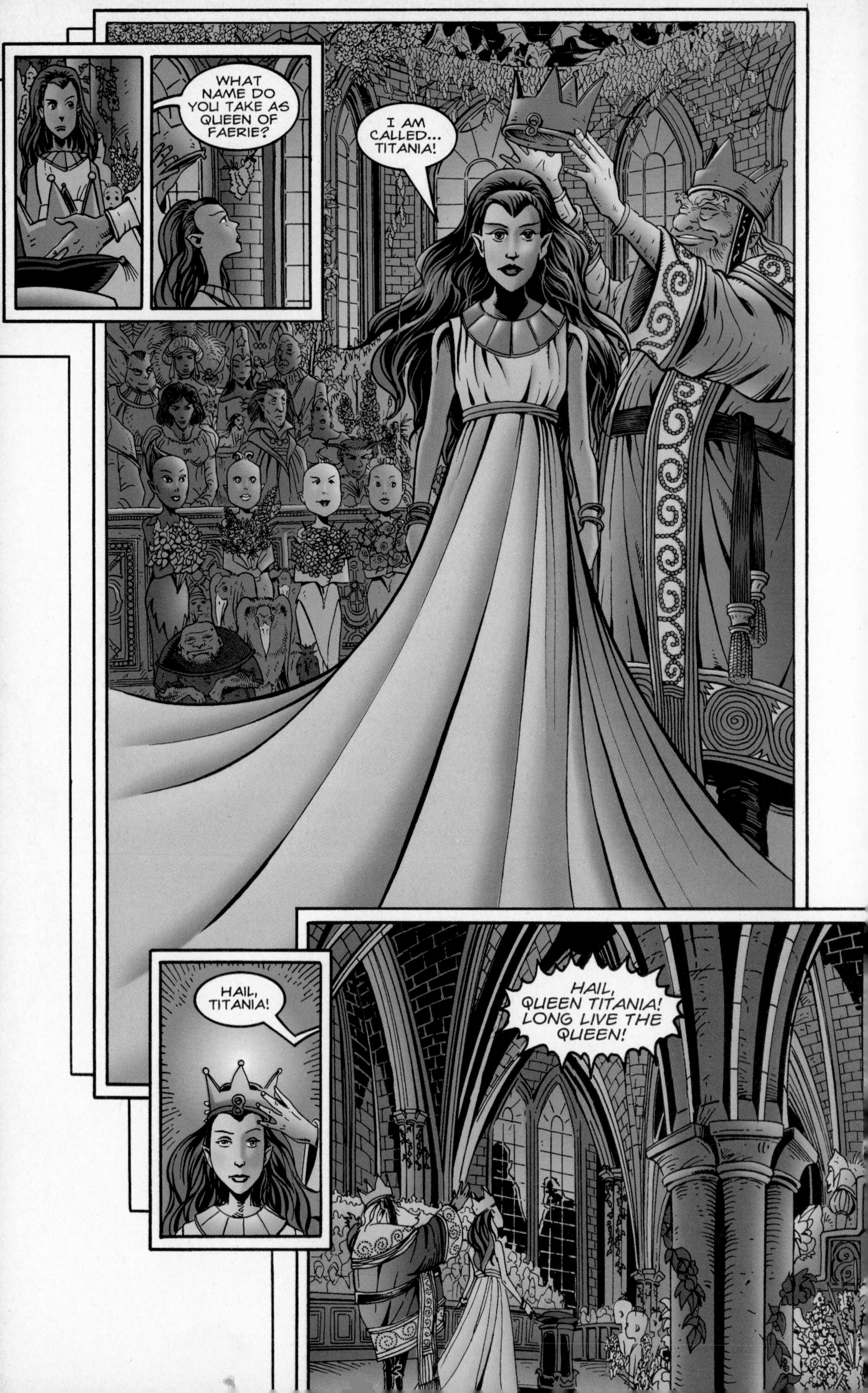
WHAT NAME DO YOU TAKE AS QUEEN OF FAERIE?
I AM CALLED... TITANIA!
HAIL, TITANIA!
HAIL, QUEEN TITANIA! LONG LIVE THE QUEEN!

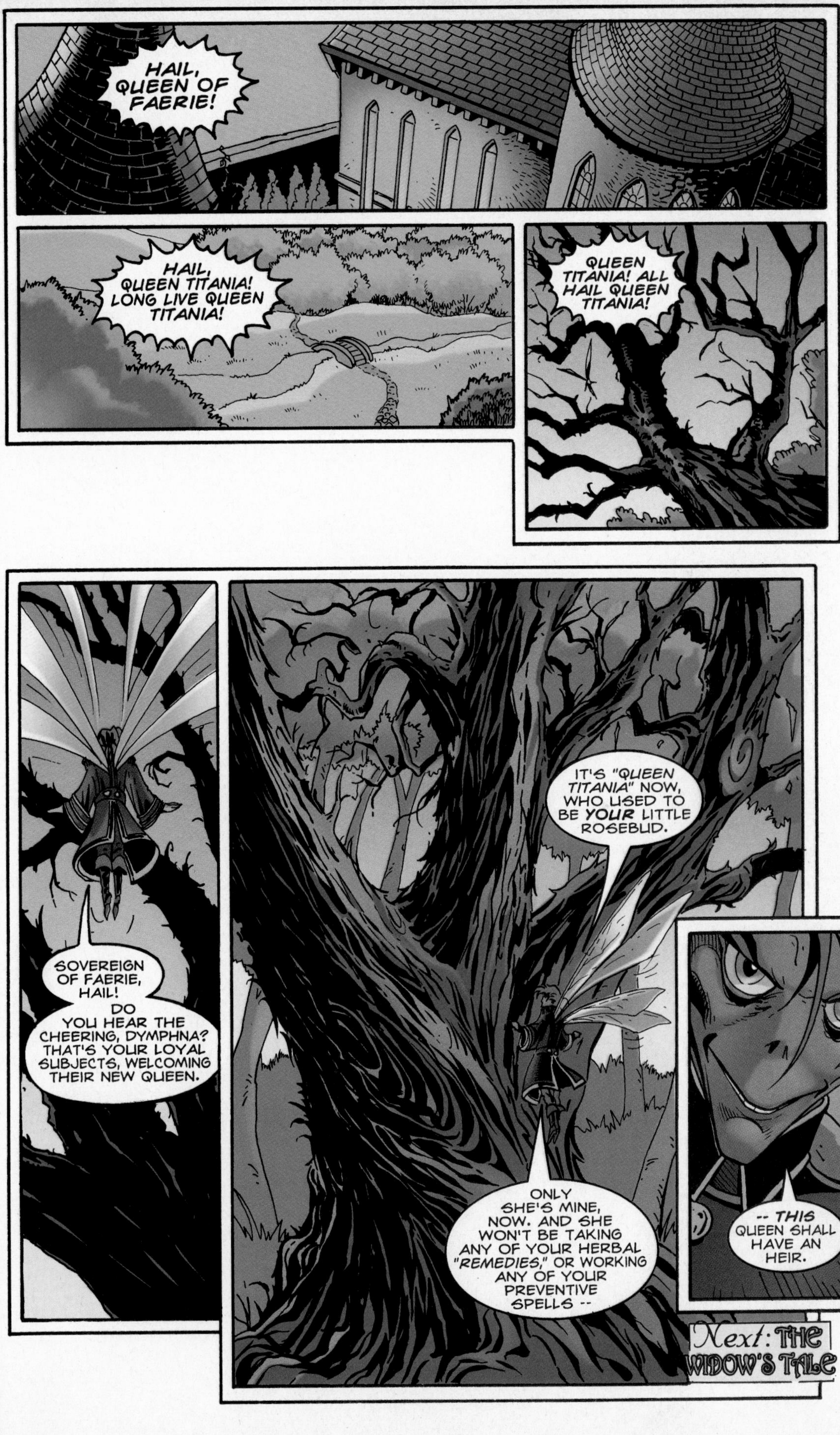
HAIL, QUEEN OF FAERIE!
HAIL, QUEEN TITANIA! LONG LIVE QUEEN TITANIA!
QUEEN TITANIA! ALL HAIL QUEEN TITANIA!
SOVEREIGN OF FAERIE, HAIL!
DO YOU HEAR THE CHEERING, DYMPHNA? THAT'S YOUR LOYAL SUBJECTS, WELCOMING THEIR NEW QUEEN.
IT'S "QUEEN TITANIA" NOW, WHO USED TO BE YOUR LITTLE ROSEBUD.
ONLY SHE'S MINE, NOW. AND SHE WON'T BE TAKING ANY OF YOUR HERBAL "REMEDIES," OR WORKING ANY OF YOUR PREVENTIVE SPELLS --
-- THIS QUEEN SHALL HAVE AN HEIR.
Next: THE WIDOW'S TALE

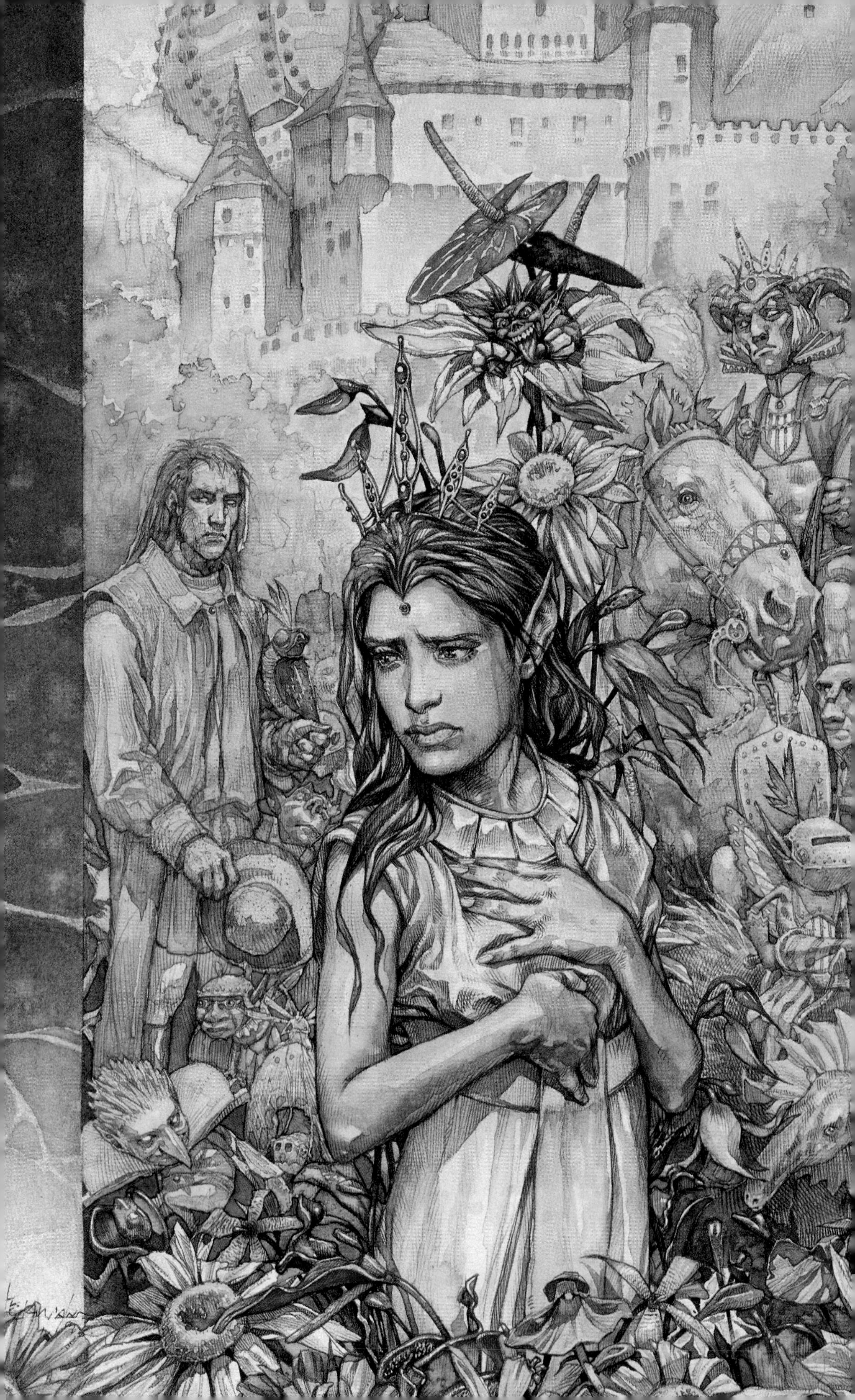

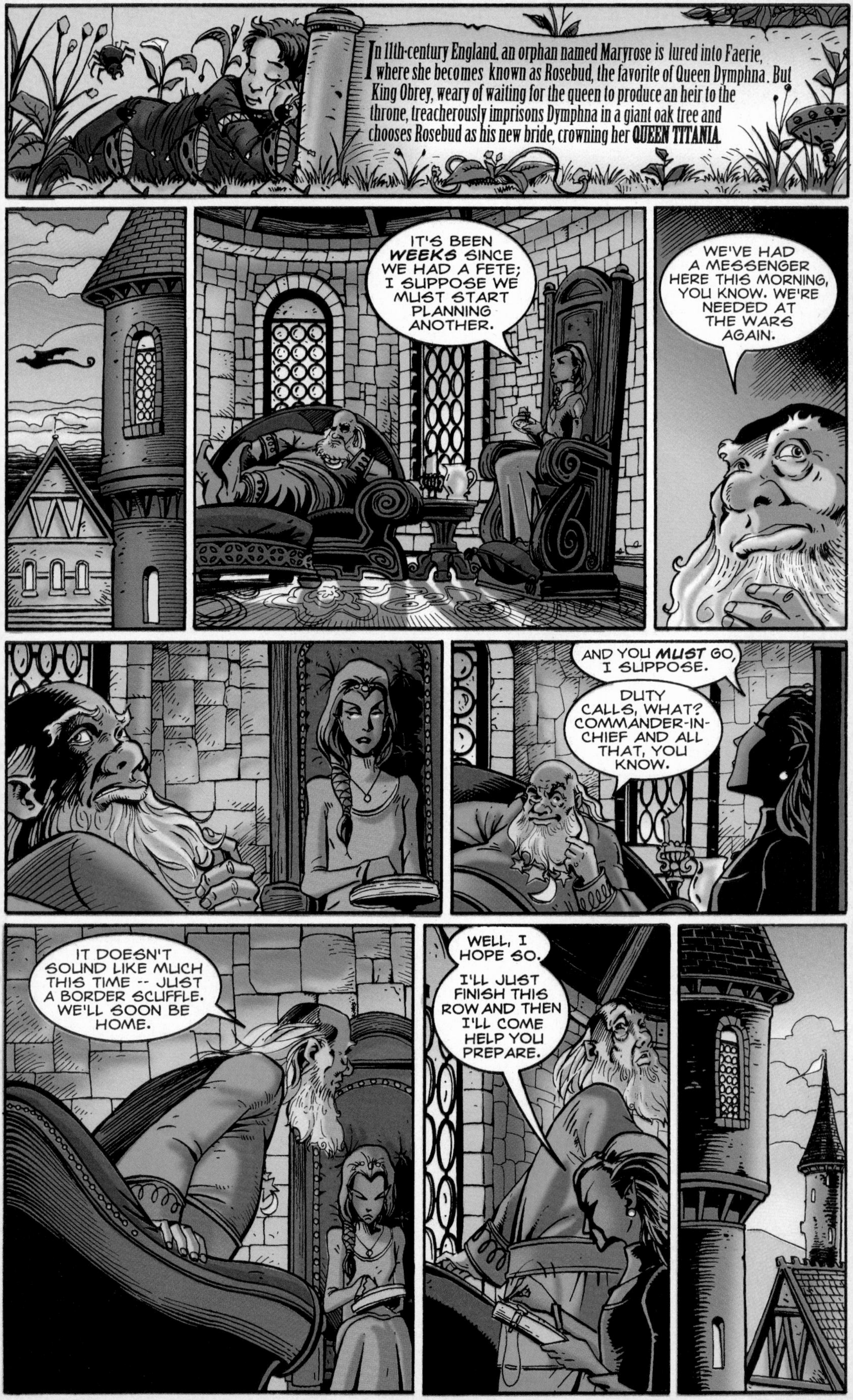
In 11th-century England, an orphan named Maryrose is lured into Faerie, where she becomes known as Rosebud, the favorite of Queen Dymphna. But King Obrey, weary of waiting for the queen to produce an heir to the throne, treacherously imprisons Dymphna in a giant oak tree and chooses Rosebud as his new bride, crowning her QUEEN TITANIA.
IT'S BEEN WEEKS SINCE WE HAD A FETE; I SUPPOSE WE MUST START PLANNING ANOTHER.
WE'VE HAD A MESSENGER HERE THIS MORNING, YOU KNOW. WE'RE NEEDED AT THE WARS AGAIN.
AND YOU MUST GO, I SUPPOSE.
DUTY CALLS, WHAT? COMMANDER-IN-CHIEF AND ALL THAT, YOU KNOW.
IT DOESN'T SOUND LIKE MUCH THIS TIME -- JUST A BORDER SCUFFLE. WE'LL SOON BE HOME.
WELL, I HOPE SO.
I'LL JUST FINISH THIS ROW AND THEN I'LL COME HELP YOU PREPARE.

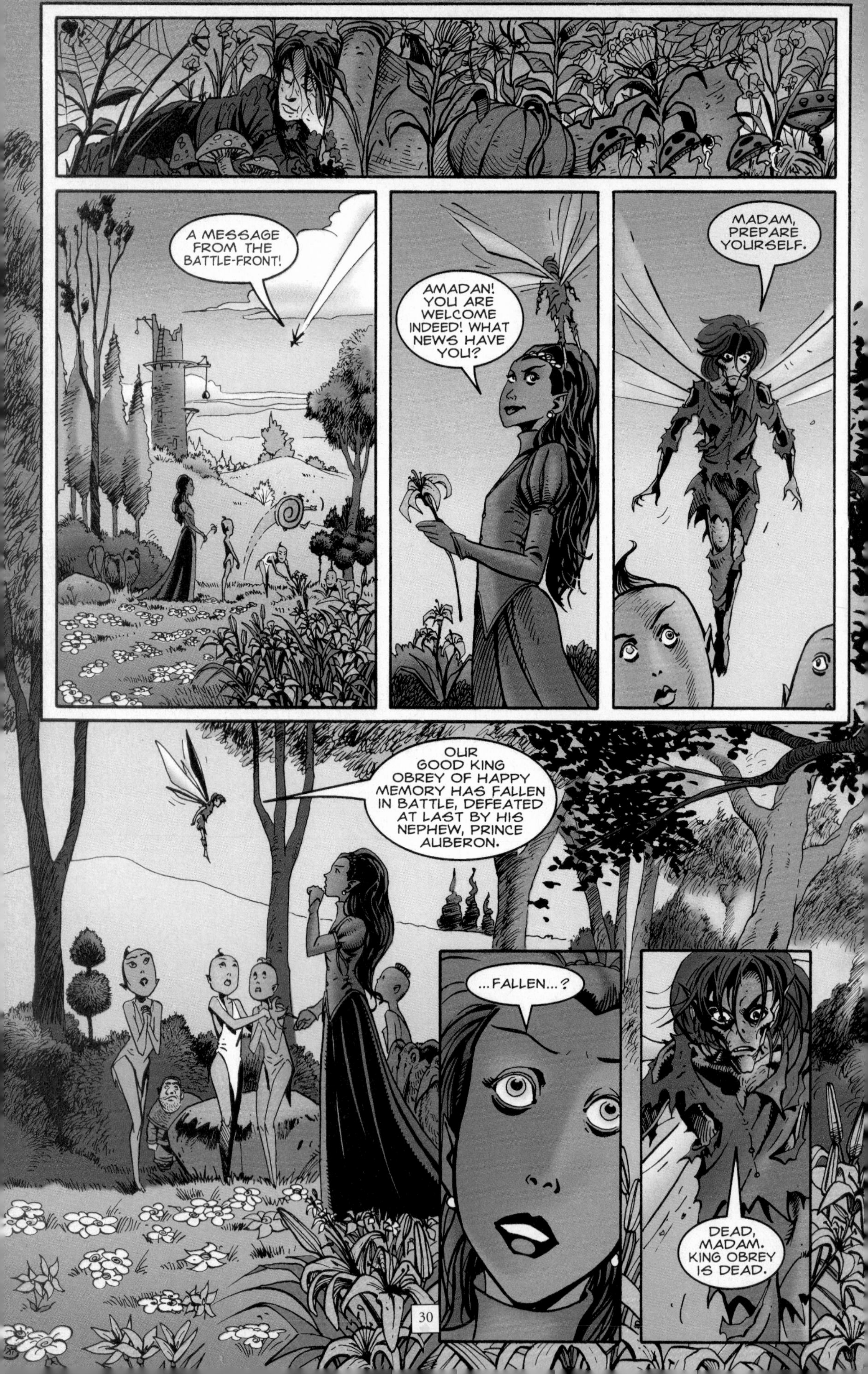
A MESSAGE FROM THE BATTLE-FRONT!
AMADAN! YOU ARE WELCOME INDEED! WHAT NEWS HAVE YOU?
MADAM, PREPARE YOURSELF.
OUR GOOD KING OBREY OF HAPPY MEMORY HAS FALLEN IN BATTLE, DEFEATED AT LAST BY HIS NEPHEW, PRINCE AUBERON.
...FALLEN...?
DEAD, MADAM. KING OBREY IS DEAD.

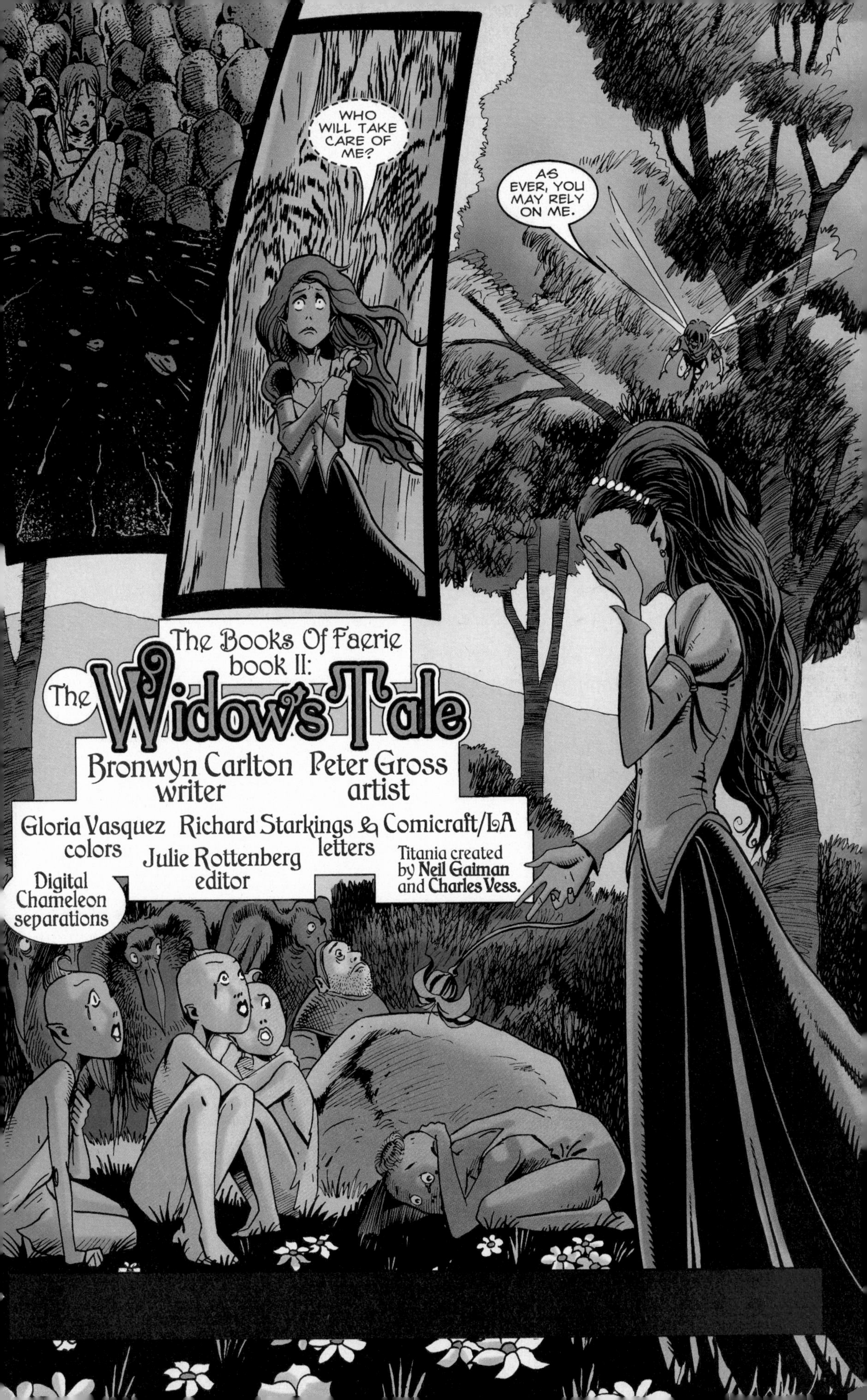
WHO WILL TAKE CARE OF ME?
AS EVER, YOU MAY RELY ON ME.
The Books Of Faerie book II:
The Widow's Tale
Bronwyn Carlton writer
Peter Gross artist
Gloria Vasquez colors
Richard Starkings & Comicraft/LA letters
Julie Rottenberg editor
Digital Chameleon separations
Titania created by Neil Gaiman and Charles Vess.

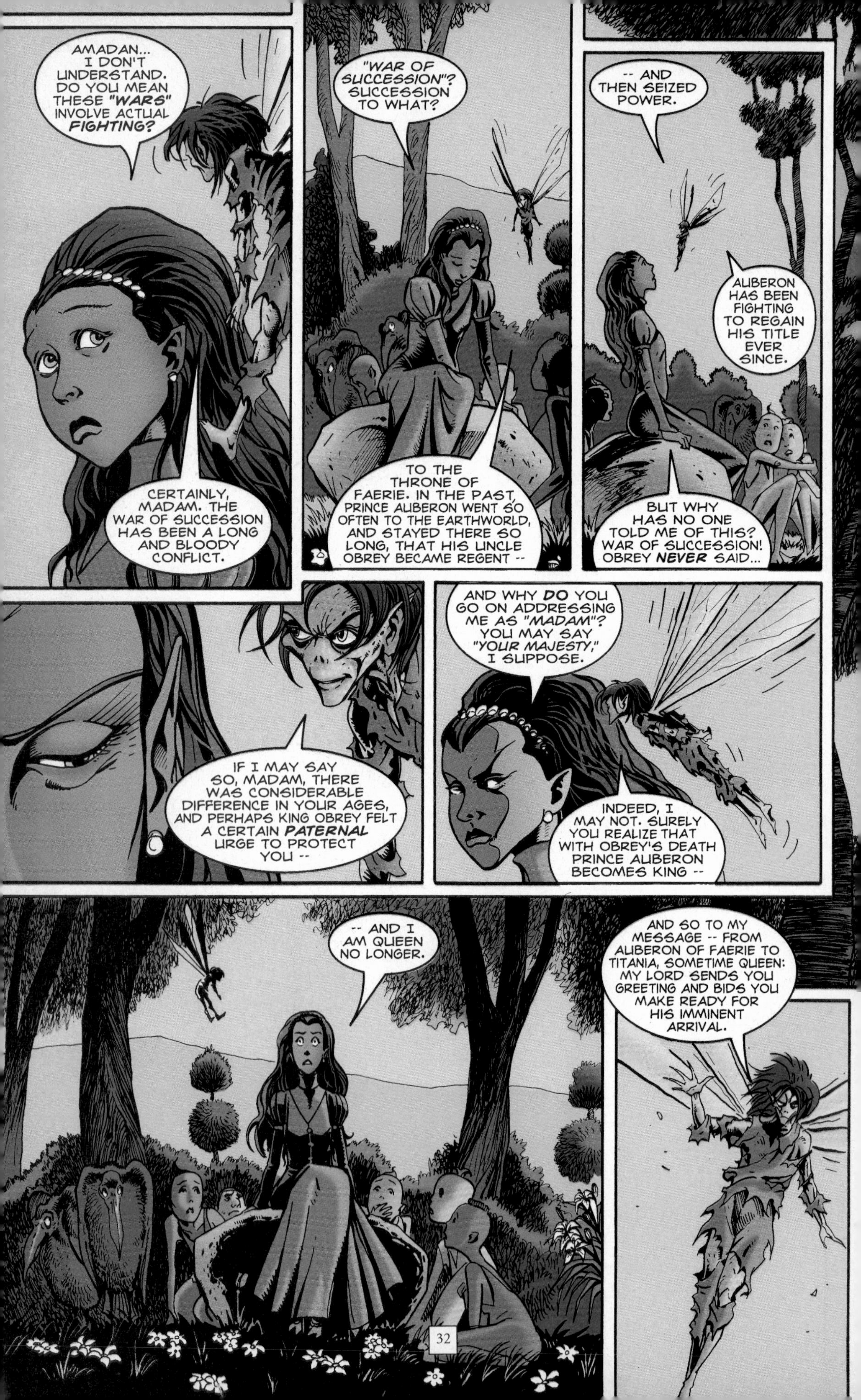
AMADAN... I DON'T UNDERSTAND. DO YOU MEAN THESE "WARS" INVOLVE ACTUAL FIGHTING?
CERTAINLY, MADAM. THE WAR OF SUCCESSION HAS BEEN A LONG AND BLOODY CONFLICT.
"WAR OF SUCCESSION"? SUCCESSION TO WHAT?
TO THE THRONE OF FAERIE. IN THE PAST, PRINCE AUBERON WENT SO OFTEN TO THE EARTHWORLD, AND STAYED THERE SO LONG, THAT HIS UNCLE OBREY BECAME REGENT --
-- AND THEN SEIZED POWER.
AUBERON HAS BEEN FIGHTING TO REGAIN HIS TITLE EVER SINCE.
BUT WHY HAS NO ONE TOLD ME OF THIS? WAR OF SUCCESSION! OBREY NEVER SAID...
IF I MAY SAY SO, MADAM, THERE WAS CONSIDERABLE DIFFERENCE IN YOUR AGES, AND PERHAPS KING OBREY FELT A CERTAIN PATERNAL URGE TO PROTECT YOU --
AND WHY DO YOU GO ON ADDRESSING ME AS "MADAM"? YOU MAY SAY "YOUR MAJESTY," I SUPPOSE.
INDEED, I MAY NOT. SURELY YOU REALIZE THAT WITH OBREY'S DEATH PRINCE AUBERON BECOMES KING --
-- AND I AM QUEEN NO LONGER.
AND SO TO MY MESSAGE -- FROM AUBERON OF FAERIE TO TITANIA, SOMETIME QUEEN: MY LORD SENDS YOU GREETING AND BIDS YOU MAKE READY FOR HIS IMMINENT ARRIVAL.

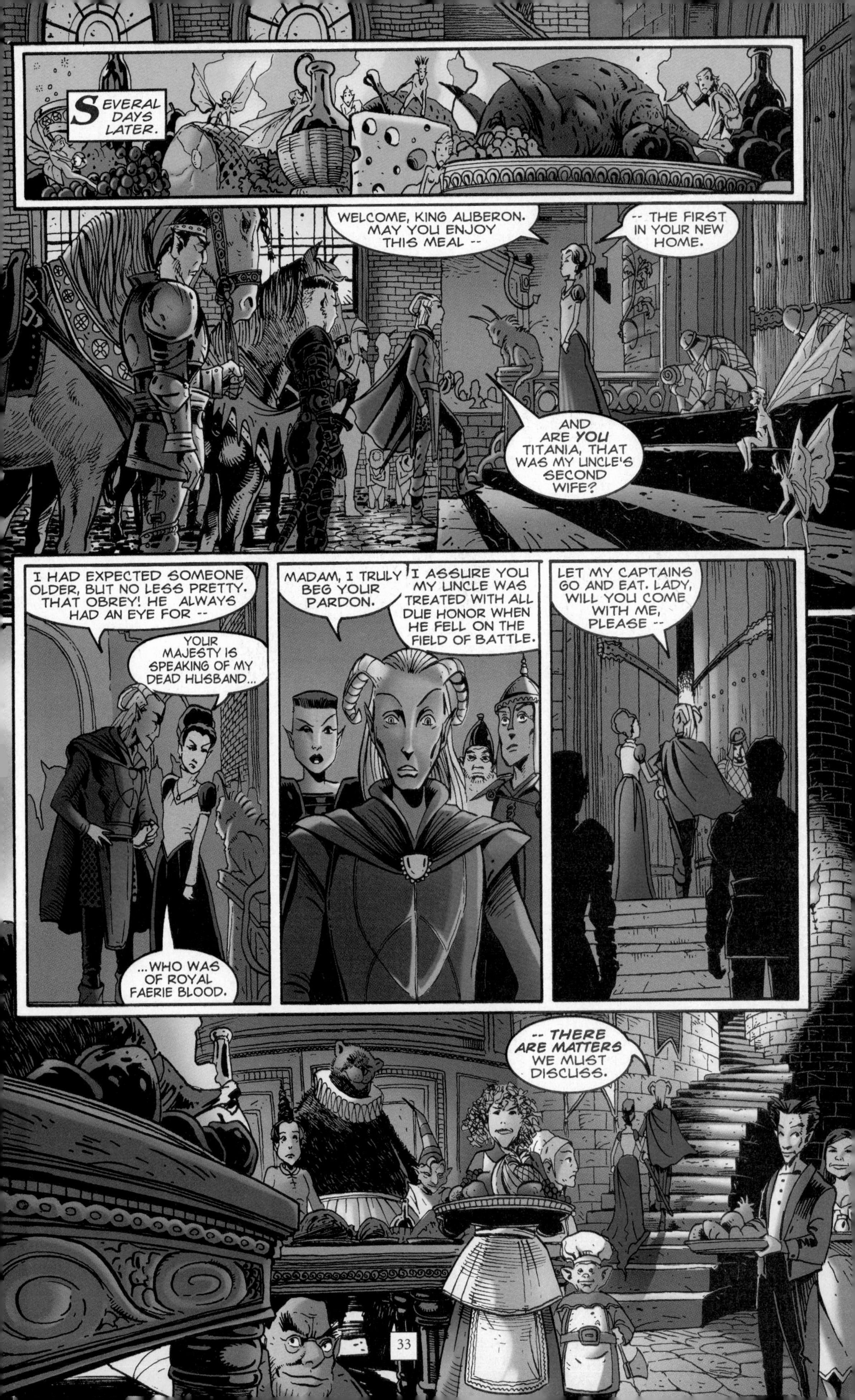
SEVERAL DAYS LATER.
WELCOME, KING AUBERON. MAY YOU ENJOY THIS MEAL --
-- THE FIRST IN YOUR NEW HOME.
AND ARE YOU TITANIA, THAT WAS MY UNCLE'S SECOND WIFE?
I HAD EXPECTED SOMEONE OLDER, BUT NO LESS PRETTY. THAT OBREY! HE ALWAYS HAD AN EYE FOR --
YOUR MAJESTY IS SPEAKING OF MY DEAD HUSBAND...
...WHO WAS OF ROYAL FAERIE BLOOD.
MADAM, I TRULY BEG YOUR PARDON.
I ASSURE YOU MY UNCLE WAS TREATED WITH ALL DUE HONOR WHEN HE FELL ON THE FIELD OF BATTLE.
LET MY CAPTAINS GO AND EAT. LADY, WILL YOU COME WITH ME, PLEASE --
-- THERE ARE MATTERS WE MUST DISCUSS.

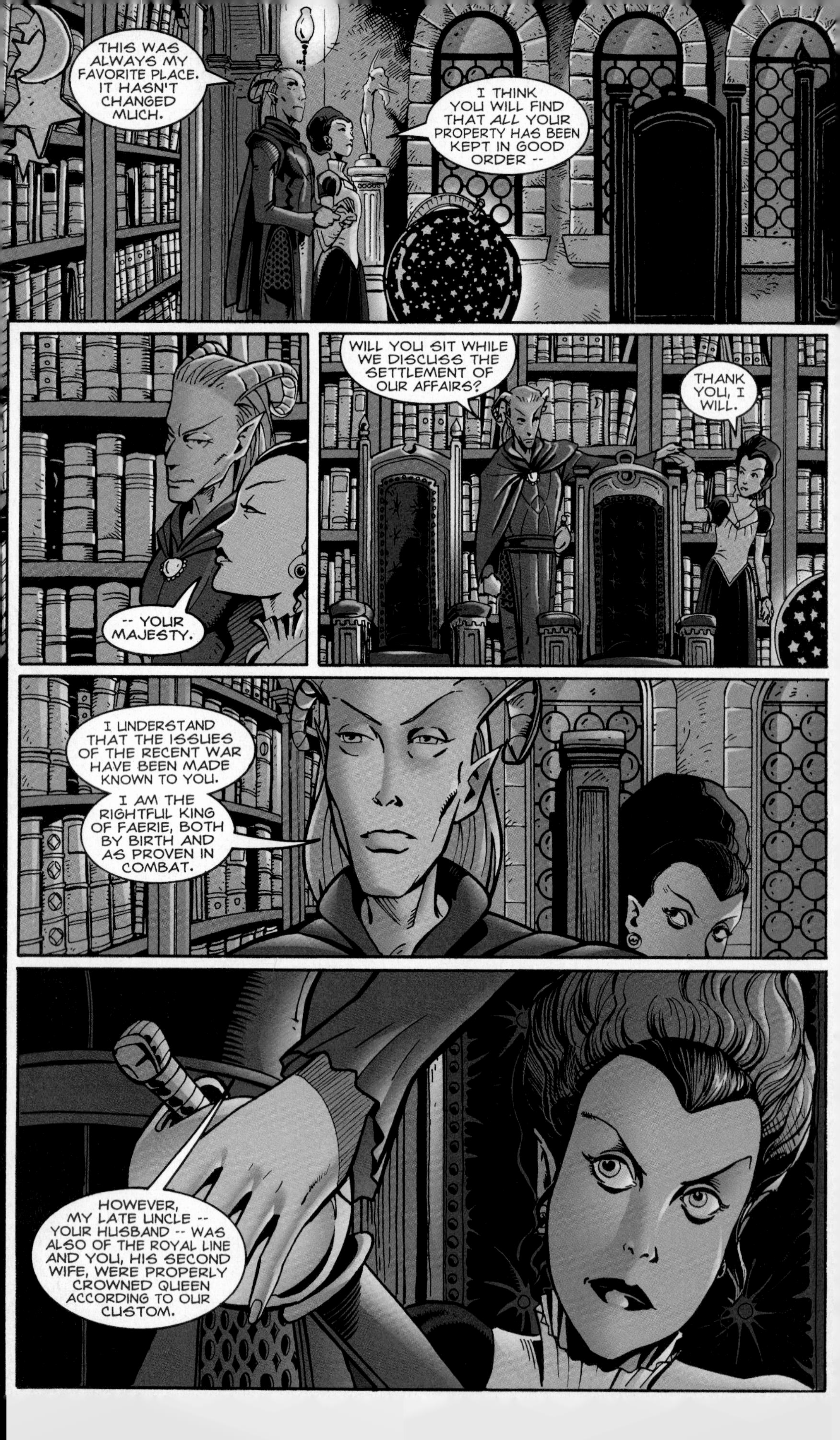
THIS WAS ALWAYS MY FAVORITE PLACE. IT HASN'T CHANGED MUCH.
I THINK YOU WILL FIND THAT *ALL* YOUR PROPERTY HAS BEEN KEPT IN GOOD ORDER --
-- YOUR MAJESTY.
WILL YOU SIT WHILE WE DISCUSS THE SETTLEMENT OF OUR AFFAIRS?
THANK YOU, I WILL.
I UNDERSTAND THAT THE ISSUES OF THE RECENT WAR HAVE BEEN MADE KNOWN TO YOU.
I AM THE RIGHTFUL KING OF FAERIE, BOTH BY BIRTH AND AS PROVEN IN COMBAT.
HOWEVER, MY LATE UNCLE -- YOUR HUSBAND -- WAS ALSO OF THE ROYAL LINE AND YOU, HIS SECOND WIFE, WERE PROPERLY CROWNED QUEEN ACCORDING TO OUR CUSTOM.

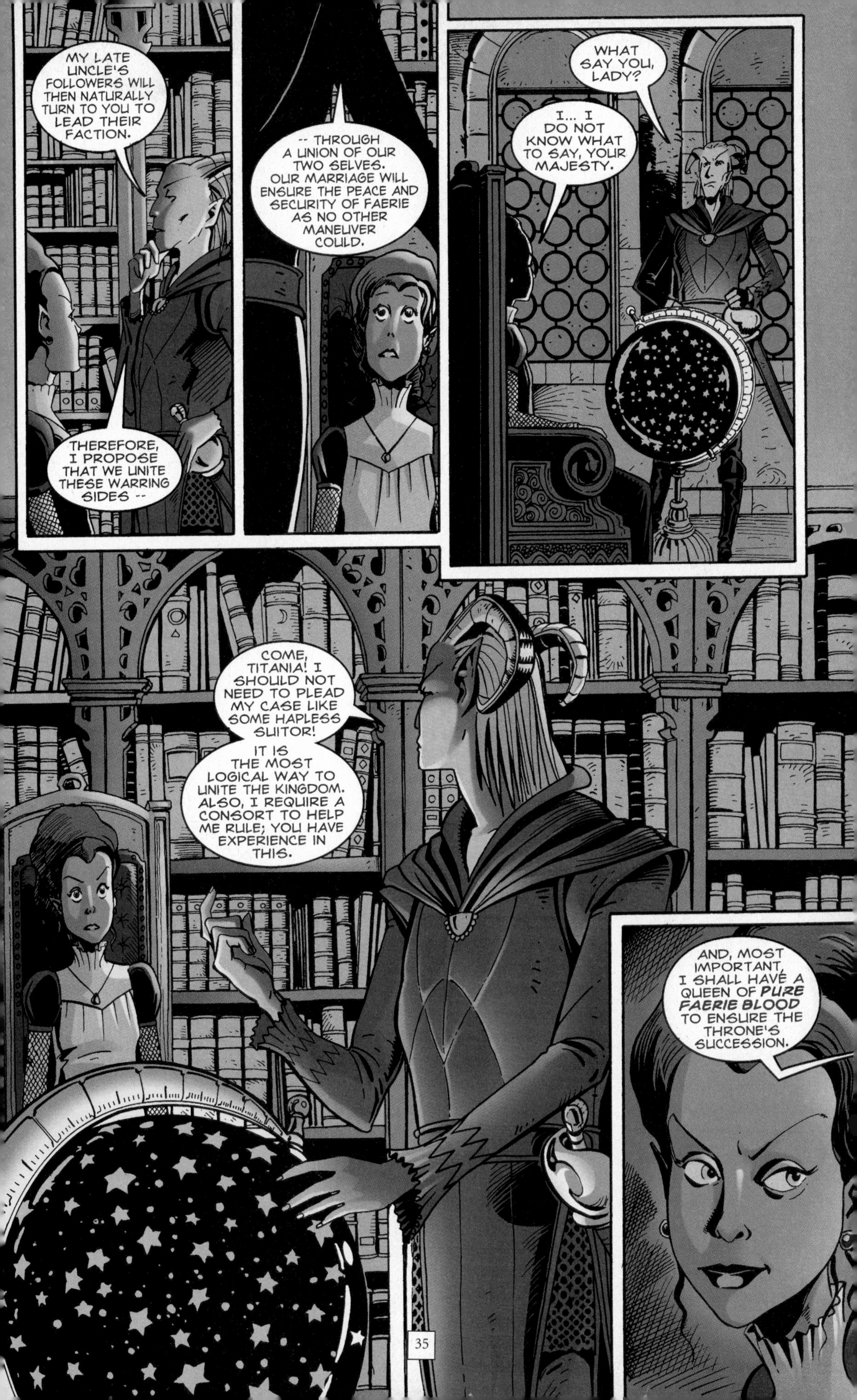
MY LATE UNCLE'S FOLLOWERS WILL THEN NATURALLY TURN TO YOU TO LEAD THEIR FACTION.
THEREFORE, I PROPOSE THAT WE UNITE THESE WARRING SIDES --
-- THROUGH A UNION OF OUR TWO SELVES. OUR MARRIAGE WILL ENSURE THE PEACE AND SECURITY OF FAERIE AS NO OTHER MANEUVER COULD.
WHAT SAY YOU, LADY?
I... I DO NOT KNOW WHAT TO SAY, YOUR MAJESTY.
COME, TITANIA! I SHOULD NOT NEED TO PLEAD MY CASE LIKE SOME HAPLESS SUITOR!
IT IS THE MOST LOGICAL WAY TO UNITE THE KINGDOM. ALSO, I REQUIRE A CONSORT TO HELP ME RULE; YOU HAVE EXPERIENCE IN THIS.
AND, MOST IMPORTANT, I SHALL HAVE A QUEEN OF *PURE FAERIE BLOOD* TO ENSURE THE THRONE'S SUCCESSION.

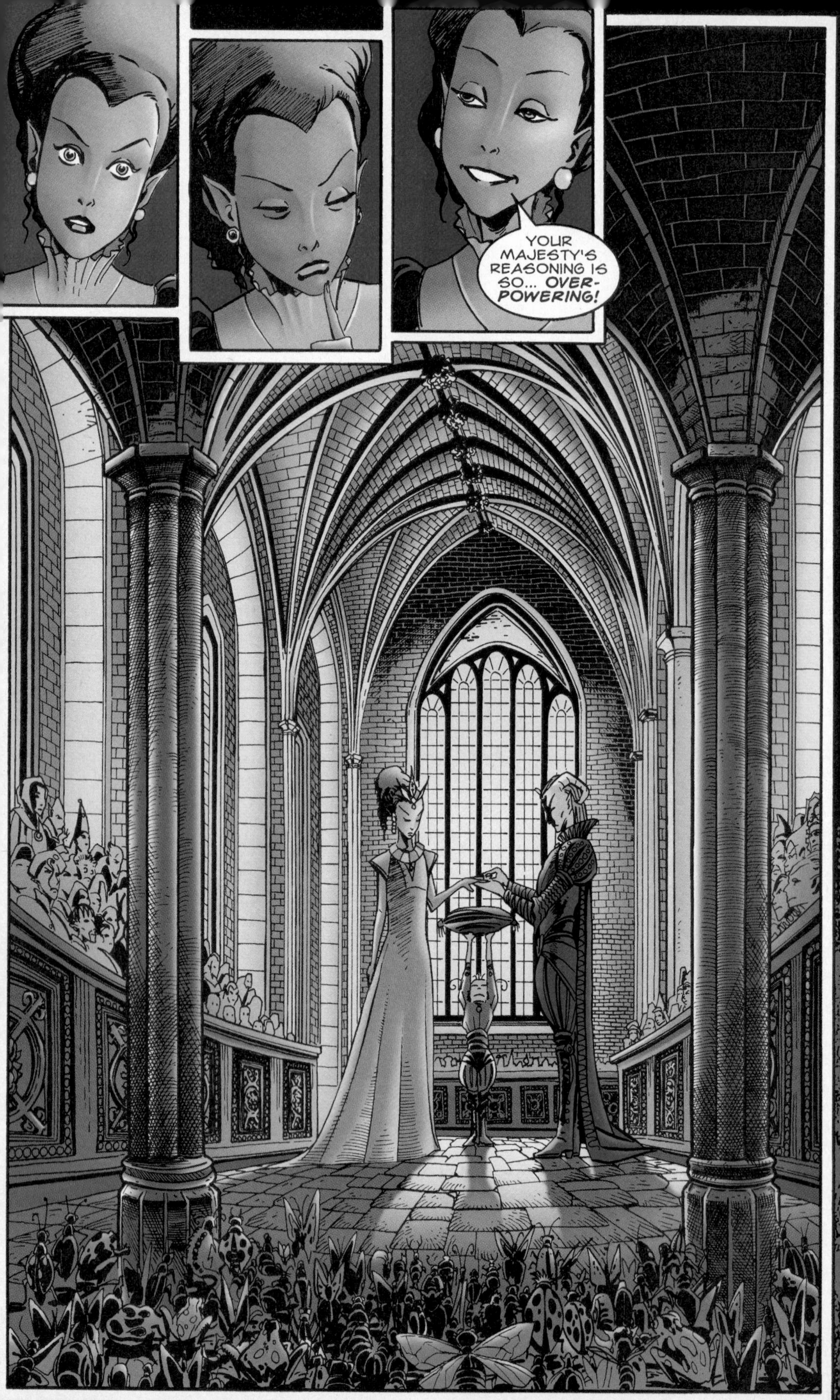
YOUR MAJESTY'S REASONING IS SO... OVER-POWERING!

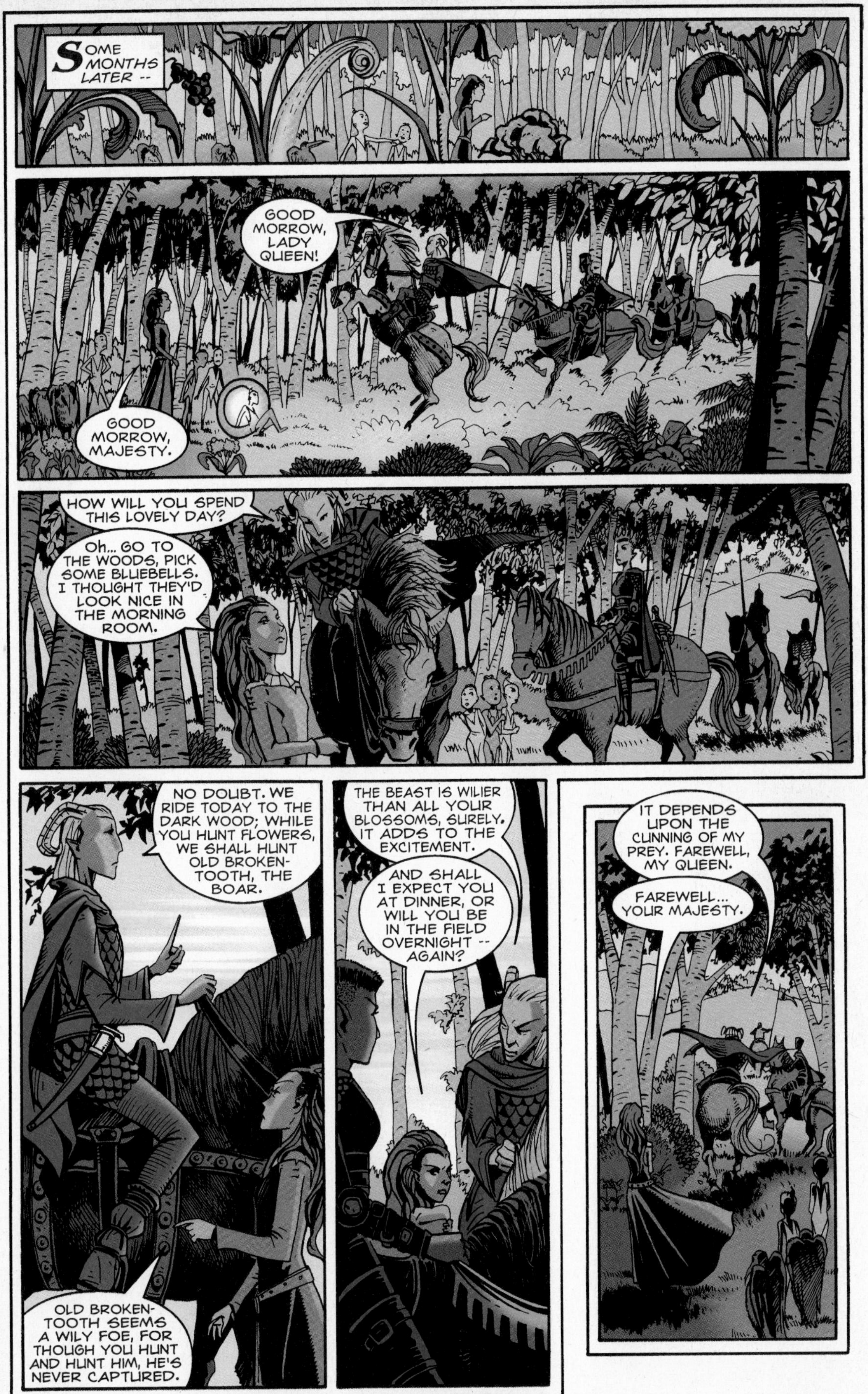
SOME MONTHS LATER --
GOOD MORROW, LADY QUEEN!
GOOD MORROW, MAJESTY.
HOW WILL YOU SPEND THIS LOVELY DAY?
Oh... GO TO THE WOODS, PICK SOME BLUEBELLS. I THOUGHT THEY'D LOOK NICE IN THE MORNING ROOM.
NO DOUBT. WE RIDE TODAY TO THE DARK WOOD; WHILE YOU HUNT FLOWERS, WE SHALL HUNT OLD BROKEN-TOOTH, THE BOAR.
OLD BROKEN-TOOTH SEEMS A WILY FOE, FOR THOUGH YOU HUNT AND HUNT HIM, HE'S NEVER CAPTURED.
THE BEAST IS WILIER THAN ALL YOUR BLOSSOMS, SURELY. IT ADDS TO THE EXCITEMENT.
AND SHALL I EXPECT YOU AT DINNER, OR WILL YOU BE IN THE FIELD OVERNIGHT -- AGAIN?
IT DEPENDS UPON THE CUNNING OF MY PREY. FAREWELL, MY QUEEN.
FAREWELL... YOUR MAJESTY.

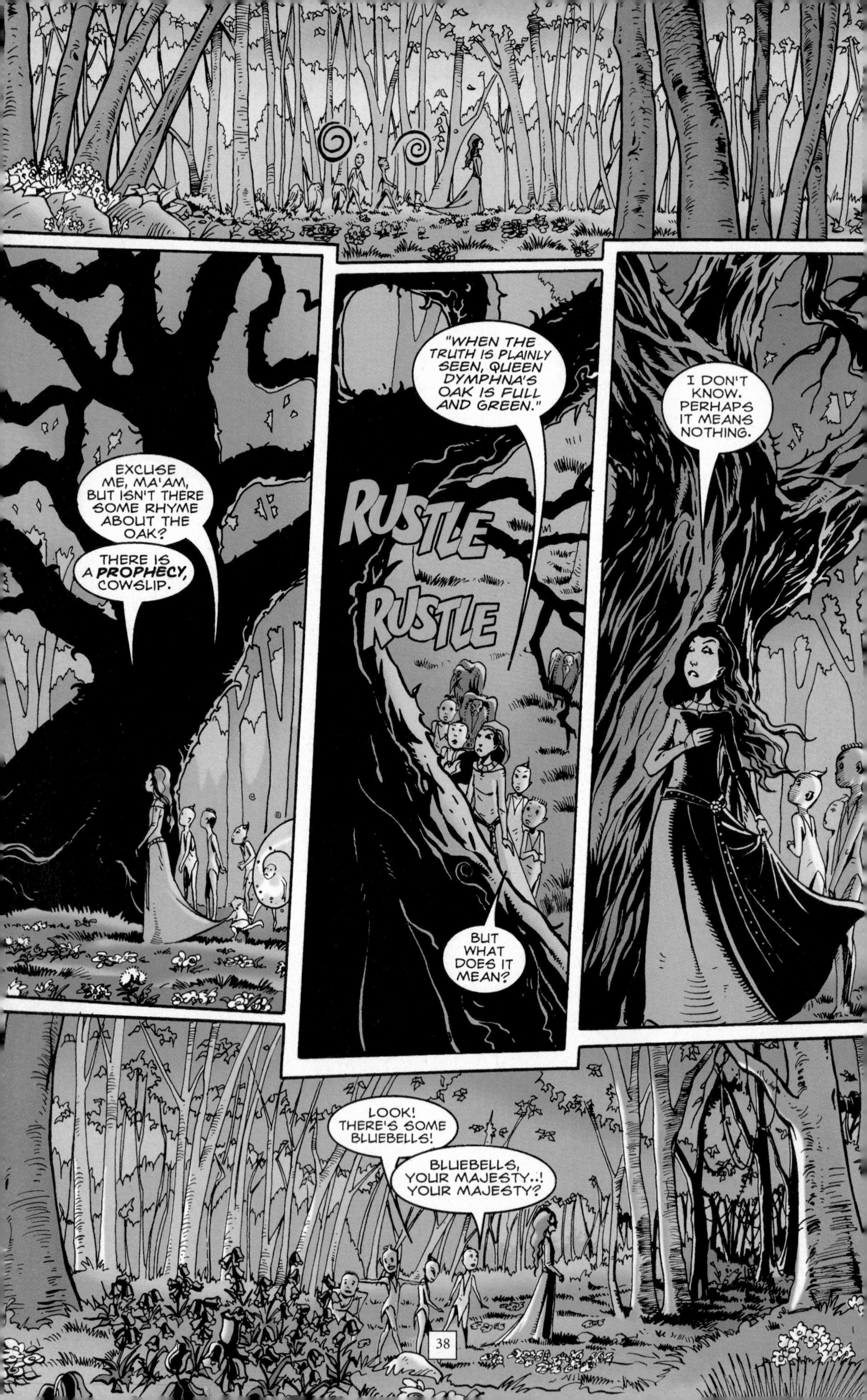
EXCUSE ME, MA'AM, BUT ISN'T THERE SOME RHYME ABOUT THE OAK?
THERE IS A **PROPHECY**, COWSLIP.
"WHEN THE TRUTH IS PLAINLY SEEN, QUEEN DYMPHNA'S OAK IS FULL AND GREEN."
RUSTLE
RUSTLE
BUT WHAT DOES IT MEAN?
I DON'T KNOW. PERHAPS IT MEANS NOTHING.
LOOK! THERE'S SOME BLUEBELLS!
BLUEBELLS, YOUR MAJESTY..! YOUR MAJESTY?

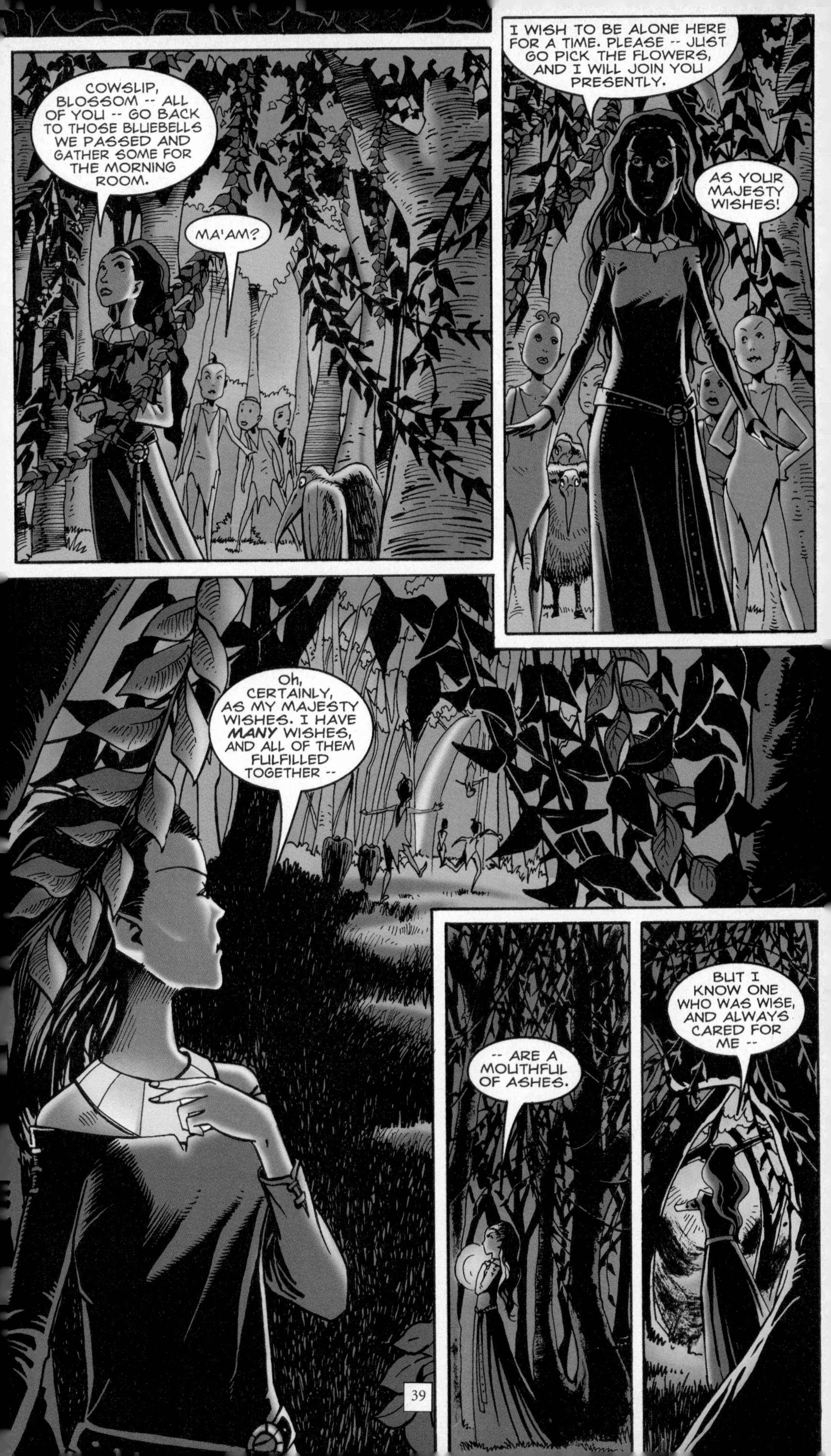
COWSLIP, BLOSSOM -- ALL OF YOU -- GO BACK TO THOSE BLUEBELLS WE PASSED AND GATHER SOME FOR THE MORNING ROOM.
MA'AM?
I WISH TO BE ALONE HERE FOR A TIME. PLEASE -- JUST GO PICK THE FLOWERS, AND I WILL JOIN YOU PRESENTLY.
AS YOUR MAJESTY WISHES!
Oh, CERTAINLY, AS MY MAJESTY WISHES. I HAVE *MANY* WISHES, AND ALL OF THEM FULFILLED TOGETHER --
-- ARE A MOUTHFUL OF ASHES.
BUT I KNOW ONE WHO WAS WISE, AND ALWAYS CARED FOR ME --

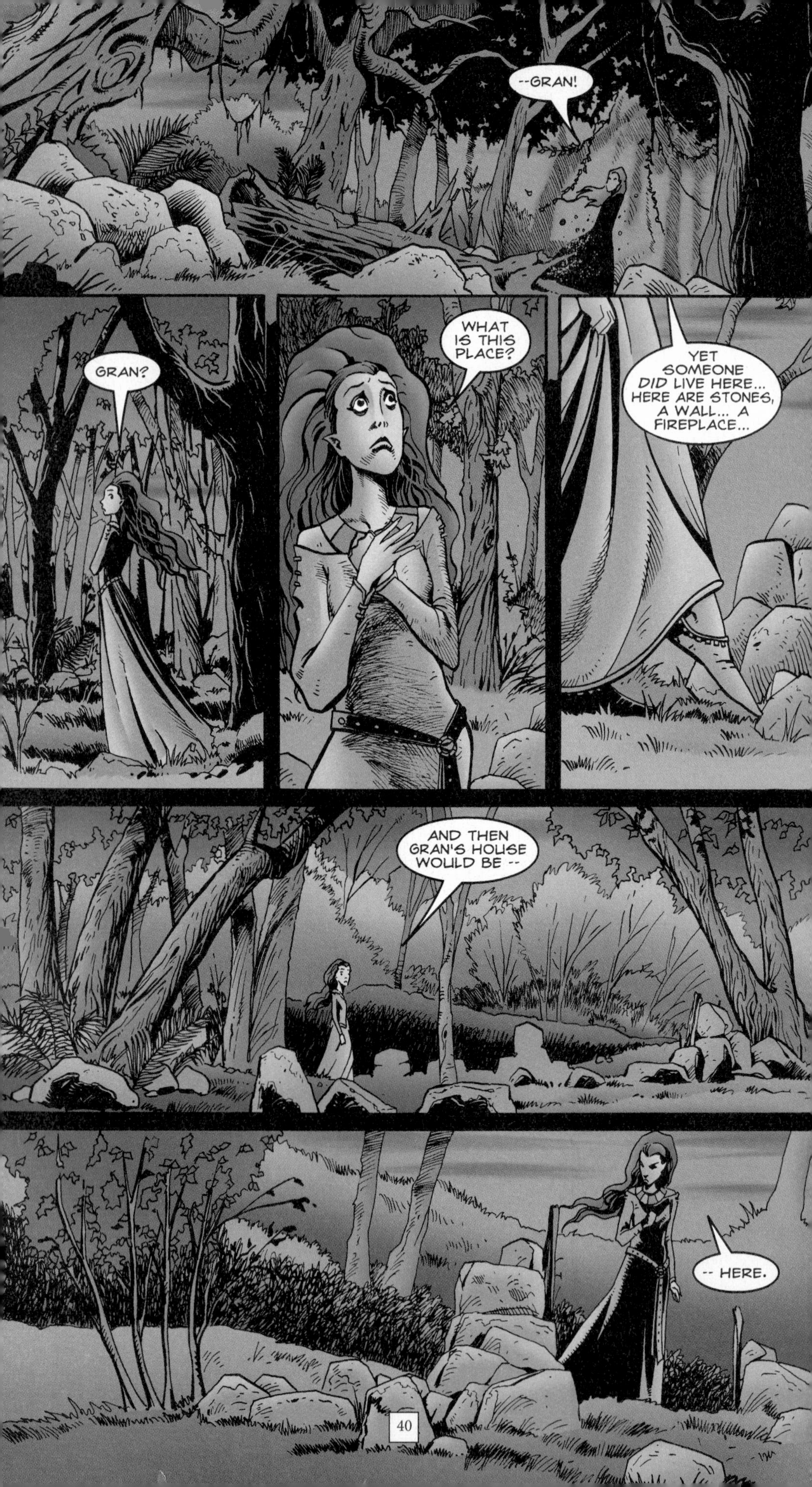
--GRAN!
GRAN?
WHAT IS THIS PLACE?
YET SOMEONE *DID* LIVE HERE... HERE ARE STONES, A WALL... A FIREPLACE...
AND THEN GRAN'S HOUSE WOULD BE --
-- HERE.

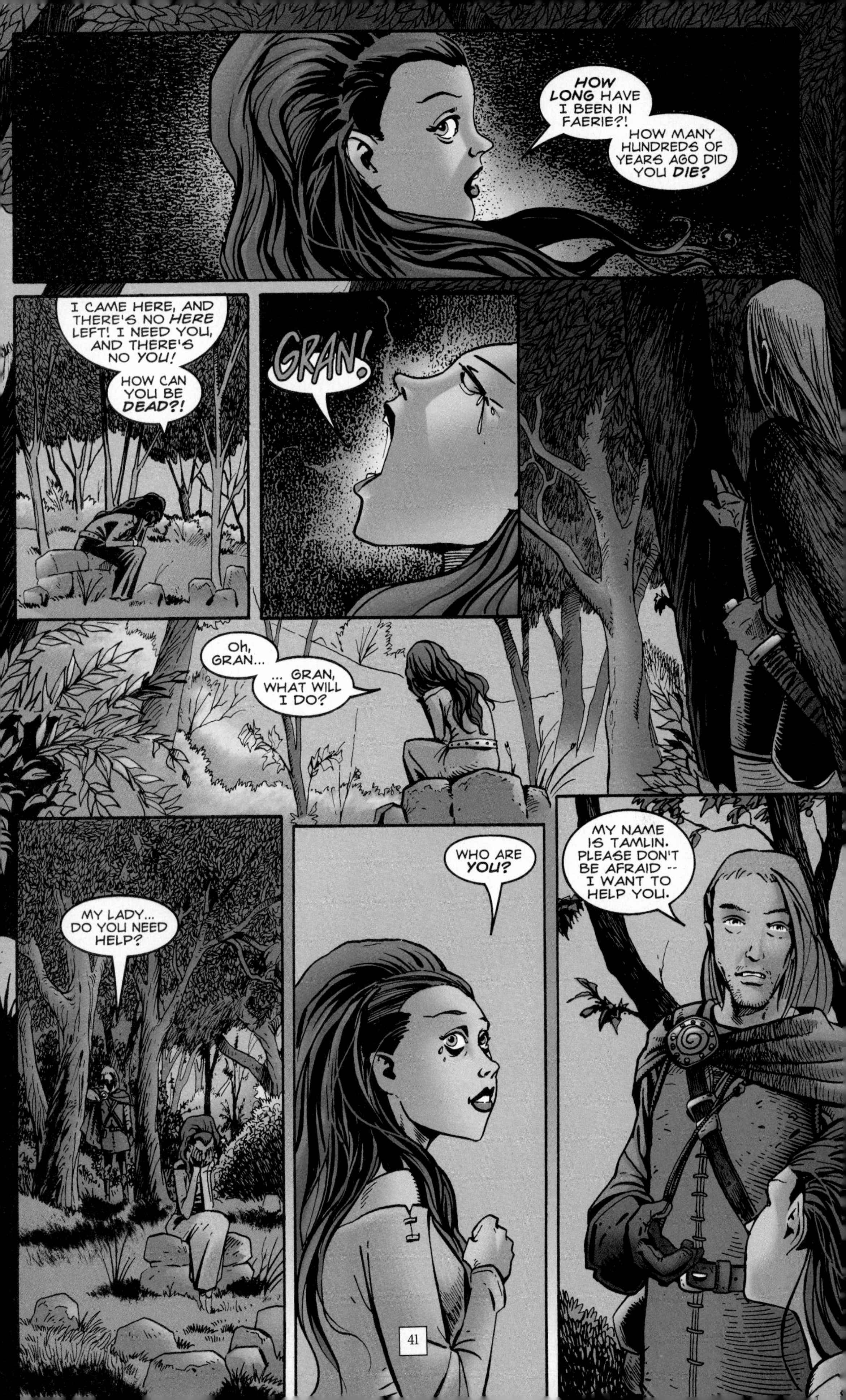
HOW LONG HAVE I BEEN IN FAERIE?!
HOW MANY HUNDREDS OF YEARS AGO DID YOU DIE?
I CAME HERE, AND THERE'S NO HERE LEFT! I NEED YOU, AND THERE'S NO YOU!
HOW CAN YOU BE DEAD?!
GRAN!
Oh, GRAN...
... GRAN, WHAT WILL I DO?
MY LADY... DO YOU NEED HELP?
WHO ARE YOU?
MY NAME IS TAMLIN. PLEASE DON'T BE AFRAID -- I WANT TO HELP YOU.

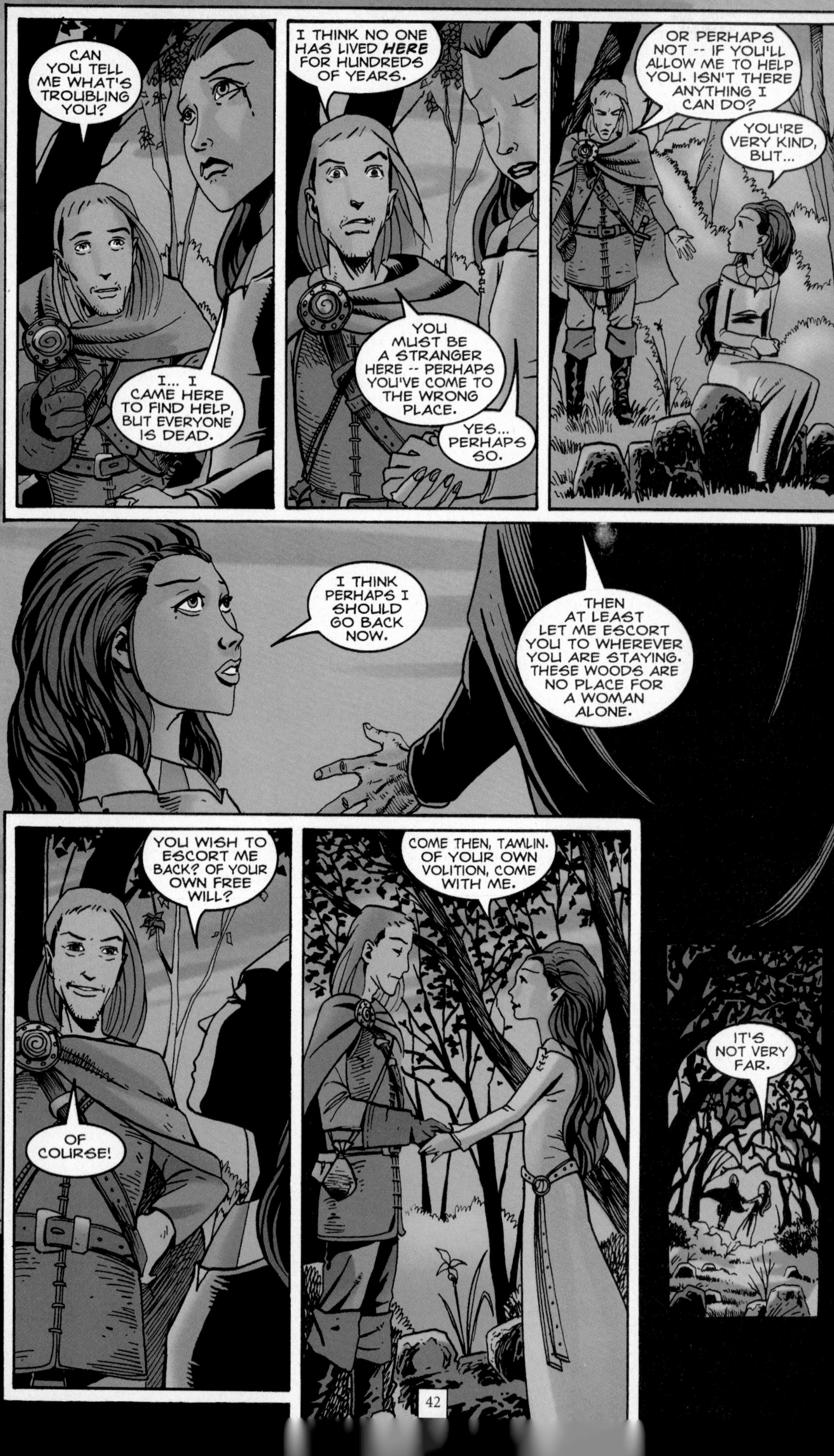
CAN YOU TELL ME WHAT'S TROUBLING YOU?
I... I CAME HERE TO FIND HELP, BUT EVERYONE IS DEAD.
I THINK NO ONE HAS LIVED HERE FOR HUNDREDS OF YEARS.
YOU MUST BE A STRANGER HERE -- PERHAPS YOU'VE COME TO THE WRONG PLACE.
YES... PERHAPS SO.
OR PERHAPS NOT -- IF YOU'LL ALLOW ME TO HELP YOU. ISN'T THERE ANYTHING I CAN DO?
YOU'RE VERY KIND, BUT...
I THINK PERHAPS I SHOULD GO BACK NOW.
THEN AT LEAST LET ME ESCORT YOU TO WHEREVER YOU ARE STAYING. THESE WOODS ARE NO PLACE FOR A WOMAN ALONE.
YOU WISH TO ESCORT ME BACK? OF YOUR OWN FREE WILL?
OF COURSE!
COME THEN, TAMLIN. OF YOUR OWN VOLITION, COME WITH ME.
IT'S NOT VERY FAR.

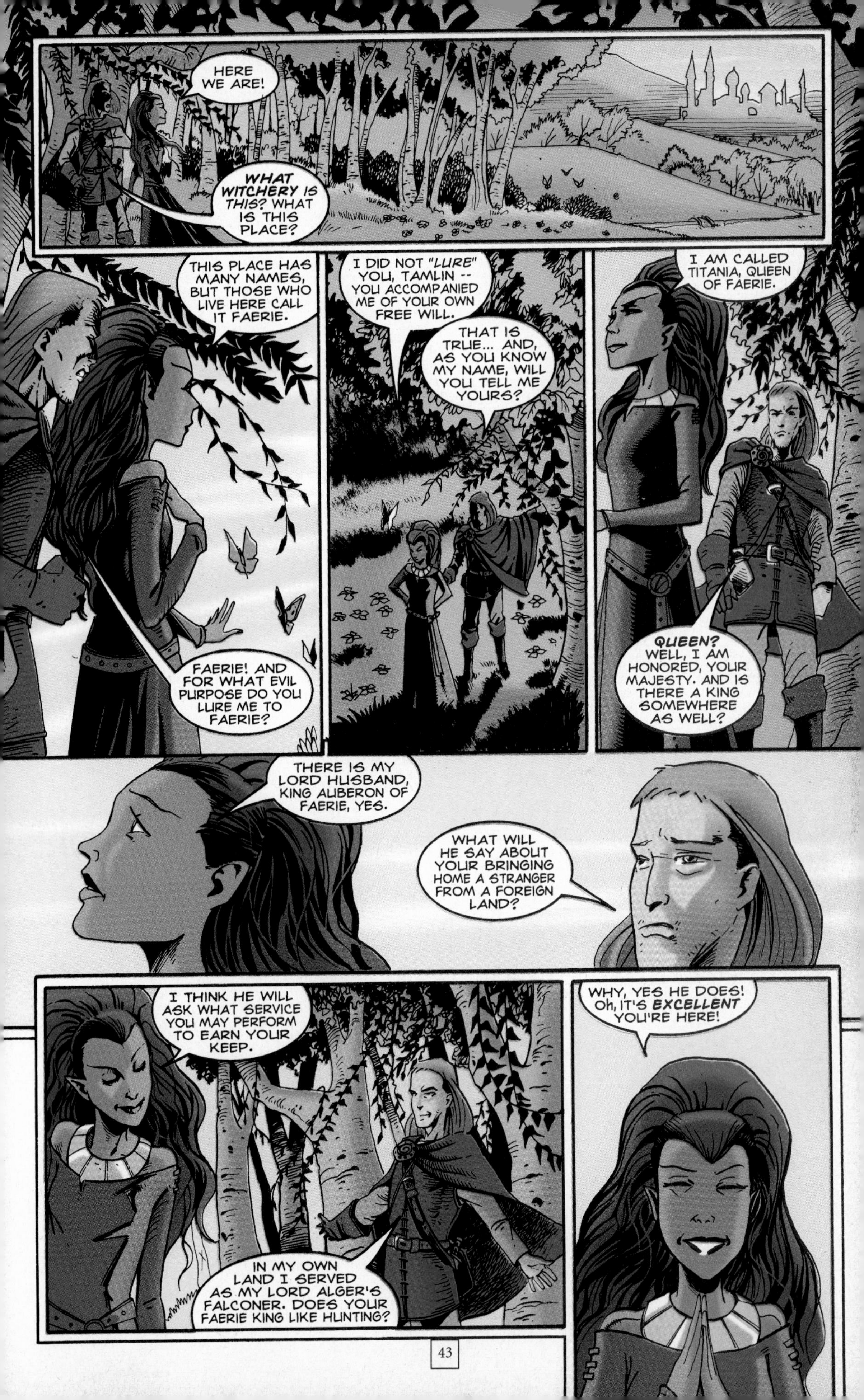

HERE WE ARE!
WHAT WITCHERY IS THIS? WHAT IS THIS PLACE?
THIS PLACE HAS MANY NAMES, BUT THOSE WHO LIVE HERE CALL IT FAERIE.
FAERIE! AND FOR WHAT EVIL PURPOSE DO YOU LURE ME TO FAERIE?
I DID NOT "LURE" YOU, TAMLIN -- YOU ACCOMPANIED ME OF YOUR OWN FREE WILL.
THAT IS TRUE... AND, AS YOU KNOW MY NAME, WILL YOU TELL ME YOURS?
I AM CALLED TITANIA, QUEEN OF FAERIE.
QUEEN? WELL, I AM HONORED, YOUR MAJESTY. AND IS THERE A KING SOMEWHERE AS WELL?
THERE IS MY LORD HUSBAND, KING AUBERON OF FAERIE, YES.
WHAT WILL HE SAY ABOUT YOUR BRINGING HOME A STRANGER FROM A FOREIGN LAND?
I THINK HE WILL ASK WHAT SERVICE YOU MAY PERFORM TO EARN YOUR KEEP.
IN MY OWN LAND I SERVED AS MY LORD ALGER'S FALCONER. DOES YOUR FAERIE KING LIKE HUNTING?
WHY, YES HE DOES! Oh, IT'S EXCELLENT YOU'RE HERE!

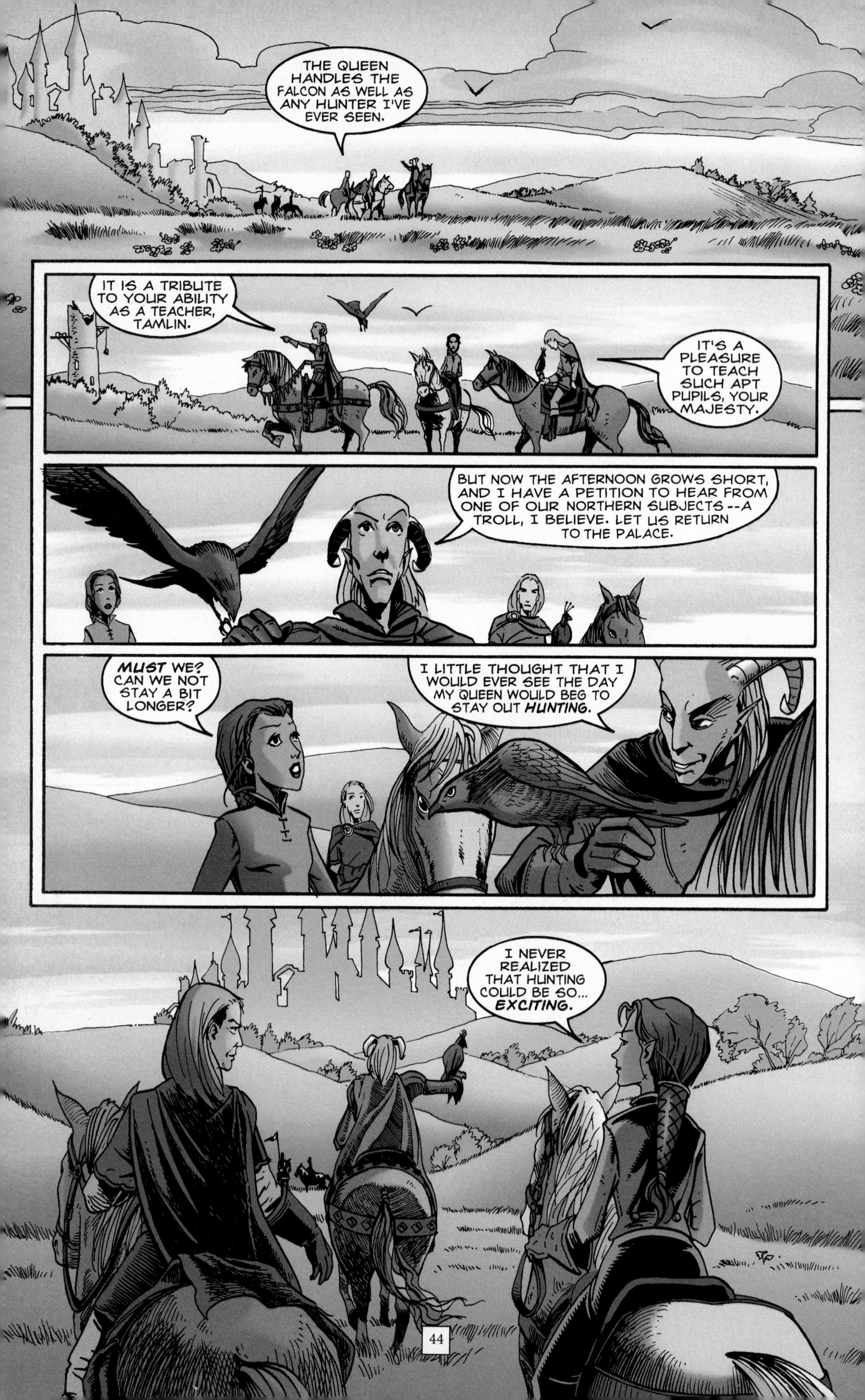
THE QUEEN HANDLES THE FALCON AS WELL AS ANY HUNTER I'VE EVER SEEN.
IT IS A TRIBUTE TO YOUR ABILITY AS A TEACHER, TAMLIN.
IT'S A PLEASURE TO TEACH SUCH APT PUPILS, YOUR MAJESTY.
BUT NOW THE AFTERNOON GROWS SHORT, AND I HAVE A PETITION TO HEAR FROM ONE OF OUR NORTHERN SUBJECTS--A TROLL, I BELIEVE. LET US RETURN TO THE PALACE.
MUST WE? CAN WE NOT STAY A BIT LONGER?
I LITTLE THOUGHT THAT I WOULD EVER SEE THE DAY MY QUEEN WOULD BEG TO STAY OUT *HUNTING*.
I NEVER REALIZED THAT HUNTING COULD BE SO... *EXCITING*.

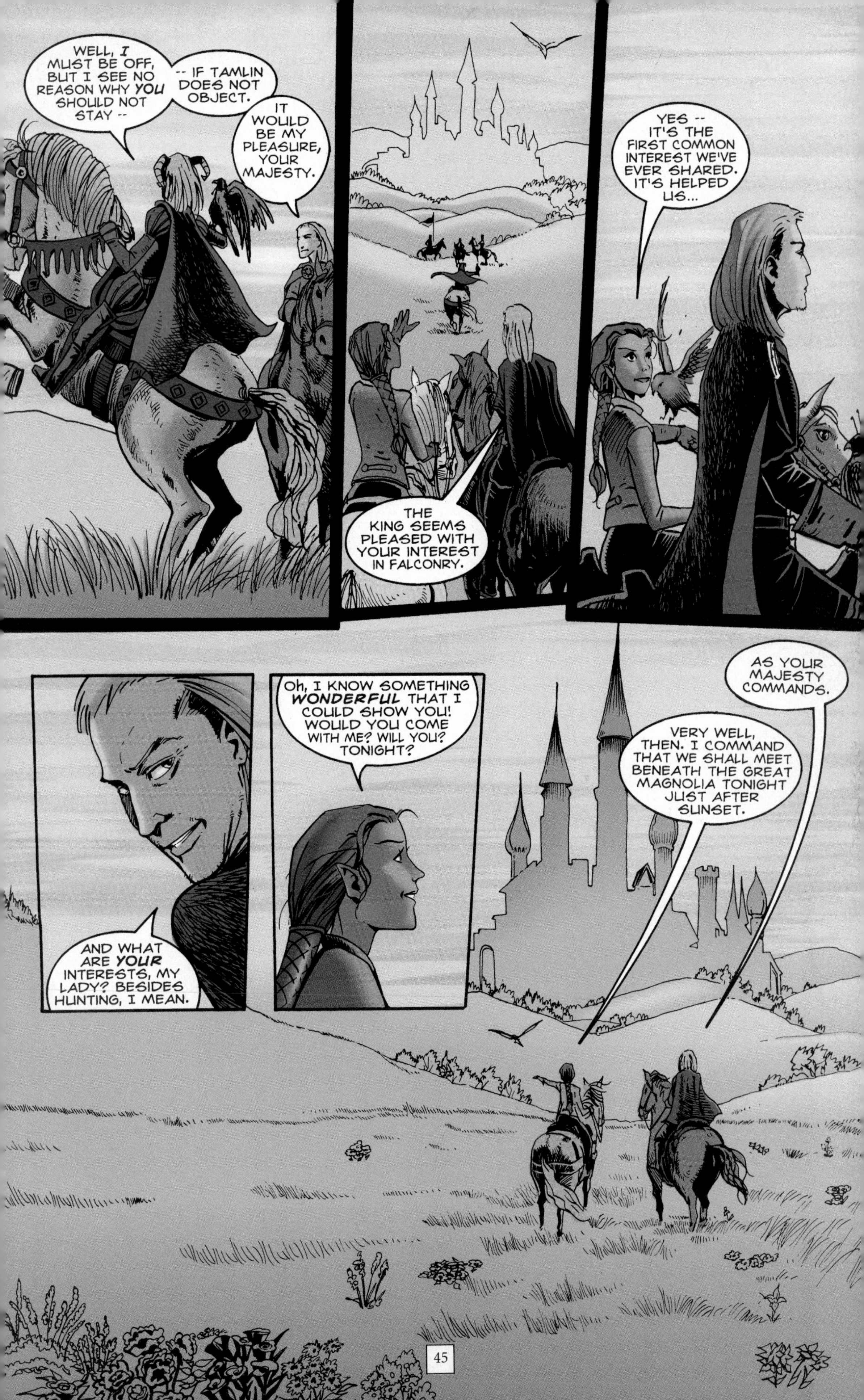
WELL, I MUST BE OFF, BUT I SEE NO REASON WHY YOU SHOULD NOT STAY --
-- IF TAMLIN DOES NOT OBJECT.
IT WOULD BE MY PLEASURE, YOUR MAJESTY.
THE KING SEEMS PLEASED WITH YOUR INTEREST IN FALCONRY.
YES -- IT'S THE FIRST COMMON INTEREST WE'VE EVER SHARED. IT'S HELPED US...
AND WHAT ARE YOUR INTERESTS, MY LADY? BESIDES HUNTING, I MEAN.
Oh, I KNOW SOMETHING WONDERFUL THAT I COULD SHOW YOU! WOULD YOU COME WITH ME? WILL YOU? TONIGHT?
AS YOUR MAJESTY COMMANDS.
VERY WELL, THEN. I COMMAND THAT WE SHALL MEET BENEATH THE GREAT MAGNOLIA TONIGHT JUST AFTER SUNSET.

WELL MET, TAMLIN!
YOUR MAJESTY?
I'M GLAD YOU'RE HERE ALREADY. HURRY, OR WE'LL MISS IT!
YOU CAN HANDLE A BOAT, I HOPE.
IF IT'S NOT TOO FAR...
IT'S JUST OVER THERE, BUT WE MUST HURRY! BEFORE THE MOON RISES TOO HIGH!
THERE IT IS! LOOK! DO YOU SEE?

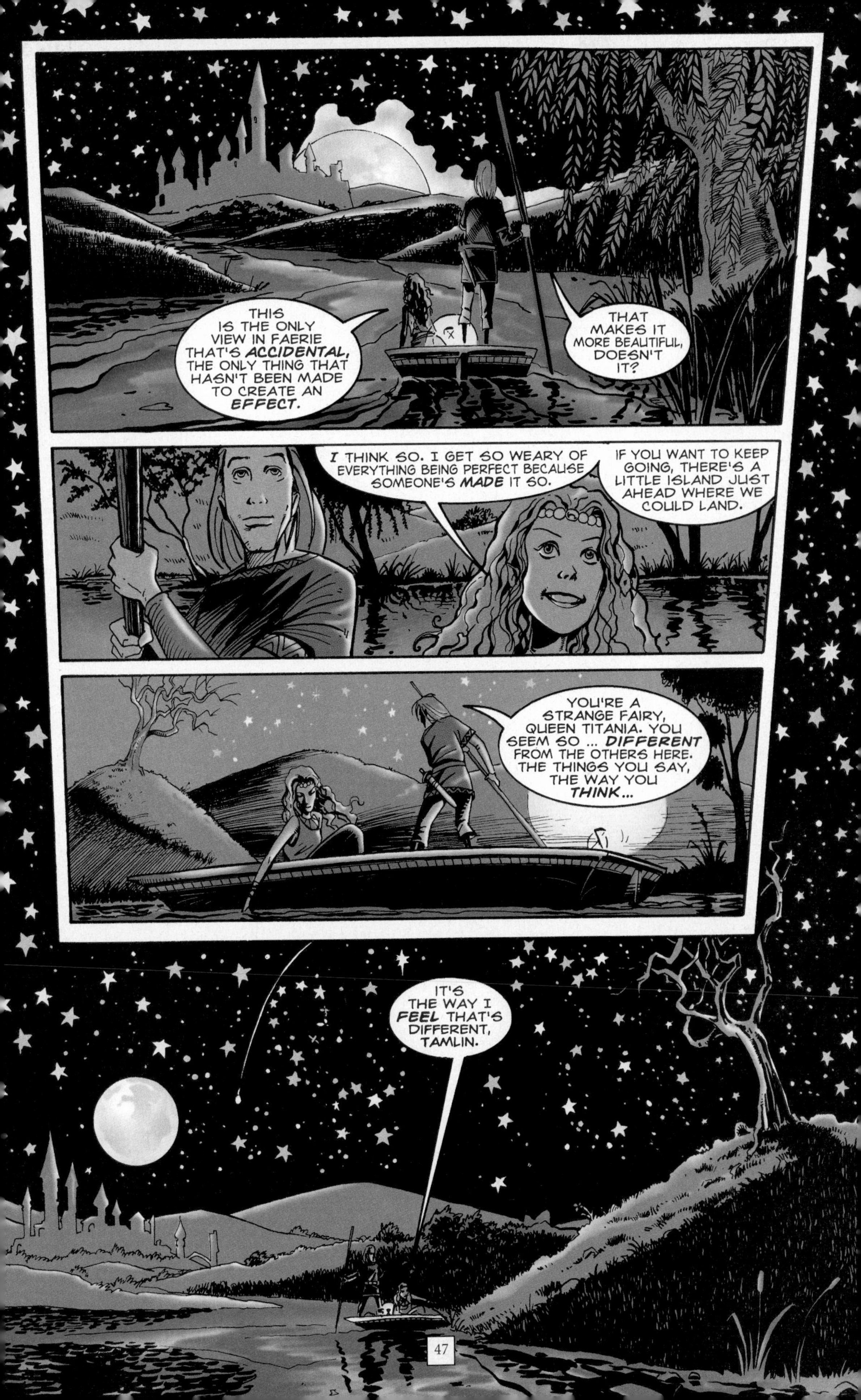
THIS IS THE ONLY VIEW IN FAERIE THAT'S ACCIDENTAL, THE ONLY THING THAT HASN'T BEEN MADE TO CREATE AN EFFECT.
THAT MAKES IT MORE BEAUTIFUL, DOESN'T IT?
I THINK SO. I GET SO WEARY OF EVERYTHING BEING PERFECT BECAUSE SOMEONE'S MADE IT SO.
IF YOU WANT TO KEEP GOING, THERE'S A LITTLE ISLAND JUST AHEAD WHERE WE COULD LAND.
YOU'RE A STRANGE FAIRY, QUEEN TITANIA. YOU SEEM SO ... DIFFERENT FROM THE OTHERS HERE. THE THINGS YOU SAY, THE WAY YOU THINK...
IT'S THE WAY I FEEL THAT'S DIFFERENT, TAMLIN.

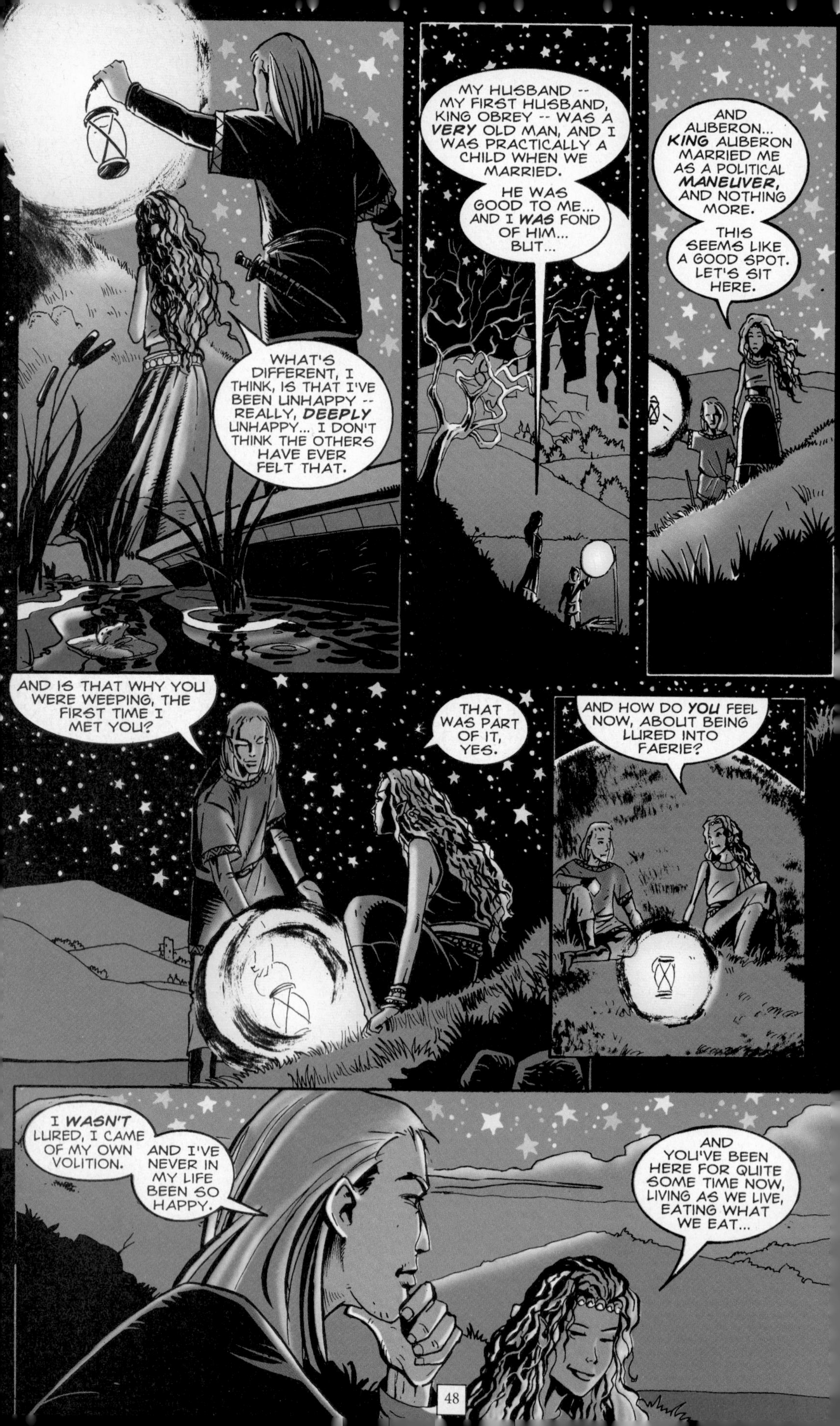
WHAT'S DIFFERENT, I THINK, IS THAT I'VE BEEN UNHAPPY -- REALLY, DEEPLY UNHAPPY... I DON'T THINK THE OTHERS HAVE EVER FELT THAT.
MY HUSBAND -- MY FIRST HUSBAND, KING OBREY -- WAS A VERY OLD MAN, AND I WAS PRACTICALLY A CHILD WHEN WE MARRIED.
HE WAS GOOD TO ME... AND I WAS FOND OF HIM... BUT...
AND AUBERON... KING AUBERON MARRIED ME AS A POLITICAL MANEUVER, AND NOTHING MORE.
THIS SEEMS LIKE A GOOD SPOT. LET'S SIT HERE.
AND IS THAT WHY YOU WERE WEEPING, THE FIRST TIME I MET YOU?
THAT WAS PART OF IT, YES.
AND HOW DO YOU FEEL NOW, ABOUT BEING LURED INTO FAERIE?
I WASN'T LURED, I CAME OF MY OWN VOLITION.
AND I'VE NEVER IN MY LIFE BEEN SO HAPPY.
AND YOU'VE BEEN HERE FOR QUITE SOME TIME NOW, LIVING AS WE LIVE, EATING WHAT WE EAT...

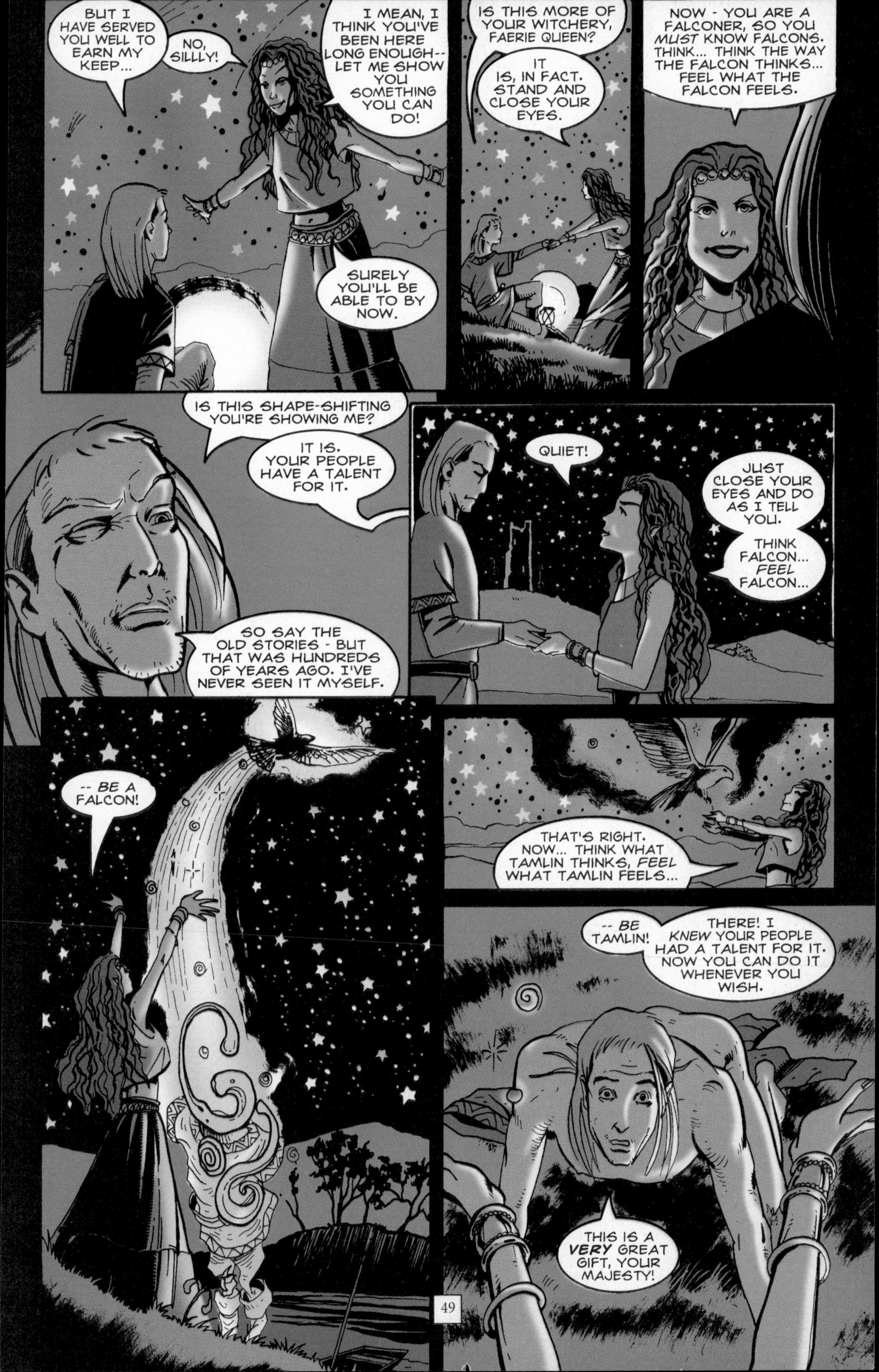
BUT I HAVE SERVED YOU WELL TO EARN MY KEEP...
NO, SILLLY!
I MEAN, I THINK YOU'VE BEEN HERE LONG ENOUGH-- LET ME SHOW YOU SOMETHING YOU CAN DO!
SURELY YOU'LL BE ABLE TO BY NOW.
IS THIS MORE OF YOUR WITCHERY, FAERIE QUEEN?
IT IS, IN FACT. STAND AND CLOSE YOUR EYES.
NOW - YOU ARE A FALCONER, SO YOU *MUST* KNOW FALCONS. THINK... THINK THE WAY THE FALCON THINKS... FEEL WHAT THE FALCON FEELS.
IS THIS SHAPE-SHIFTING YOU'RE SHOWING ME?
IT IS. YOUR PEOPLE HAVE A TALENT FOR IT.
SO SAY THE OLD STORIES - BUT THAT WAS HUNDREDS OF YEARS AGO. I'VE NEVER SEEN IT MYSELF.
QUIET!
JUST CLOSE YOUR EYES AND DO AS I TELL YOU.
THINK FALCON... *FEEL* FALCON...
-- *BE* A FALCON!
THAT'S RIGHT. NOW... THINK WHAT TAMLIN THINKS, *FEEL* WHAT TAMLIN FEELS...
-- *BE* TAMLIN!
THERE! I *KNEW* YOUR PEOPLE HAD A TALENT FOR IT. NOW YOU CAN DO IT WHENEVER YOU WISH.
THIS IS A ***VERY*** GREAT GIFT, YOUR MAJESTY!

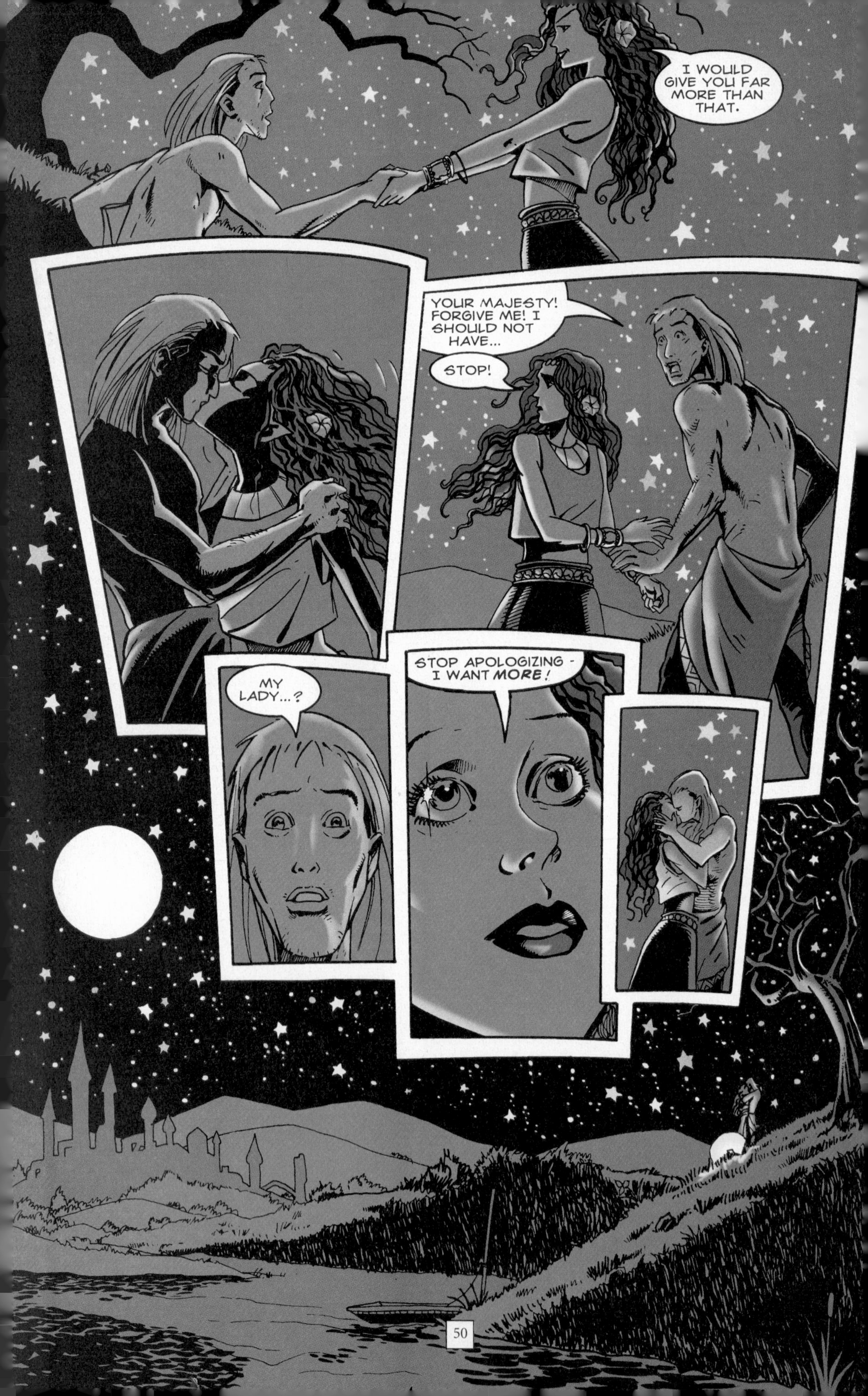
I WOULD GIVE YOU FAR MORE THAN THAT.
YOUR MAJESTY! FORGIVE ME! I SHOULD NOT HAVE...
STOP!
MY LADY...?
STOP APOLOGIZING - I WANT MORE!

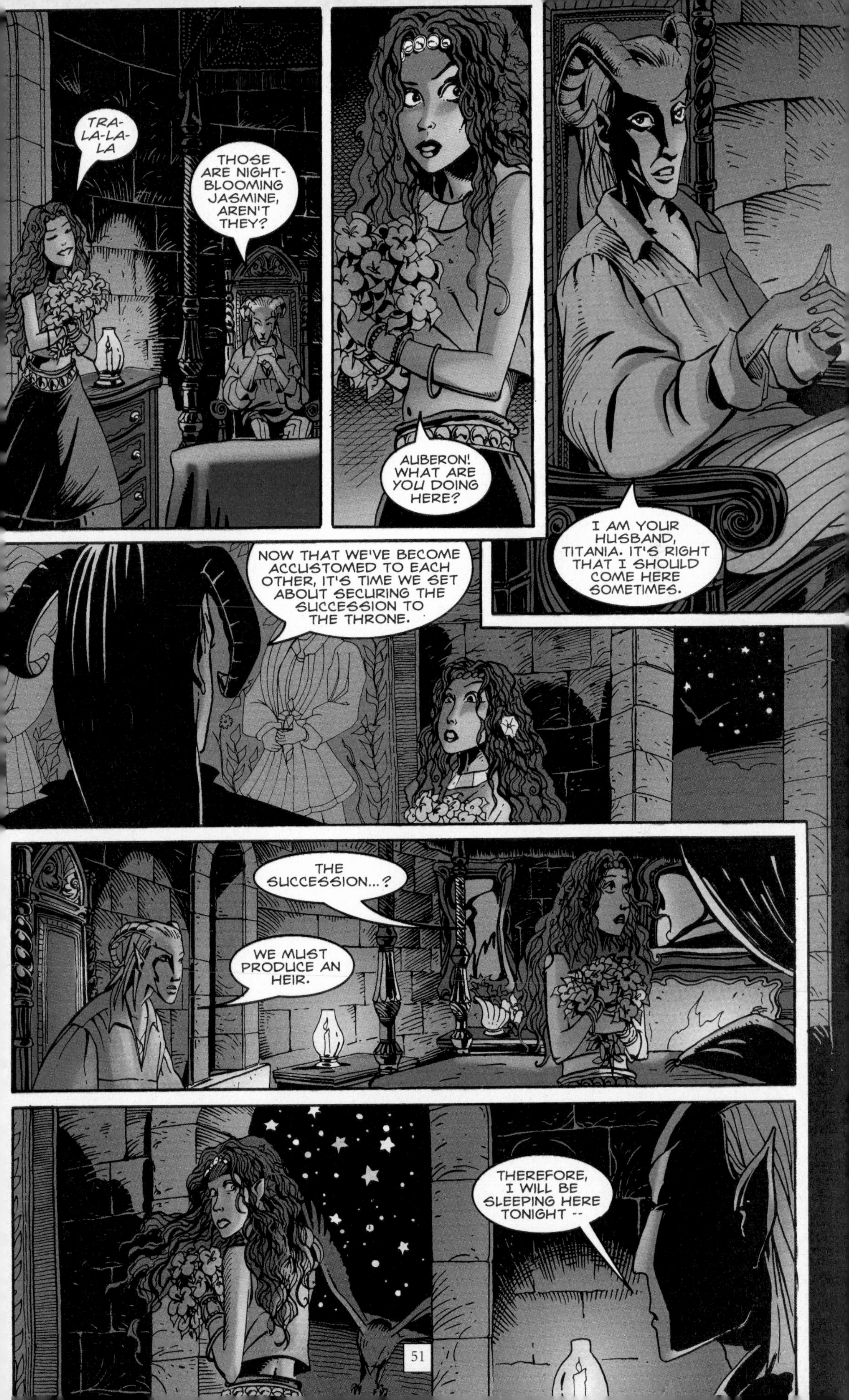

TRA-LA-LA-LA
THOSE ARE NIGHT-BLOOMING JASMINE, AREN'T THEY?
AUBERON! WHAT ARE YOU DOING HERE?
I AM YOUR HUSBAND, TITANIA. IT'S RIGHT THAT I SHOULD COME HERE SOMETIMES.
NOW THAT WE'VE BECOME ACCUSTOMED TO EACH OTHER, IT'S TIME WE SET ABOUT SECURING THE SUCCESSION TO THE THRONE.
THE SUCCESSION...?
WE MUST PRODUCE AN HEIR.
THEREFORE, I WILL BE SLEEPING HERE TONIGHT --

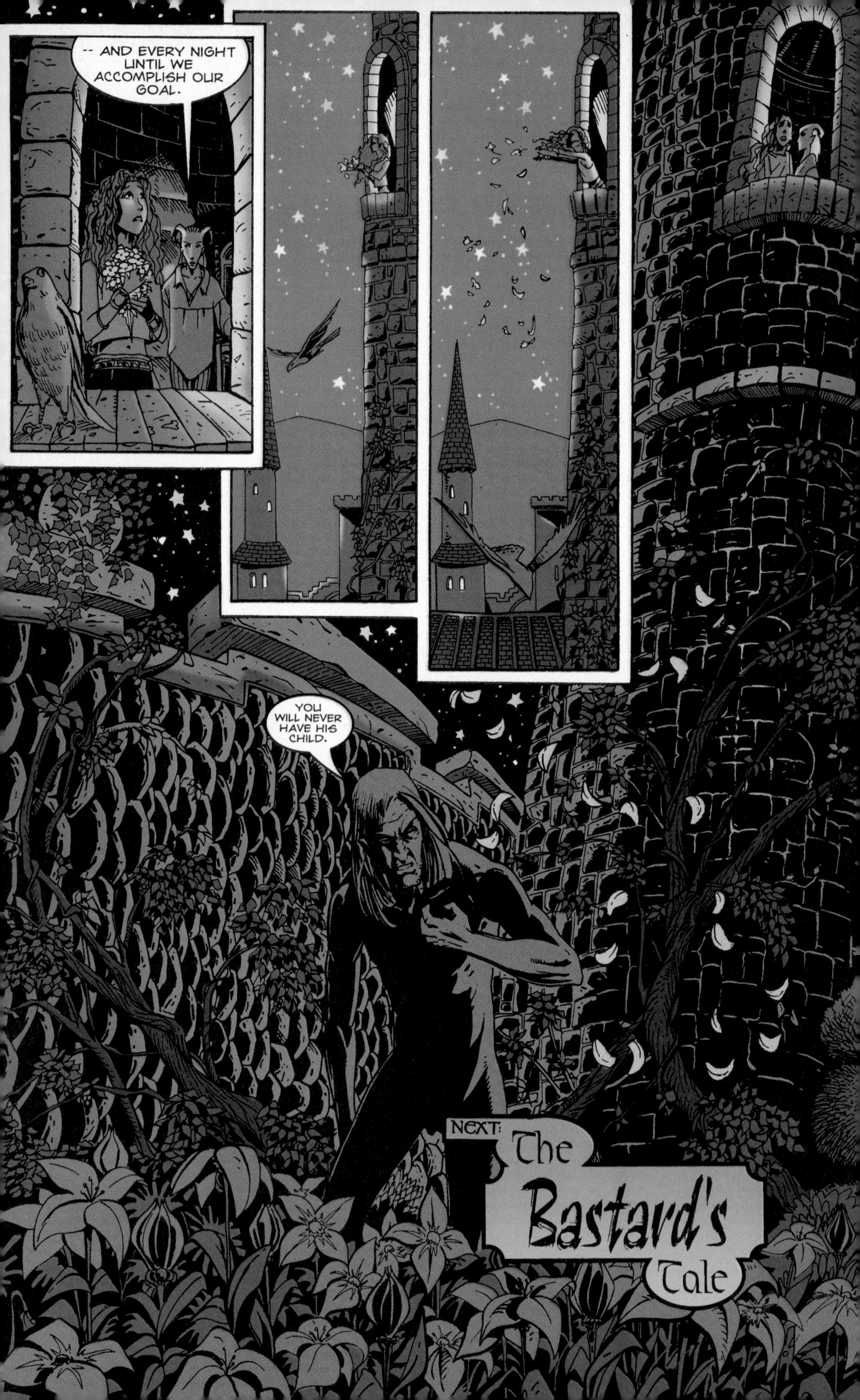
-- AND EVERY NIGHT UNTIL WE ACCOMPLISH OUR GOAL.
YOU WILL NEVER HAVE HIS CHILD.
NEXT: The Bastard's Tale

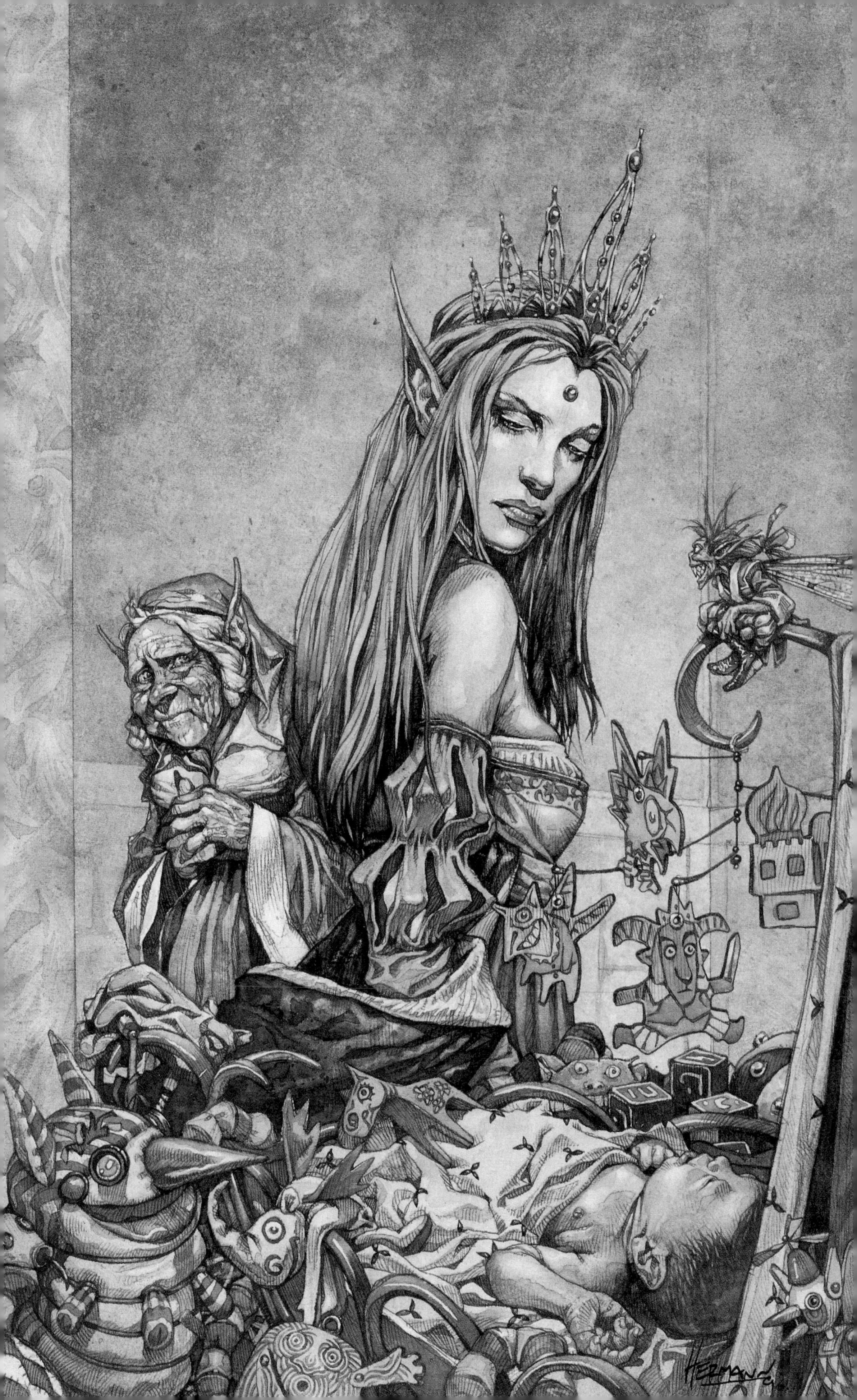
HERMAN

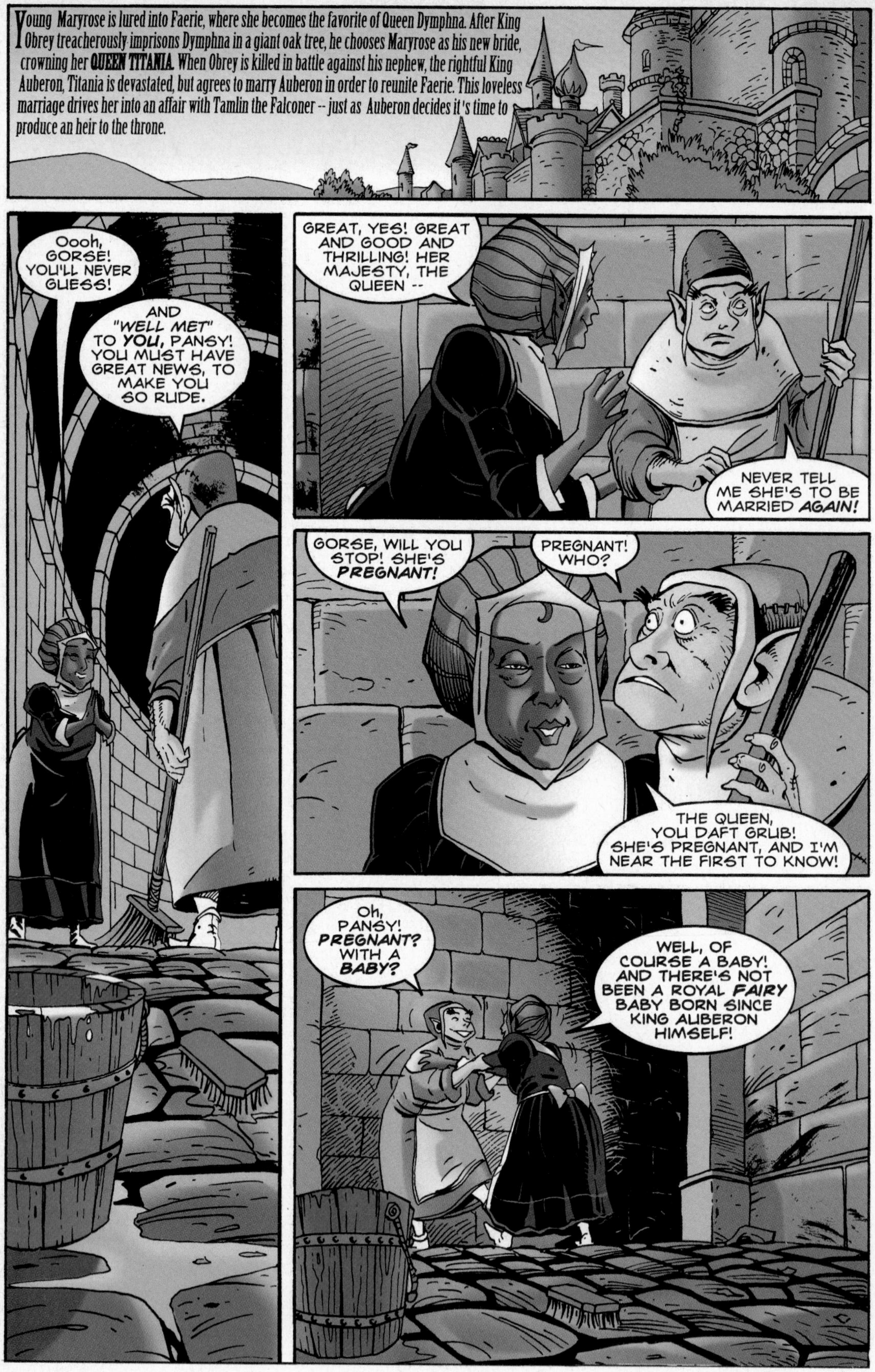

Young Maryrose is lured into Faerie, where she becomes the favorite of Queen Dymphna. After King Obrey treacherously imprisons Dymphna in a giant oak tree, he chooses Maryrose as his new bride, crowning her QUEEN TITANIA. When Obrey is killed in battle against his nephew, the rightful King Auberon, Titania is devastated, but agrees to marry Auberon in order to reunite Faerie. This loveless marriage drives her into an affair with Tamlin the Falconer -- just as Auberon decides it's time to produce an heir to the throne.
Oooh, GORSE! YOU'LL NEVER GUESS!
AND "WELL MET" TO YOU, PANSY! YOU MUST HAVE GREAT NEWS, TO MAKE YOU SO RUDE.
GREAT, YES! GREAT AND GOOD AND THRILLING! HER MAJESTY, THE QUEEN --
NEVER TELL ME SHE'S TO BE MARRIED AGAIN!
GORSE, WILL YOU STOP! SHE'S PREGNANT!
PREGNANT! WHO?
THE QUEEN, YOU DAFT GRUB! SHE'S PREGNANT, AND I'M NEAR THE FIRST TO KNOW!
Oh, PANSY! PREGNANT? WITH A BABY?
WELL, OF COURSE A BABY! AND THERE'S NOT BEEN A ROYAL FAIRY BABY BORN SINCE KING AUBERON HIMSELF!

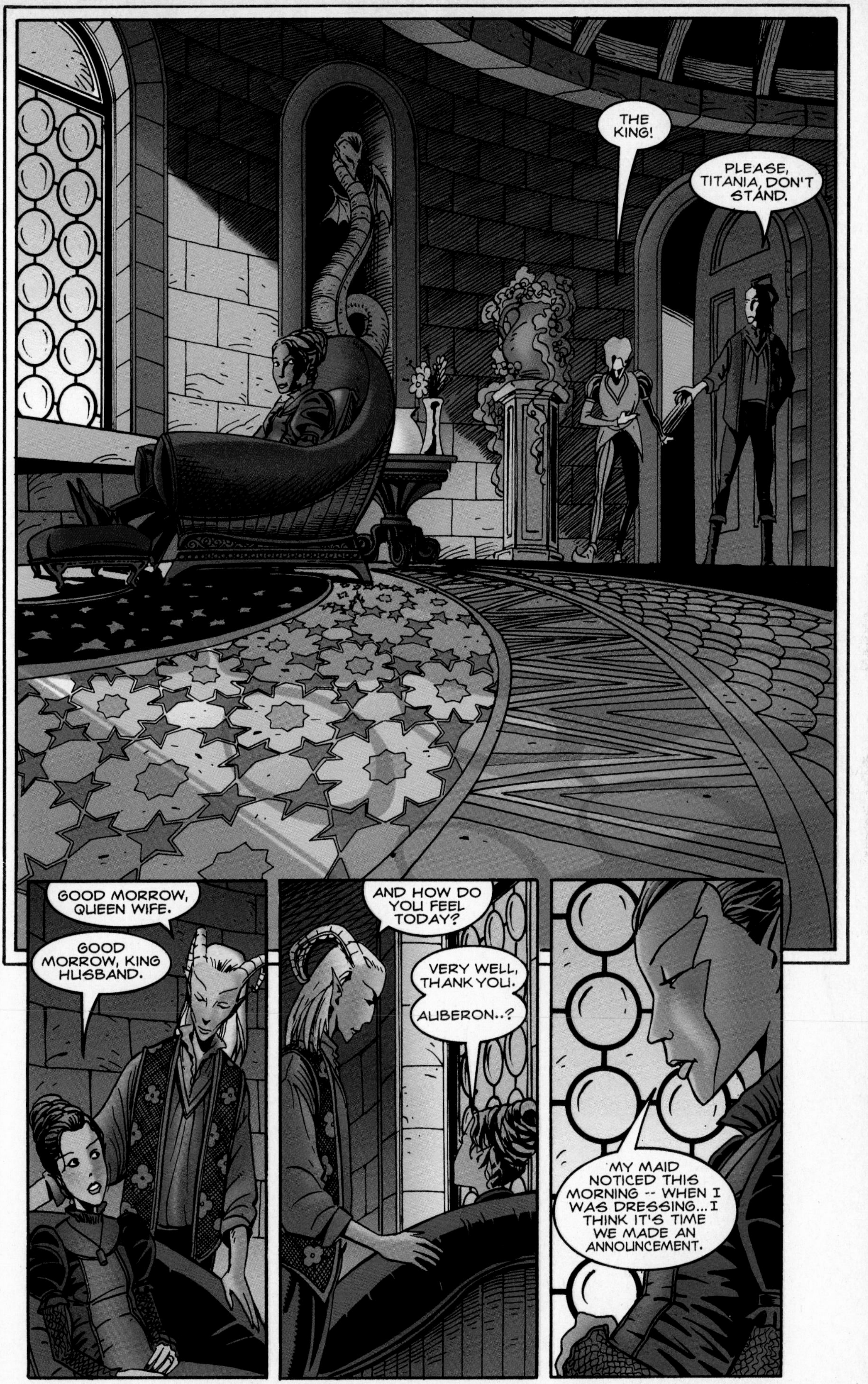
THE KING!
PLEASE, TITANIA, DON'T STAND.
GOOD MORROW, QUEEN WIFE.
GOOD MORROW, KING HUSBAND.
AND HOW DO YOU FEEL TODAY?
VERY WELL, THANK YOU.
AUBERON..?
MY MAID NOTICED THIS MORNING -- WHEN I WAS DRESSING... I THINK IT'S TIME WE MADE AN ANNOUNCEMENT.

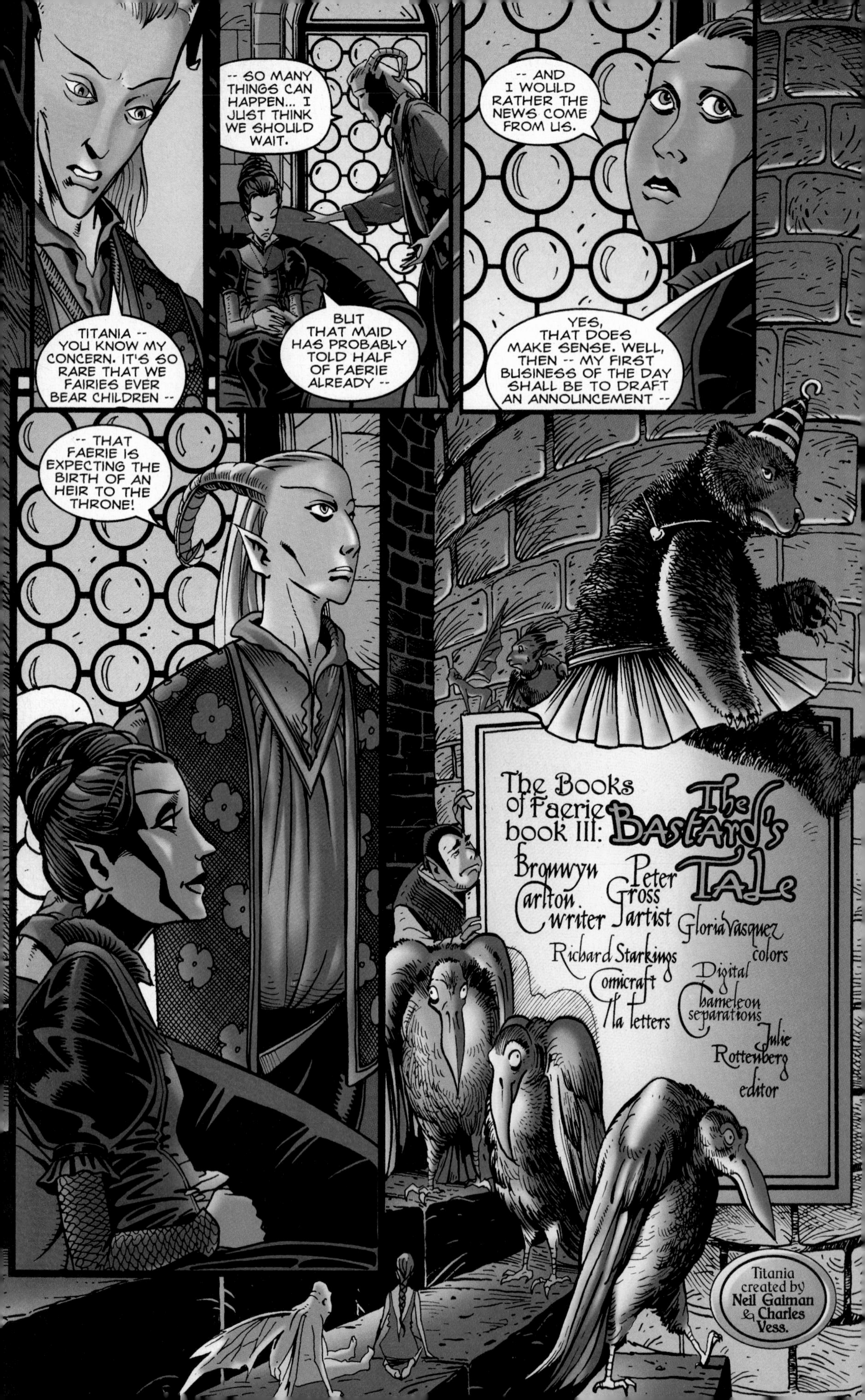
TITANIA -- YOU KNOW MY CONCERN. IT'S SO RARE THAT WE FAIRIES EVER BEAR CHILDREN --
-- SO MANY THINGS CAN HAPPEN... I JUST THINK WE SHOULD WAIT.
BUT THAT MAID HAS PROBABLY TOLD HALF OF FAERIE ALREADY --
-- AND I WOULD RATHER THE NEWS COME FROM US.
YES, THAT DOES MAKE SENSE. WELL, THEN -- MY FIRST BUSINESS OF THE DAY SHALL BE TO DRAFT AN ANNOUNCEMENT --
-- THAT FAERIE IS EXPECTING THE BIRTH OF AN HEIR TO THE THRONE!
The Books of Faerie book III: The Bastard's Tale
Bronwyn Carlton writer
Peter Gross artist
Gloria Vasquez colors
Richard Starkings Comicraft
/la letters
Digital Chameleon separations
Julie Rottenberg editor
Titania created by Neil Gaiman & Charles Vess.

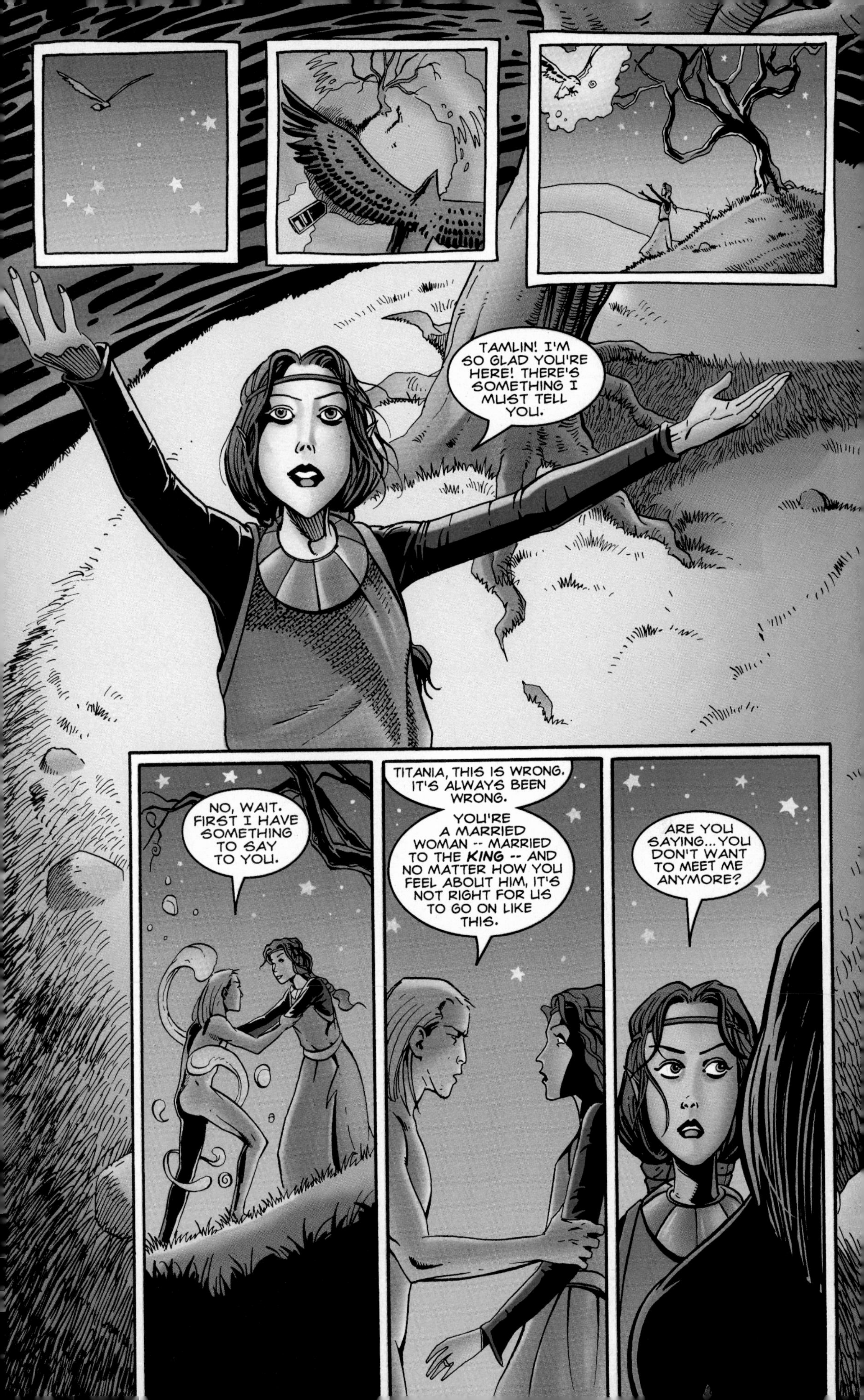
TAMLIN! I'M SO GLAD YOU'RE HERE! THERE'S SOMETHING I MUST TELL YOU.
NO, WAIT. FIRST I HAVE SOMETHING TO SAY TO YOU.
TITANIA, THIS IS WRONG. IT'S ALWAYS BEEN WRONG.
YOU'RE A MARRIED WOMAN -- MARRIED TO THE **KING** -- AND NO MATTER HOW YOU FEEL ABOUT HIM, IT'S NOT RIGHT FOR US TO GO ON LIKE THIS.
ARE YOU SAYING... YOU DON'T WANT TO MEET ME ANYMORE?

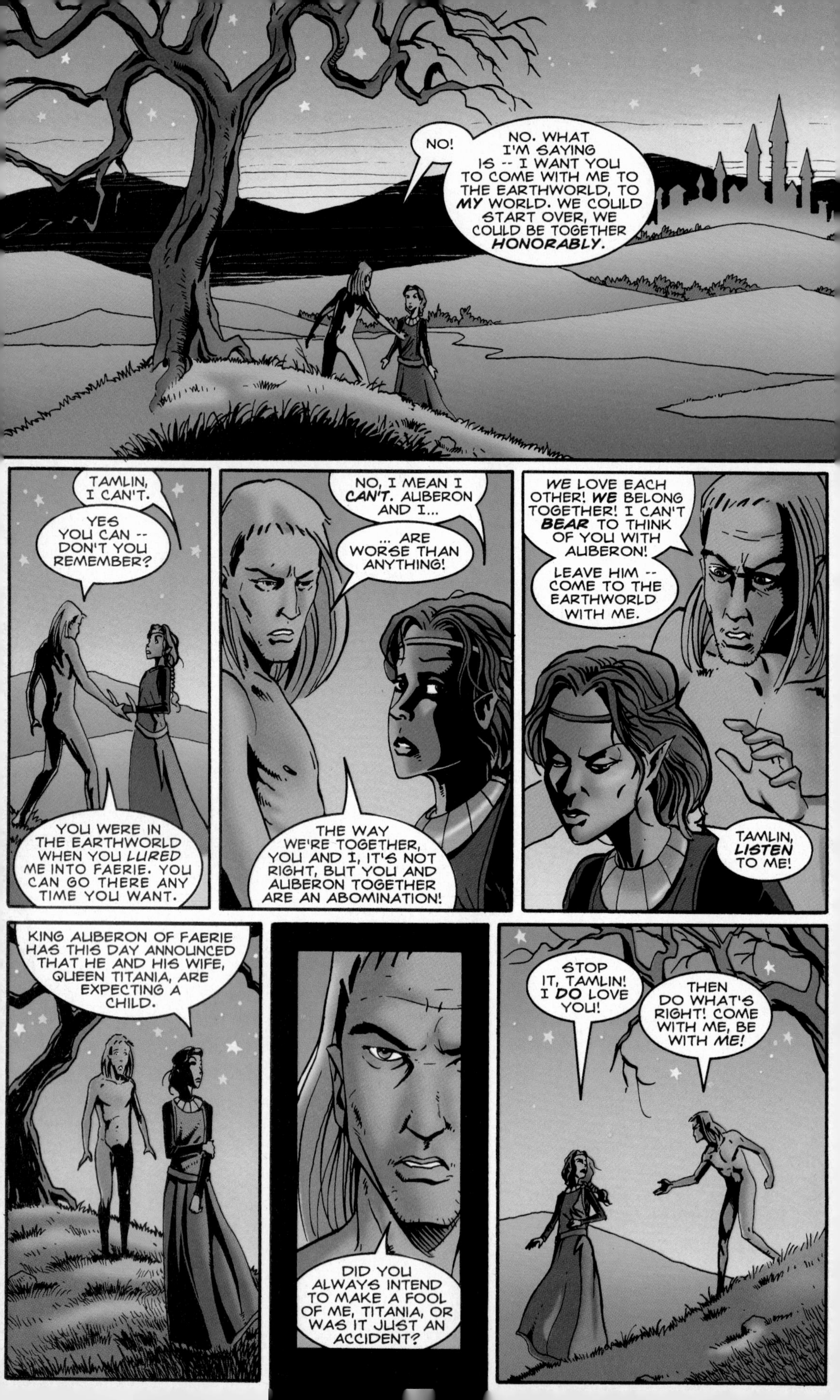
NO!
NO. WHAT I'M SAYING IS -- I WANT YOU TO COME WITH ME TO THE EARTHWORLD, TO *MY* WORLD. WE COULD START OVER, WE COULD BE TOGETHER *HONORABLY.*
TAMLIN, I CAN'T.
YES YOU CAN -- DON'T YOU REMEMBER?
YOU WERE IN THE EARTHWORLD WHEN YOU *LURED* ME INTO FAERIE. YOU CAN GO THERE ANY TIME YOU WANT.
NO, I MEAN I *CAN'T.* AUBERON AND I...
... ARE WORSE THAN ANYTHING!
THE WAY WE'RE TOGETHER, YOU AND I, IT'S NOT RIGHT, BUT YOU AND AUBERON TOGETHER ARE AN ABOMINATION!
WE LOVE EACH OTHER! *WE* BELONG TOGETHER! I CAN'T *BEAR* TO THINK OF YOU WITH AUBERON!
LEAVE HIM -- COME TO THE EARTHWORLD WITH ME.
TAMLIN, *LISTEN* TO ME!
KING AUBERON OF FAERIE HAS THIS DAY ANNOUNCED THAT HE AND HIS WIFE, QUEEN TITANIA, ARE EXPECTING A CHILD.
DID YOU ALWAYS INTEND TO MAKE A FOOL OF ME, TITANIA, OR WAS IT JUST AN ACCIDENT?
STOP IT, TAMLIN! I *DO* LOVE YOU!
THEN DO WHAT'S RIGHT! COME WITH ME, BE WITH *ME!*

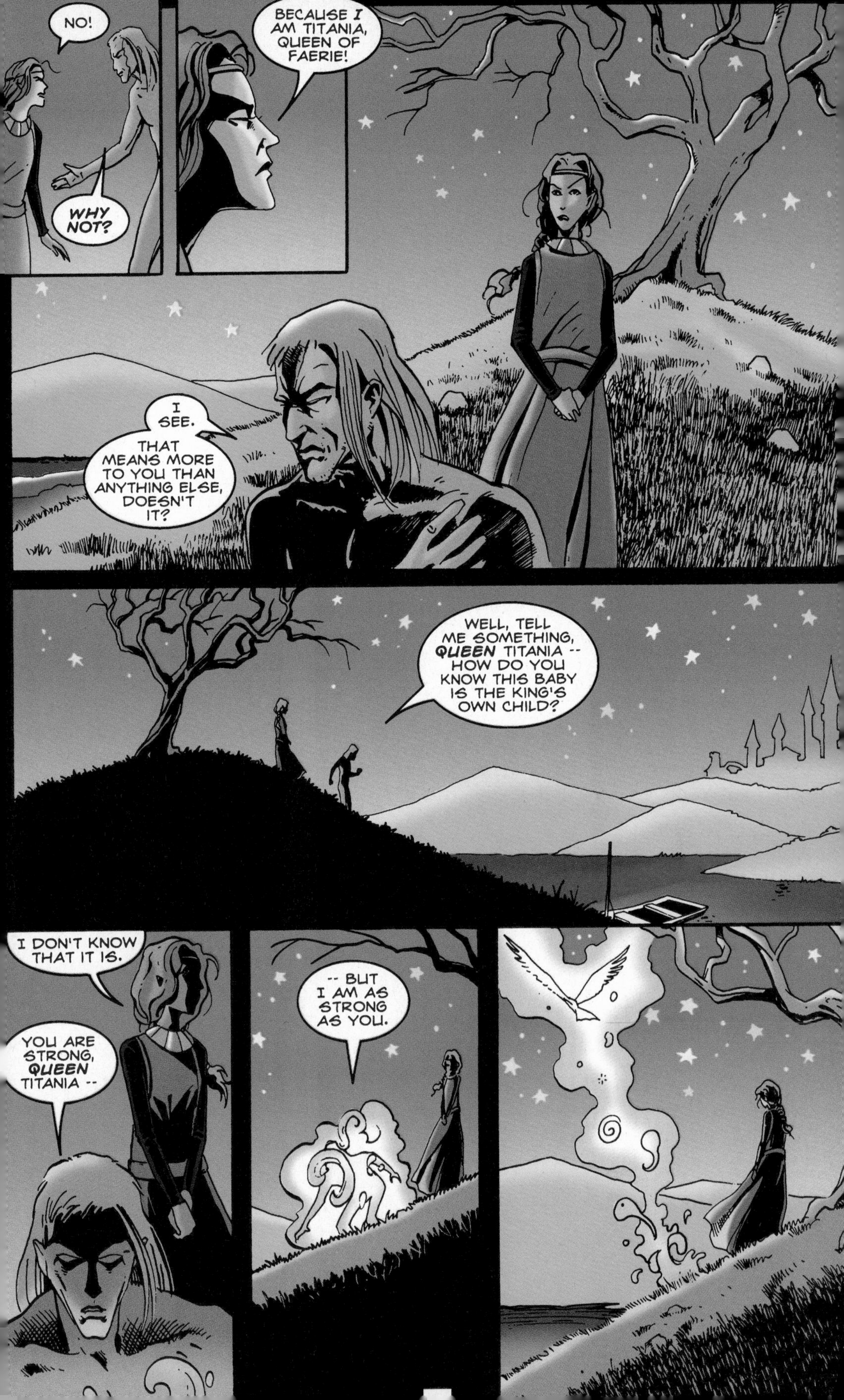
NO!
WHY NOT?
BECAUSE I AM TITANIA, QUEEN OF FAERIE!
I SEE.
THAT MEANS MORE TO YOU THAN ANYTHING ELSE, DOESN'T IT?
WELL, TELL ME SOMETHING, QUEEN TITANIA -- HOW DO YOU KNOW THIS BABY IS THE KING'S OWN CHILD?
I DON'T KNOW THAT IT IS.
YOU ARE STRONG, QUEEN TITANIA --
-- BUT I AM AS STRONG AS YOU.

GOOD MORROW, AMADAN! WE WELCOME YOUR RETURN!

GOOD MORROW, PANSY. IS THE QUEEN ABLE TO RECEIVE VISITORS?

IF YOU MEAN, IS SHE DRESSED, SHE IS. I'VE JUST FINISHED WITH HER.

BUT AS FOR HER *ABILITY*, I'M SURE I CAN'T SAY.

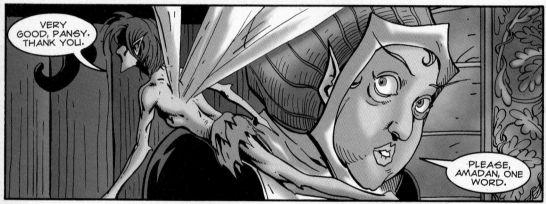

VERY GOOD, PANSY. THANK YOU.

PLEASE, AMADAN, ONE WORD.

YOU'VE BEEN AWAY, AND YOU MAY NOT KNOW HOW IT'S BEEN FOR THE QUEEN THESE PAST MONTHS, BUT BE WARNED -- SHE'S SUFFERED GREATLY CARRYING THIS CHILD.

THERE'VE BEEN TIMES WE'VE THOUGHT SHE WAS LIKE TO DIE.

WE ALL -- ALL OF US BELOW STAIRS -- WE HOPE FOR HER HEALTH, AND FOR THE HEALTH OF THE BABY. COULD YOU SOMEHOW LET HER KNOW THAT, PLEASE?

CERTAINLY I SHALL.

MY THANKS, GOOD AMADAN.

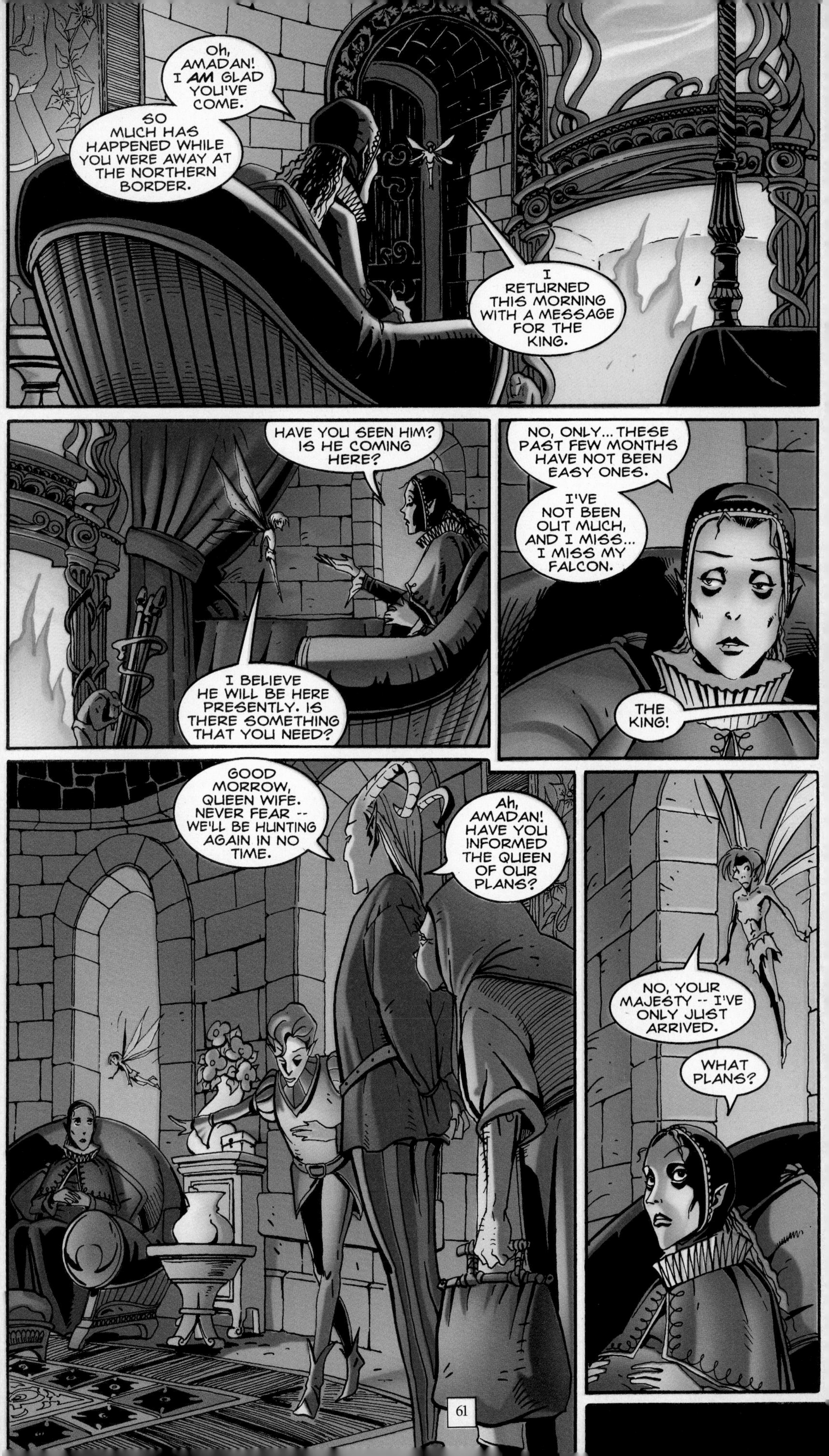

Oh, AMADAN! I AM GLAD YOU'VE COME.
SO MUCH HAS HAPPENED WHILE YOU WERE AWAY AT THE NORTHERN BORDER.
I RETURNED THIS MORNING WITH A MESSAGE FOR THE KING.
HAVE YOU SEEN HIM? IS HE COMING HERE?
I BELIEVE HE WILL BE HERE PRESENTLY. IS THERE SOMETHING THAT YOU NEED?
NO, ONLY... THESE PAST FEW MONTHS HAVE NOT BEEN EASY ONES.
I'VE NOT BEEN OUT MUCH, AND I MISS... I MISS MY FALCON.
THE KING!
GOOD MORROW, QUEEN WIFE. NEVER FEAR -- WE'LL BE HUNTING AGAIN IN NO TIME.
Ah, AMADAN! HAVE YOU INFORMED THE QUEEN OF OUR PLANS?
NO, YOUR MAJESTY -- I'VE ONLY JUST ARRIVED.
WHAT PLANS?

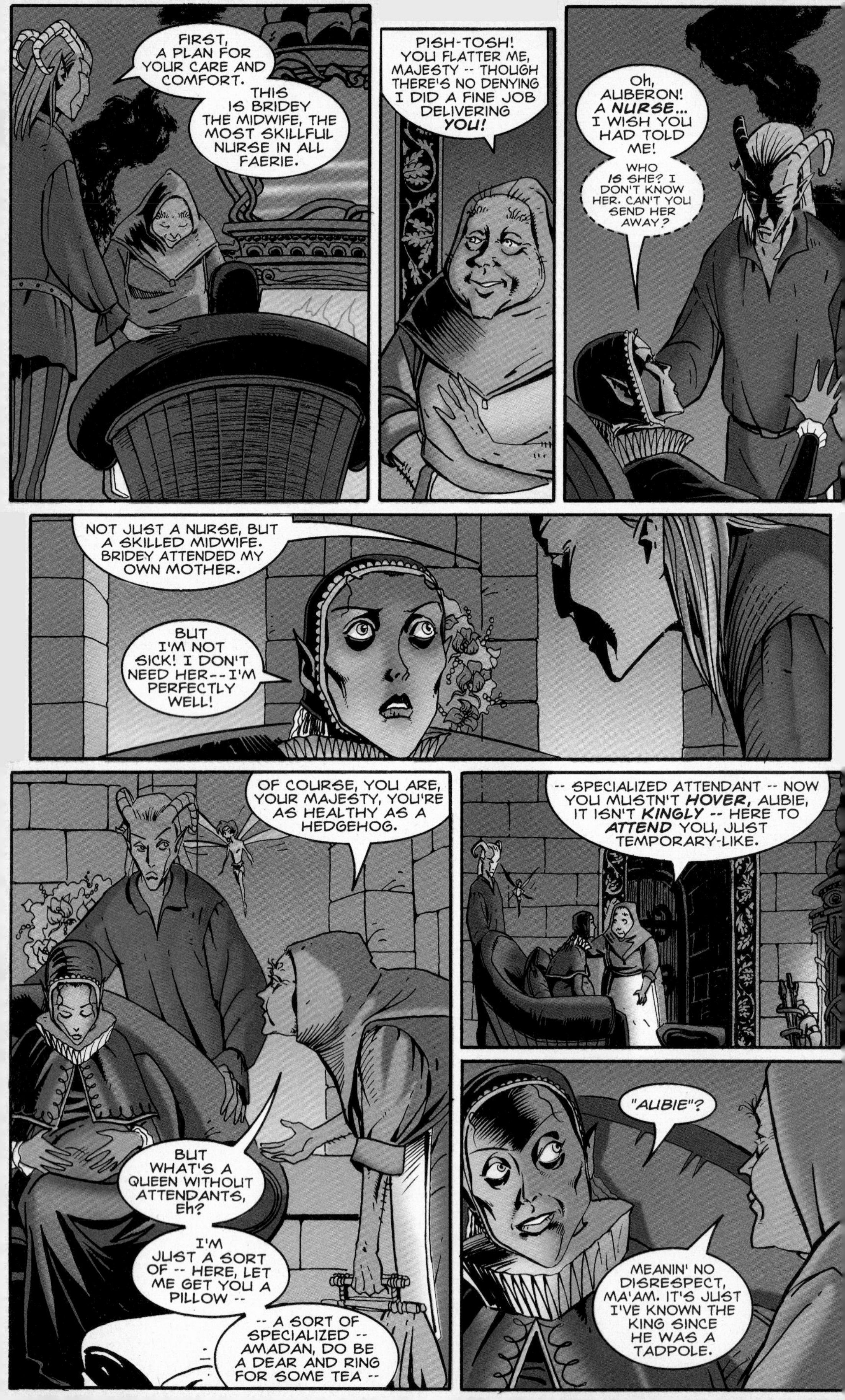
FIRST, A PLAN FOR YOUR CARE AND COMFORT.
THIS IS BRIDEY THE MIDWIFE, THE MOST SKILLFUL NURSE IN ALL FAERIE.
PISH-TOSH! YOU FLATTER ME, MAJESTY -- THOUGH THERE'S NO DENYING I DID A FINE JOB DELIVERING YOU!
Oh, AUBERON! A NURSE... I WISH YOU HAD TOLD ME!
WHO IS SHE? I DON'T KNOW HER. CAN'T YOU SEND HER AWAY?
NOT JUST A NURSE, BUT A SKILLED MIDWIFE. BRIDEY ATTENDED MY OWN MOTHER.
BUT I'M NOT SICK! I DON'T NEED HER--I'M PERFECTLY WELL!
OF COURSE, YOU ARE, YOUR MAJESTY, YOU'RE AS HEALTHY AS A HEDGEHOG.
BUT WHAT'S A QUEEN WITHOUT ATTENDANTS, Eh?
I'M JUST A SORT OF -- HERE, LET ME GET YOU A PILLOW --
-- A SORT OF SPECIALIZED -- AMADAN, DO BE A DEAR AND RING FOR SOME TEA --
-- SPECIALIZED ATTENDANT -- NOW YOU MUSTN'T HOVER, AUBIE, IT ISN'T KINGLY -- HERE TO ATTEND YOU, JUST TEMPORARY-LIKE.
"AUBIE"?
MEANIN' NO DISRESPECT, MA'AM. IT'S JUST I'VE KNOWN THE KING SINCE HE WAS A TADPOLE.

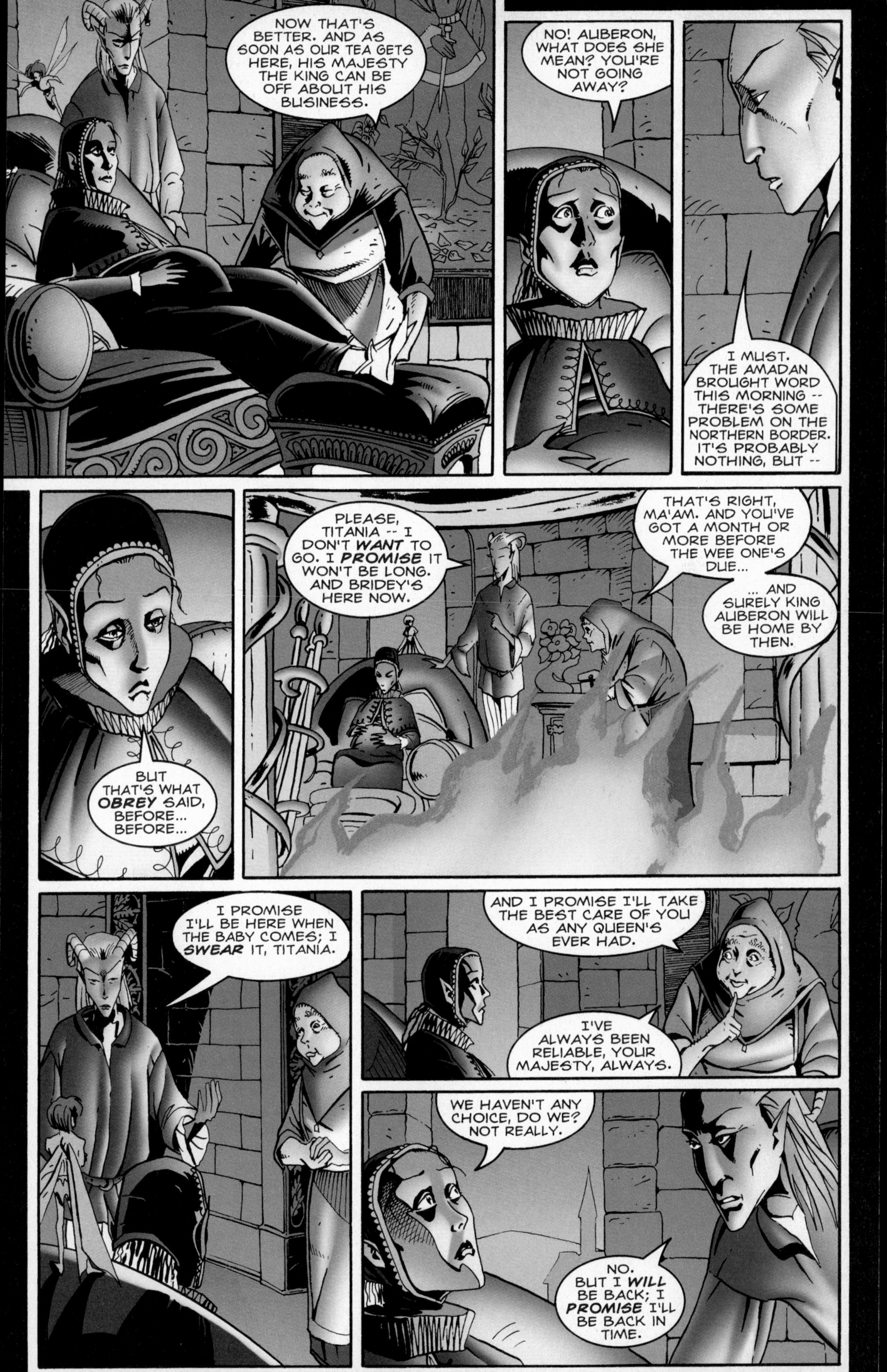
NOW THAT'S BETTER. AND AS SOON AS OUR TEA GETS HERE, HIS MAJESTY THE KING CAN BE OFF ABOUT HIS BUSINESS.
NO! AUBERON, WHAT DOES SHE MEAN? YOU'RE NOT GOING AWAY?
I MUST. THE AMADAN BROUGHT WORD THIS MORNING -- THERE'S SOME PROBLEM ON THE NORTHERN BORDER. IT'S PROBABLY NOTHING, BUT --
BUT THAT'S WHAT OBREY SAID, BEFORE... BEFORE...
PLEASE, TITANIA -- I DON'T WANT TO GO. I PROMISE IT WON'T BE LONG. AND BRIDEY'S HERE NOW.
THAT'S RIGHT, MA'AM. AND YOU'VE GOT A MONTH OR MORE BEFORE THE WEE ONE'S DUE...
... AND SURELY KING AUBERON WILL BE HOME BY THEN.
I PROMISE I'LL BE HERE WHEN THE BABY COMES; I SWEAR IT, TITANIA.
AND I PROMISE I'LL TAKE THE BEST CARE OF YOU AS ANY QUEEN'S EVER HAD.
I'VE ALWAYS BEEN RELIABLE, YOUR MAJESTY, ALWAYS.
WE HAVEN'T ANY CHOICE, DO WE? NOT REALLY.
NO. BUT I WILL BE BACK; I PROMISE I'LL BE BACK IN TIME.

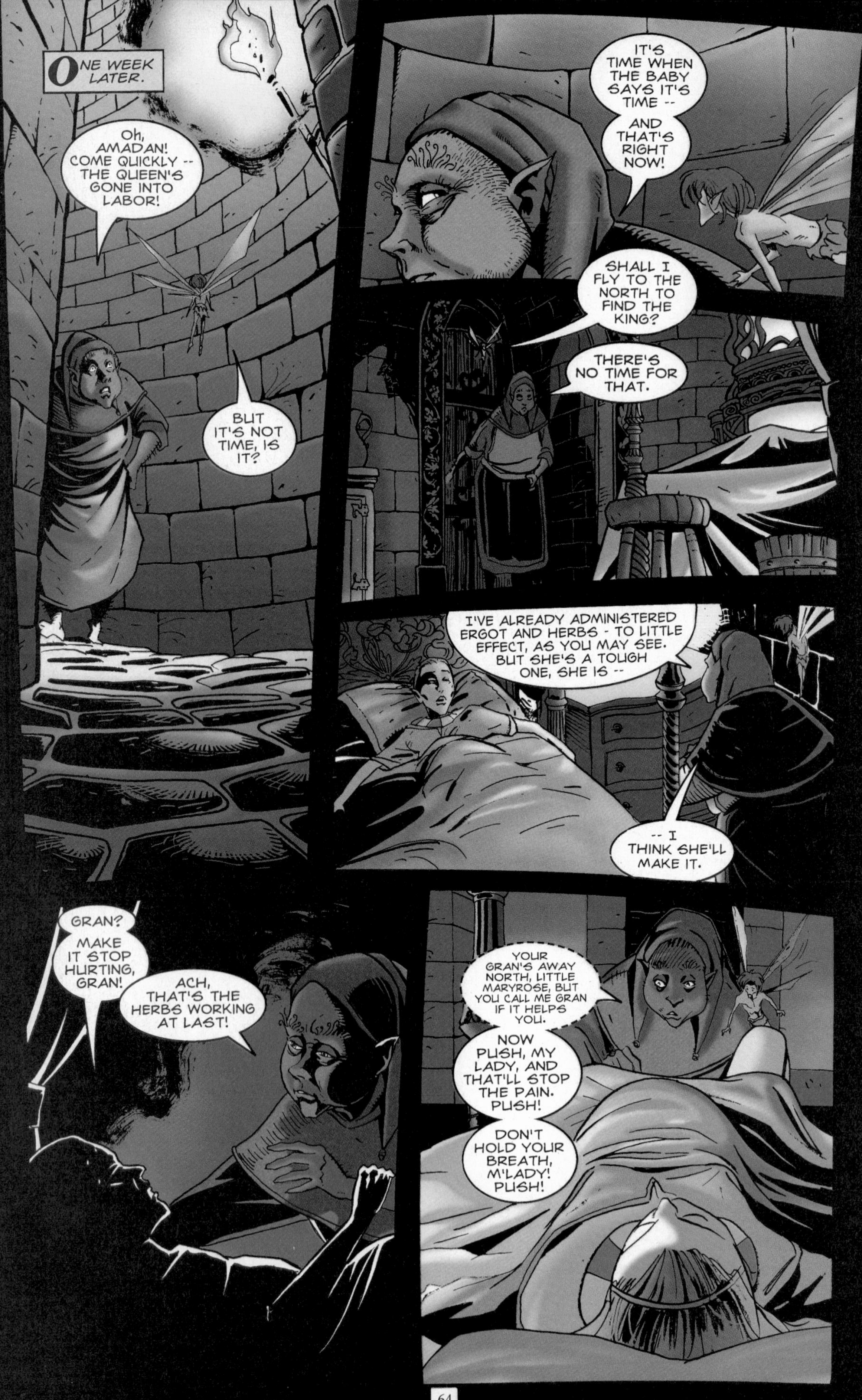
ONE WEEK LATER.
Oh, AMADAN! COME QUICKLY -- THE QUEEN'S GONE INTO LABOR!
BUT IT'S NOT TIME, IS IT?
IT'S TIME WHEN THE BABY SAYS IT'S TIME --
AND THAT'S RIGHT NOW!
SHALL I FLY TO THE NORTH TO FIND THE KING?
THERE'S NO TIME FOR THAT.
I'VE ALREADY ADMINISTERED ERGOT AND HERBS - TO LITTLE EFFECT, AS YOU MAY SEE. BUT SHE'S A TOUGH ONE, SHE IS --
-- I THINK SHE'LL MAKE IT.
GRAN?
MAKE IT STOP HURTING, GRAN!
ACH, THAT'S THE HERBS WORKING AT LAST!
YOUR GRAN'S AWAY NORTH, LITTLE MARYROSE, BUT YOU CALL ME GRAN IF IT HELPS YOU.
NOW PUSH, MY LADY, AND THAT'LL STOP THE PAIN. PUSH!
DON'T HOLD YOUR BREATH, M'LADY! PUSH!

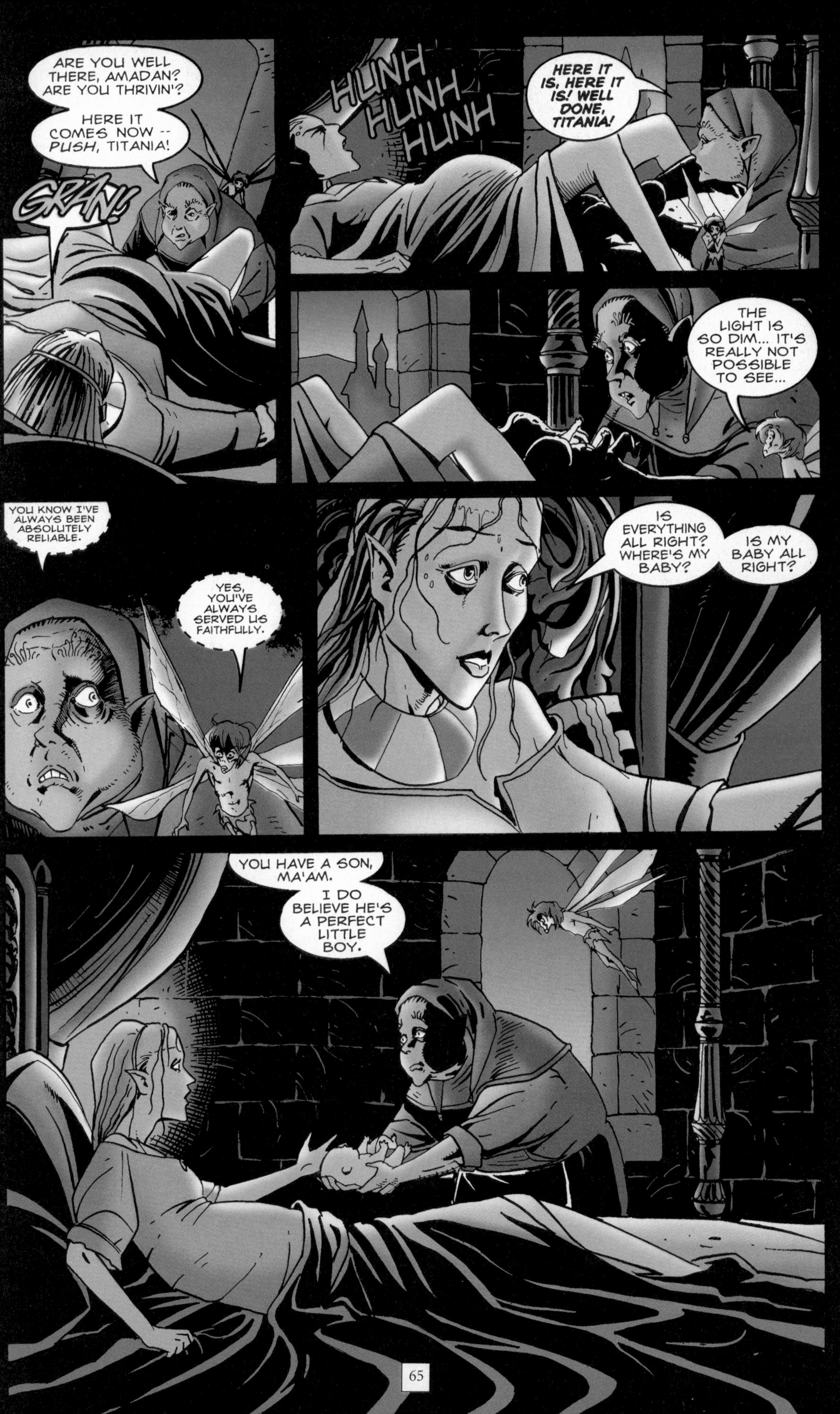
ARE YOU WELL THERE, AMADAN? ARE YOU THRIVIN'?
HERE IT COMES NOW -- *PUSH*, TITANIA!
GRAN!
HUNH HUNH HUNH
HERE IT IS, HERE IT IS! WELL DONE, TITANIA!
THE LIGHT IS SO DIM... IT'S REALLY NOT POSSIBLE TO SEE...
YOU KNOW I'VE ALWAYS BEEN ABSOLUTELY RELIABLE.
YES, YOU'VE ALWAYS SERVED US FAITHFULLY.
IS EVERYTHING ALL RIGHT? WHERE'S MY BABY?
IS MY BABY ALL RIGHT?
YOU HAVE A SON, MA'AM.
I DO BELIEVE HE'S A PERFECT LITTLE BOY.

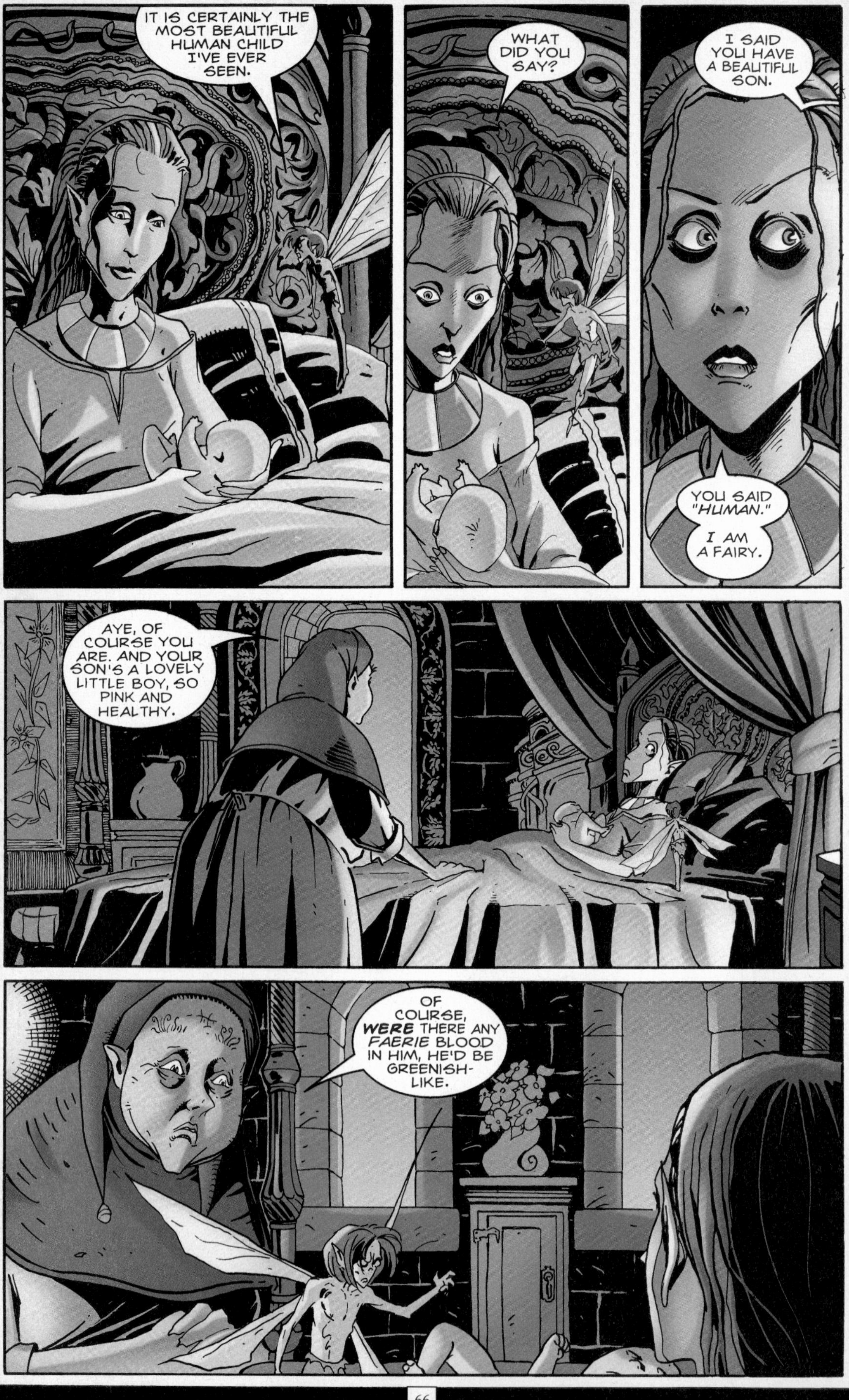
IT IS CERTAINLY THE MOST BEAUTIFUL HUMAN CHILD I'VE EVER SEEN.
WHAT DID YOU SAY?
I SAID YOU HAVE A BEAUTIFUL SON.
YOU SAID "HUMAN."
I AM A FAIRY.
AYE, OF COURSE YOU ARE. AND YOUR SON'S A LOVELY LITTLE BOY, SO PINK AND HEALTHY.
OF COURSE, WERE THERE ANY FAERIE BLOOD IN HIM, HE'D BE GREENISH-LIKE.

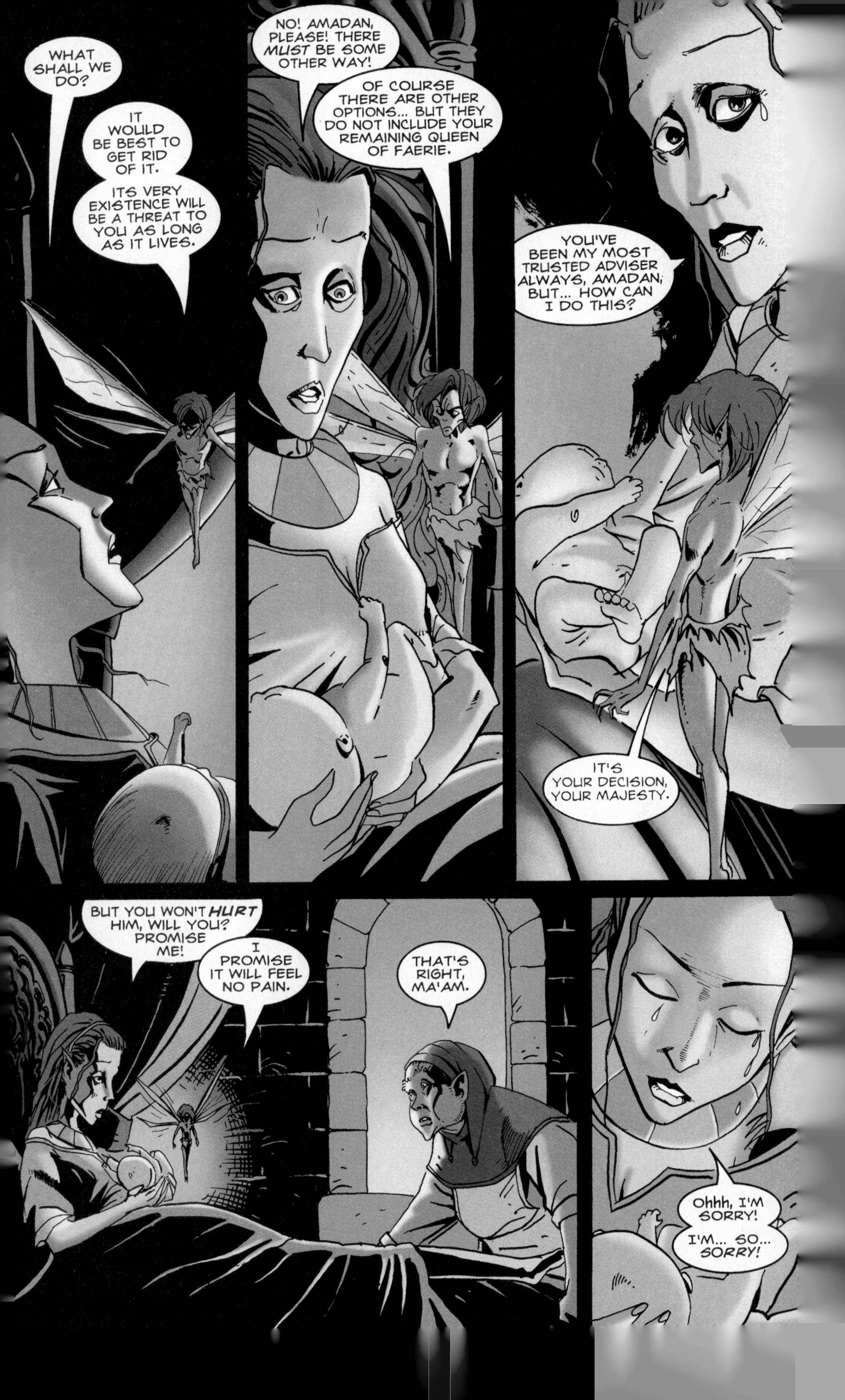
WHAT SHALL WE DO?
IT WOULD BE BEST TO GET RID OF IT.
ITS VERY EXISTENCE WILL BE A THREAT TO YOU AS LONG AS IT LIVES.
NO! AMADAN, PLEASE! THERE *MUST* BE SOME OTHER WAY!
OF COURSE THERE ARE OTHER OPTIONS... BUT THEY DO NOT INCLUDE YOUR REMAINING QUEEN OF FAERIE.
YOU'VE BEEN MY MOST TRUSTED ADVISER ALWAYS, AMADAN, BUT... HOW CAN I DO THIS?
IT'S YOUR DECISION, YOUR MAJESTY.
BUT YOU WON'T ***HURT*** HIM, WILL YOU? PROMISE ME!
I PROMISE IT WILL FEEL NO PAIN.
THAT'S RIGHT, MA'AM.
Ohhh, I'M SORRY!
I'M... SO... SORRY!

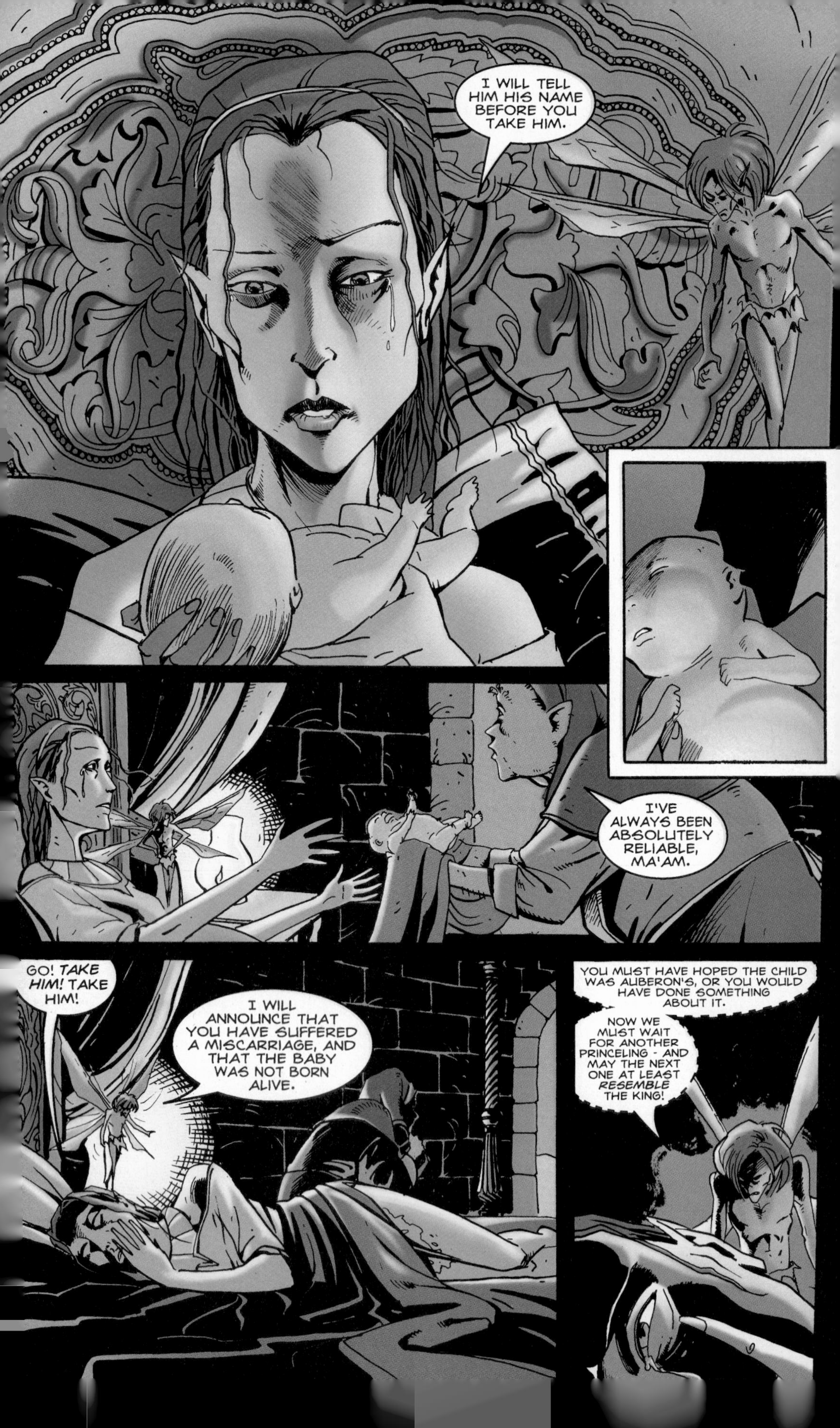
I WILL TELL HIM HIS NAME BEFORE YOU TAKE HIM.
I'VE ALWAYS BEEN ABSOLUTELY RELIABLE, MA'AM.
GO! *TAKE HIM!* TAKE HIM!
I WILL ANNOUNCE THAT YOU HAVE SUFFERED A MISCARRIAGE, AND THAT THE BABY WAS NOT BORN ALIVE.
YOU MUST HAVE HOPED THE CHILD WAS AUBERON'S, OR YOU WOULD HAVE DONE SOMETHING ABOUT IT.
NOW WE MUST WAIT FOR ANOTHER PRINCELING - AND MAY THE NEXT ONE AT LEAST *RESEMBLE* THE KING!

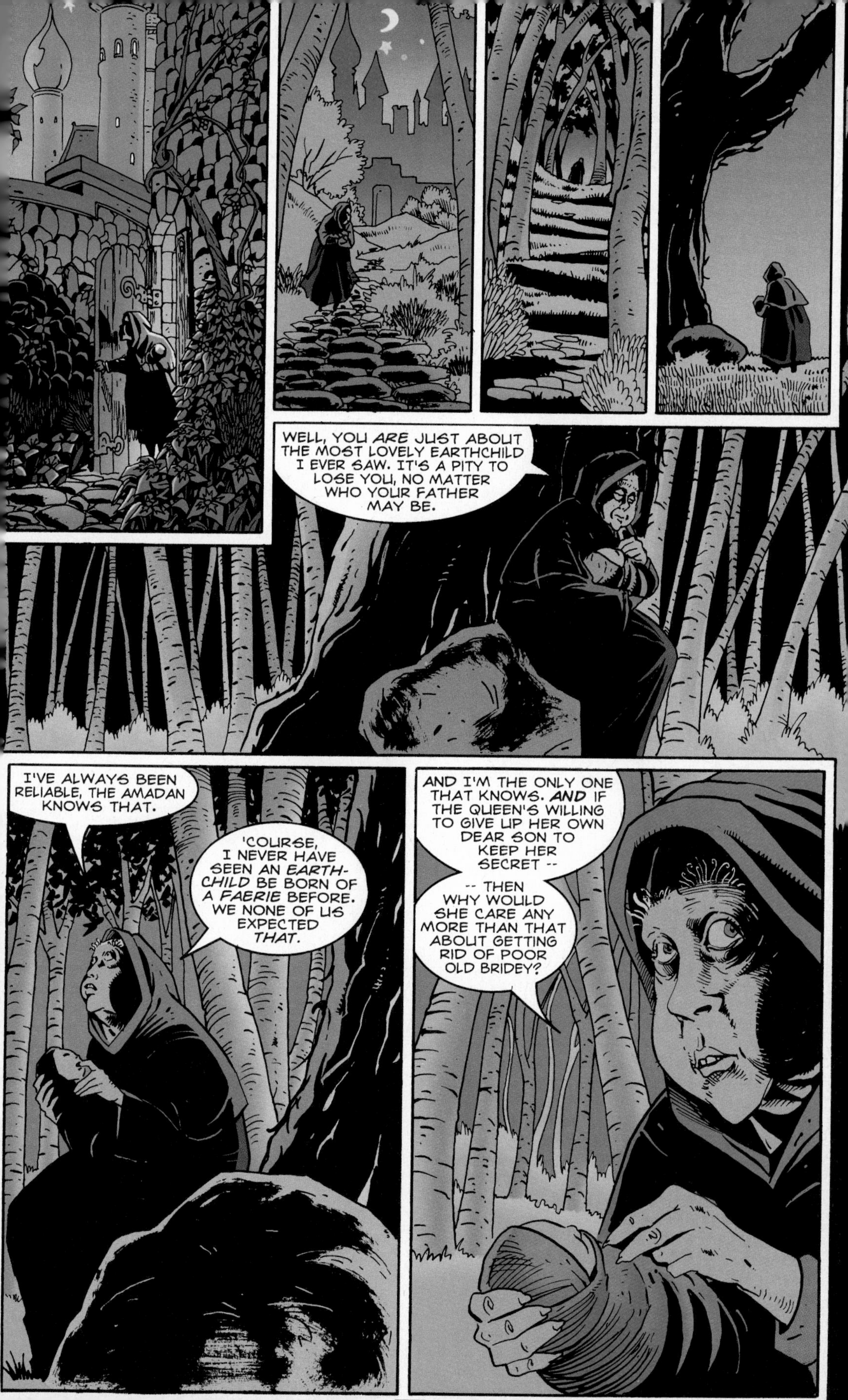
WELL, YOU ARE JUST ABOUT THE MOST LOVELY EARTHCHILD I EVER SAW. IT'S A PITY TO LOSE YOU, NO MATTER WHO YOUR FATHER MAY BE.
I'VE ALWAYS BEEN RELIABLE, THE AMADAN KNOWS THAT.
'COURSE, I NEVER HAVE SEEN AN EARTH-CHILD BE BORN OF A FAERIE BEFORE. WE NONE OF US EXPECTED THAT.
AND I'M THE ONLY ONE THAT KNOWS. AND IF THE QUEEN'S WILLING TO GIVE UP HER OWN DEAR SON TO KEEP HER SECRET --
-- THEN WHY WOULD SHE CARE ANY MORE THAN THAT ABOUT GETTING RID OF POOR OLD BRIDEY?

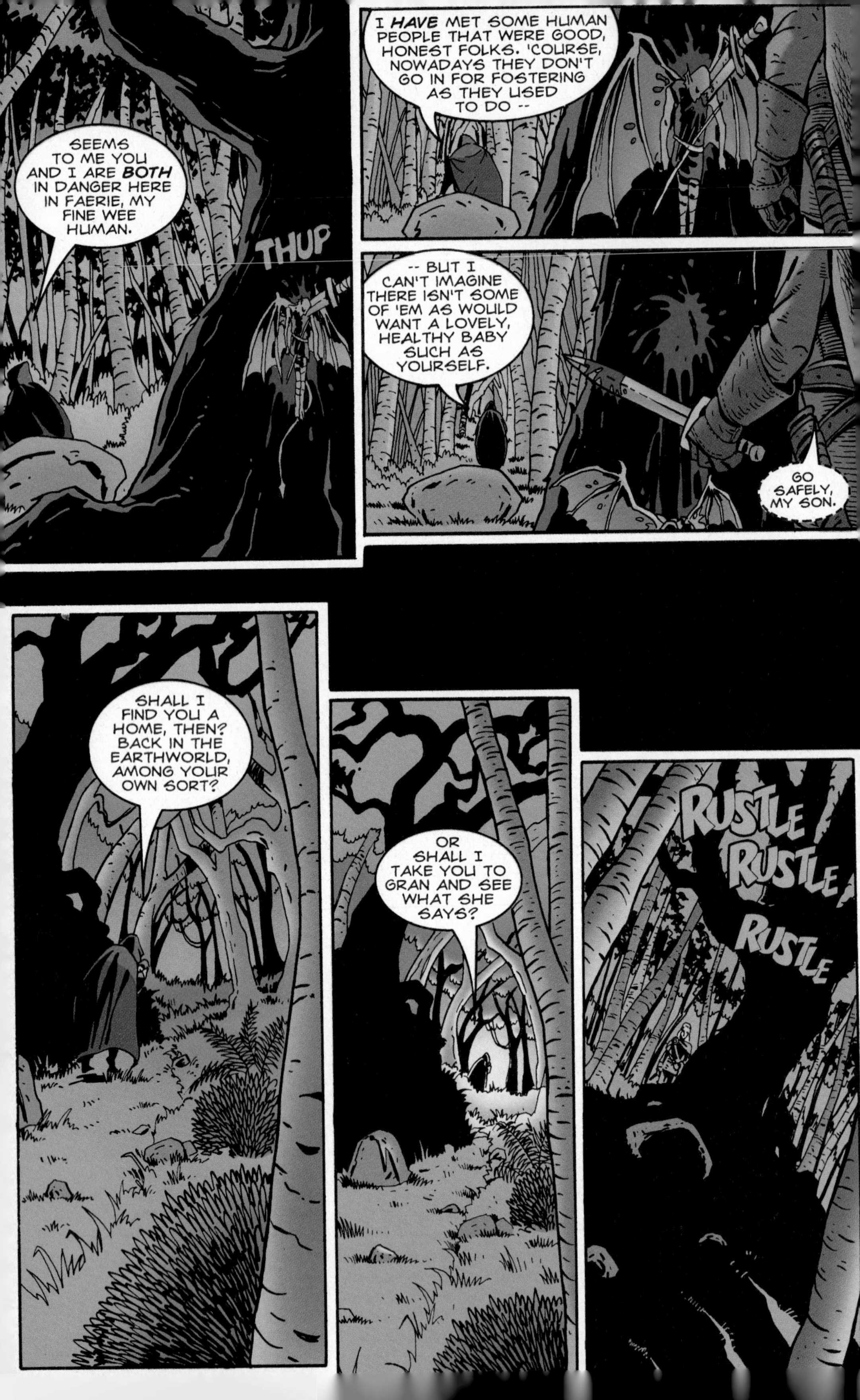
SEEMS TO ME YOU AND I ARE BOTH IN DANGER HERE IN FAERIE, MY FINE WEE HUMAN.
THUP
I HAVE MET SOME HUMAN PEOPLE THAT WERE GOOD, HONEST FOLKS. 'COURSE, NOWADAYS THEY DON'T GO IN FOR FOSTERING AS THEY USED TO DO --
-- BUT I CAN'T IMAGINE THERE ISN'T SOME OF 'EM AS WOULD WANT A LOVELY, HEALTHY BABY SUCH AS YOURSELF.
GO SAFELY, MY SON.
SHALL I FIND YOU A HOME, THEN? BACK IN THE EARTHWORLD, AMONG YOUR OWN SORT?
OR SHALL I TAKE YOU TO GRAN AND SEE WHAT SHE SAYS?
RUSTLE
RUSTLE
RUSTLE

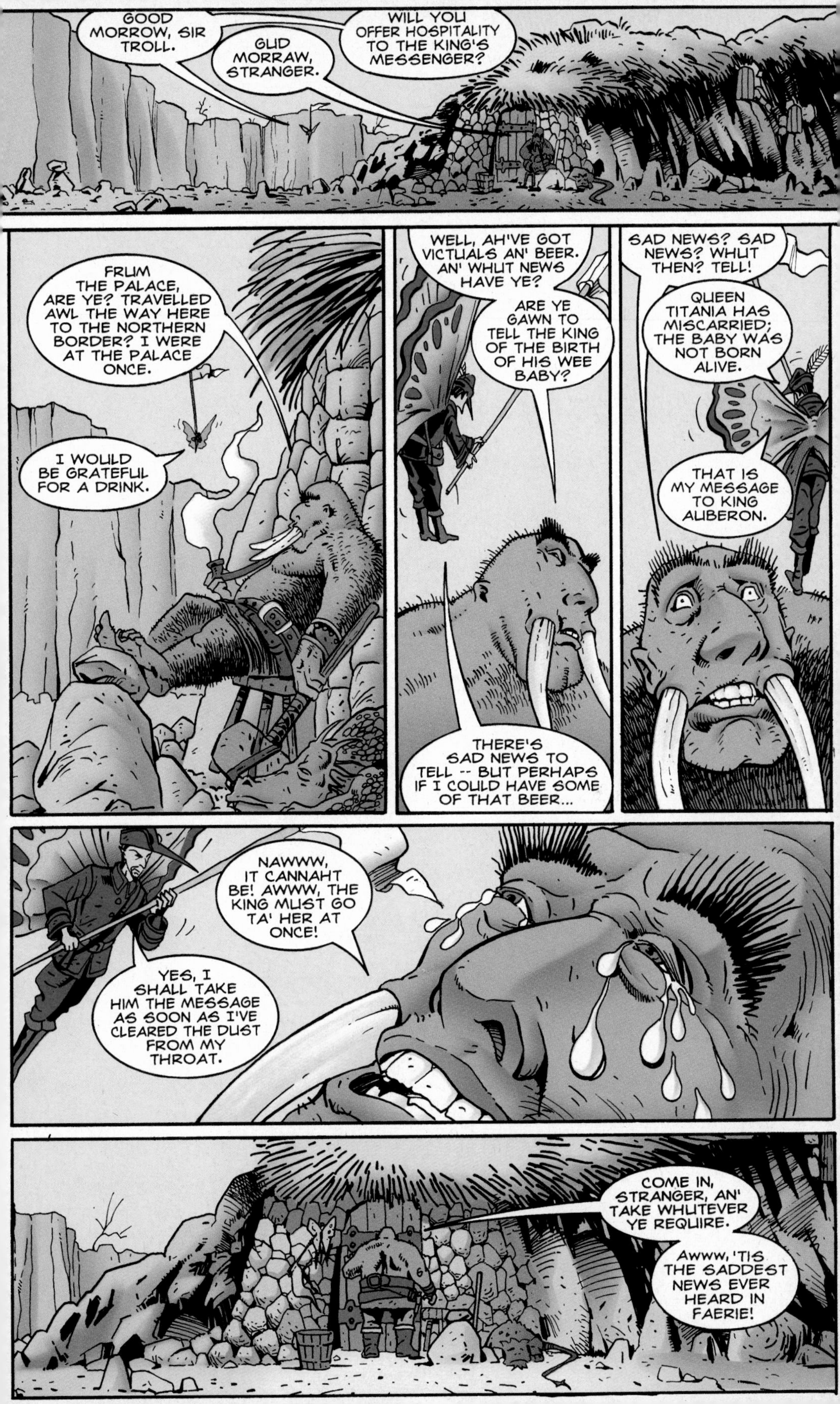
GOOD MORROW, SIR TROLL.
GUD MORRAW, STRANGER.
WILL YOU OFFER HOSPITALITY TO THE KING'S MESSENGER?
FRUM THE PALACE, ARE YE? TRAVELLED AWL THE WAY HERE TO THE NORTHERN BORDER? I WERE AT THE PALACE ONCE.
I WOULD BE GRATEFUL FOR A DRINK.
WELL, AH'VE GOT VICTUALS AN' BEER. AN' WHUT NEWS HAVE YE?
ARE YE GAWN TO TELL THE KING OF THE BIRTH OF HIS WEE BABY?
THERE'S SAD NEWS TO TELL -- BUT PERHAPS IF I COULD HAVE SOME OF THAT BEER...
SAD NEWS? SAD NEWS? WHUT THEN? TELL!
QUEEN TITANIA HAS MISCARRIED; THE BABY WAS NOT BORN ALIVE.
THAT IS MY MESSAGE TO KING AUBERON.
NAWWW, IT CANNAHT BE! AWWW, THE KING MUST GO TA' HER AT ONCE!
YES, I SHALL TAKE HIM THE MESSAGE AS SOON AS I'VE CLEARED THE DUST FROM MY THROAT.
COME IN, STRANGER, AN' TAKE WHUTEVER YE REQUIRE.
Awww, 'TIS THE SADDEST NEWS EVER HEARD IN FAERIE!

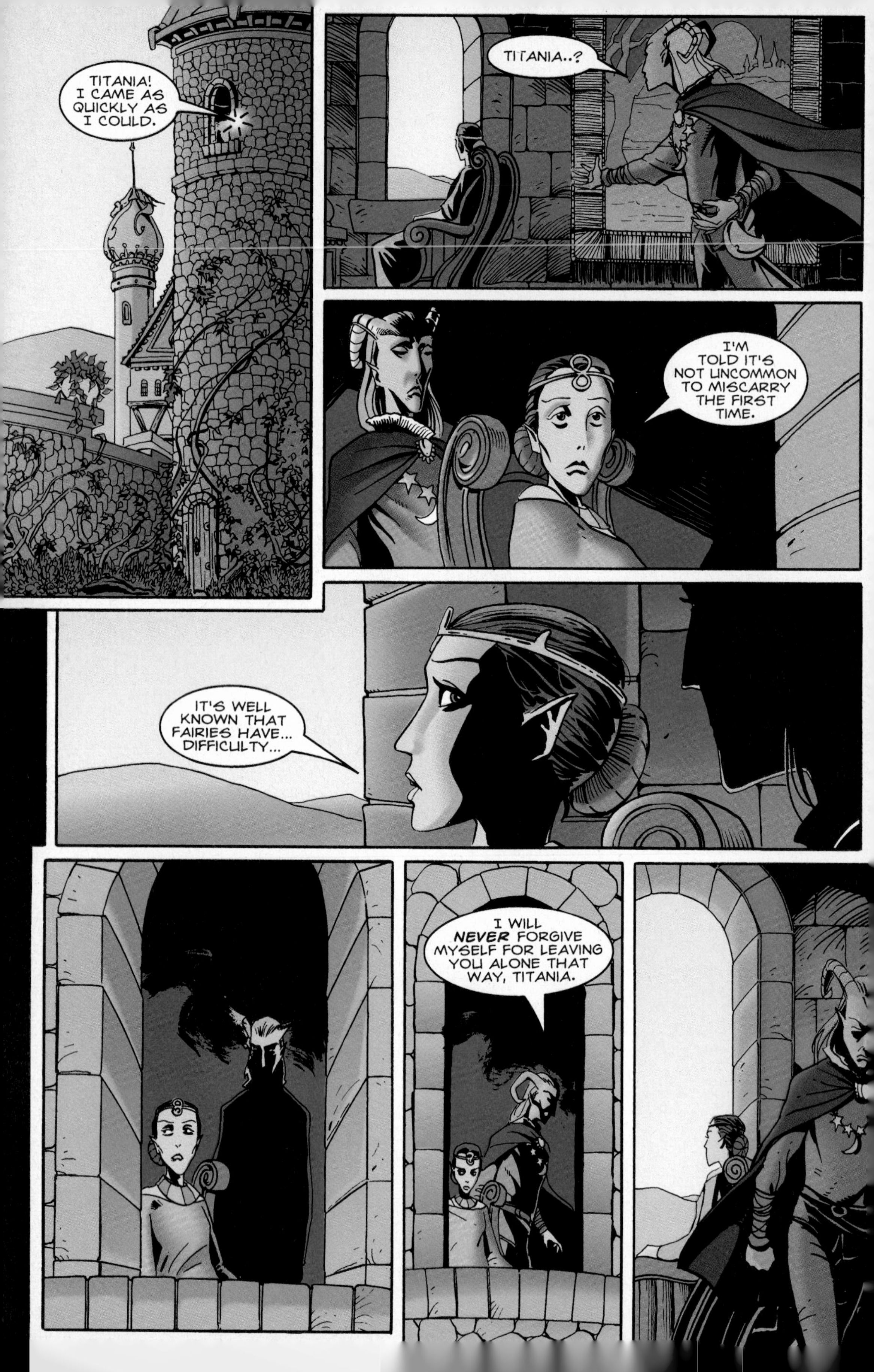
TITANIA! I CAME AS QUICKLY AS I COULD.
TITANIA..?
I'M TOLD IT'S NOT UNCOMMON TO MISCARRY THE FIRST TIME.
IT'S WELL KNOWN THAT FAIRIES HAVE... DIFFICULTY...
I WILL **NEVER** FORGIVE MYSELF FOR LEAVING YOU ALONE THAT WAY, TITANIA.

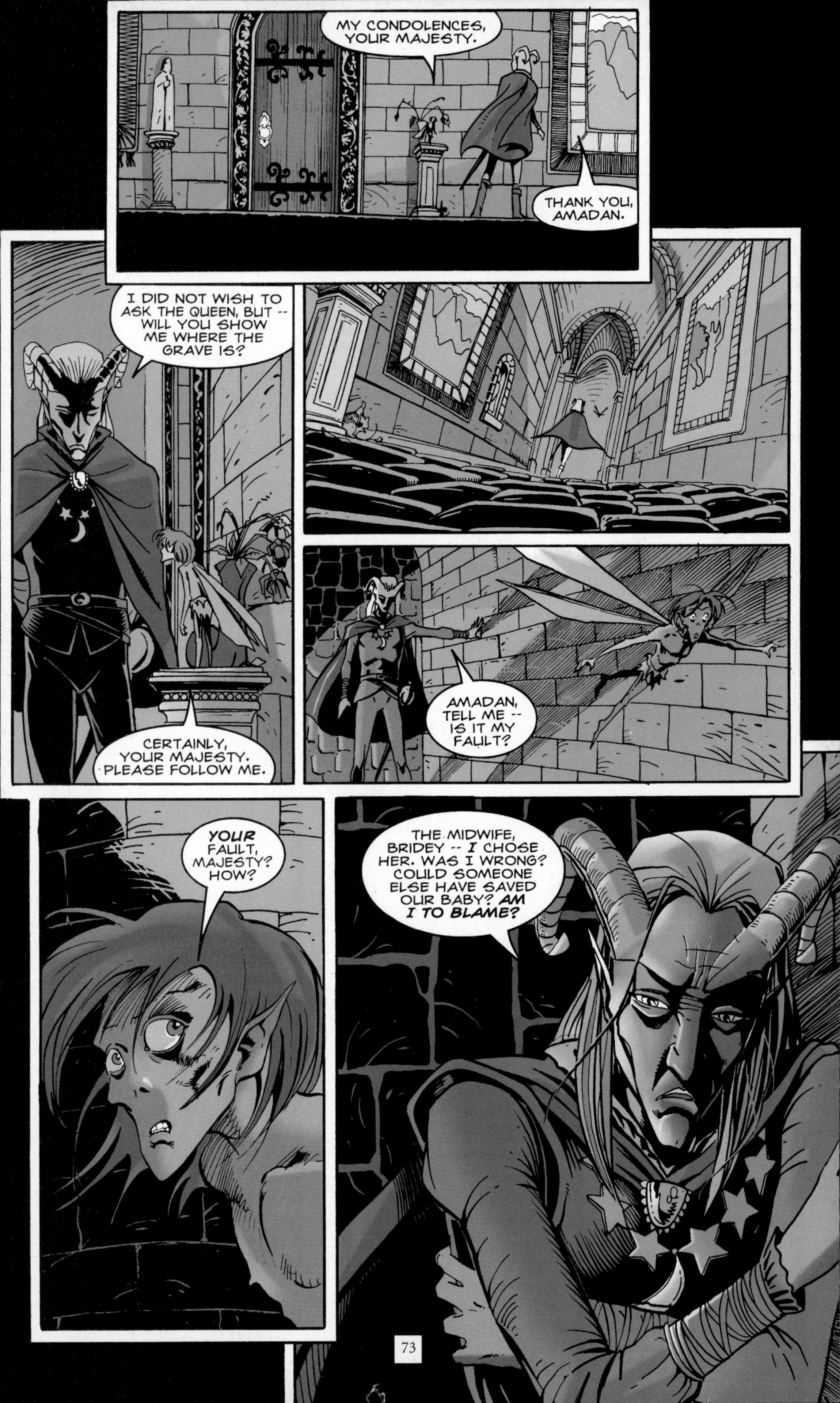

MY CONDOLENCES, YOUR MAJESTY.
THANK YOU, AMADAN.
I DID NOT WISH TO ASK THE QUEEN, BUT -- WILL YOU SHOW ME WHERE THE GRAVE IS?
CERTAINLY, YOUR MAJESTY. PLEASE FOLLOW ME.
AMADAN, TELL ME -- IS IT MY FAULT?
YOUR FAULT, MAJESTY? HOW?
THE MIDWIFE, BRIDEY -- I CHOSE HER. WAS I WRONG? COULD SOMEONE ELSE HAVE SAVED OUR BABY? AM I TO BLAME?

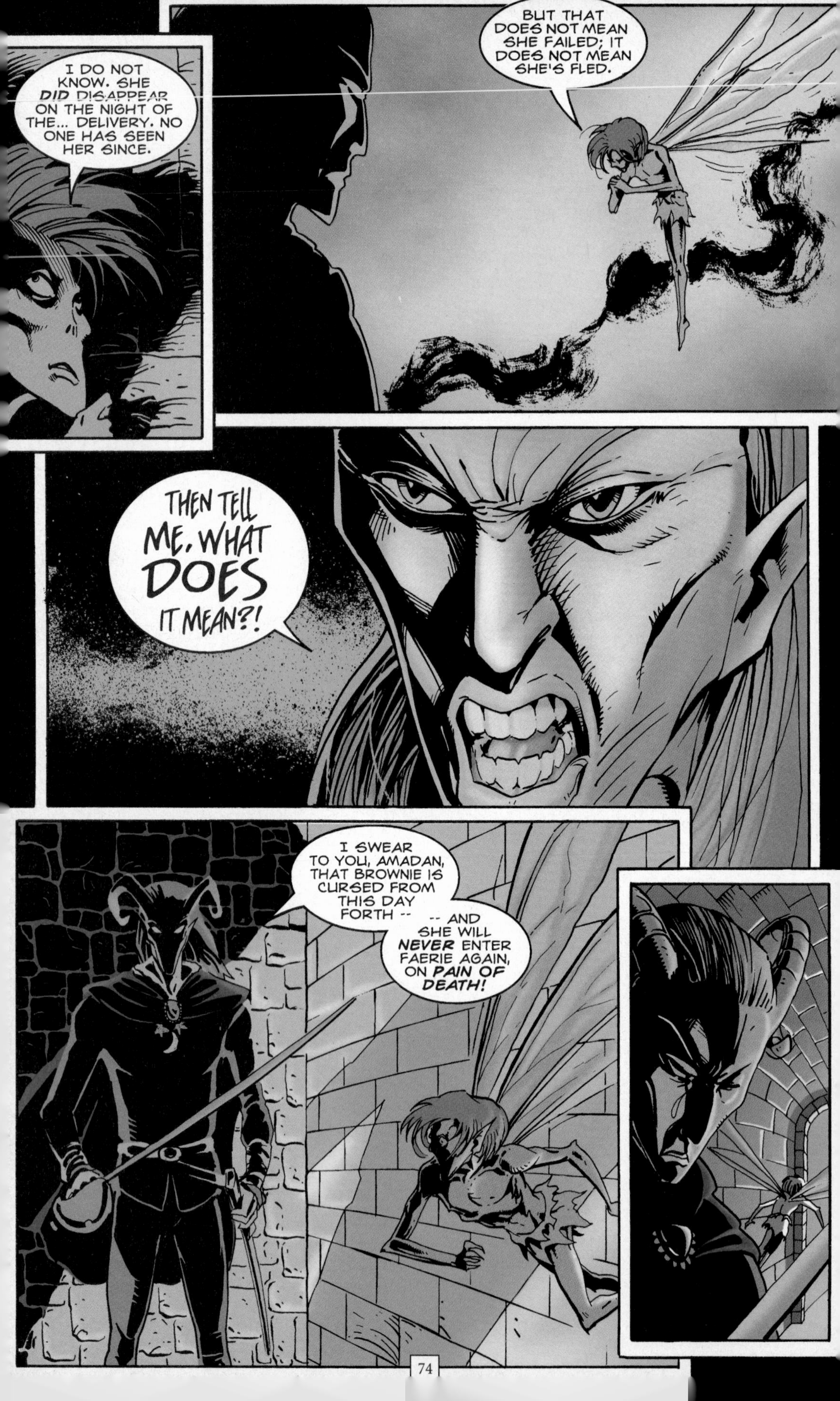
I DO NOT KNOW. SHE *DID* DISAPPEAR ON THE NIGHT OF THE... DELIVERY. NO ONE HAS SEEN HER SINCE.
BUT THAT DOES NOT MEAN SHE FAILED; IT DOES NOT MEAN SHE'S FLED.
THEN TELL ME, WHAT DOES IT MEAN?!
I SWEAR TO YOU, AMADAN, THAT BROWNIE IS CURSED FROM THIS DAY FORTH --
-- AND SHE WILL *NEVER* ENTER FAERIE AGAIN, ON *PAIN OF DEATH!*

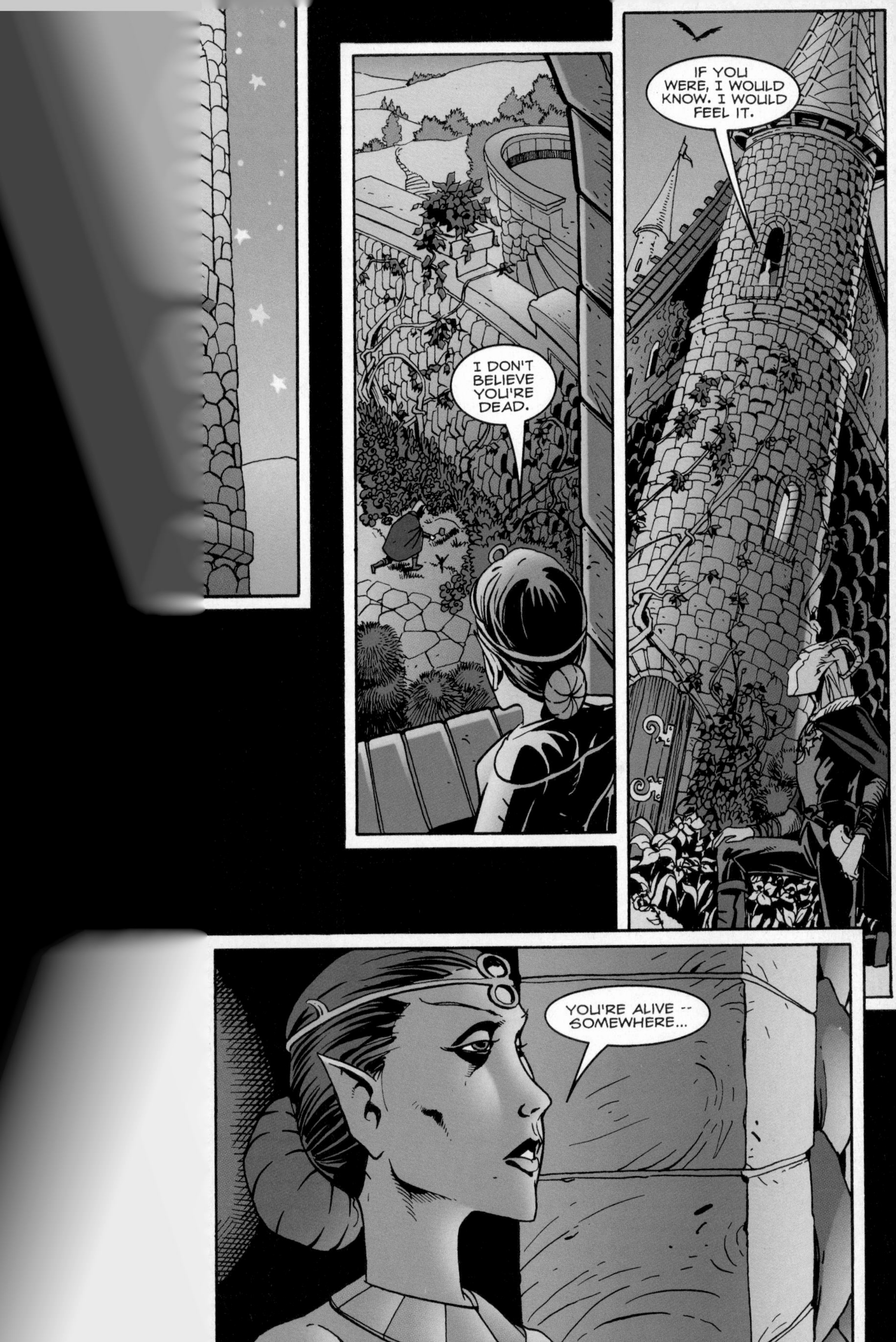
I DON'T BELIEVE YOU'RE DEAD.
IF YOU WERE, I WOULD KNOW. I WOULD FEEL IT.
YOU'RE ALIVE -- SOMEWHERE...

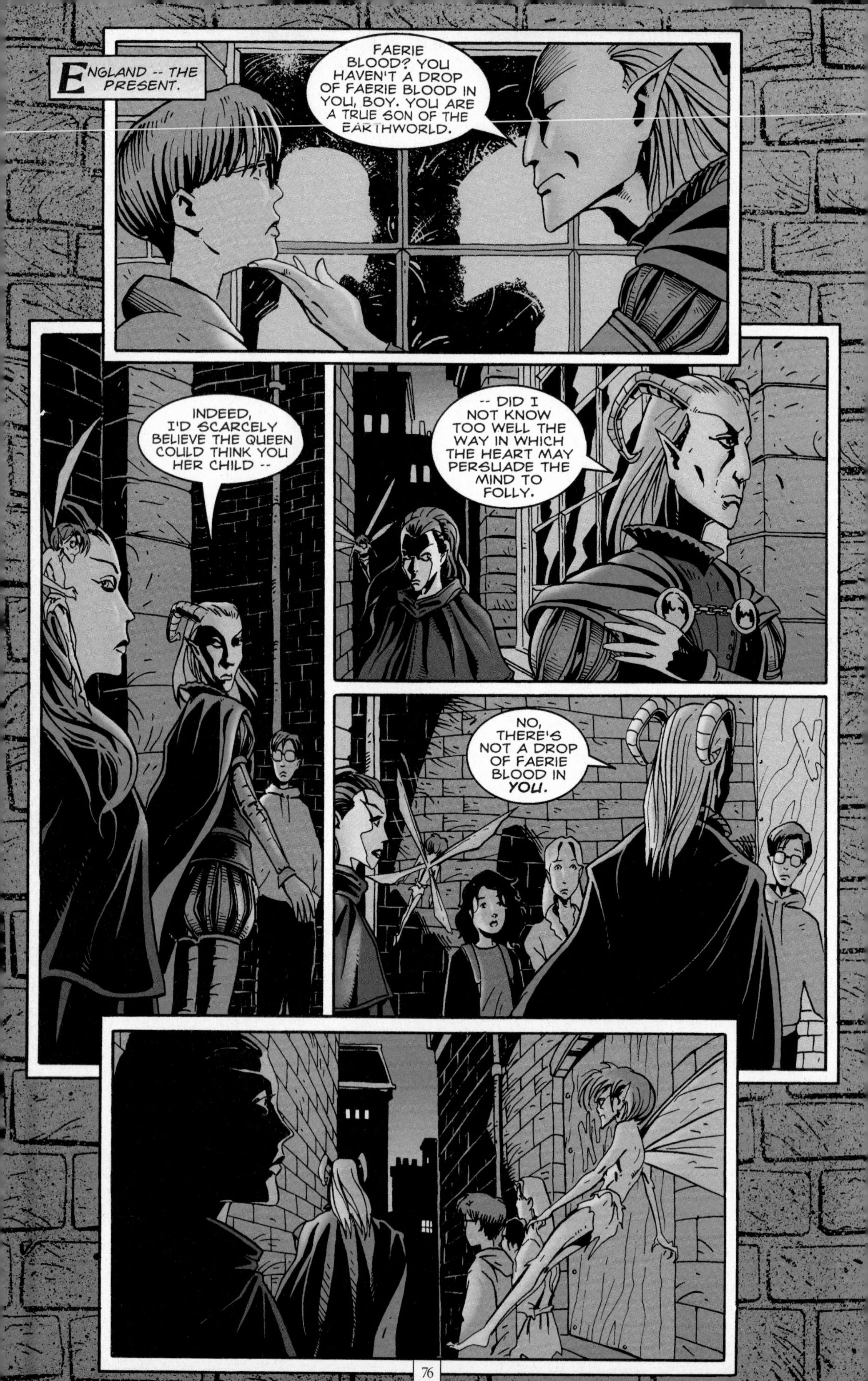
ENGLAND -- THE PRESENT.
FAERIE BLOOD? YOU HAVEN'T A DROP OF FAERIE BLOOD IN YOU, BOY. YOU ARE A TRUE SON OF THE EARTHWORLD.
INDEED, I'D SCARCELY BELIEVE THE QUEEN COULD THINK YOU HER CHILD --
-- DID I NOT KNOW TOO WELL THE WAY IN WHICH THE HEART MAY PERSUADE THE MIND TO FOLLY.
NO, THERE'S NOT A DROP OF FAERIE BLOOD IN *YOU*.

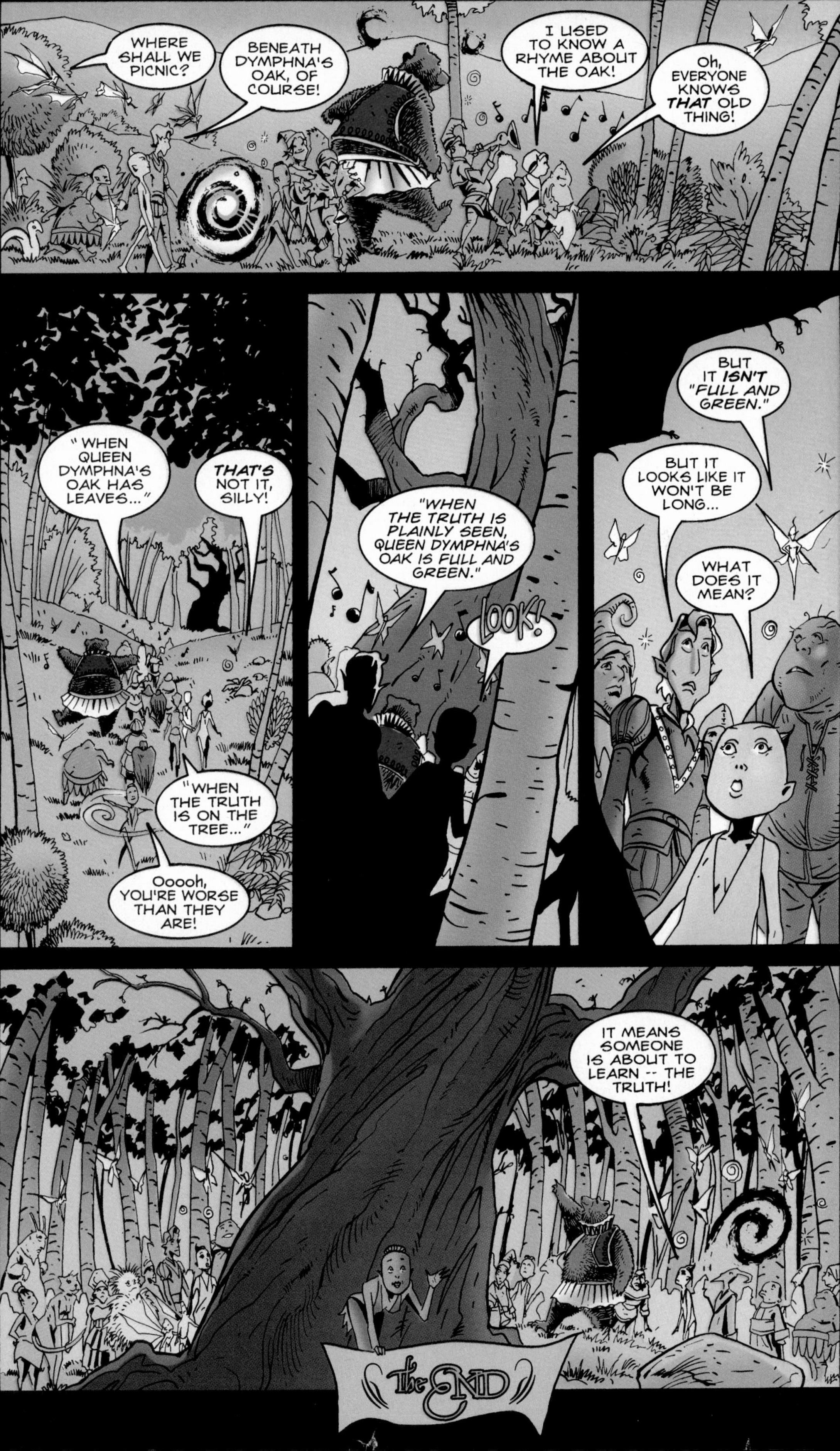
WHERE SHALL WE PICNIC?
BENEATH DYMPHNA'S OAK, OF COURSE!
I USED TO KNOW A RHYME ABOUT THE OAK!
Oh, EVERYONE KNOWS THAT OLD THING!
"WHEN QUEEN DYMPHNA'S OAK HAS LEAVES..."
THAT'S NOT IT, SILLY!
"WHEN THE TRUTH IS ON THE TREE..."
Ooooh, YOU'RE WORSE THAN THEY ARE!
"WHEN THE TRUTH IS PLAINLY SEEN, QUEEN DYMPHNA'S OAK IS FULL AND GREEN."
LOOK!
BUT IT ISN'T "FULL AND GREEN."
BUT IT LOOKS LIKE IT WON'T BE LONG...
WHAT DOES IT MEAN?
IT MEANS SOMEONE IS ABOUT TO LEARN -- THE TRUTH!
The END

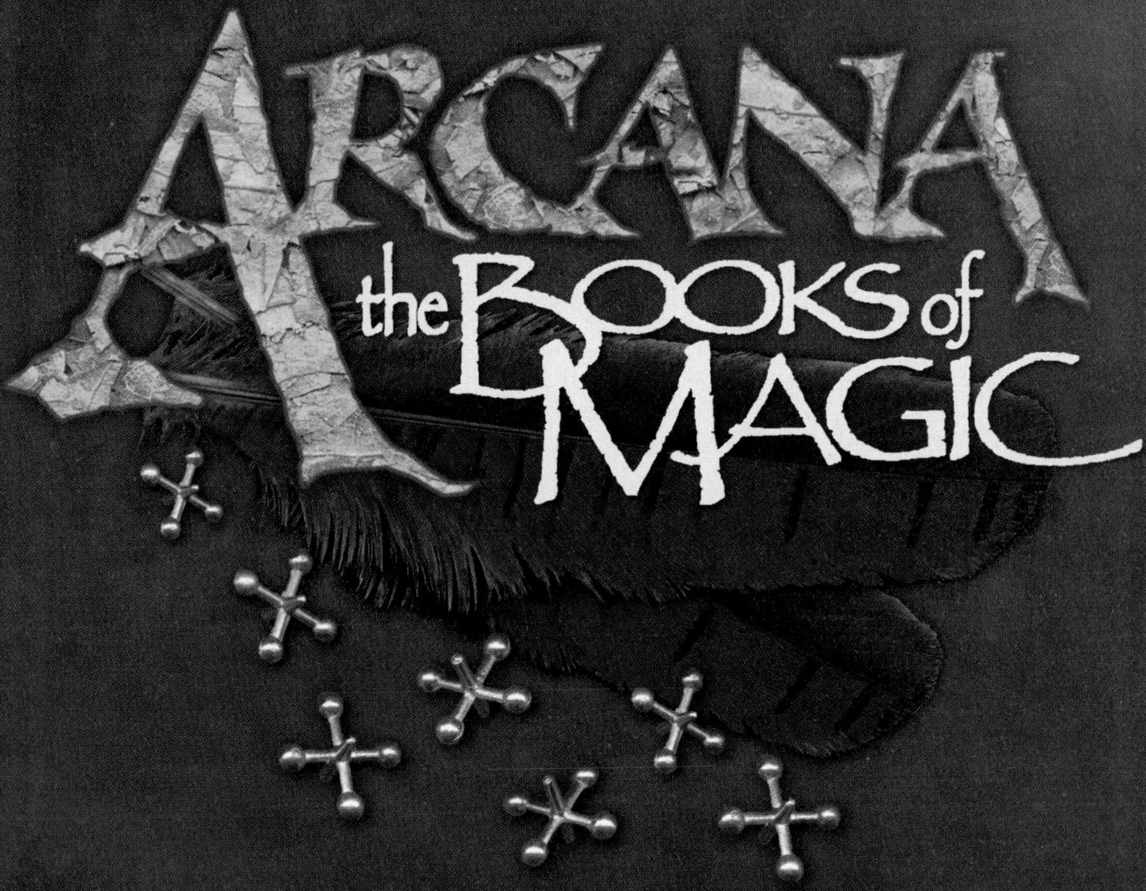
ARCANA
the BOOKS of
MAGIC

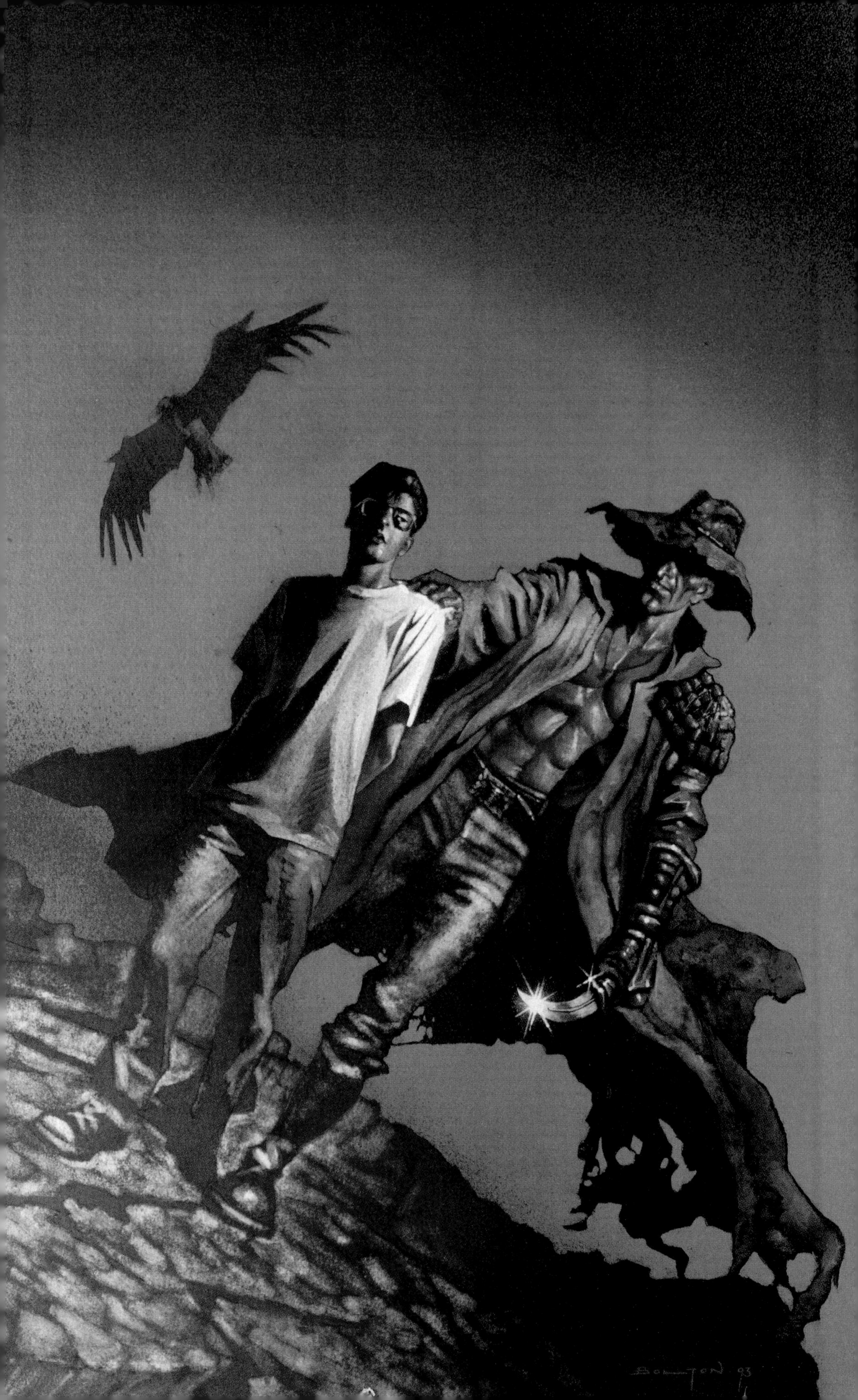
BOLTON 93

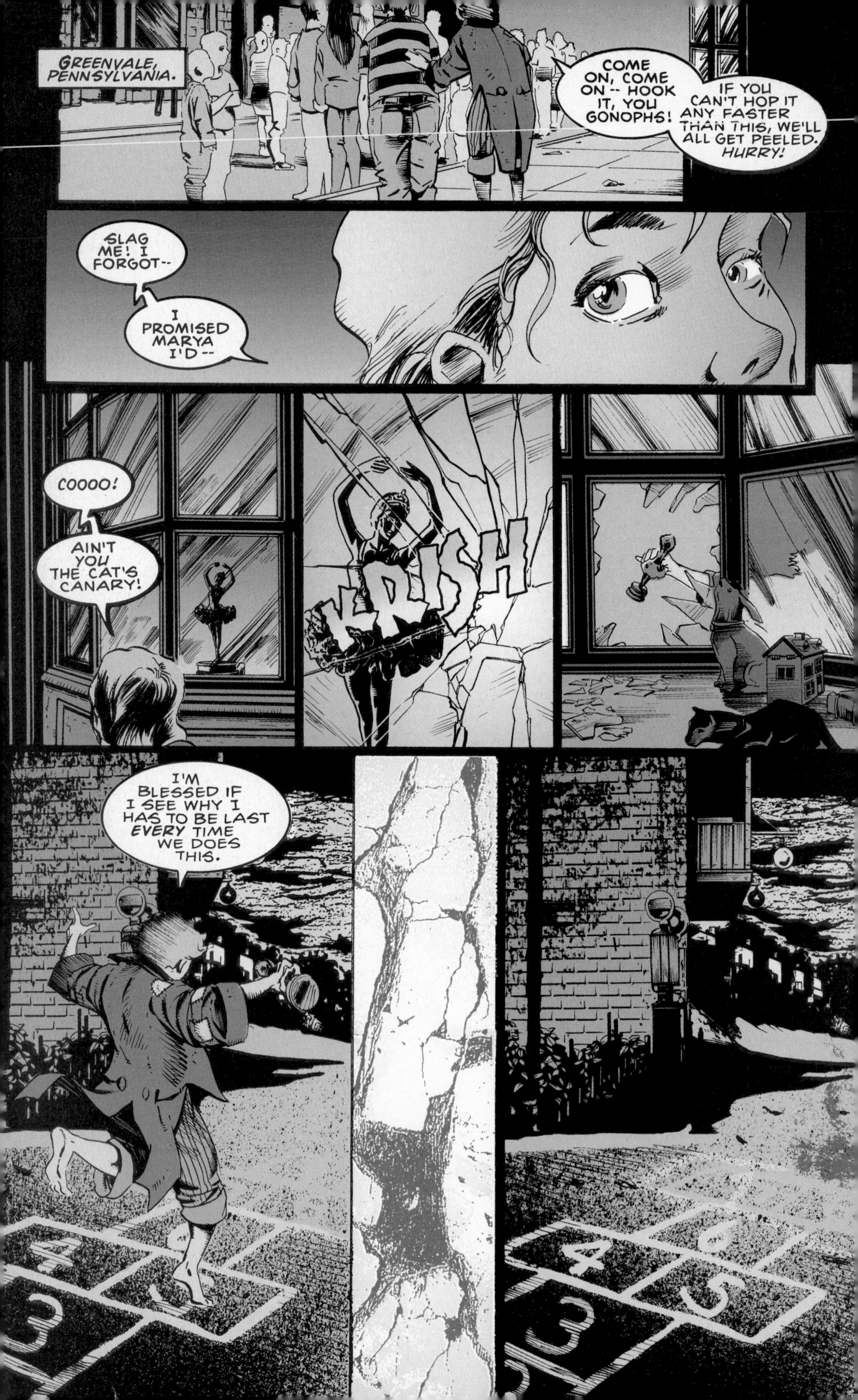
GREENVALE, PENNSYLVANIA.
COME ON, COME ON -- HOOK IT, YOU GONOPHS!
IF YOU CAN'T HOP IT ANY FASTER THAN THIS, WE'LL ALL GET PEELED. HURRY!
SLAG ME! I FORGOT--
I PROMISED MARYA I'D --
COOOO!
AIN'T YOU THE CAT'S CANARY!
KRISH
I'M BLESSED IF I SEE WHY I HAS TO BE LAST EVERY TIME WE DOES THIS.

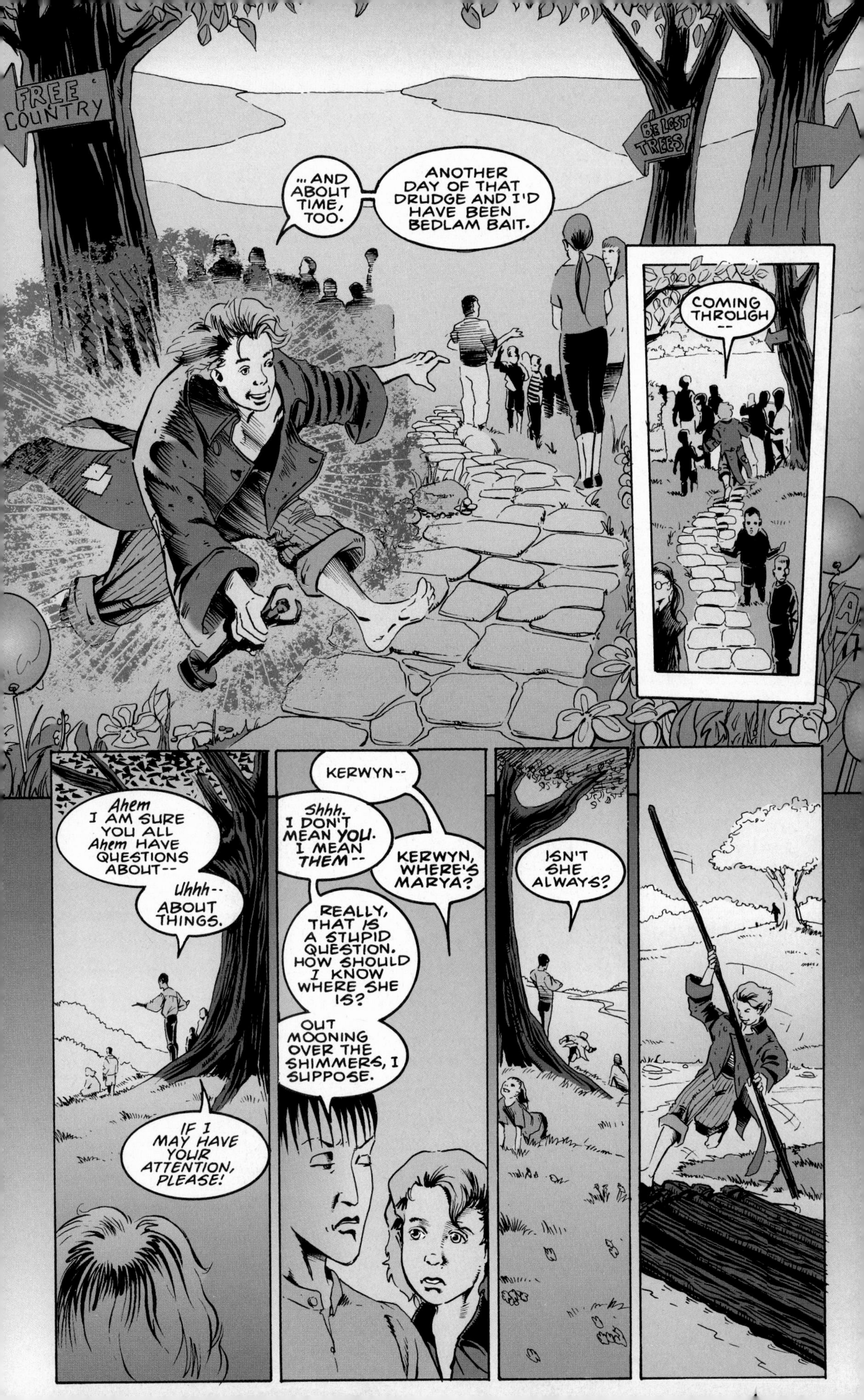
FREE COUNTRY
BE LOST TREES
...AND ABOUT TIME, TOO.
ANOTHER DAY OF THAT DRUDGE AND I'D HAVE BEEN BEDLAM BAIT.
COMING THROUGH --
Ahem I AM SURE YOU ALL *Ahem* HAVE QUESTIONS ABOUT--
Uhhh-- ABOUT THINGS.
IF I MAY HAVE YOUR ATTENTION, PLEASE!
KERWYN--
Shhh. I DON'T MEAN **YOU**. I MEAN ***THEM***--
KERWYN, WHERE'S MARYA?
REALLY, THAT IS A STUPID QUESTION. HOW SHOULD I KNOW WHERE SHE IS?
OUT MOONING OVER THE SHIMMERS, I SUPPOSE.
ISN'T SHE ALWAYS?

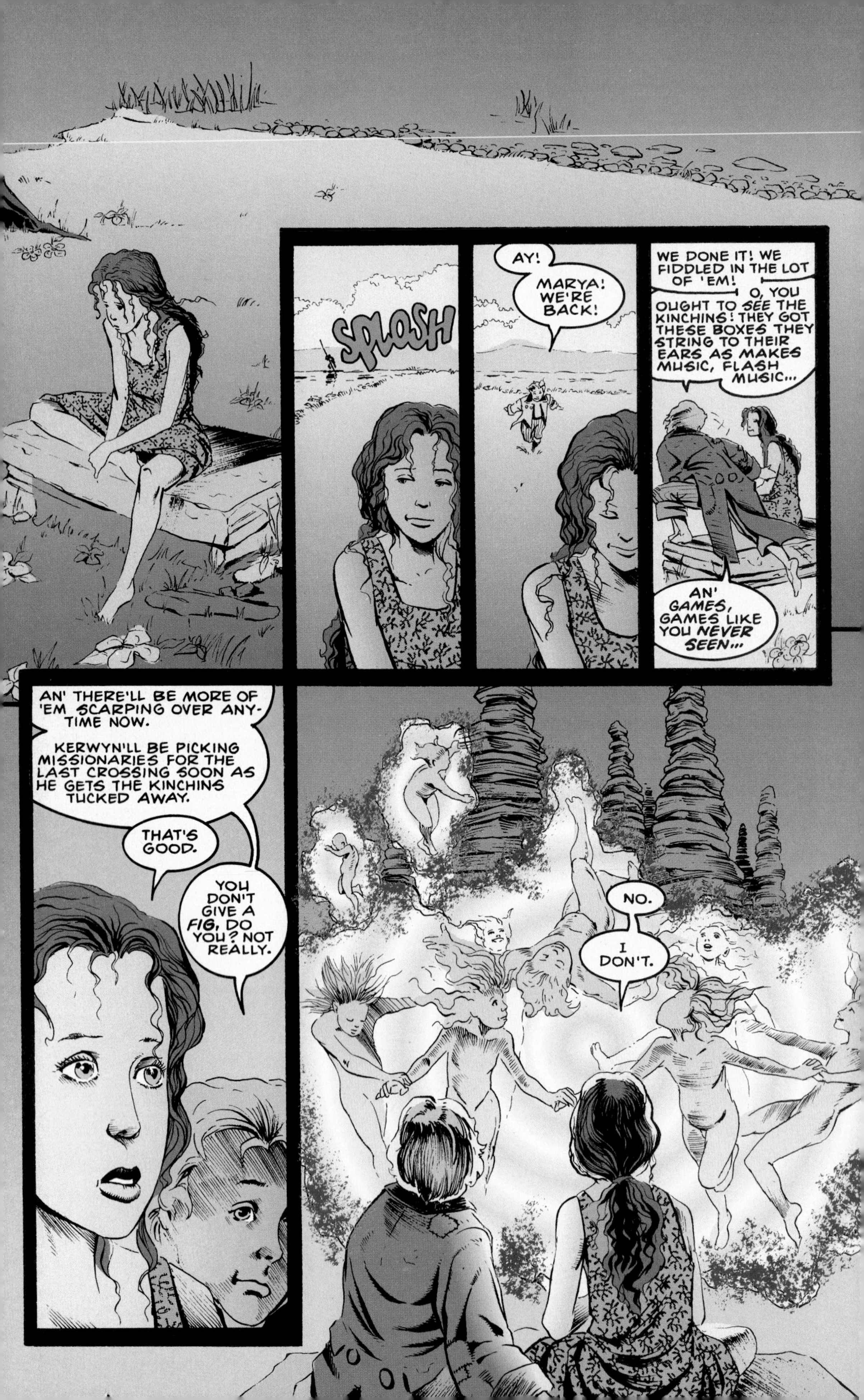
SPLOSH
AY!
MARYA! WE'RE BACK!
WE DONE IT! WE FIDDLED IN THE LOT OF 'EM!
O, YOU OUGHT TO SEE THE KINCHINS! THEY GOT THESE BOXES THEY STRING TO THEIR EARS AS MAKES MUSIC, FLASH MUSIC...
AN' GAMES, GAMES LIKE YOU NEVER SEEN...
AN' THERE'LL BE MORE OF 'EM SCARPING OVER ANY-TIME NOW.
KERWYN'LL BE PICKING MISSIONARIES FOR THE LAST CROSSING SOON AS HE GETS THE KINCHINS TUCKED AWAY.
THAT'S GOOD.
YOU DON'T GIVE A FIG, DO YOU? NOT REALLY.
NO.
I DON'T.

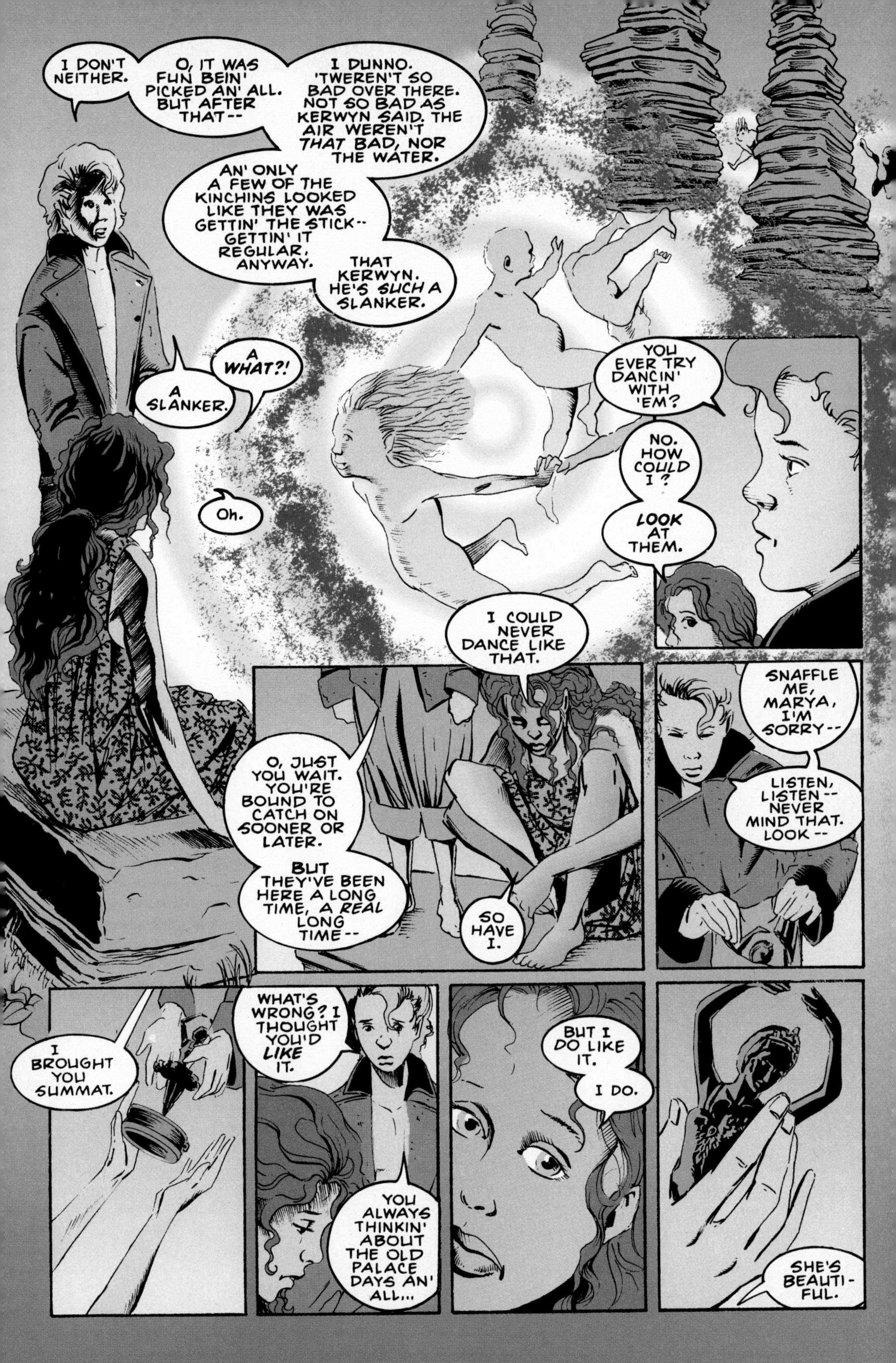
I DON'T NEITHER.
O, IT WAS FUN BEIN' PICKED AN' ALL. BUT AFTER THAT--
I DUNNO. 'TWEREN'T SO BAD OVER THERE. NOT SO BAD AS KERWYN SAID. THE AIR WEREN'T THAT BAD, NOR THE WATER.
AN' ONLY A FEW OF THE KINCHINS LOOKED LIKE THEY WAS GETTIN' THE STICK-- GETTIN' IT REGULAR, ANYWAY.
THAT KERWYN. HE'S SUCH A SLANKER.
A WHAT?!
A SLANKER.
Oh.
YOU EVER TRY DANCIN' WITH 'EM?
NO. HOW COULD I?
LOOK AT THEM.
I COULD NEVER DANCE LIKE THAT.
O, JUST YOU WAIT. YOU'RE BOUND TO CATCH ON SOONER OR LATER.
BUT THEY'VE BEEN HERE A LONG TIME, A REAL LONG TIME--
SO HAVE I.
SNAFFLE ME, MARYA, I'M SORRY--
LISTEN, LISTEN-- NEVER MIND THAT. LOOK--
I BROUGHT YOU SUMMAT.
WHAT'S WRONG? I THOUGHT YOU'D LIKE IT.
YOU ALWAYS THINKIN' ABOUT THE OLD PALACE DAYS AN' ALL...
BUT I DO LIKE IT.
I DO.
SHE'S BEAUTI-FUL.

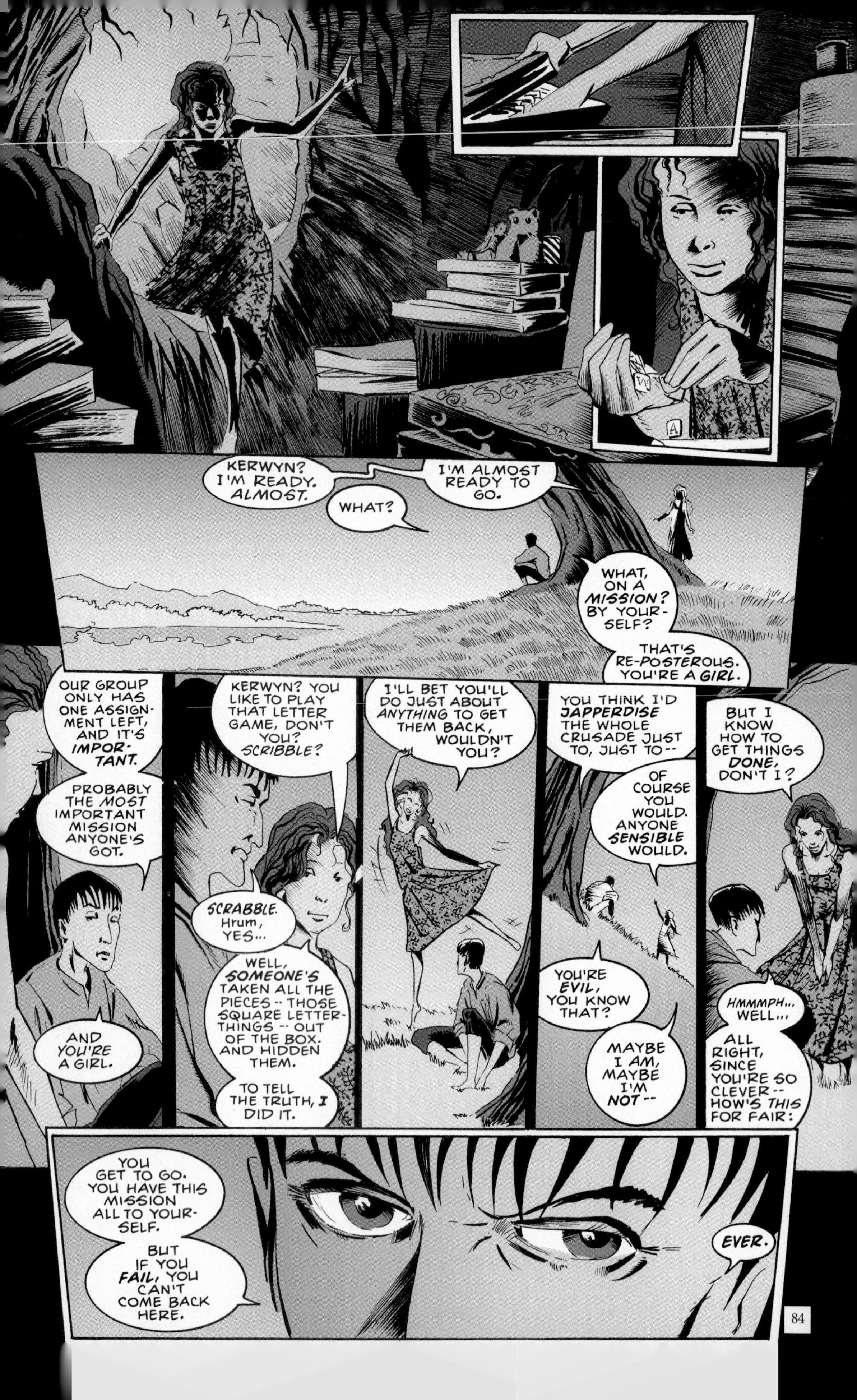
KERWYN? I'M READY. ALMOST.
WHAT?
I'M ALMOST READY TO GO.
WHAT, ON A MISSION? BY YOURSELF?
THAT'S RE-POSTEROUS. YOU'RE A GIRL.
OUR GROUP ONLY HAS ONE ASSIGNMENT LEFT, AND IT'S IMPORTANT.
PROBABLY THE MOST IMPORTANT MISSION ANYONE'S GOT.
AND YOU'RE A GIRL.
KERWYN? YOU LIKE TO PLAY THAT LETTER GAME, DON'T YOU? SCRIBBLE?
SCRABBLE. Hrum, YES...
WELL, SOMEONE'S TAKEN ALL THE PIECES -- THOSE SQUARE LETTER-THINGS -- OUT OF THE BOX. AND HIDDEN THEM.
TO TELL THE TRUTH, I DID IT.
I'LL BET YOU'LL DO JUST ABOUT ANYTHING TO GET THEM BACK, WOULDN'T YOU?
YOU THINK I'D JAPPERDISE THE WHOLE CRUSADE JUST TO, JUST TO--
OF COURSE YOU WOULD. ANYONE SENSIBLE WOULD.
YOU'RE EVIL, YOU KNOW THAT?
MAYBE I AM, MAYBE I'M NOT--
BUT I KNOW HOW TO GET THINGS DONE, DON'T I?
HMMMPH... WELL...
ALL RIGHT, SINCE YOU'RE SO CLEVER-- HOW'S THIS FOR FAIR:
YOU GET TO GO. YOU HAVE THIS MISSION ALL TO YOURSELF.
BUT IF YOU FAIL, YOU CAN'T COME BACK HERE.
EVER.

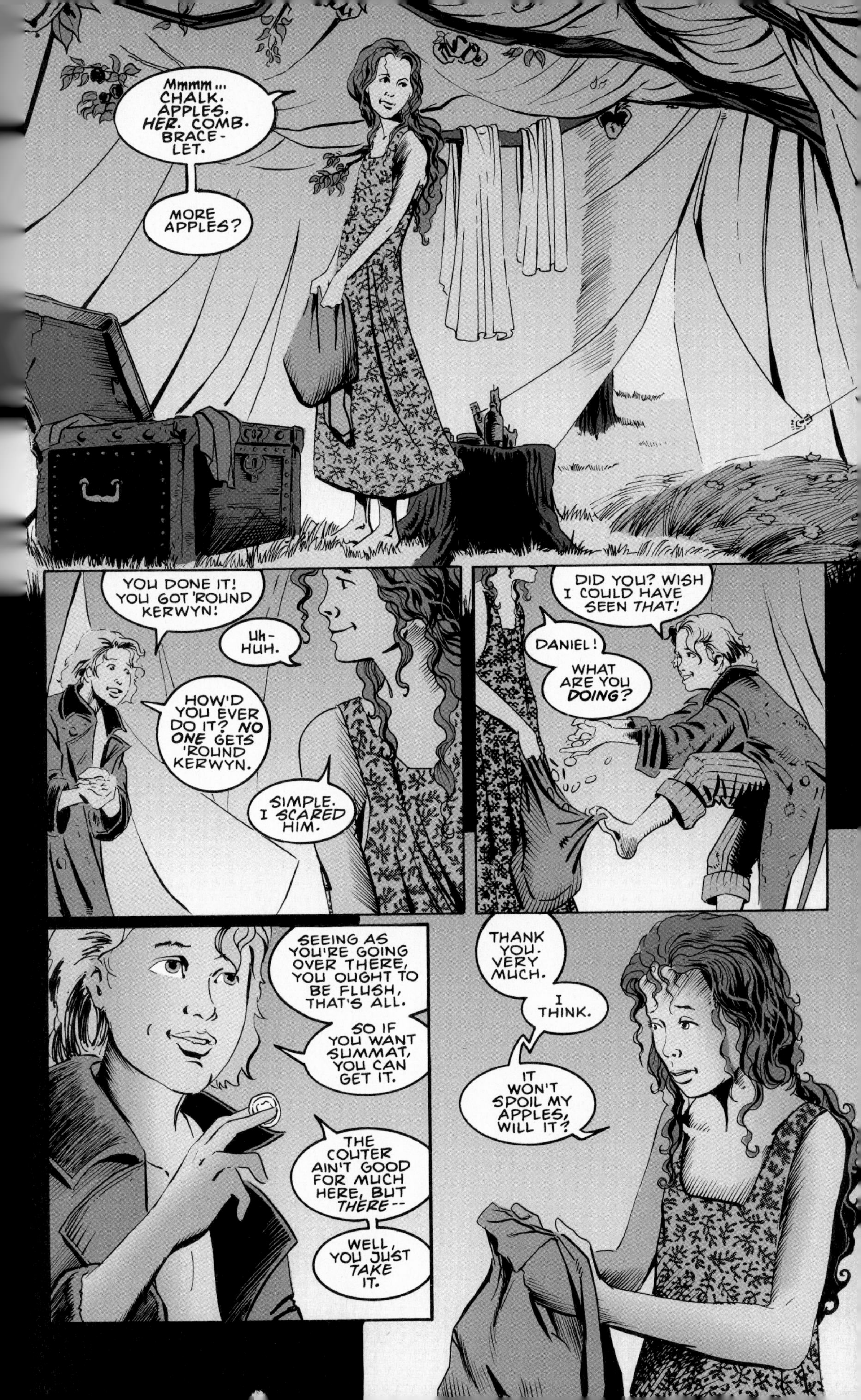

Mmmm... CHALK. APPLES. HER. COMB. BRACE-LET.
MORE APPLES?
YOU DONE IT! YOU GOT 'ROUND KERWYN!
UH-HUH.
HOW'D YOU EVER DO IT? NO ONE GETS 'ROUND KERWYN.
SIMPLE. I SCARED HIM.
DID YOU? WISH I COULD HAVE SEEN THAT!
DANIEL!
WHAT ARE YOU DOING?
SEEING AS YOU'RE GOING OVER THERE, YOU OUGHT TO BE FLUSH, THAT'S ALL.
SO IF YOU WANT SUMMAT, YOU CAN GET IT.
THE COUTER AIN'T GOOD FOR MUCH HERE, BUT THERE--
WELL, YOU JUST TAKE IT.
THANK YOU. VERY MUCH.
I THINK.
IT WON'T SPOIL MY APPLES, WILL IT?

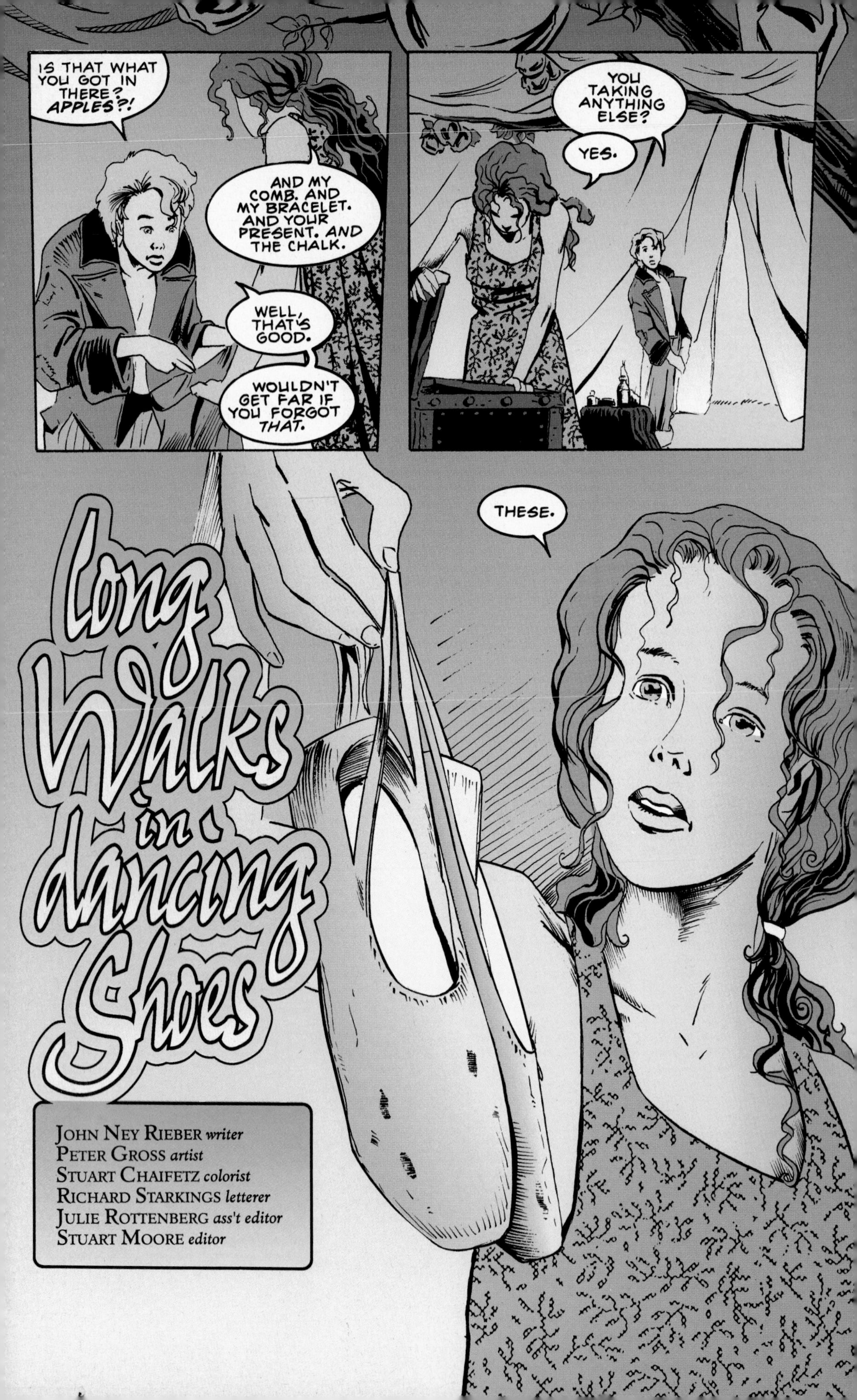
IS THAT WHAT YOU GOT IN THERE? APPLES?!
AND MY COMB. AND MY BRACELET. AND YOUR PRESENT. AND THE CHALK.
WELL, THAT'S GOOD.
WOULDN'T GET FAR IF YOU FORGOT THAT.
YOU TAKING ANYTHING ELSE?
YES.
THESE.
Long Walks in dancing Shoes
JOHN NEY RIEBER writer
PETER GROSS artist
STUART CHAIFETZ colorist
RICHARD STARKINGS letterer
JULIE ROTTENBERG ass't editor
STUART MOORE editor

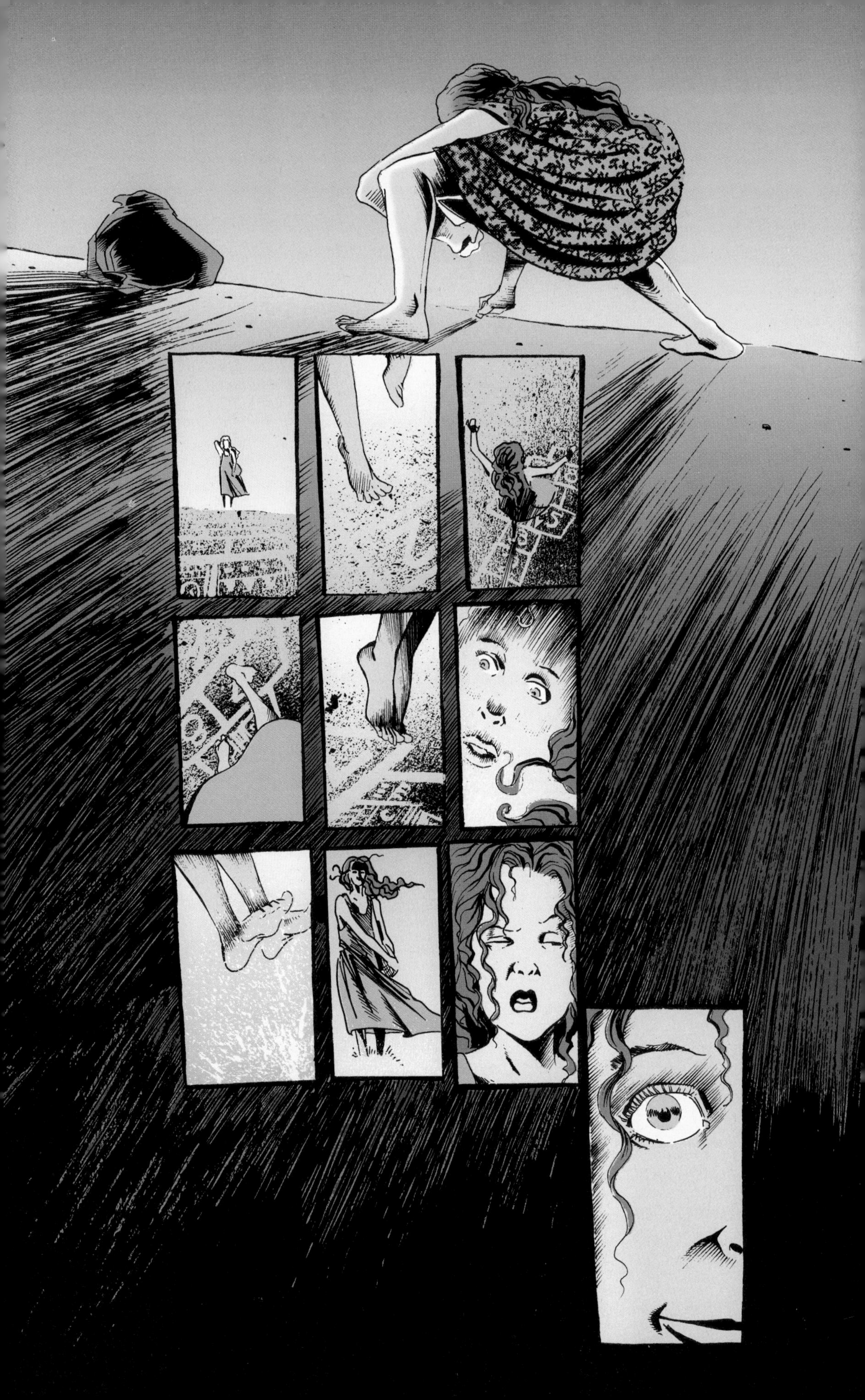

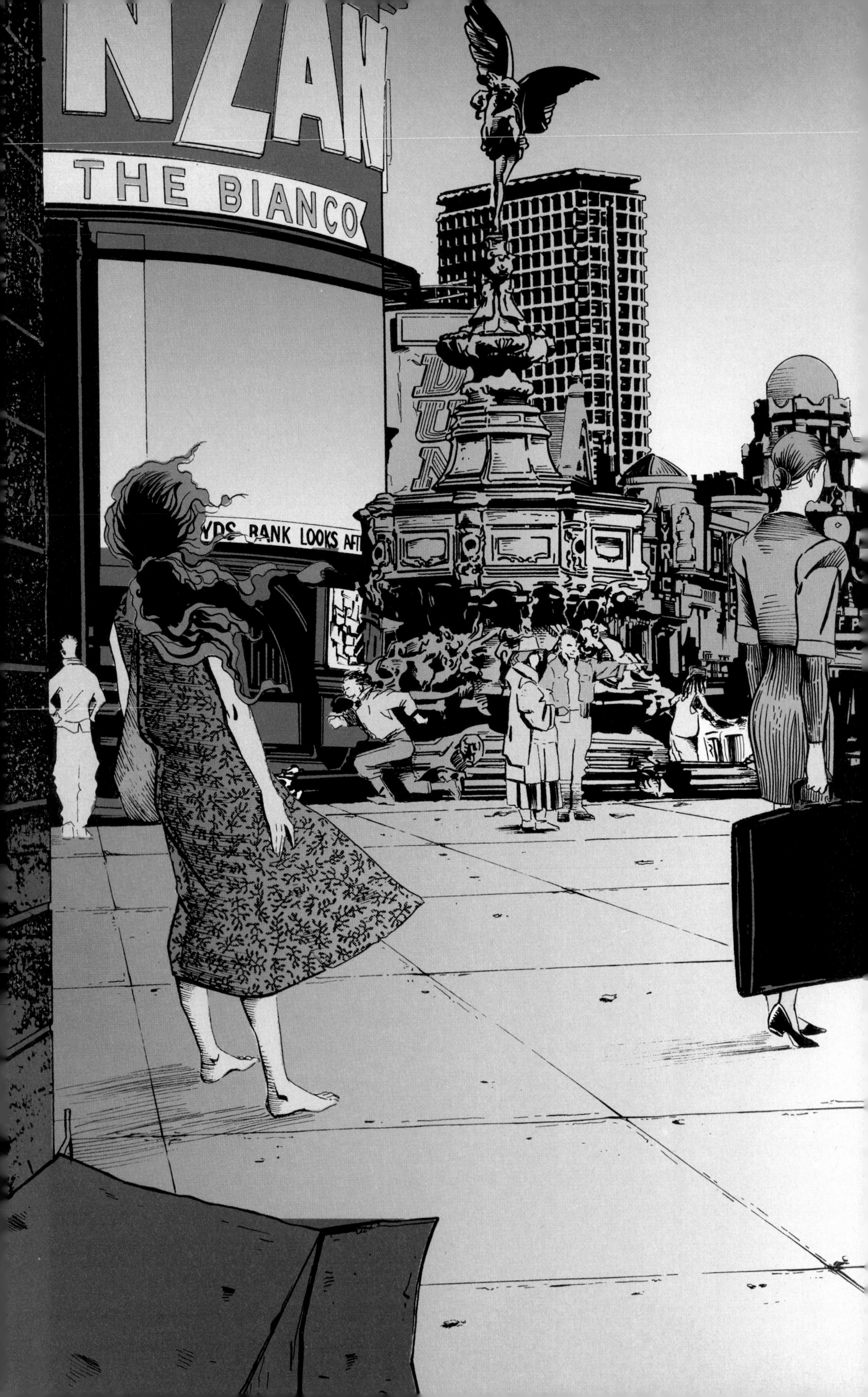
THE BIANCO
YDS BANK LOOKS AFT
LYRIC

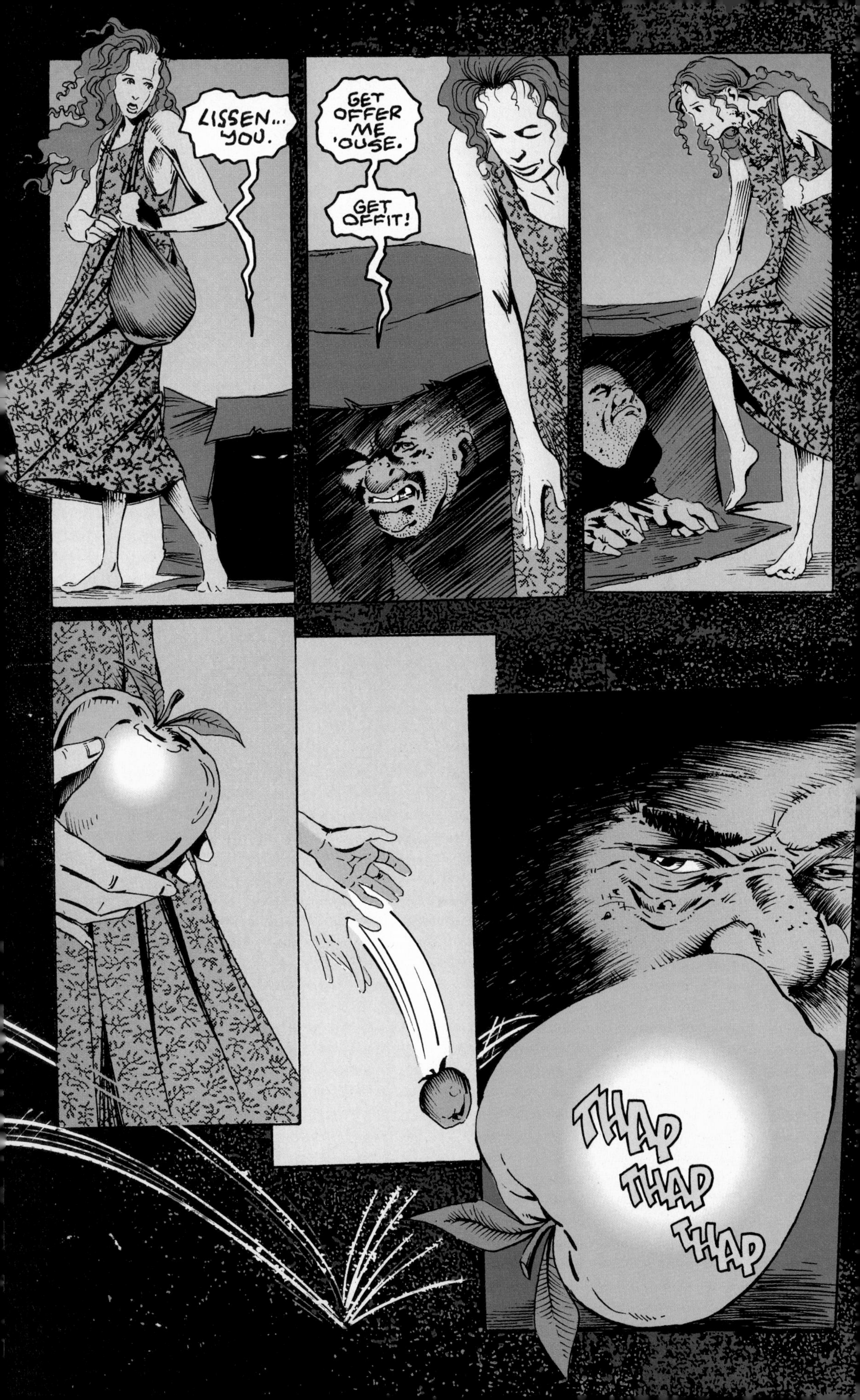
LISSEN... YOU.
GET OFFER ME 'OUSE.
GET OFFIT!
THAP THAP THAP

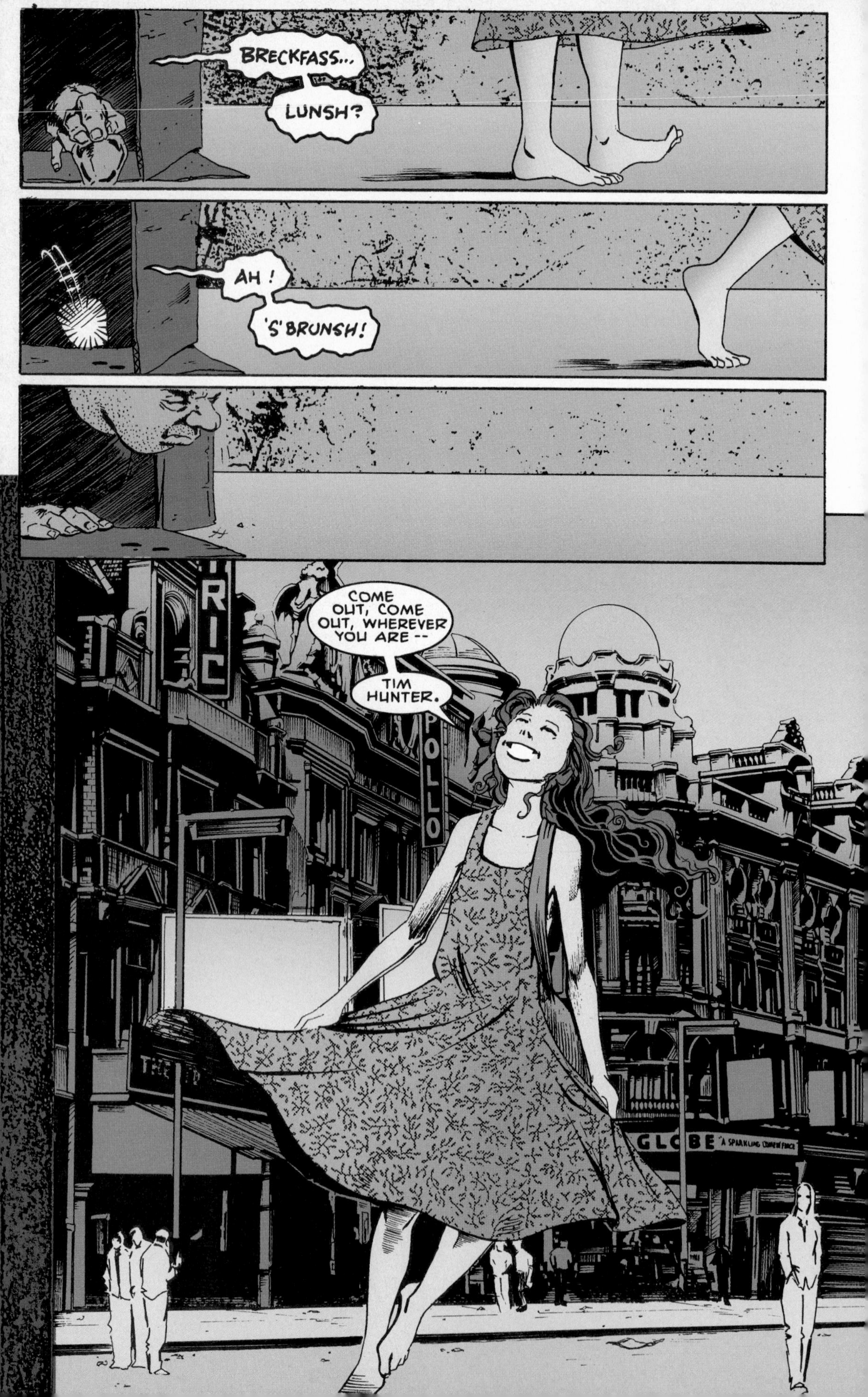
BRECKFASS...
LUNSH?
AH!
'S' BRUNSH!
COME OUT, COME OUT, WHEREVER YOU ARE --
TIM HUNTER.
GLOBE
A SPARKLING COMEDY FARCE

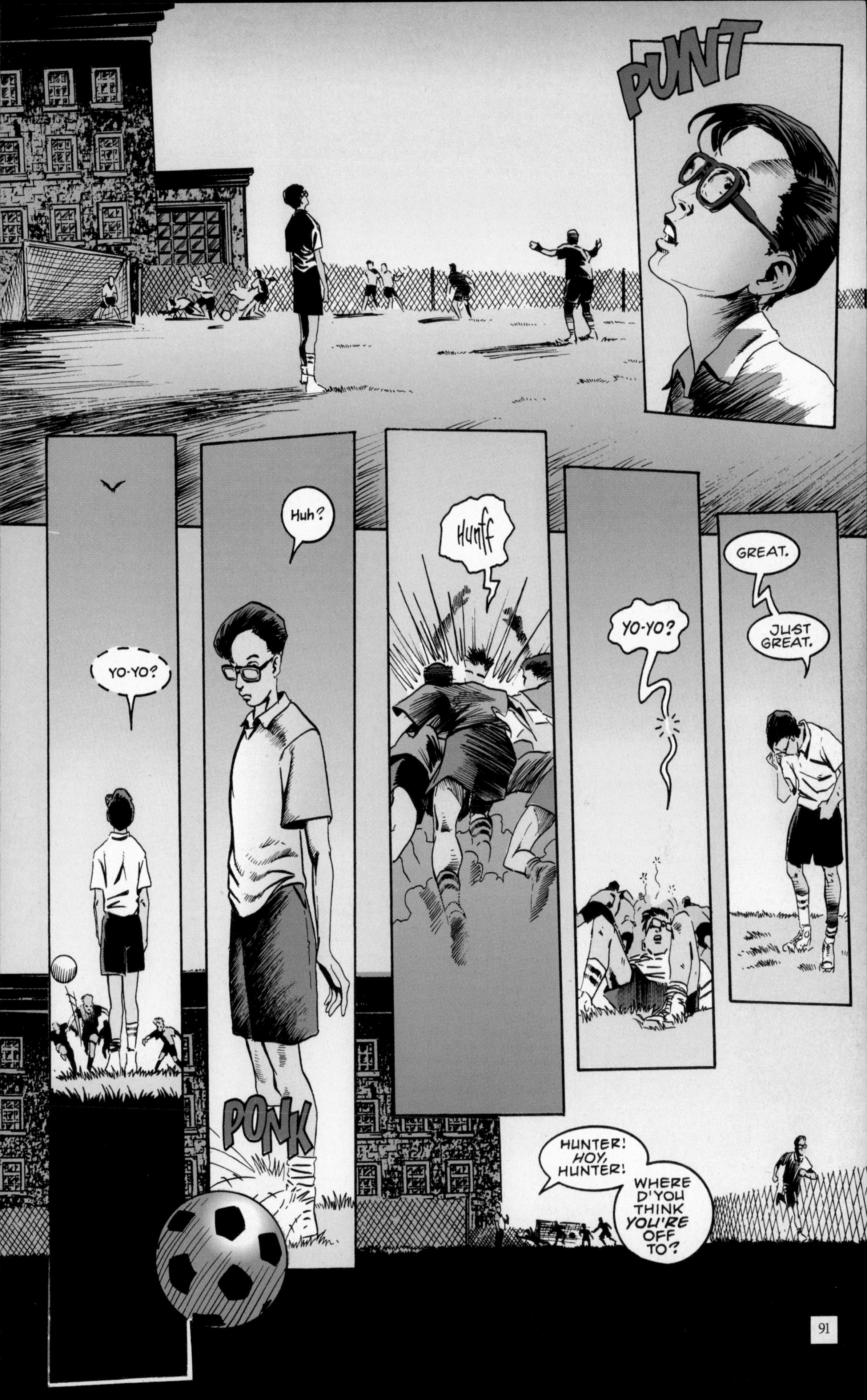
PUNT
YO-YO?
Huh?
PONK
Hunf
YO-YO?
GREAT.
JUST GREAT.
HUNTER! HOY, HUNTER!
WHERE D'YOU THINK YOU'RE OFF TO?

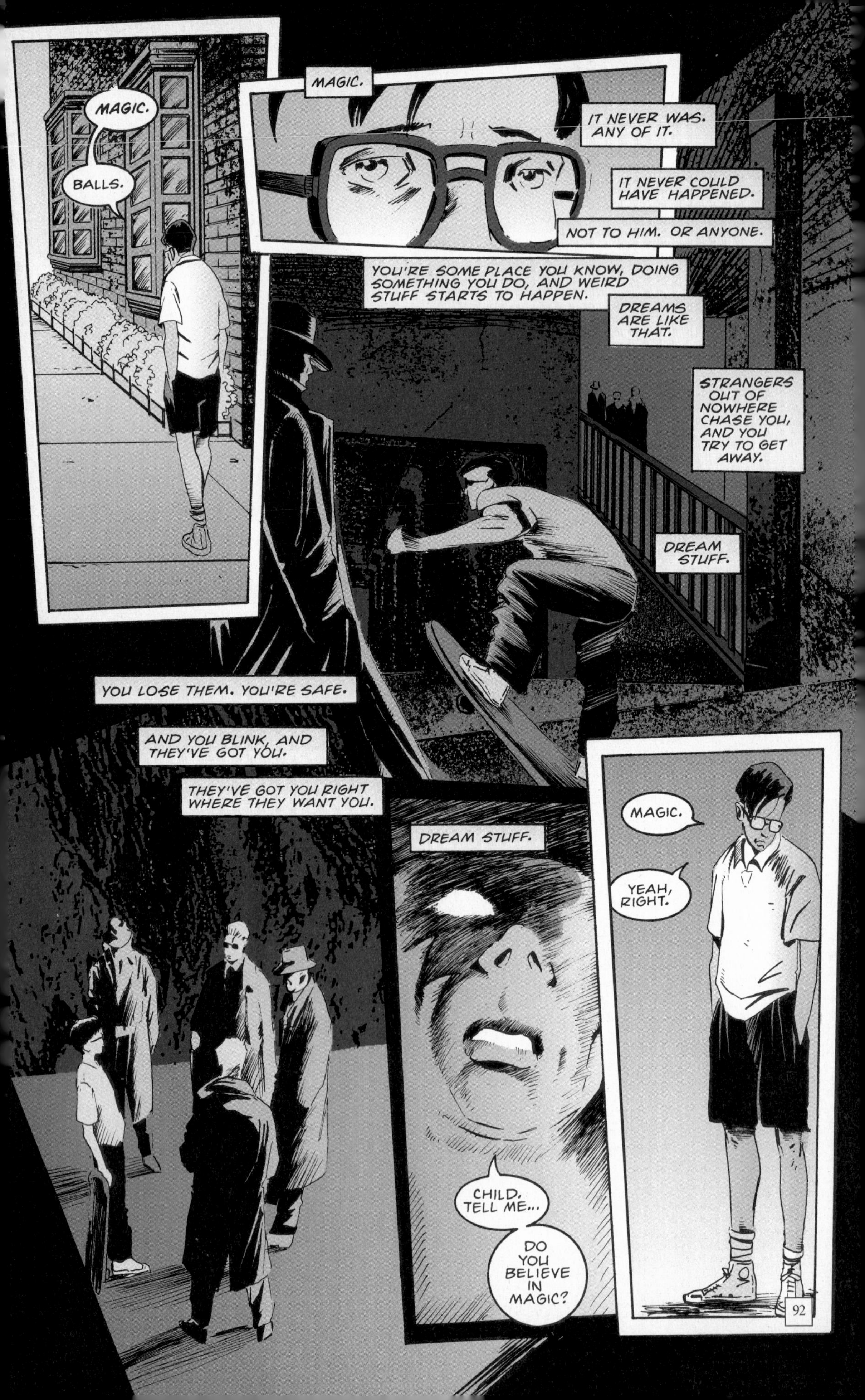
MAGIC.
BALLS.
MAGIC.
IT NEVER WAS. ANY OF IT.
IT NEVER COULD HAVE HAPPENED.
NOT TO HIM. OR ANYONE.
YOU'RE SOME PLACE YOU KNOW, DOING SOMETHING YOU DO, AND WEIRD STUFF STARTS TO HAPPEN.
DREAMS ARE LIKE THAT.
STRANGERS OUT OF NOWHERE CHASE YOU, AND YOU TRY TO GET AWAY.
DREAM STUFF.
YOU LOSE THEM. YOU'RE SAFE.
AND YOU BLINK, AND THEY'VE GOT YOU.
THEY'VE GOT YOU RIGHT WHERE THEY WANT YOU.
DREAM STUFF.
CHILD. TELL ME...
DO YOU BELIEVE IN MAGIC?
MAGIC.
YEAH, RIGHT.

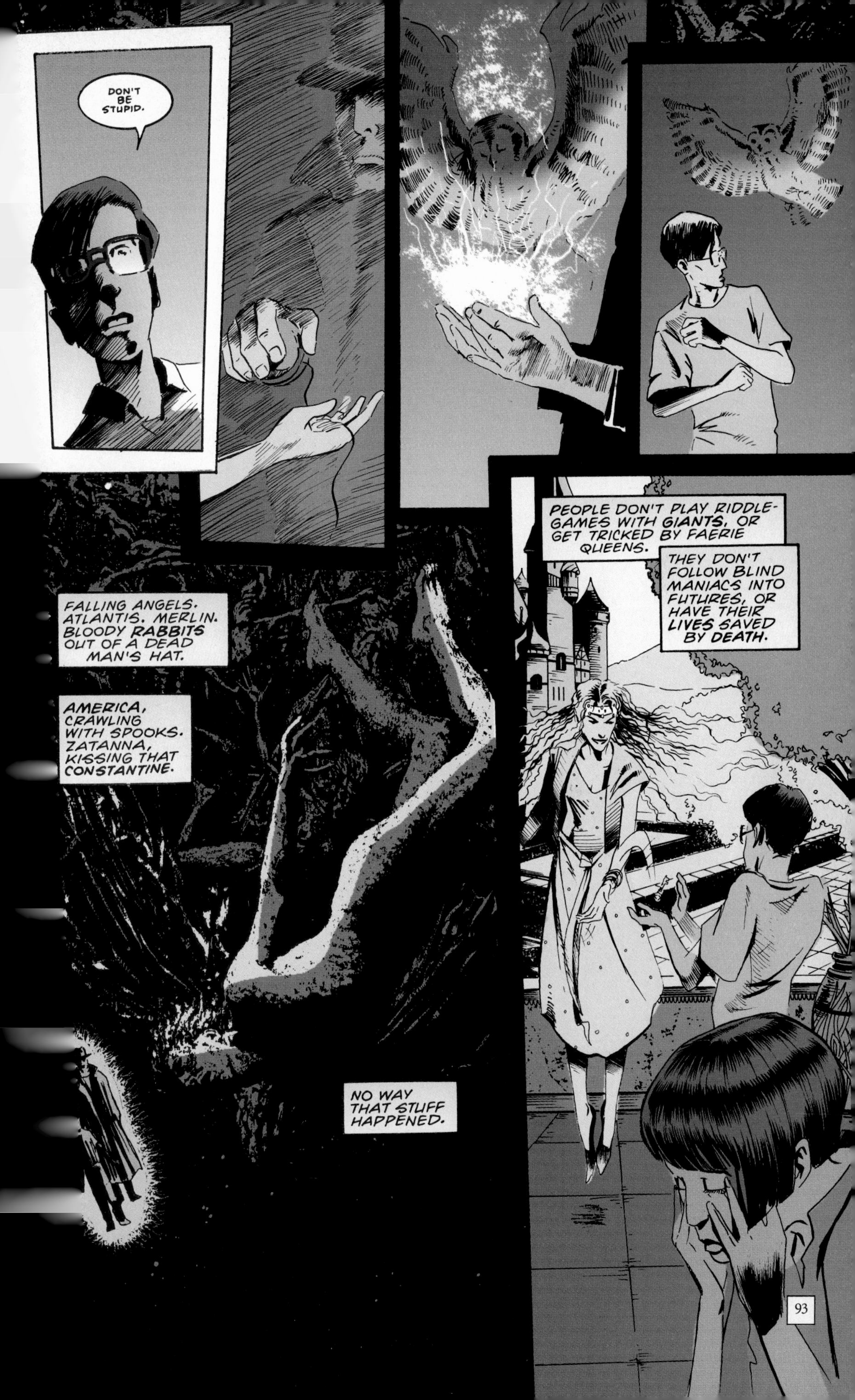
DON'T BE STUPID.
PEOPLE DON'T PLAY RIDDLE-GAMES WITH GIANTS, OR GET TRICKED BY FAERIE QUEENS.
THEY DON'T FOLLOW BLIND MANIACS INTO FUTURES, OR HAVE THEIR LIVES SAVED BY DEATH.
FALLING ANGELS. ATLANTIS. MERLIN. BLOODY RABBITS OUT OF A DEAD MAN'S HAT.
AMERICA, CRAWLING WITH SPOOKS. ZATANNA, KISSING THAT CONSTANTINE.
NO WAY THAT STUFF HAPPENED.

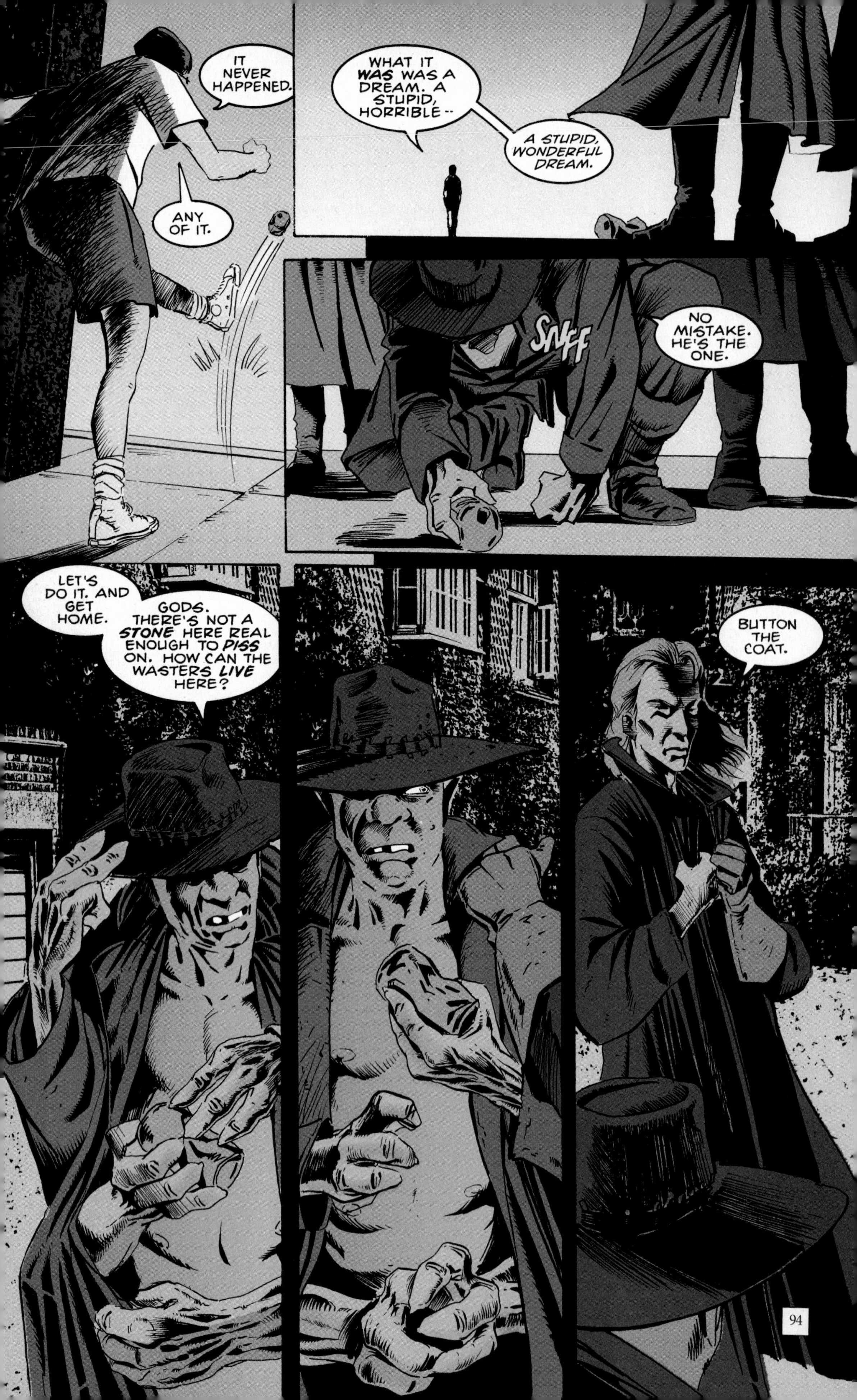
IT NEVER HAPPENED.
ANY OF IT.
WHAT IT WAS WAS A DREAM. A STUPID, HORRIBLE --
A STUPID, WONDERFUL DREAM.
SNIFF
NO MISTAKE. HE'S THE ONE.
LET'S DO IT. AND GET HOME.
GODS. THERE'S NOT A STONE HERE REAL ENOUGH TO PISS ON. HOW CAN THE WASTERS LIVE HERE?
BUTTON THE COAT.

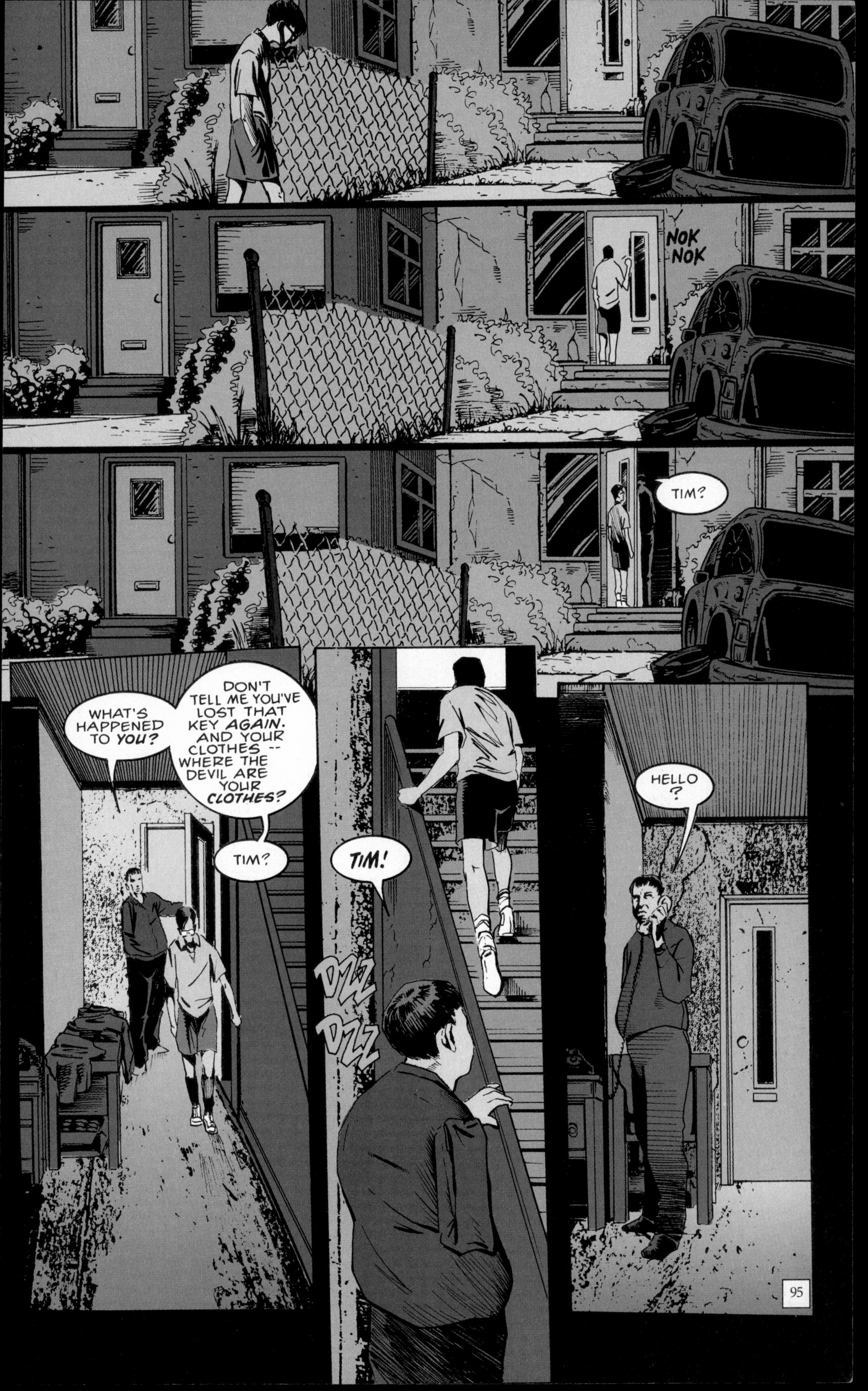
NOK
NOK
TIM?
WHAT'S HAPPENED TO YOU?
DON'T TELL ME YOU'VE LOST THAT KEY AGAIN. AND YOUR CLOTHES -- WHERE THE DEVIL ARE YOUR CLOTHES?
TIM?
TIM!
DZZ
DZZ
HELLO ?

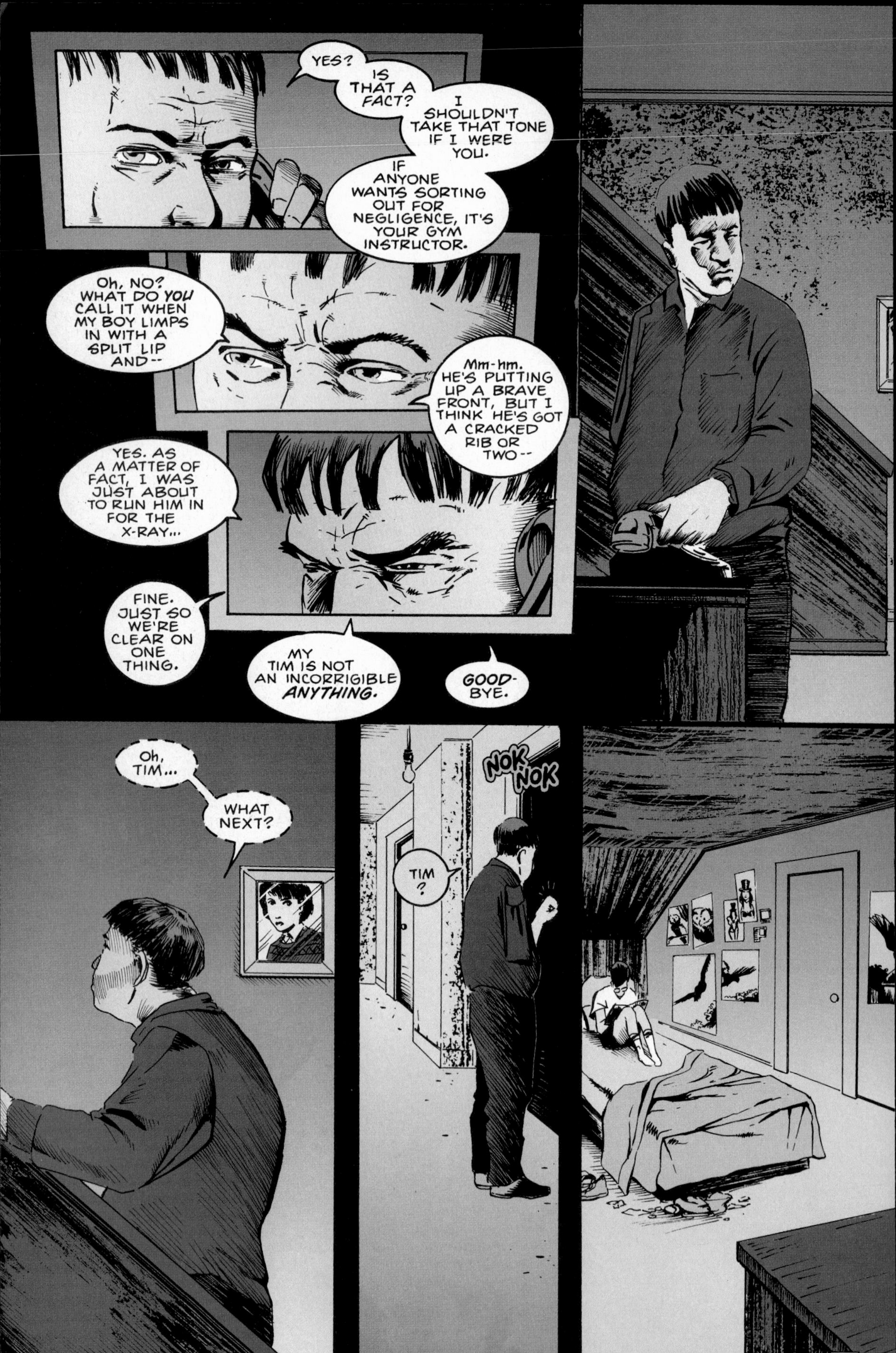
YES?
IS THAT A FACT?
I SHOULDN'T TAKE THAT TONE IF I WERE YOU.
IF ANYONE WANTS SORTING OUT FOR NEGLIGENCE, IT'S YOUR GYM INSTRUCTOR.
Oh, NO? WHAT DO YOU CALL IT WHEN MY BOY LIMPS IN WITH A SPLIT LIP AND--
Mm-hm. HE'S PUTTING UP A BRAVE FRONT, BUT I THINK HE'S GOT A CRACKED RIB OR TWO--
YES. AS A MATTER OF FACT, I WAS JUST ABOUT TO RUN HIM IN FOR THE X-RAY...
FINE. JUST SO WE'RE CLEAR ON ONE THING.
MY TIM IS NOT AN INCORRIGIBLE ANYTHING.
GOOD-BYE.
Oh, TIM...
WHAT NEXT?
NOK NOK
TIM?

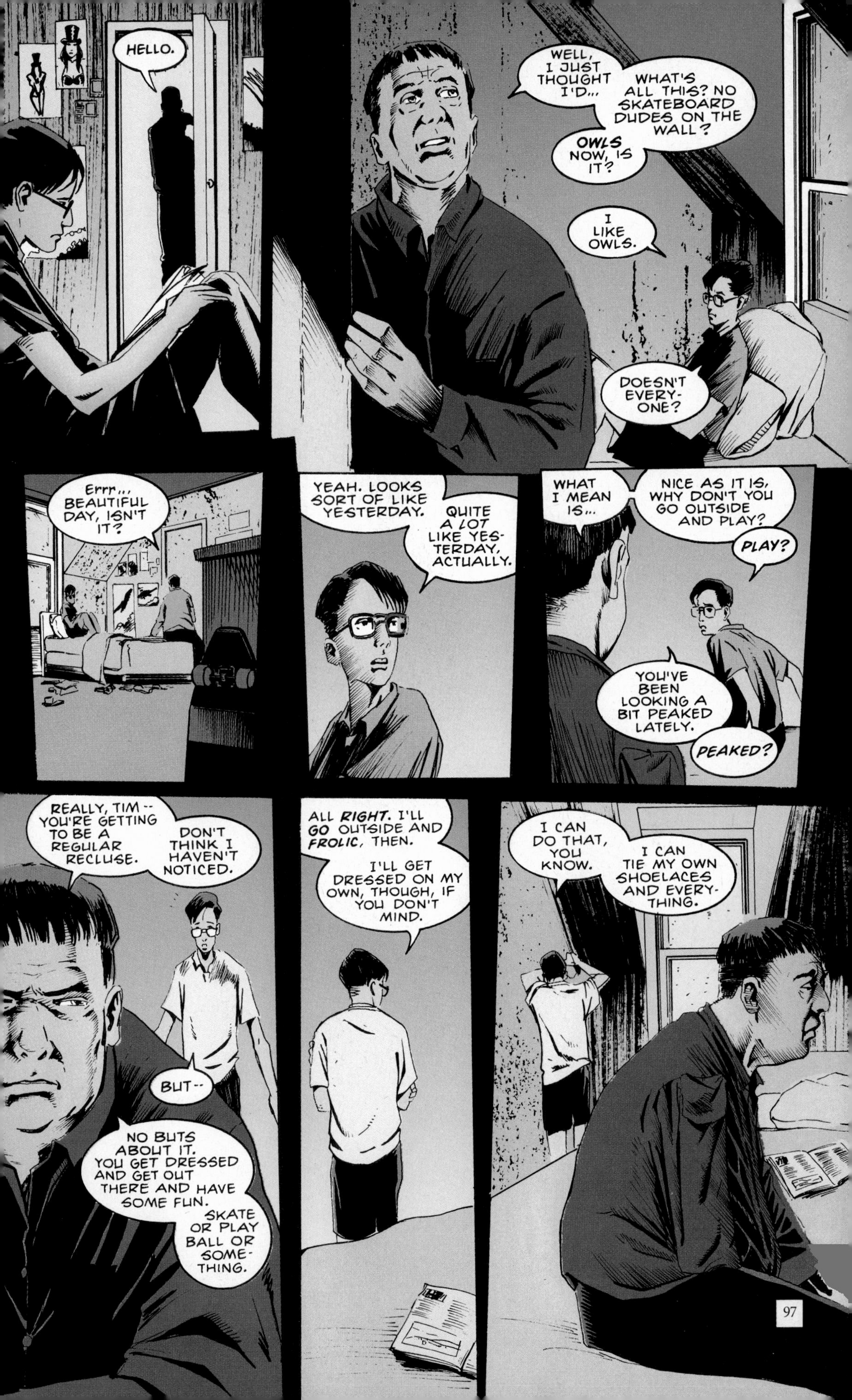

HELLO.
WELL, I JUST THOUGHT I'D...
WHAT'S ALL THIS? NO SKATEBOARD DUDES ON THE WALL?
OWLS NOW, IS IT?
I LIKE OWLS.
DOESN'T EVERY-ONE?
Errr... BEAUTIFUL DAY, ISN'T IT?
YEAH. LOOKS SORT OF LIKE YESTERDAY.
QUITE A LOT LIKE YES-TERDAY, ACTUALLY.
WHAT I MEAN IS...
NICE AS IT IS, WHY DON'T YOU GO OUTSIDE AND PLAY?
PLAY?
YOU'VE BEEN LOOKING A BIT PEAKED LATELY.
PEAKED?
REALLY, TIM -- YOU'RE GETTING TO BE A REGULAR RECLUSE.
DON'T THINK I HAVEN'T NOTICED.
BUT--
NO BUTS ABOUT IT. YOU GET DRESSED AND GET OUT THERE AND HAVE SOME FUN.
SKATE OR PLAY BALL OR SOME-THING.
ALL RIGHT. I'LL GO OUTSIDE AND FROLIC, THEN.
I'LL GET DRESSED ON MY OWN, THOUGH, IF YOU DON'T MIND.
I CAN DO THAT, YOU KNOW.
I CAN TIE MY OWN SHOELACES AND EVERY-THING.

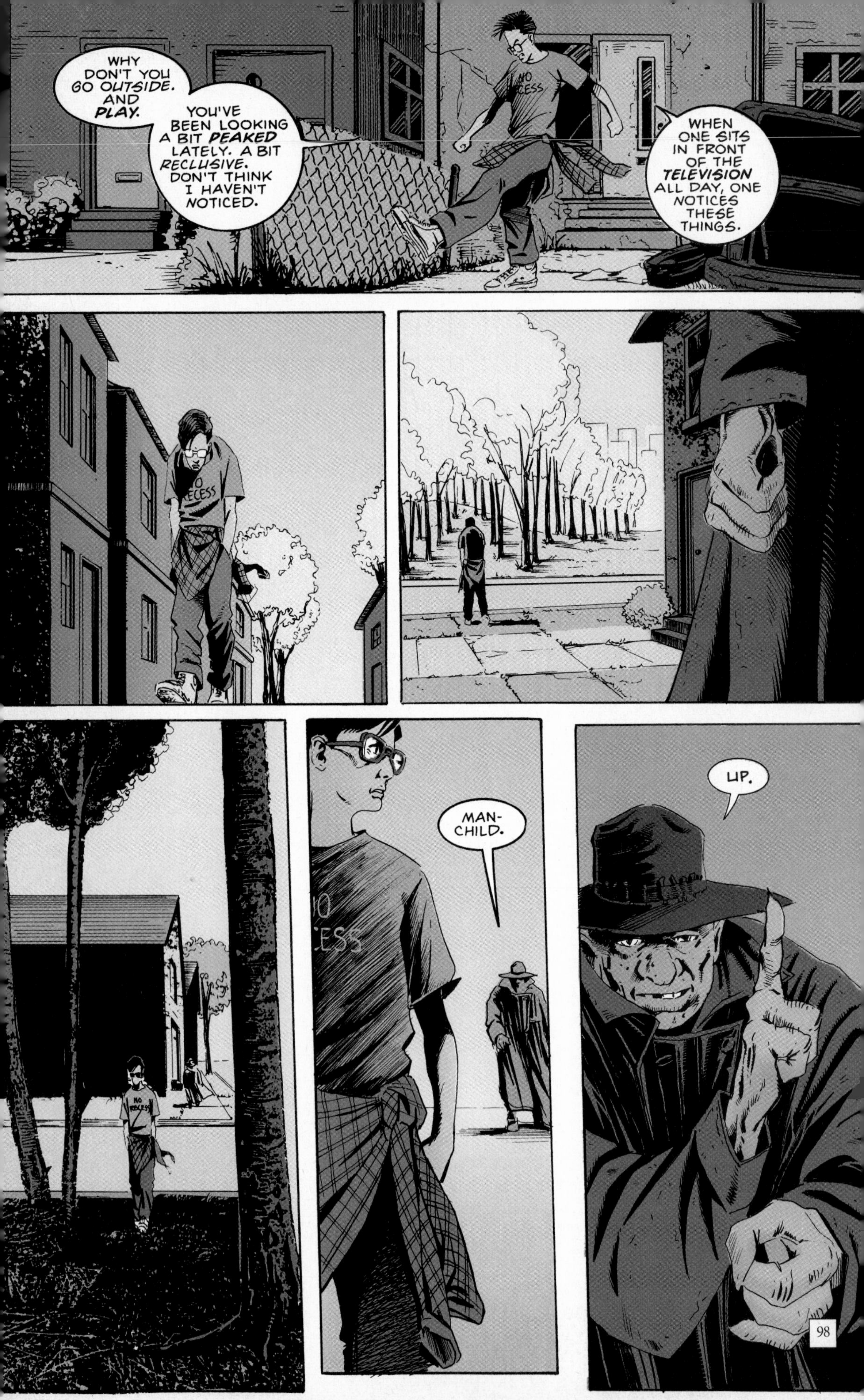
WHY DON'T YOU GO OUTSIDE. AND PLAY.
YOU'VE BEEN LOOKING A BIT PEAKED LATELY. A BIT RECLUSIVE. DON'T THINK I HAVEN'T NOTICED.
WHEN ONE SITS IN FRONT OF THE TELEVISION ALL DAY, ONE NOTICES THESE THINGS.
NO RECESS
MAN-CHILD.
UP.

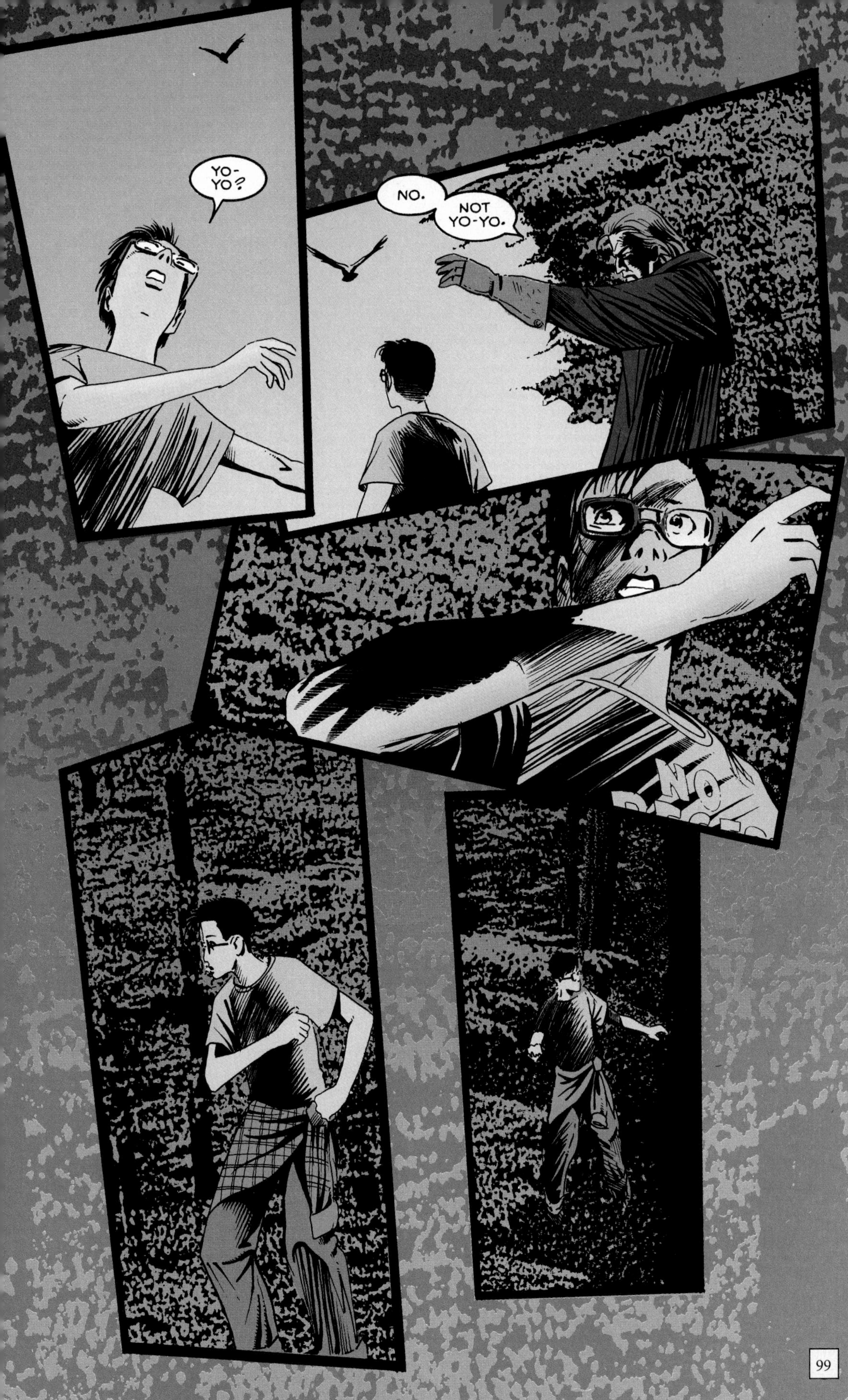
YO-YO?
NO.
NOT YO-YO.

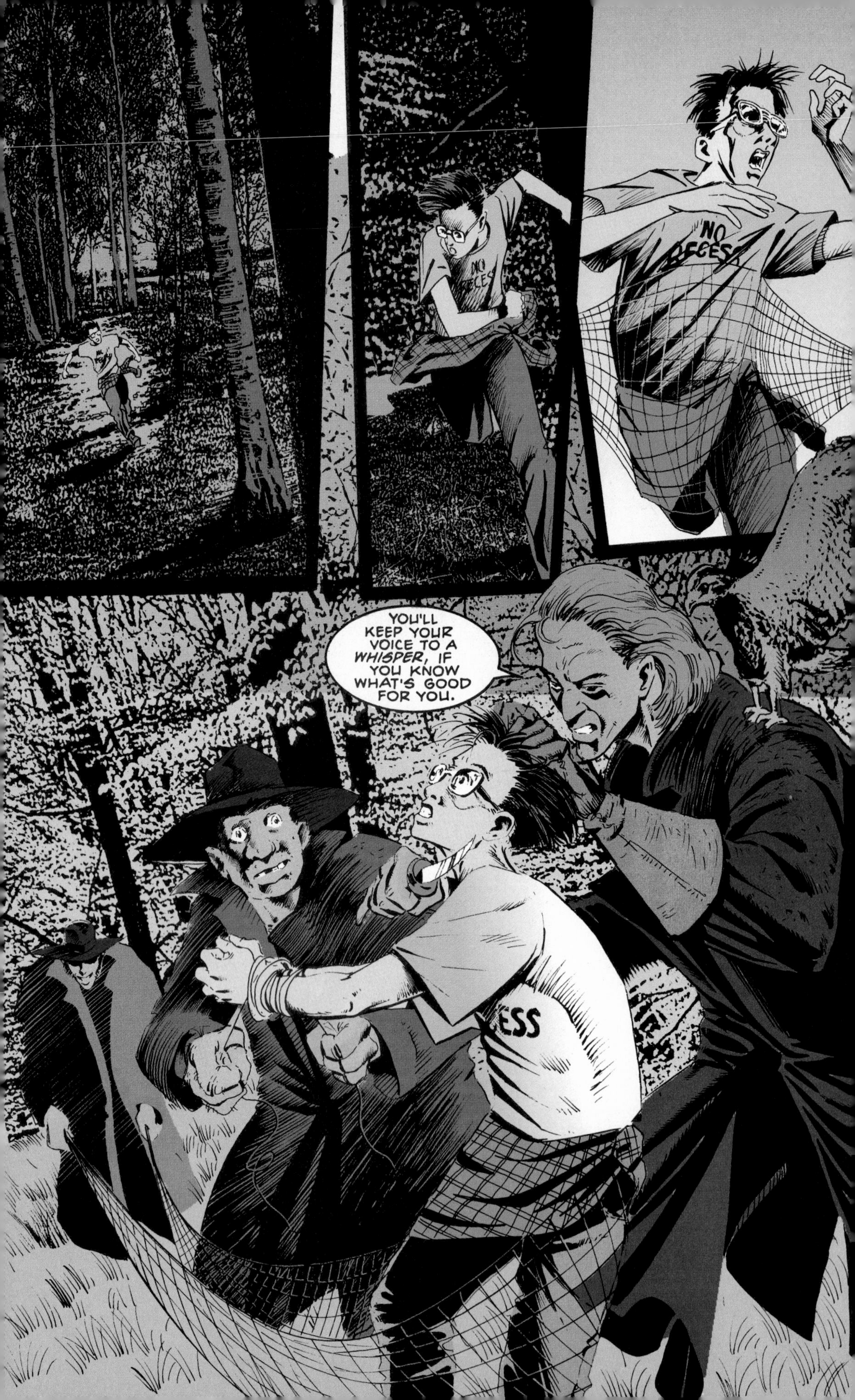
YOU'LL KEEP YOUR VOICE TO A WHISPER, IF YOU KNOW WHAT'S GOOD FOR YOU.

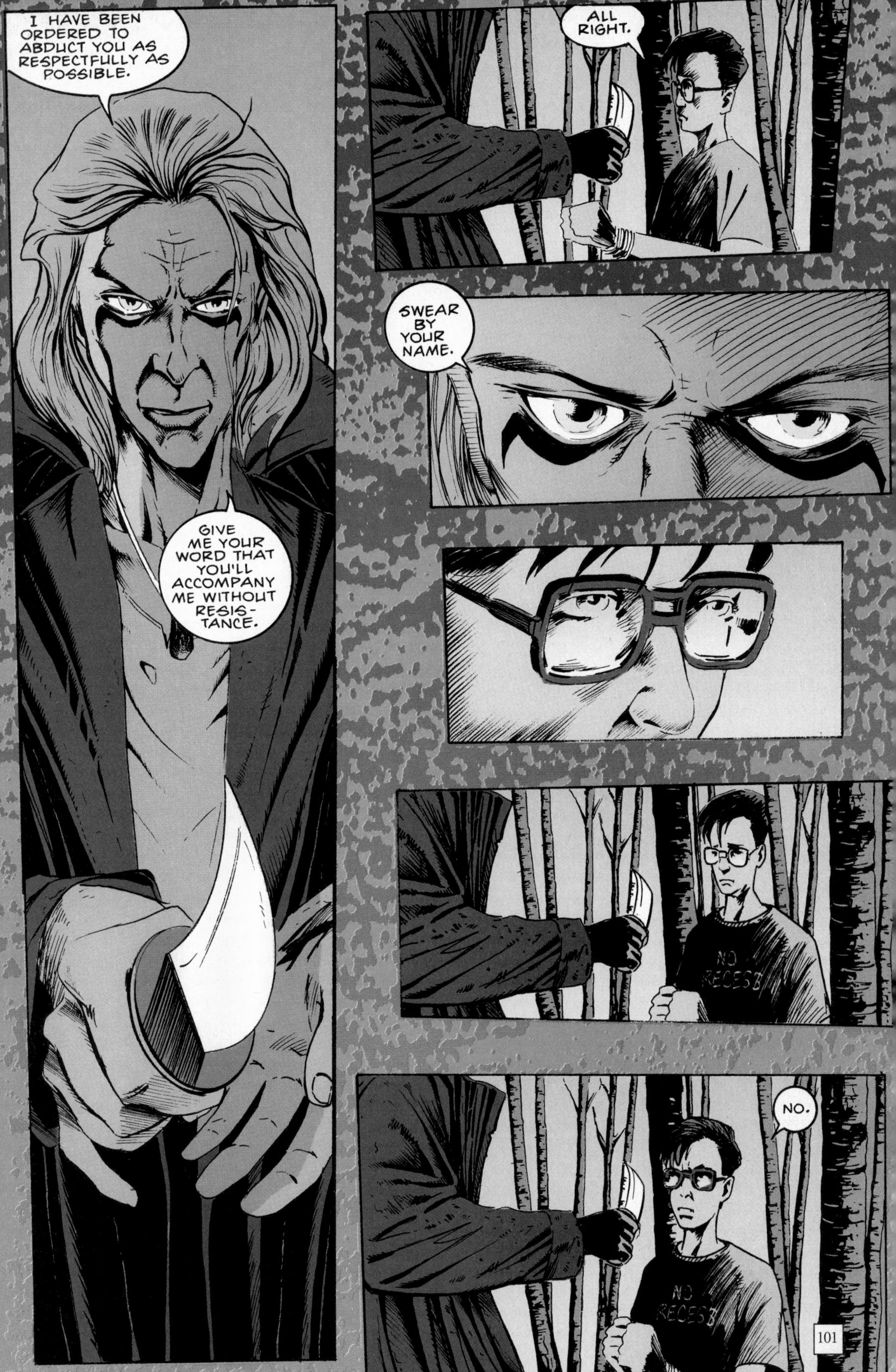
I HAVE BEEN ORDERED TO ABDUCT YOU AS RESPECTFULLY AS POSSIBLE.
GIVE ME YOUR WORD THAT YOU'LL ACCOMPANY ME WITHOUT RESIS-TANCE.
ALL RIGHT.
SWEAR BY YOUR NAME.
NO RECESS
NO.
NO RECESS

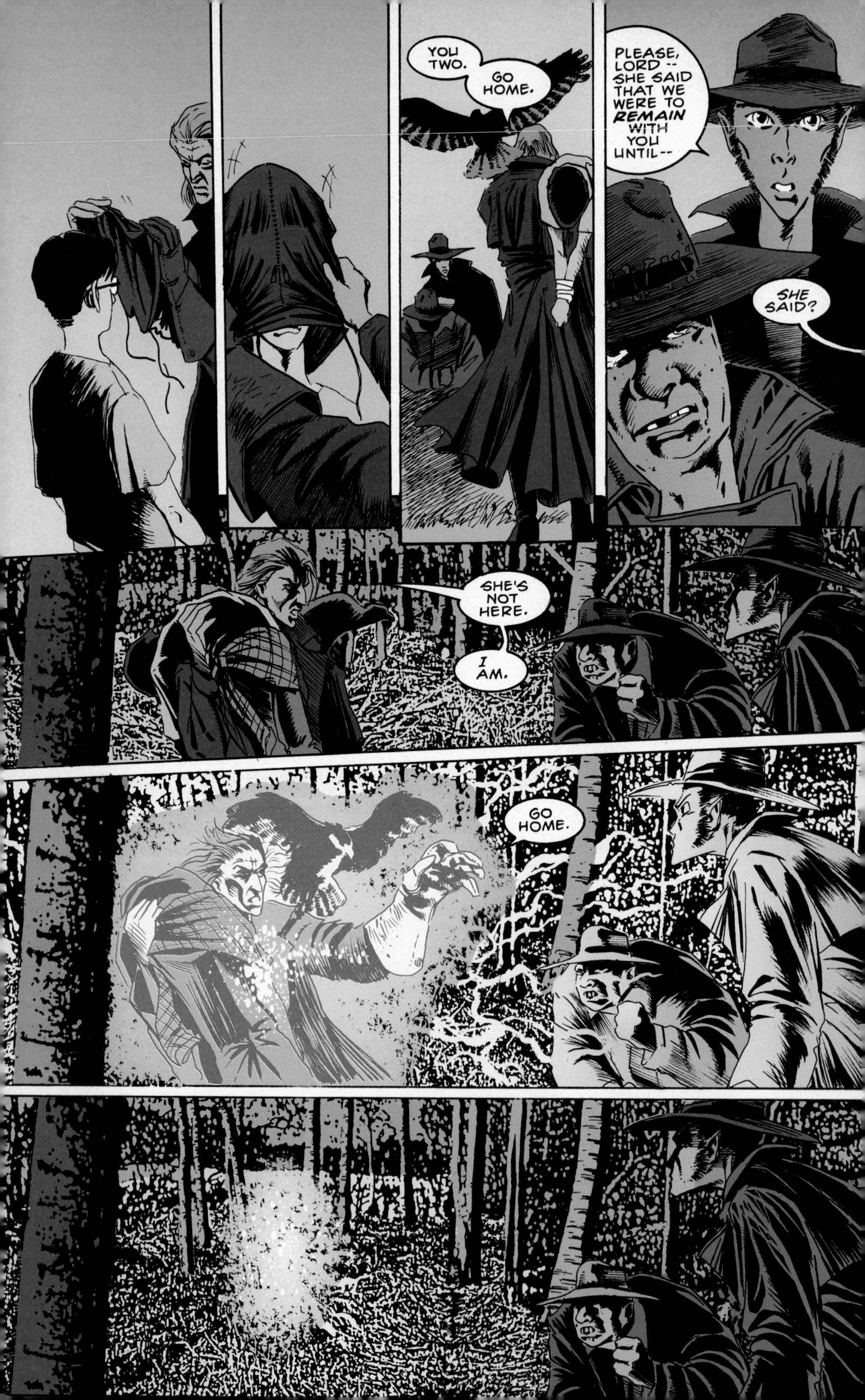
YOU TWO.
GO HOME.
PLEASE, LORD -- SHE SAID THAT WE WERE TO *REMAIN* WITH YOU UNTIL--
SHE SAID?
SHE'S NOT HERE.
I AM.
GO HOME.

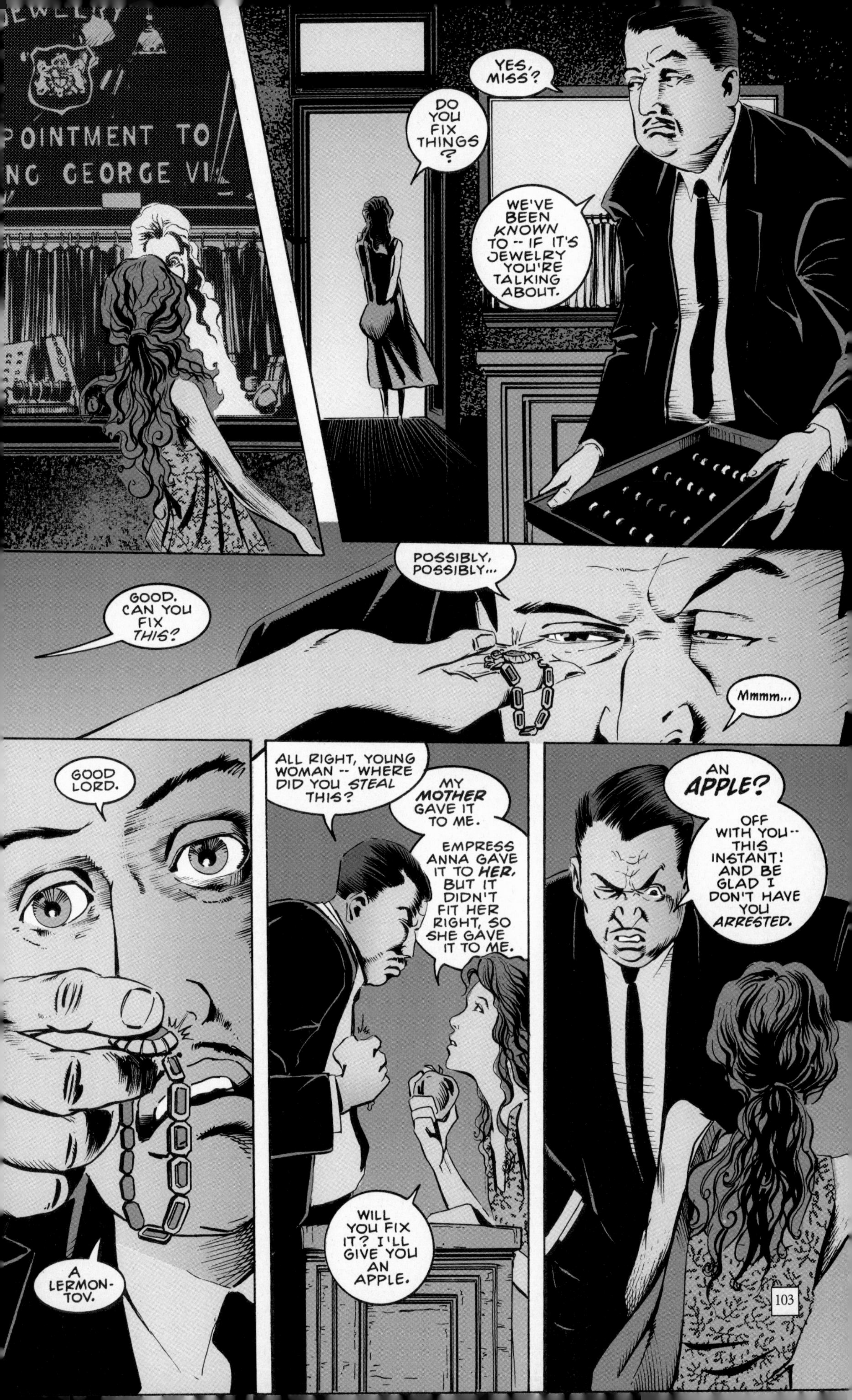

JEWELRY
POINTMENT TO
NG GEORGE VI
YES, MISS?
DO YOU FIX THINGS?
WE'VE BEEN *KNOWN* TO -- IF IT'S JEWELRY YOU'RE TALKING ABOUT.
GOOD. CAN YOU FIX *THIS*?
POSSIBLY, POSSIBLY...
Mmmm...
GOOD LORD.
A LERMON-TOV.
ALL RIGHT, YOUNG WOMAN -- WHERE DID YOU *STEAL* THIS?
MY ***MOTHER*** GAVE IT TO ME.
EMPRESS ANNA GAVE IT TO ***HER***, BUT IT DIDN'T FIT HER RIGHT, SO SHE GAVE IT TO ME.
WILL YOU FIX IT? I'LL GIVE YOU AN APPLE.
AN ***APPLE?***
OFF WITH YOU -- THIS INSTANT! AND BE GLAD I DON'T HAVE YOU *ARRESTED*.

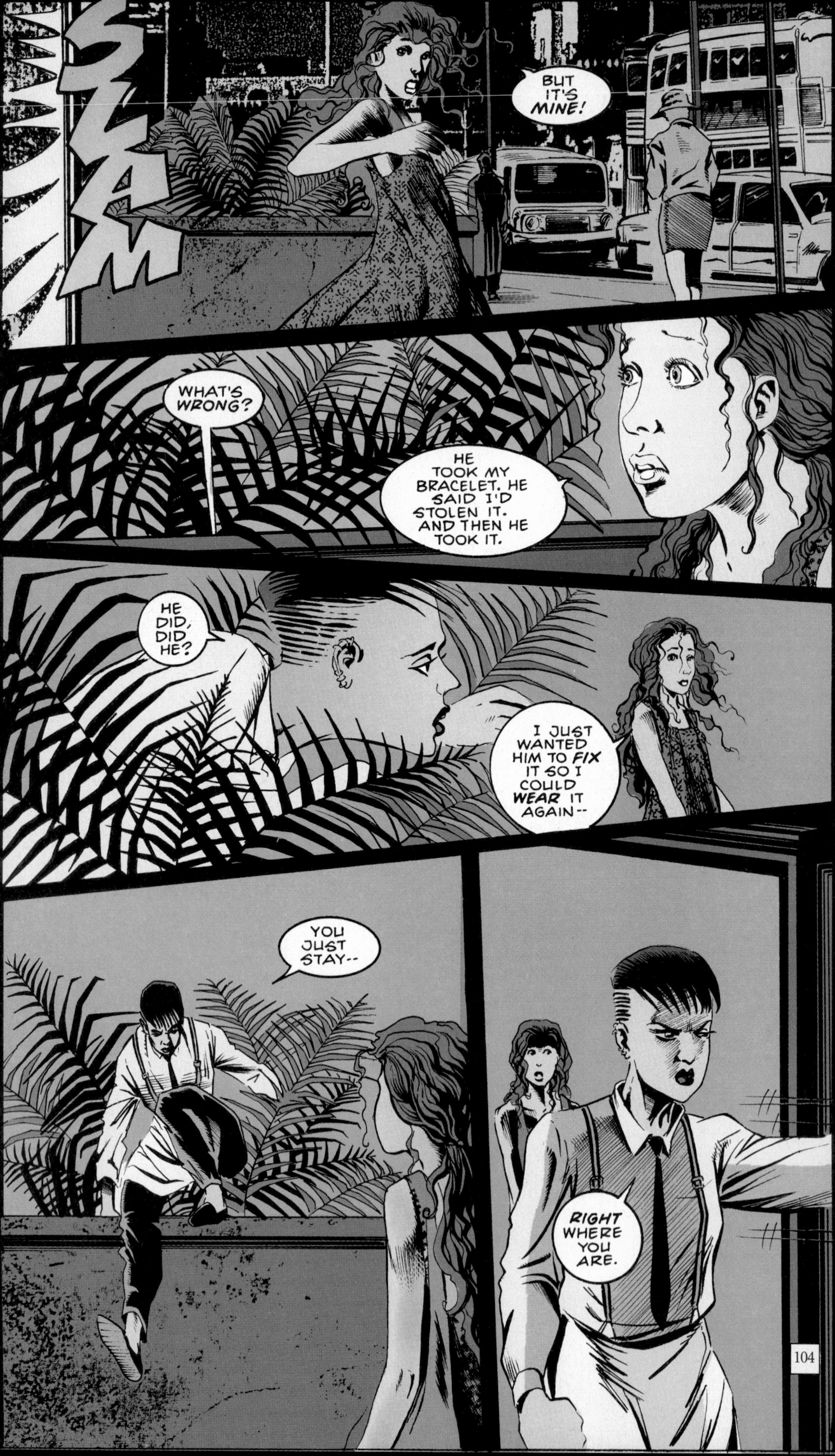
SLAM
BUT IT'S MINE!
WHAT'S WRONG?
HE TOOK MY BRACELET. HE SAID I'D STOLEN IT. AND THEN HE TOOK IT.
HE DID, DID HE?
I JUST WANTED HIM TO FIX IT SO I COULD WEAR IT AGAIN--
YOU JUST STAY--
RIGHT WHERE YOU ARE.

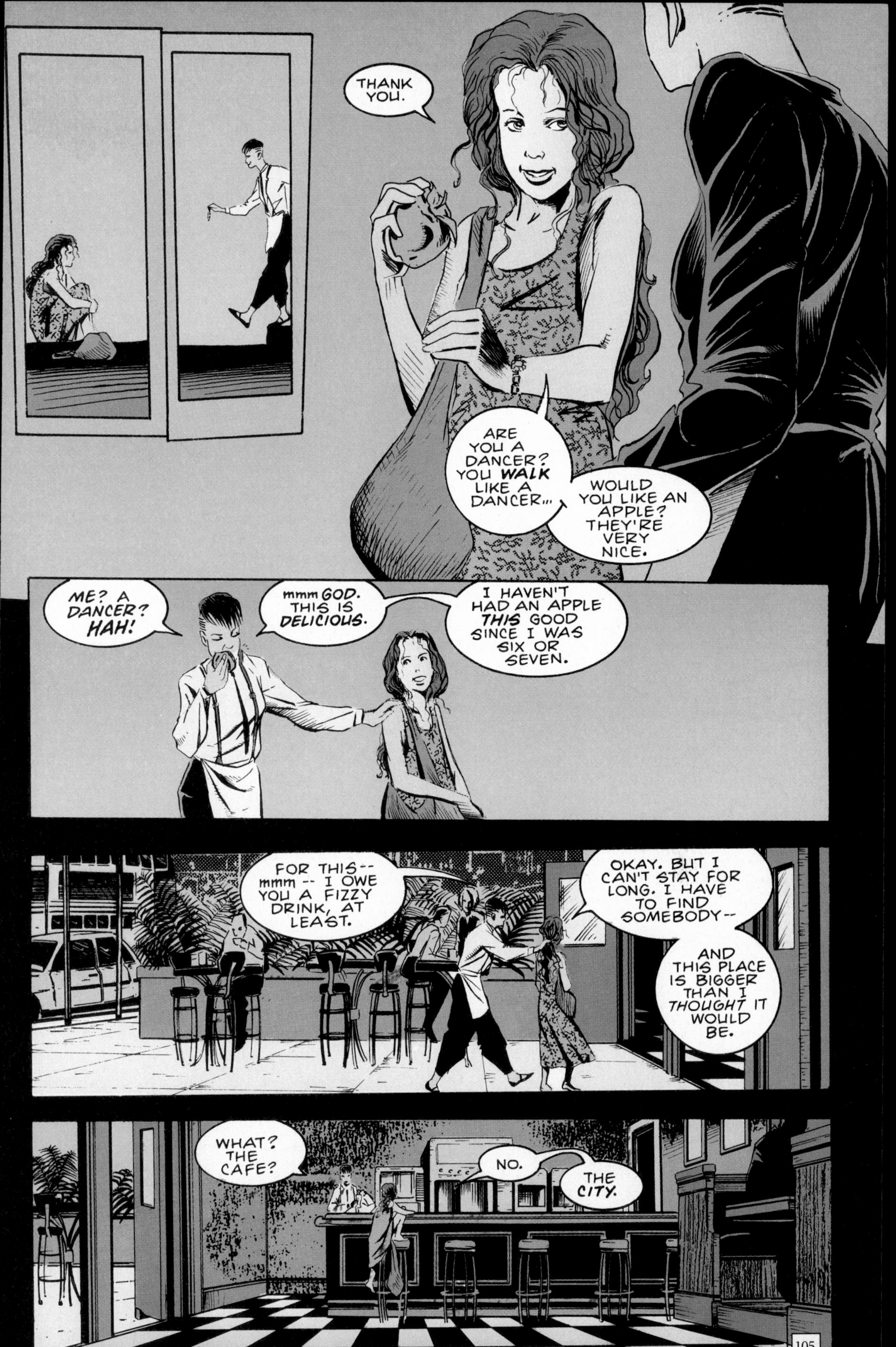
THANK YOU.
ARE YOU A DANCER? YOU WALK LIKE A DANCER...
WOULD YOU LIKE AN APPLE? THEY'RE VERY NICE.
ME? A DANCER? HAH!
mmm GOD. THIS IS DELICIOUS.
I HAVEN'T HAD AN APPLE THIS GOOD SINCE I WAS SIX OR SEVEN.
FOR THIS-- mmm -- I OWE YOU A FIZZY DRINK, AT LEAST.
OKAY. BUT I CAN'T STAY FOR LONG. I HAVE TO FIND SOMEBODY--
AND THIS PLACE IS BIGGER THAN I THOUGHT IT WOULD BE.
WHAT? THE CAFE?
NO.
THE CITY.

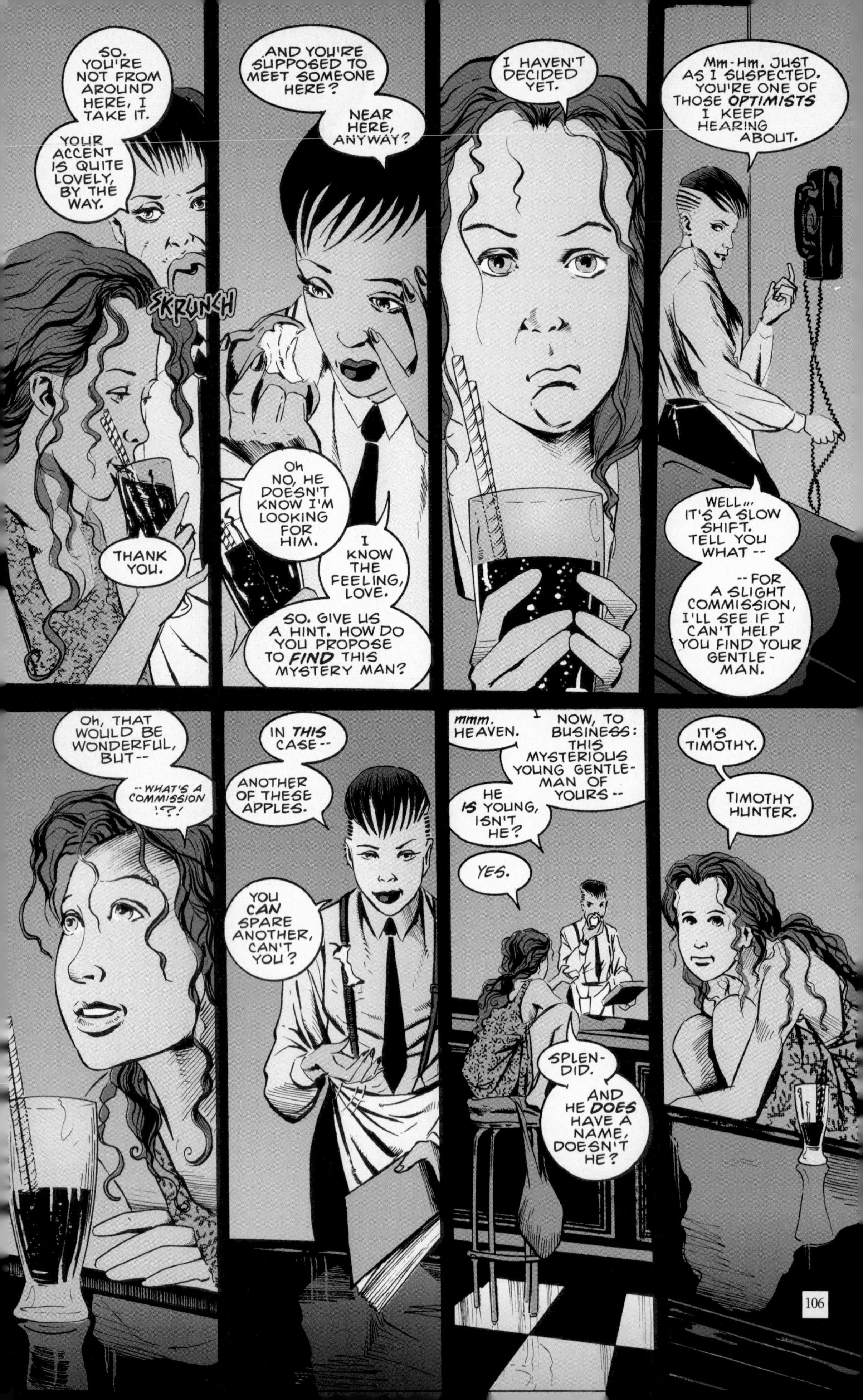
SO. YOU'RE NOT FROM AROUND HERE, I TAKE IT.
YOUR ACCENT IS QUITE LOVELY, BY THE WAY.
SKRUNCH
THANK YOU.
AND YOU'RE SUPPOSED TO MEET SOMEONE HERE?
NEAR HERE, ANYWAY?
Oh NO, HE DOESN'T KNOW I'M LOOKING FOR HIM.
I KNOW THE FEELING, LOVE.
SO. GIVE US A HINT. HOW DO YOU PROPOSE TO FIND THIS MYSTERY MAN?
I HAVEN'T DECIDED YET.
Mm-Hm. JUST AS I SUSPECTED. YOU'RE ONE OF THOSE OPTIMISTS I KEEP HEARING ABOUT.
WELL... IT'S A SLOW SHIFT. TELL YOU WHAT --
-- FOR A SLIGHT COMMISSION, I'LL SEE IF I CAN'T HELP YOU FIND YOUR GENTLEMAN.
Oh, THAT WOULD BE WONDERFUL, BUT--
-- WHAT'S A COMMISSION !?!
IN THIS CASE --
ANOTHER OF THESE APPLES.
YOU CAN SPARE ANOTHER, CAN'T YOU?
mmm. HEAVEN.
NOW, TO BUSINESS: THIS MYSTERIOUS YOUNG GENTLEMAN OF YOURS --
HE IS YOUNG, ISN'T HE?
YES.
SPLENDID.
AND HE DOES HAVE A NAME, DOESN'T HE?
IT'S TIMOTHY.
TIMOTHY HUNTER.

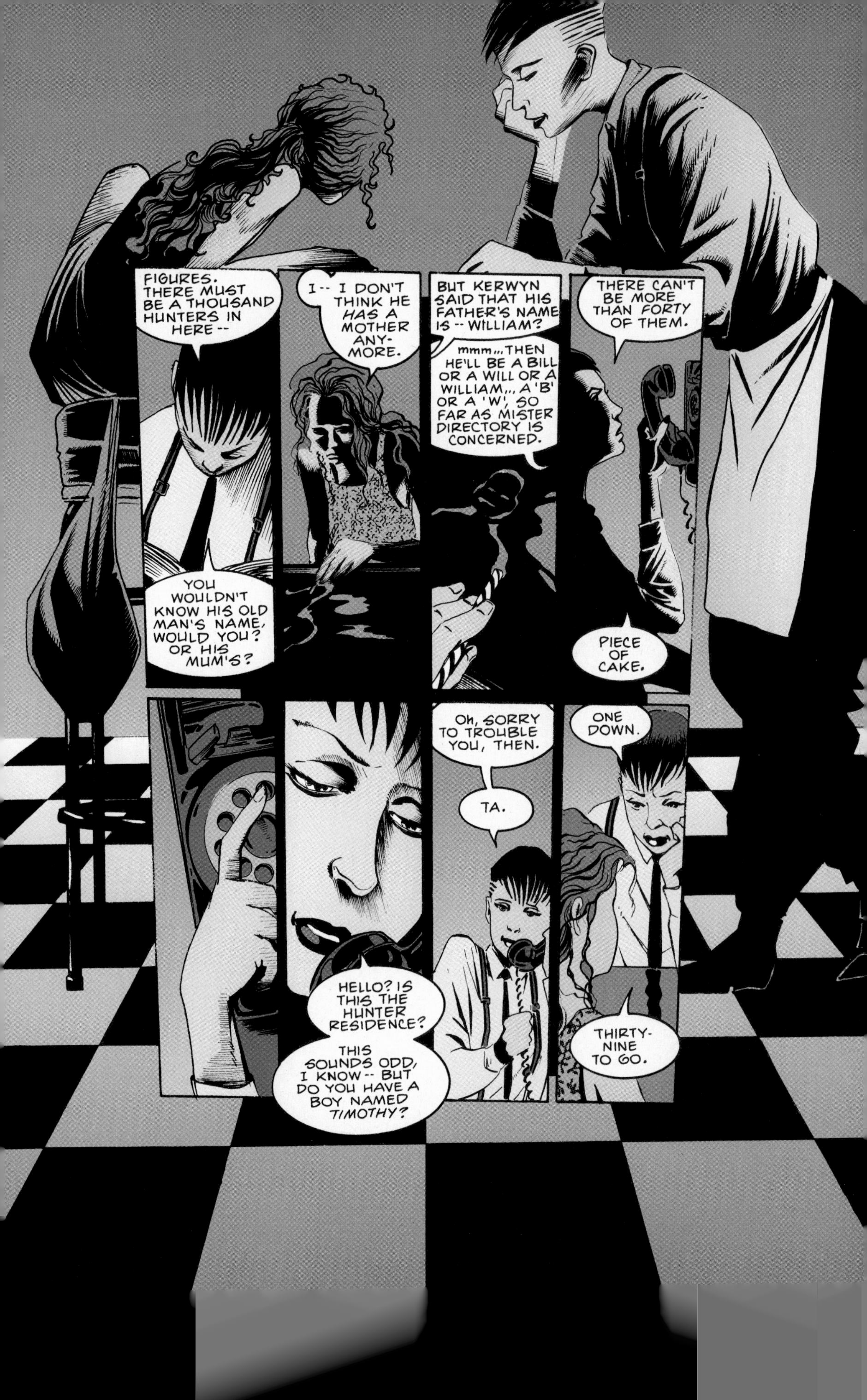
FIGURES. THERE MUST BE A THOUSAND HUNTERS IN HERE --
YOU WOULDN'T KNOW HIS OLD MAN'S NAME, WOULD YOU? OR HIS MUM'S?
I -- I DON'T THINK HE HAS A MOTHER ANYMORE.
BUT KERWYN SAID THAT HIS FATHER'S NAME IS -- WILLIAM?
mmm... THEN HE'LL BE A BILL OR A WILL OR A WILLIAM... A 'B' OR A 'W', SO FAR AS MISTER DIRECTORY IS CONCERNED.
THERE CAN'T BE MORE THAN FORTY OF THEM.
PIECE OF CAKE.
HELLO? IS THIS THE HUNTER RESIDENCE?
THIS SOUNDS ODD, I KNOW -- BUT DO YOU HAVE A BOY NAMED TIMOTHY?
OH, SORRY TO TROUBLE YOU, THEN.
TA.
ONE DOWN.
THIRTY-NINE TO GO.

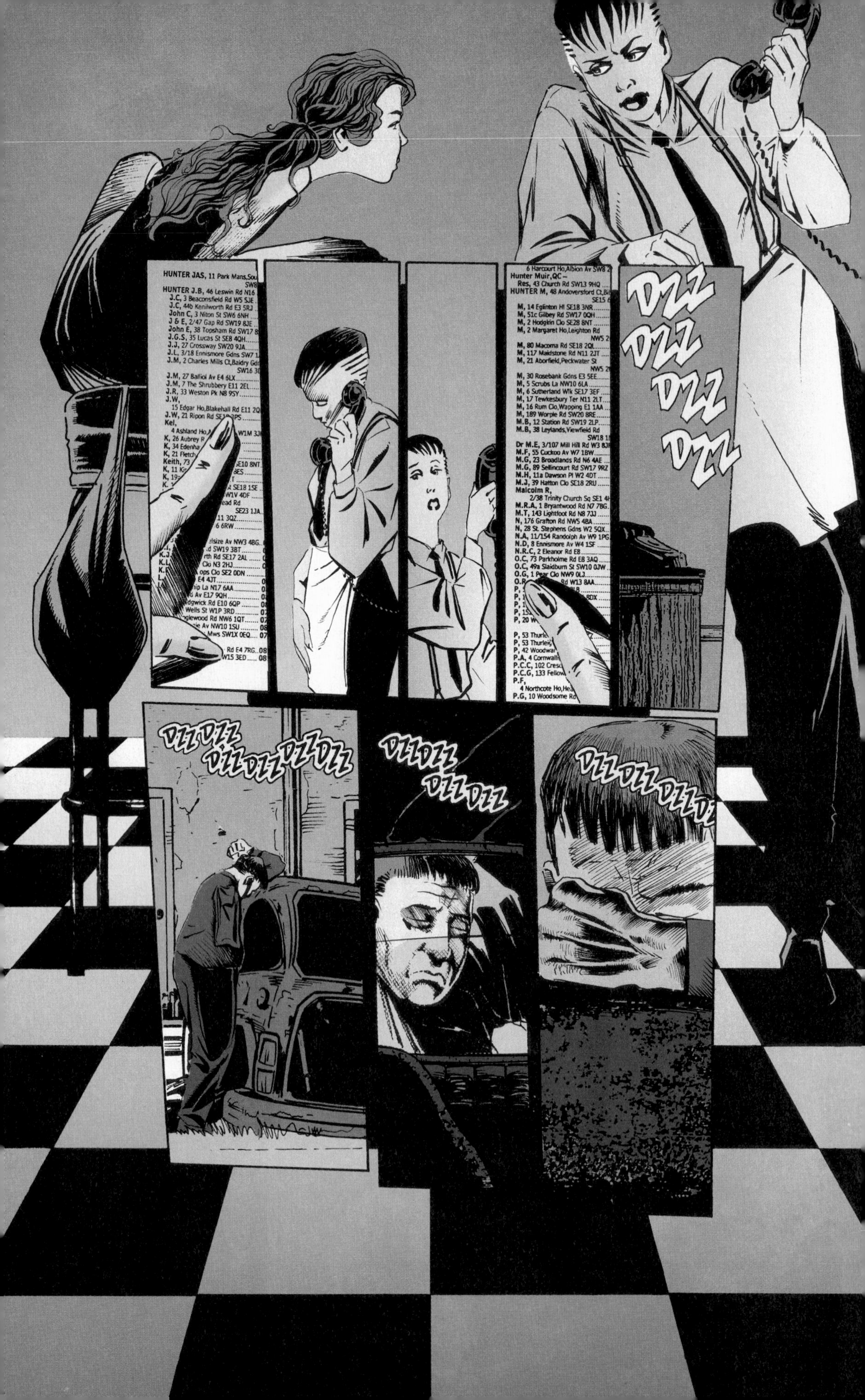

HUNTER JAS, 11 Park Mans,Sou
SW8
HUNTER J.B, 46 Leswin Rd N16
J.C, 3 Beaconsfield Rd W5 5JE
J.C, 44b Kenilworth Rd E3 5RJ
John C, 3 Niton St SW6 6NH
J & E, 2/47 Gap Rd SW19 8JE
John E, 38 Topsham Rd SW17
J.G.S, 35 Lucas St SE8 4QH
J.J, 27 Crossway SW20 9JA
J.L, 3/18 Ennismore Gdns SW7
J.M, 2 Charles Mills Ct,Baldry Gd
SW16
J.M, 27 Balliol Av E4 6LX
J.M, 7 The Shrubbery E11 2EL
J.R, 33 Weston Pk N8 9SY
J.W,
15 Edgar Ho,Blakehall Rd E11
Kel,
6 Harcourt Ho,Albion Av SW8
Hunter Muir,QC –
Res, 43 Church Rd SW13 9HQ
HUNTER M, 48 Andoversford Ct,
SE15
M, 14 Eglinton Hl SE18 3NR
M, 51c Gilbey Rd SW17 0QH
M, 2 Hodgkin Clo SE28 8NT
M, 2 Margaret Ho,Leighton Rd
NW5
M, 80 Macoma Rd SE18 2QL
M, 117 Maidstone Rd N11 2JT
M, 21 Aborfield,Peckwater St
NW5
M, 30 Rosebank Gdns E3 5EE
M, 5 Scrubs La NW10 6LA
M, 6 Sutherland Wlk SE17 3EF
M, 17 Tewkesbury Ter N11 2LT
M, 16 Rum Clo,Wapping E1 1AA
M, 189 Worple Rd SW20 8RE
M.B, 12 Station Rd SW19 2LP
M.B, 38 Leylands,Viewfield Rd
SW18
Dr M.E, 3/107 Mill Hill Rd W3
M.F, 55 Cuckoo Av W7 1BW
M.G, 23 Broadlands Rd N6 4AE
M.G, 89 Sellincourt Rd SW17 9RZ
M.H, 11a Dawson Pl W2 4DT
M.J, 39 Hatton Clo SE18 2RU
Malcolm R,
2/38 Trinity Church Sq SE1
M.R.A, 1 Bryantwood Rd N7 7BG
M.T, 143 Lightfoot Rd N8 7JJ
N, 176 Grafton Rd NW5 4BA
N, 28 St. Stephens Gdns W2 5QX
N.A, 11/154 Randolph Av W9 1PG
N.D, 8 Ennismore Av W4 1SF
N.R.C, 2 Eleanor Rd E8
O.C, 73 Parkholme Rd E8 3AQ
O.C, 49a Slaidburn St SW10 0JW
DZZ
DZZ
DZZ
DZZ
DZZ DZZ
DZZ DZZ DZZ DZZ
DZZ DZZ
DZZ DZZ
DZZ DZZ DZZ DZ

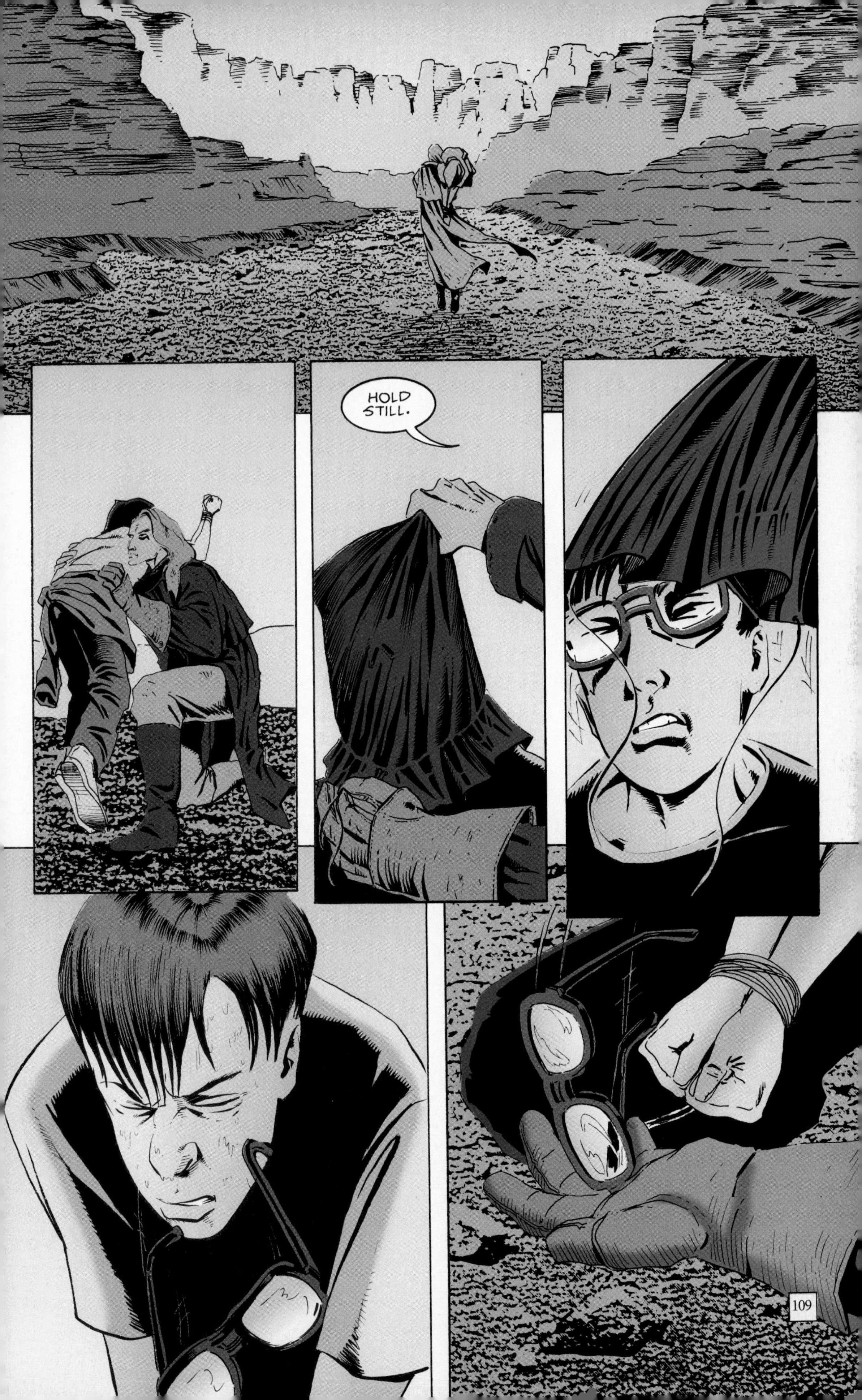
HOLD STILL.

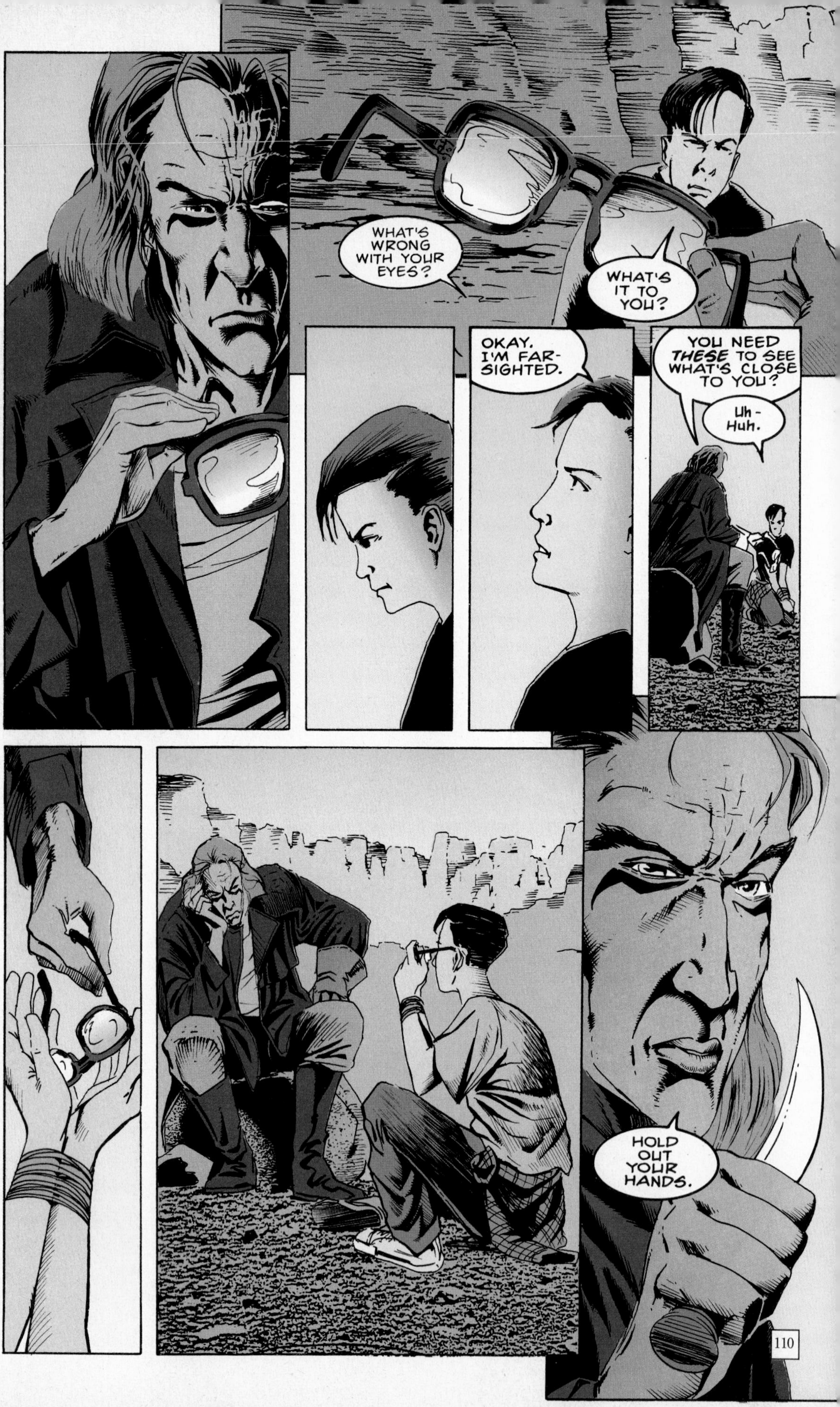
WHAT'S WRONG WITH YOUR EYES?
WHAT'S IT TO YOU?
OKAY. I'M FAR-SIGHTED.
YOU NEED *THESE* TO SEE WHAT'S CLOSE TO YOU?
Uh-Huh.
HOLD OUT YOUR HANDS.

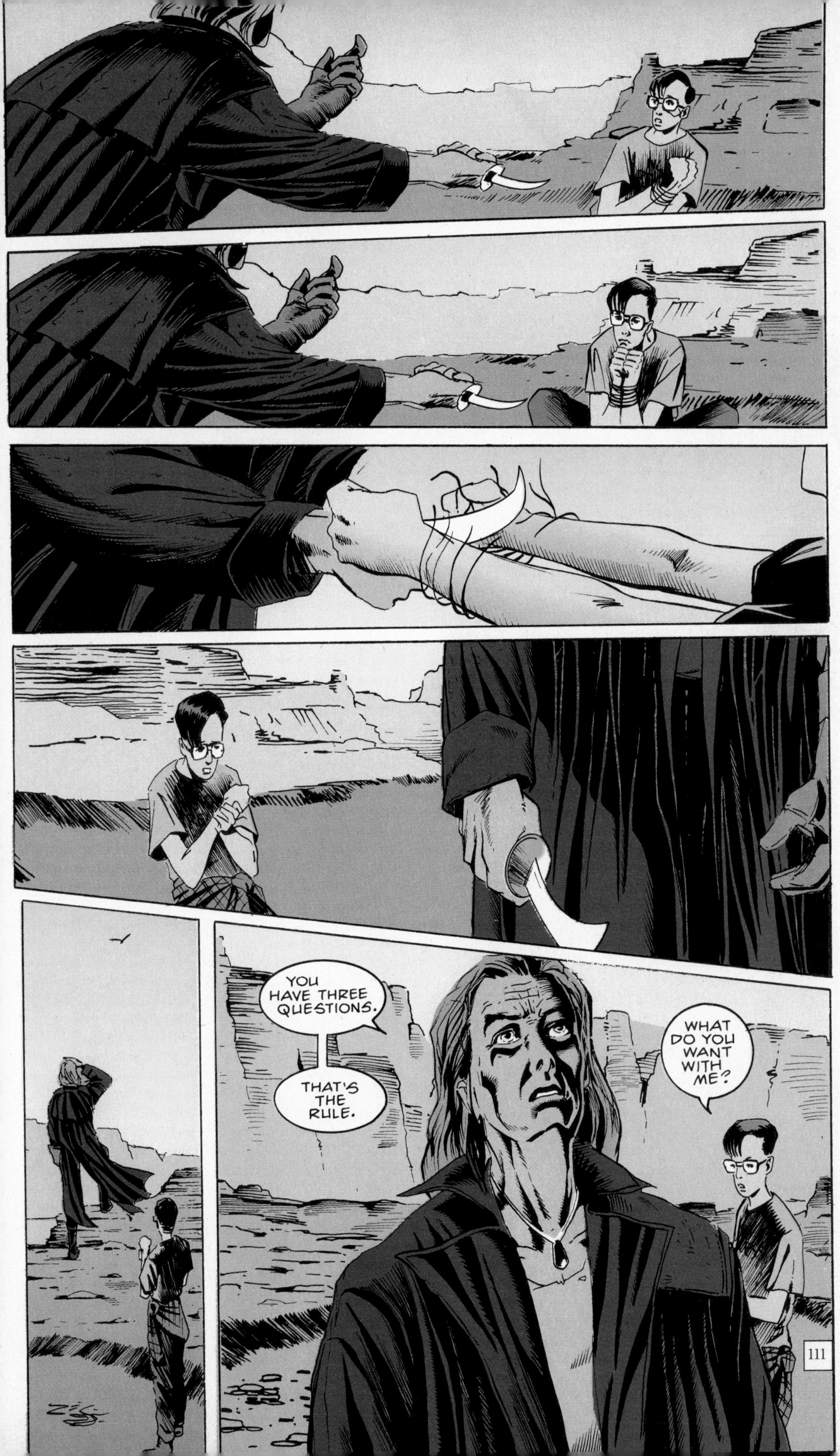
YOU HAVE THREE QUESTIONS.
THAT'S THE RULE.
WHAT DO YOU WANT WITH ME?

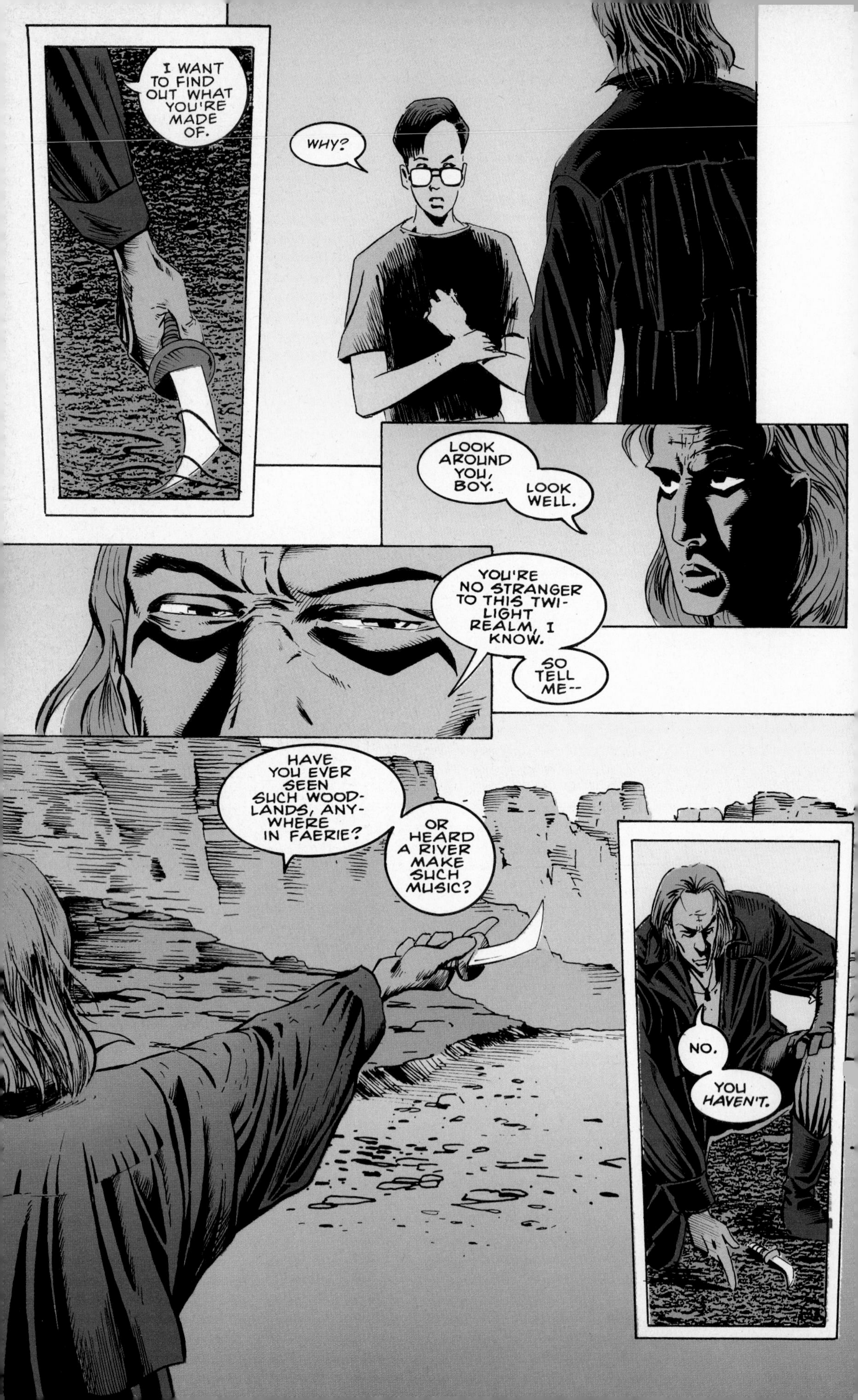
I WANT TO FIND OUT WHAT YOU'RE MADE OF.
WHY?
LOOK AROUND YOU, BOY.
LOOK WELL.
YOU'RE NO STRANGER TO THIS TWI-LIGHT REALM, I KNOW.
SO TELL ME--
HAVE YOU EVER SEEN SUCH WOOD-LANDS, ANY-WHERE IN FAERIE?
OR HEARD A RIVER MAKE SUCH MUSIC?
NO.
YOU HAVEN'T.

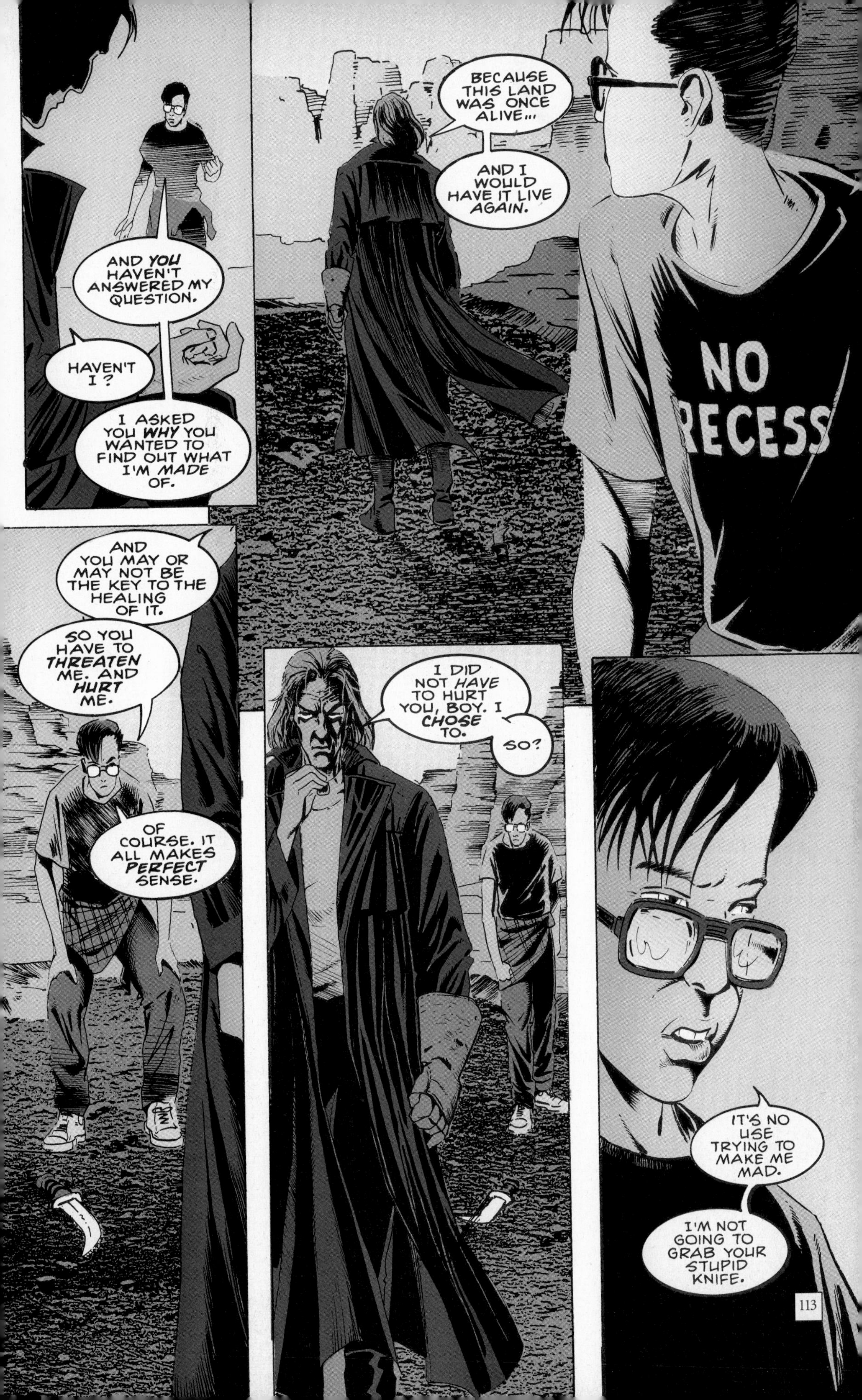

AND YOU HAVEN'T ANSWERED MY QUESTION.
HAVEN'T I?
I ASKED YOU WHY YOU WANTED TO FIND OUT WHAT I'M MADE OF.
BECAUSE THIS LAND WAS ONCE ALIVE...
AND I WOULD HAVE IT LIVE AGAIN.
NO RECESS
AND YOU MAY OR MAY NOT BE THE KEY TO THE HEALING OF IT.
SO YOU HAVE TO THREATEN ME. AND HURT ME.
OF COURSE. IT ALL MAKES PERFECT SENSE.
I DID NOT HAVE TO HURT YOU, BOY. I CHOSE TO.
SO?
IT'S NO USE TRYING TO MAKE ME MAD.
I'M NOT GOING TO GRAB YOUR STUPID KNIFE.

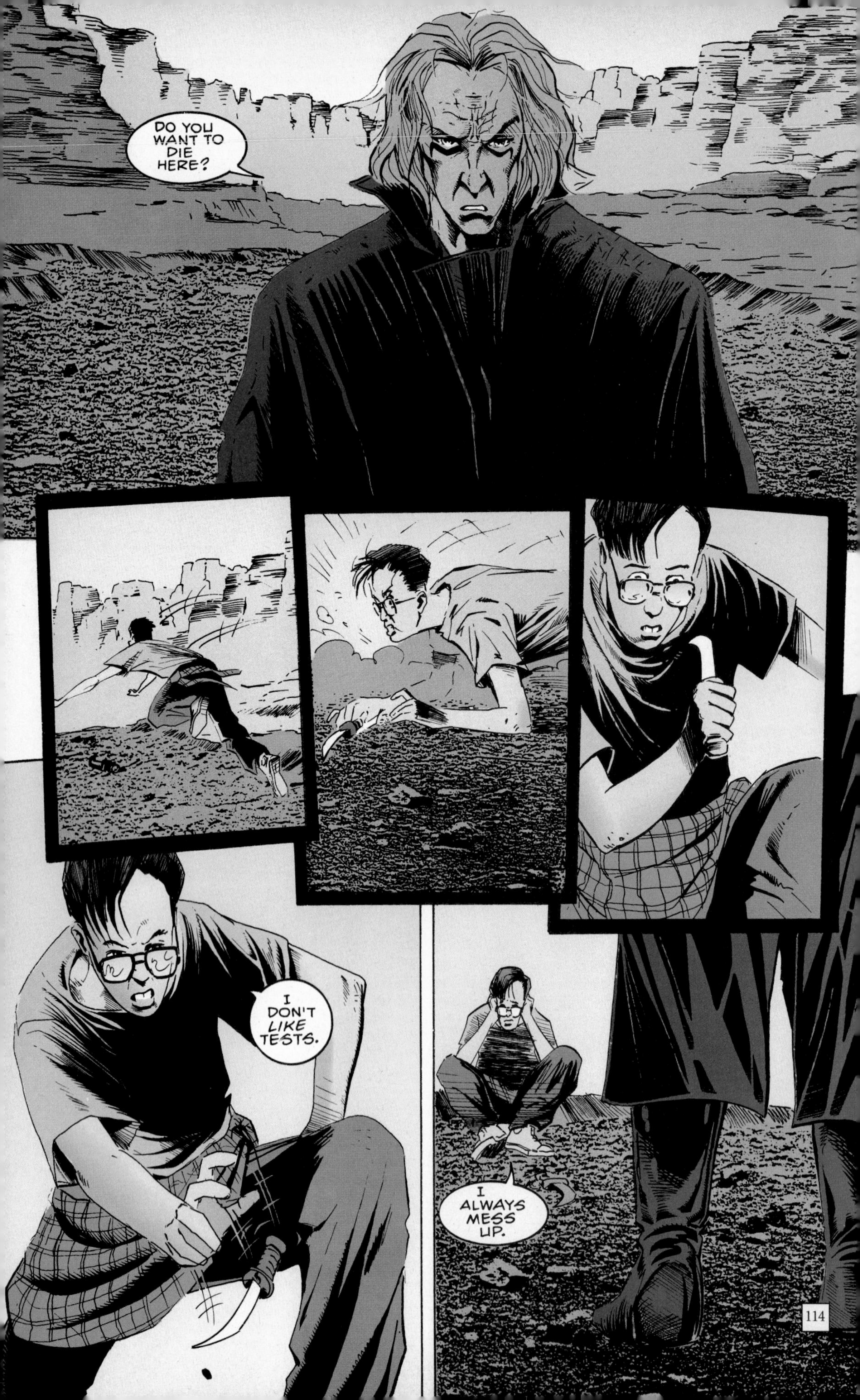
DO YOU WANT TO DIE HERE?
I DON'T LIKE TESTS.
I ALWAYS MESS UP.

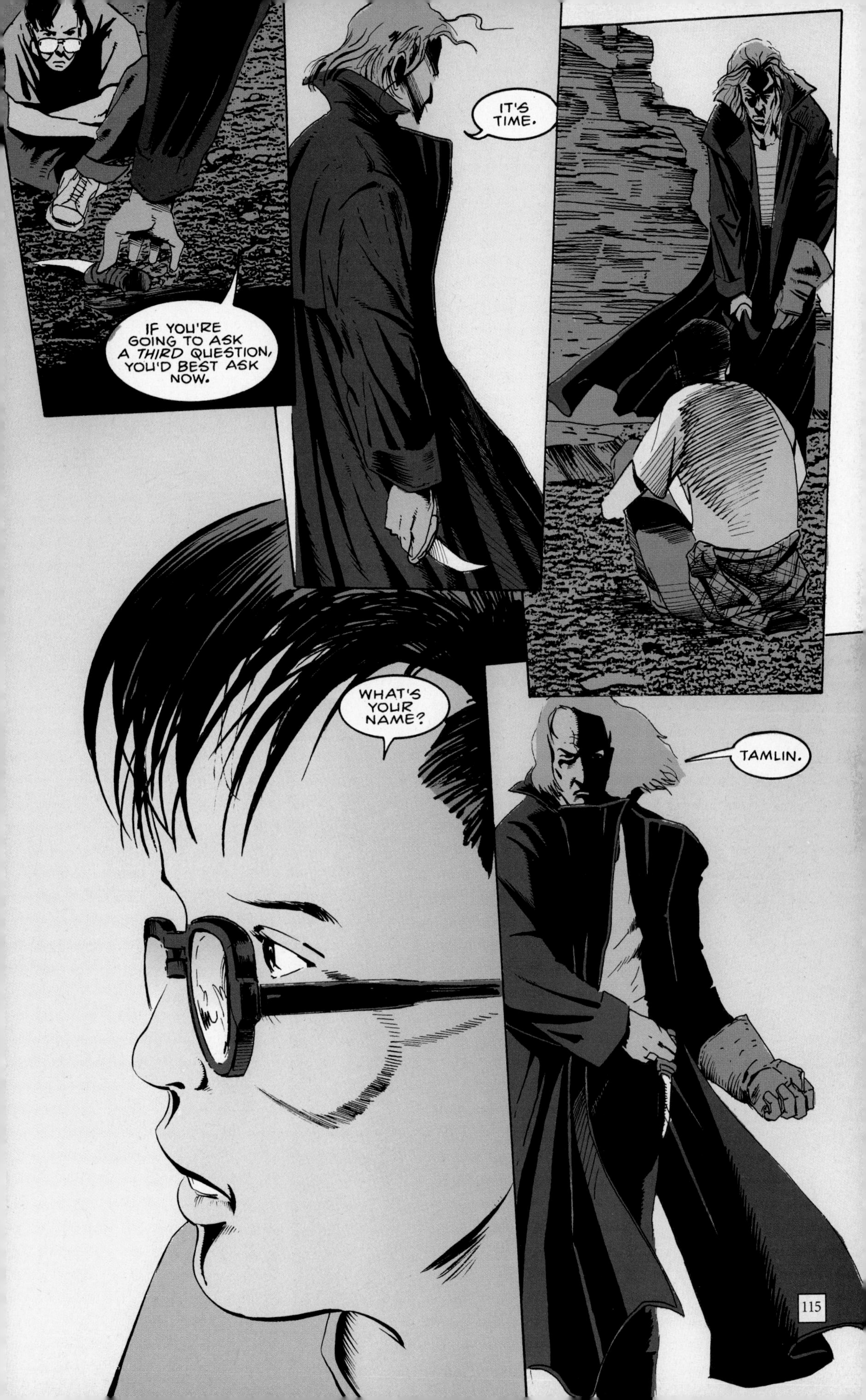
IF YOU'RE GOING TO ASK A *THIRD* QUESTION, YOU'D BEST ASK NOW.
IT'S TIME.
WHAT'S YOUR NAME?
TAMLIN.

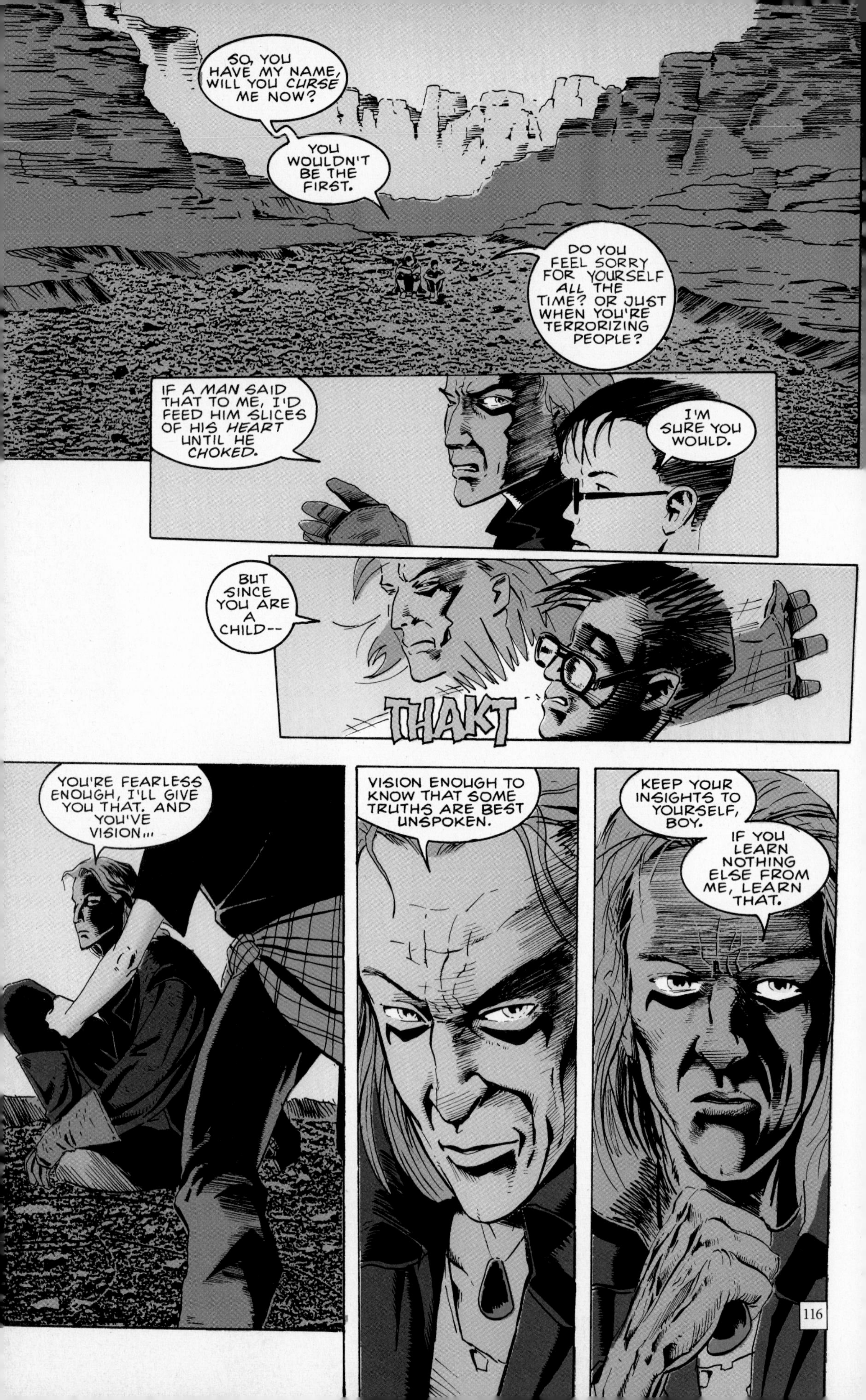
SO, YOU HAVE MY NAME, WILL YOU CURSE ME NOW?
YOU WOULDN'T BE THE FIRST.
DO YOU FEEL SORRY FOR YOURSELF ALL THE TIME? OR JUST WHEN YOU'RE TERRORIZING PEOPLE?
IF A MAN SAID THAT TO ME, I'D FEED HIM SLICES OF HIS HEART UNTIL HE CHOKED.
I'M SURE YOU WOULD.
BUT SINCE YOU ARE A CHILD--
THAKT
YOU'RE FEARLESS ENOUGH, I'LL GIVE YOU THAT. AND YOU'VE VISION...
VISION ENOUGH TO KNOW THAT SOME TRUTHS ARE BEST UNSPOKEN.
KEEP YOUR INSIGHTS TO YOURSELF, BOY.
IF YOU LEARN NOTHING ELSE FROM ME, LEARN THAT.

YOU'VE DONE *WELL*, HUNTER.

VERY *WELL.*

SNAP

unhh...

I HAD NOT THOUGHT YOU WOULD.

THIS IS YOURS *NOW.*

TAKE IT.

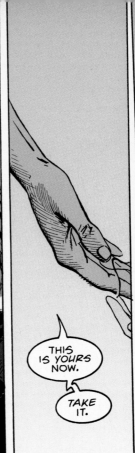

WHAT-- WHAT IS IT?

IN *YOUR* HAND? I CAN'T SAY. IT COULD BE I'VE DARED MY QUEEN'S ANGER AND MUCH ELSE TO GIVE YOU *NOTHING.*

SOME THINGS ARE WHAT YOU MAKE OF THEM.

TAKE THESE TOO.

IF YOU WANT THEM.

117

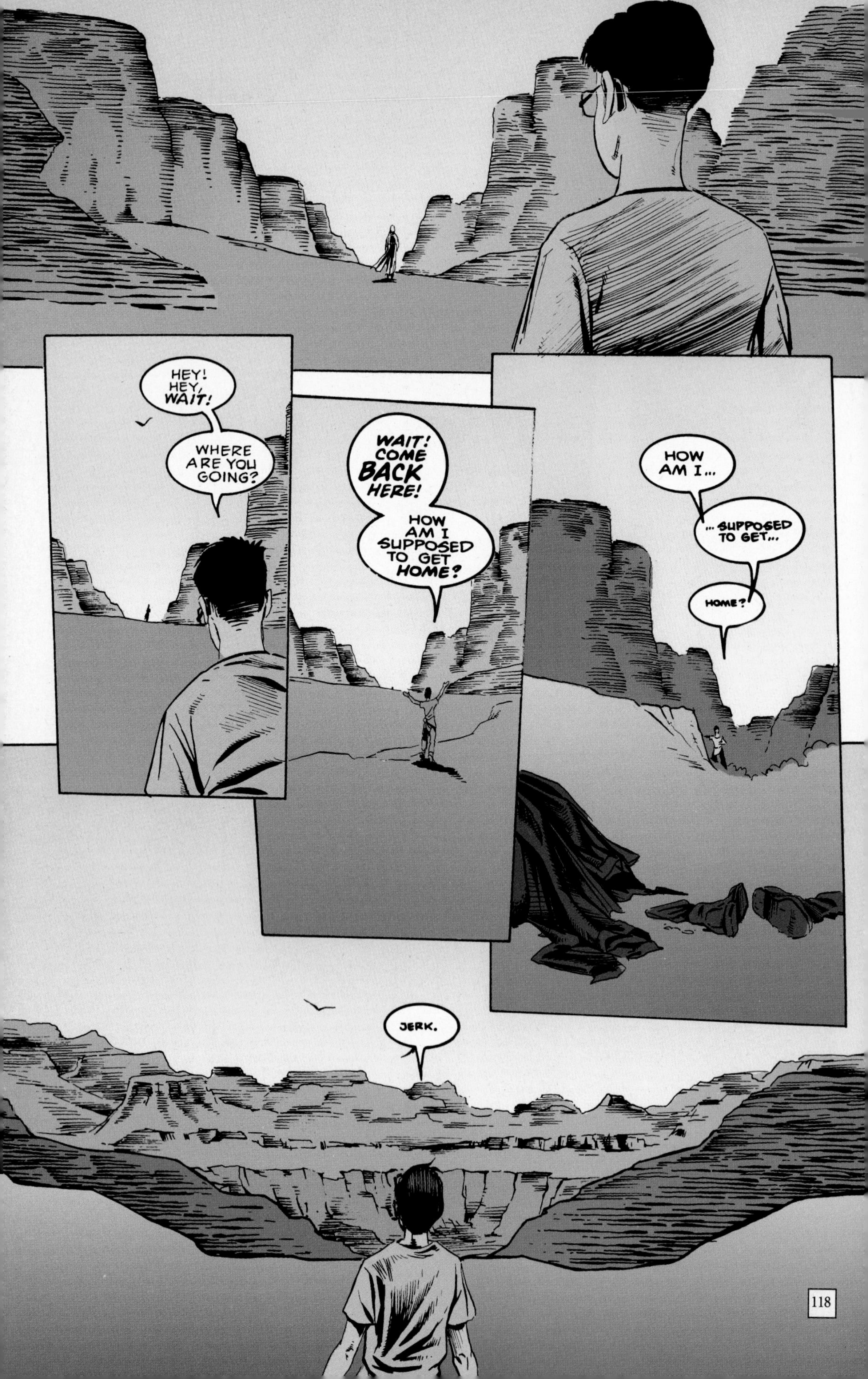
HEY! HEY, WAIT!
WHERE ARE YOU GOING?
WAIT! COME BACK HERE!
HOW AM I SUPPOSED TO GET HOME?
HOW AM I...
...SUPPOSED TO GET...
HOME?
JERK.

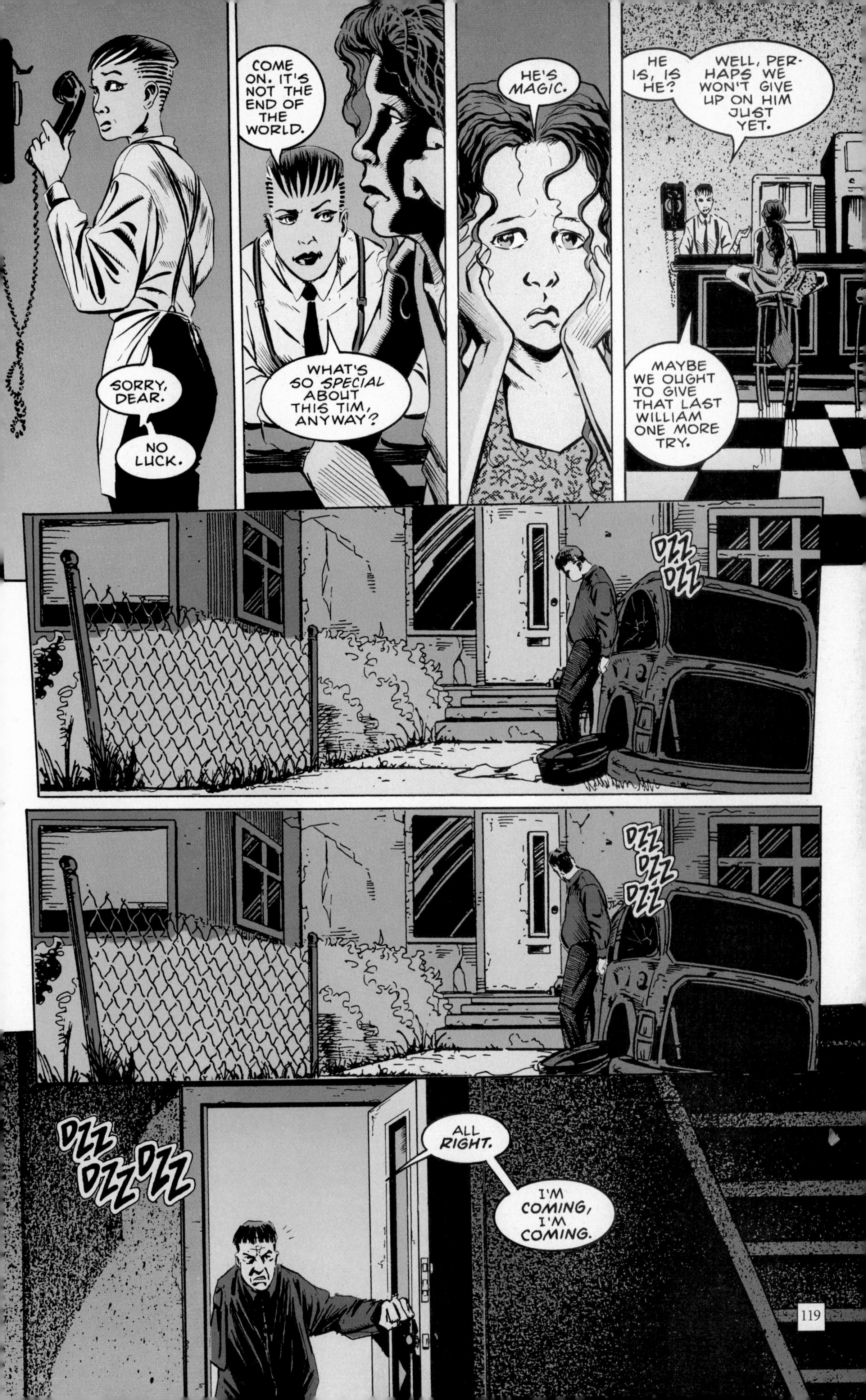
SORRY, DEAR.
NO LUCK.
COME ON. IT'S NOT THE END OF THE WORLD.
WHAT'S SO SPECIAL ABOUT THIS TIM, ANYWAY?
HE'S MAGIC.
HE IS, IS HE?
WELL, PERHAPS WE WON'T GIVE UP ON HIM JUST YET.
MAYBE WE OUGHT TO GIVE THAT LAST WILLIAM ONE MORE TRY.
DZZ DZZ
DZZ DZZ DZZ
DZZ DZZ DZZ
ALL RIGHT.
I'M COMING, I'M COMING.

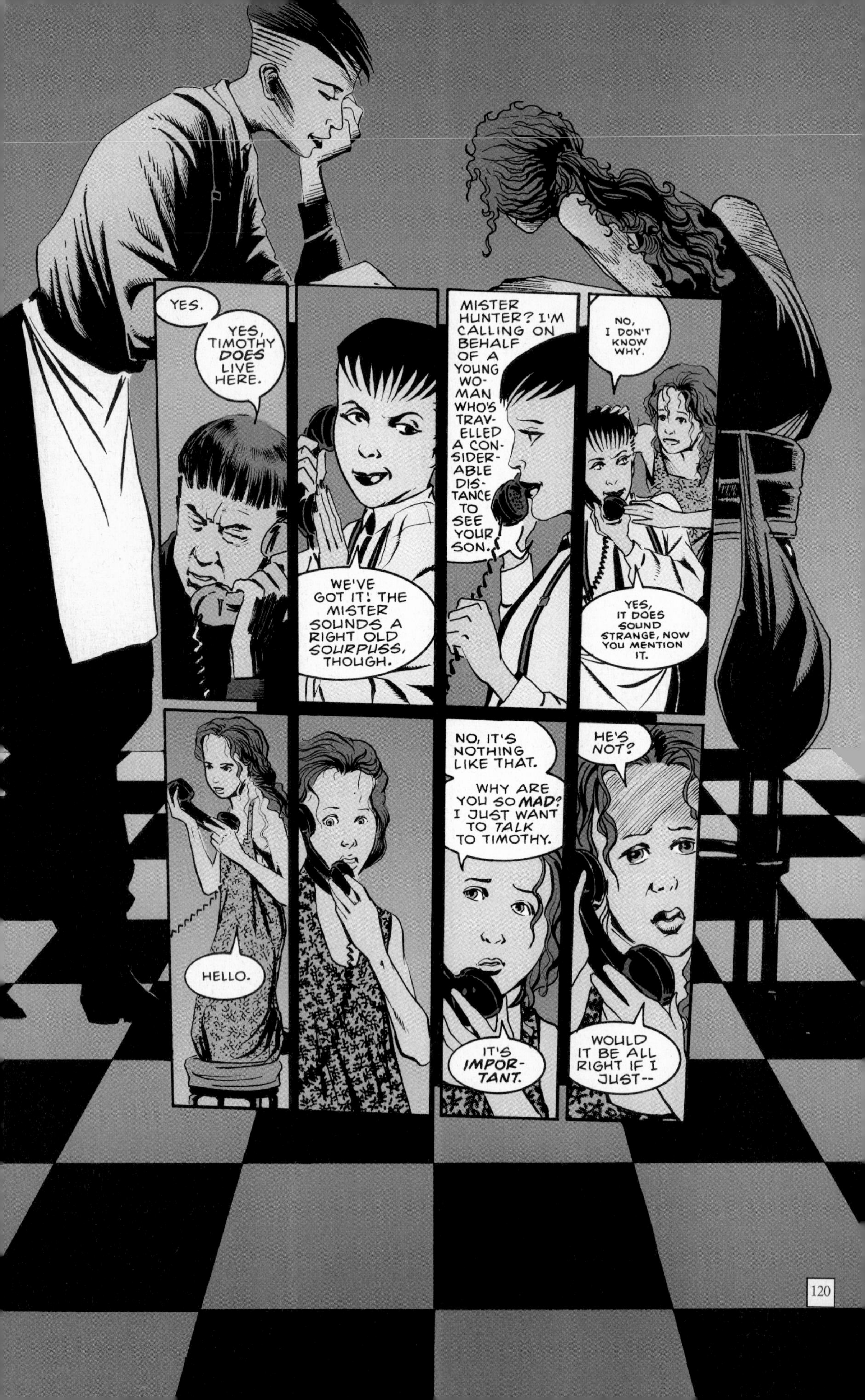
YES.
YES, TIMOTHY DOES LIVE HERE.
WE'VE GOT IT! THE MISTER SOUNDS A RIGHT OLD SOURPUSS, THOUGH.
MISTER HUNTER? I'M CALLING ON BEHALF OF A YOUNG WO-MAN WHO'S TRAV-ELLED A CON-SIDER-ABLE DIS-TANCE TO SEE YOUR SON.
NO, I DON'T KNOW WHY.
YES, IT DOES SOUND STRANGE, NOW YOU MENTION IT.
HELLO.
NO, IT'S NOTHING LIKE THAT.
WHY ARE YOU SO MAD? I JUST WANT TO TALK TO TIMOTHY.
IT'S IMPOR-TANT.
HE'S NOT?
WOULD IT BE ALL RIGHT IF I JUST--

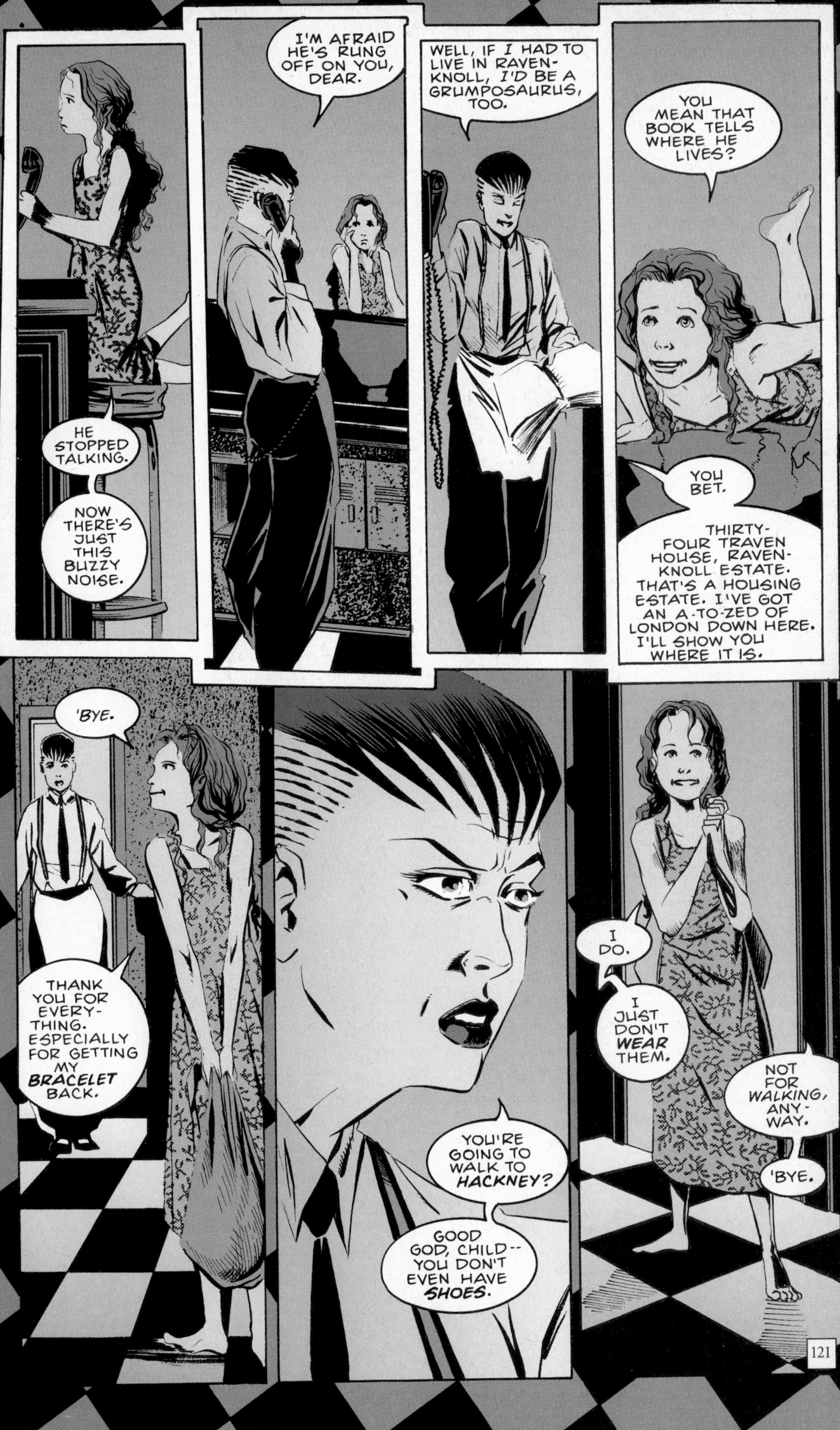

HE STOPPED TALKING.
NOW THERE'S JUST THIS BUZZY NOISE.
I'M AFRAID HE'S RUNG OFF ON YOU, DEAR.
WELL, IF *I* HAD TO LIVE IN RAVEN-KNOLL, *I'D* BE A GRUMPOSAURUS, TOO.
YOU MEAN THAT BOOK TELLS WHERE HE LIVES?
YOU BET.
THIRTY-FOUR TRAVEN HOUSE, RAVEN-KNOLL ESTATE. THAT'S A HOUSING ESTATE. I'VE GOT AN A-TO-ZED OF LONDON DOWN HERE. I'LL SHOW YOU WHERE IT IS.
'BYE.
THANK YOU FOR EVERY-THING. ESPECIALLY FOR GETTING MY ***BRACELET*** BACK.
YOU'RE GOING TO WALK TO *HACKNEY*?
GOOD GOD, CHILD-- YOU DON'T EVEN HAVE ***SHOES***.
I DO.
I JUST DON'T ***WEAR*** THEM.
NOT FOR *WALKING*, ANY-WAY.
'BYE.

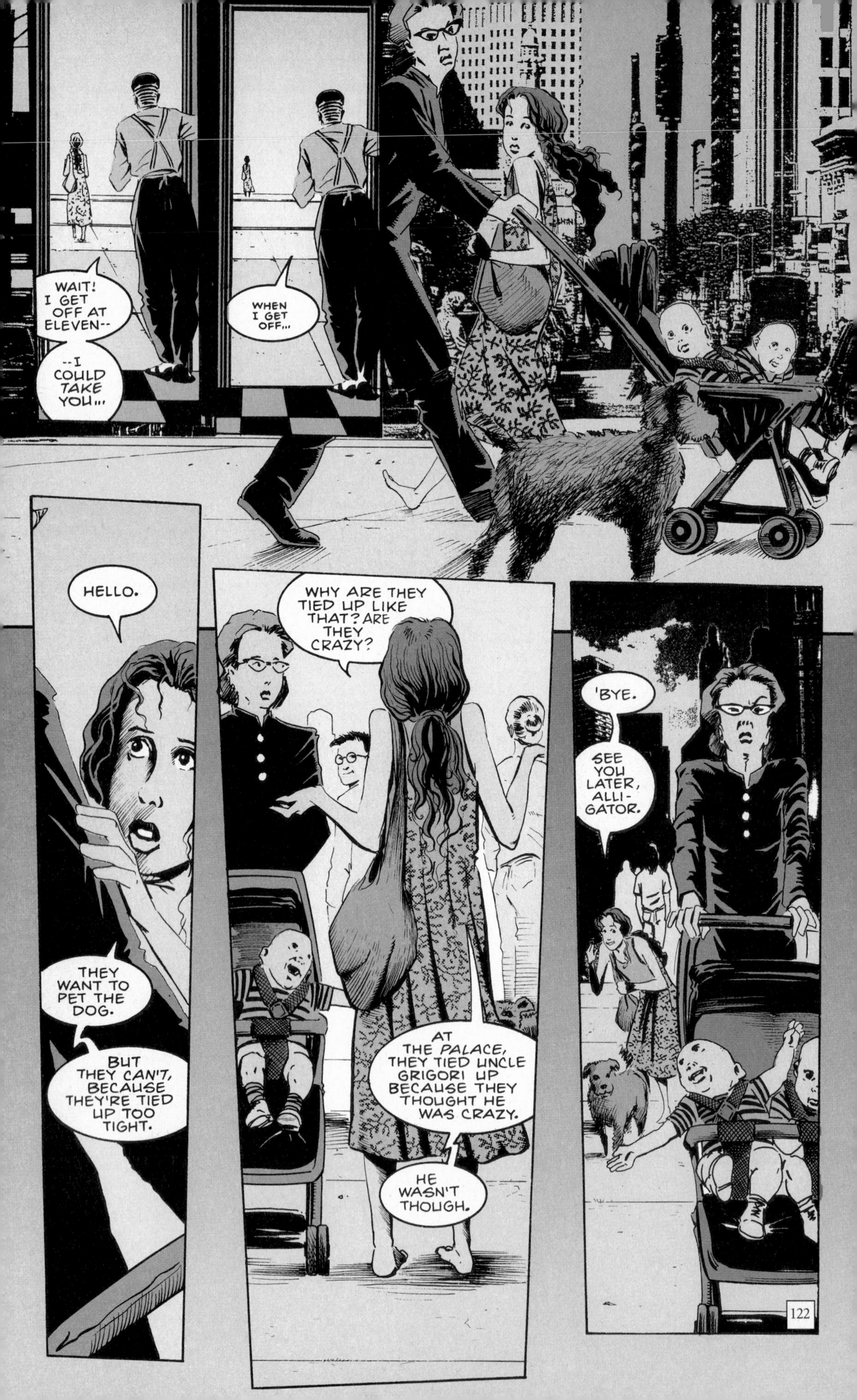
WAIT! I GET OFF AT ELEVEN--
--I COULD TAKE YOU...
WHEN I GET OFF...
HELLO.
THEY WANT TO PET THE DOG.
BUT THEY CAN'T, BECAUSE THEY'RE TIED UP TOO TIGHT.
WHY ARE THEY TIED UP LIKE THAT? ARE THEY CRAZY?
AT THE PALACE, THEY TIED UNCLE GRIGORI UP BECAUSE THEY THOUGHT HE WAS CRAZY.
HE WASN'T THOUGH.
'BYE.
SEE YOU LATER, ALLI-GATOR.

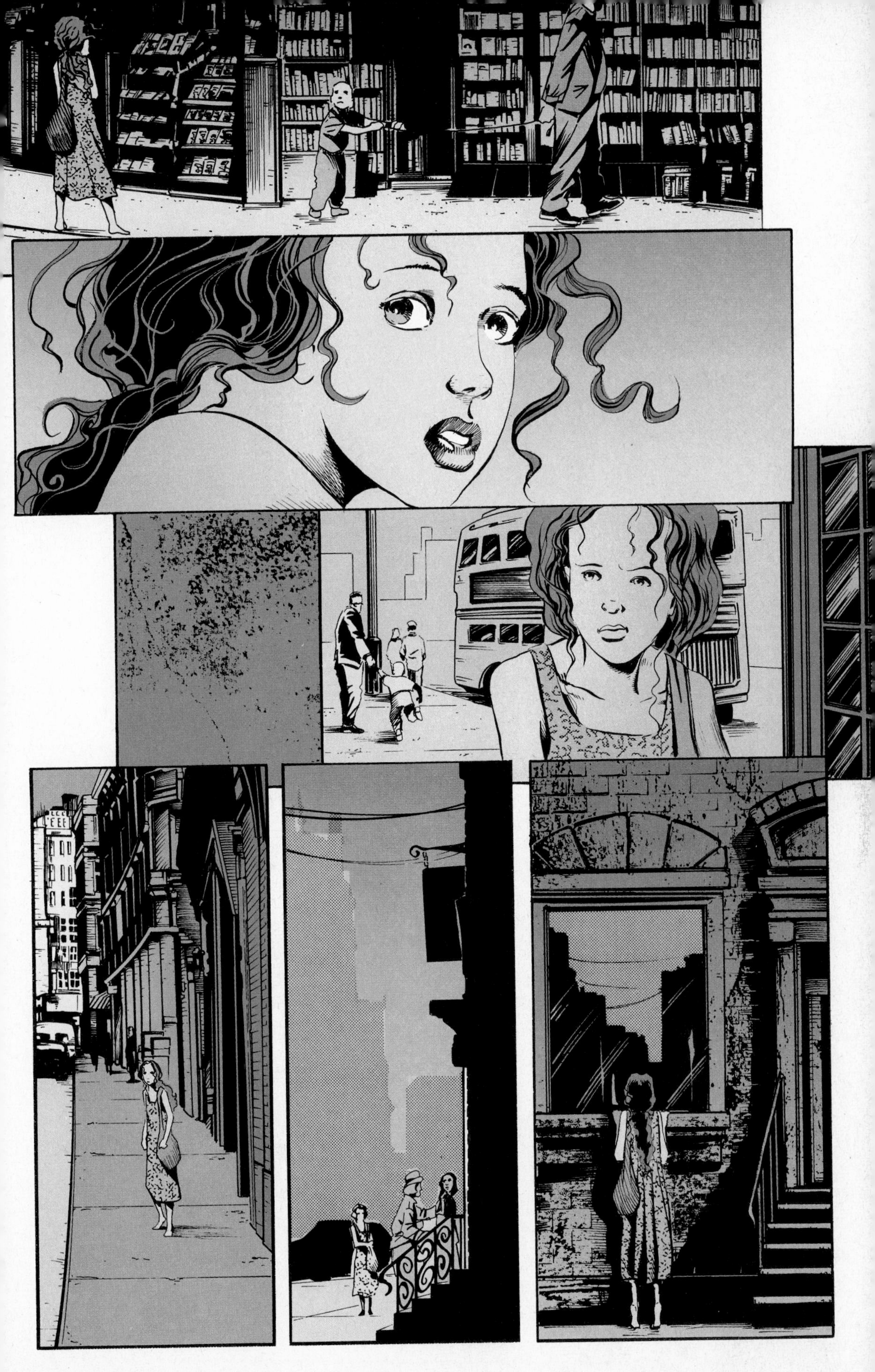

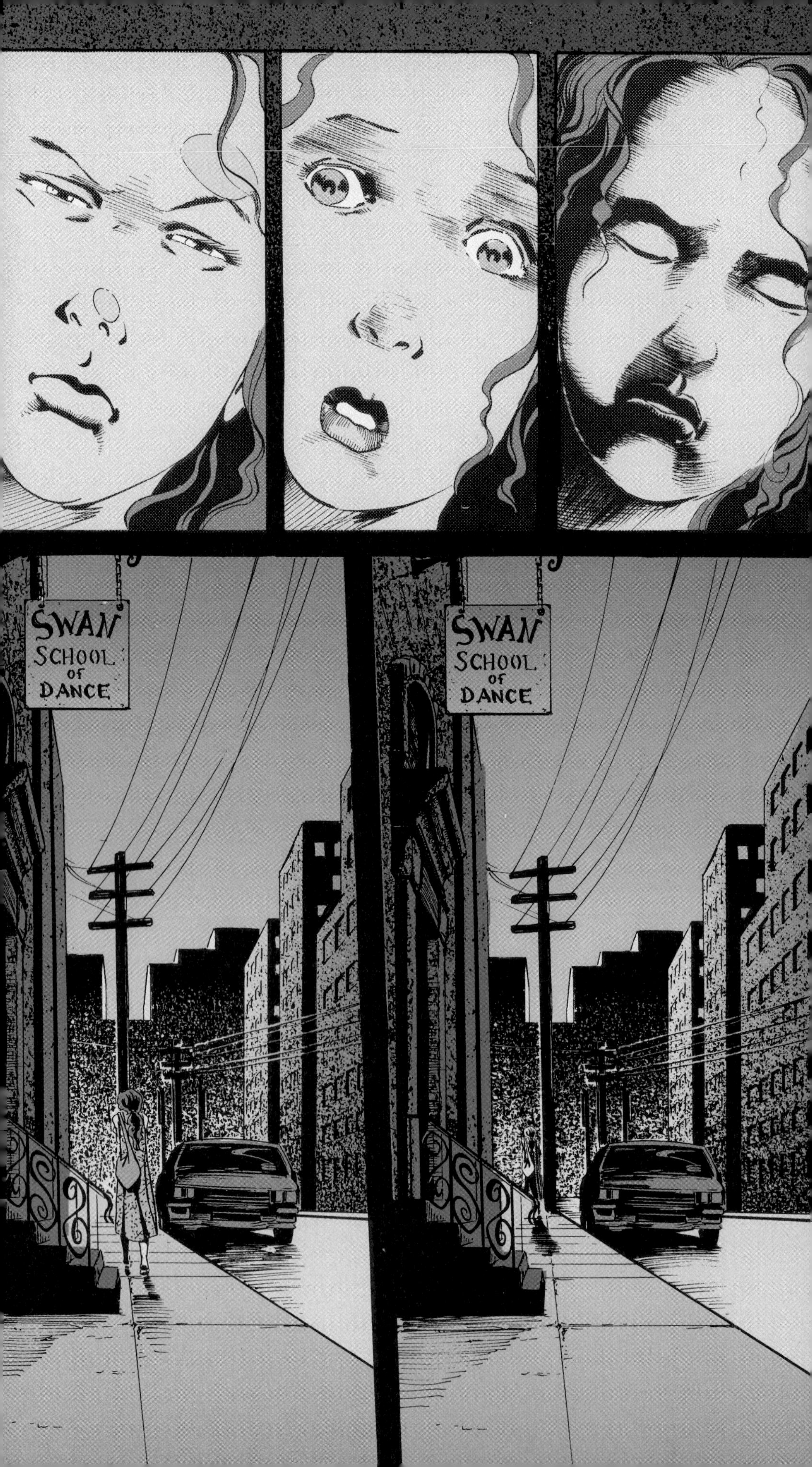
SWAN
SCHOOL
of
DANCE
SWAN
SCHOOL
of
DANCE

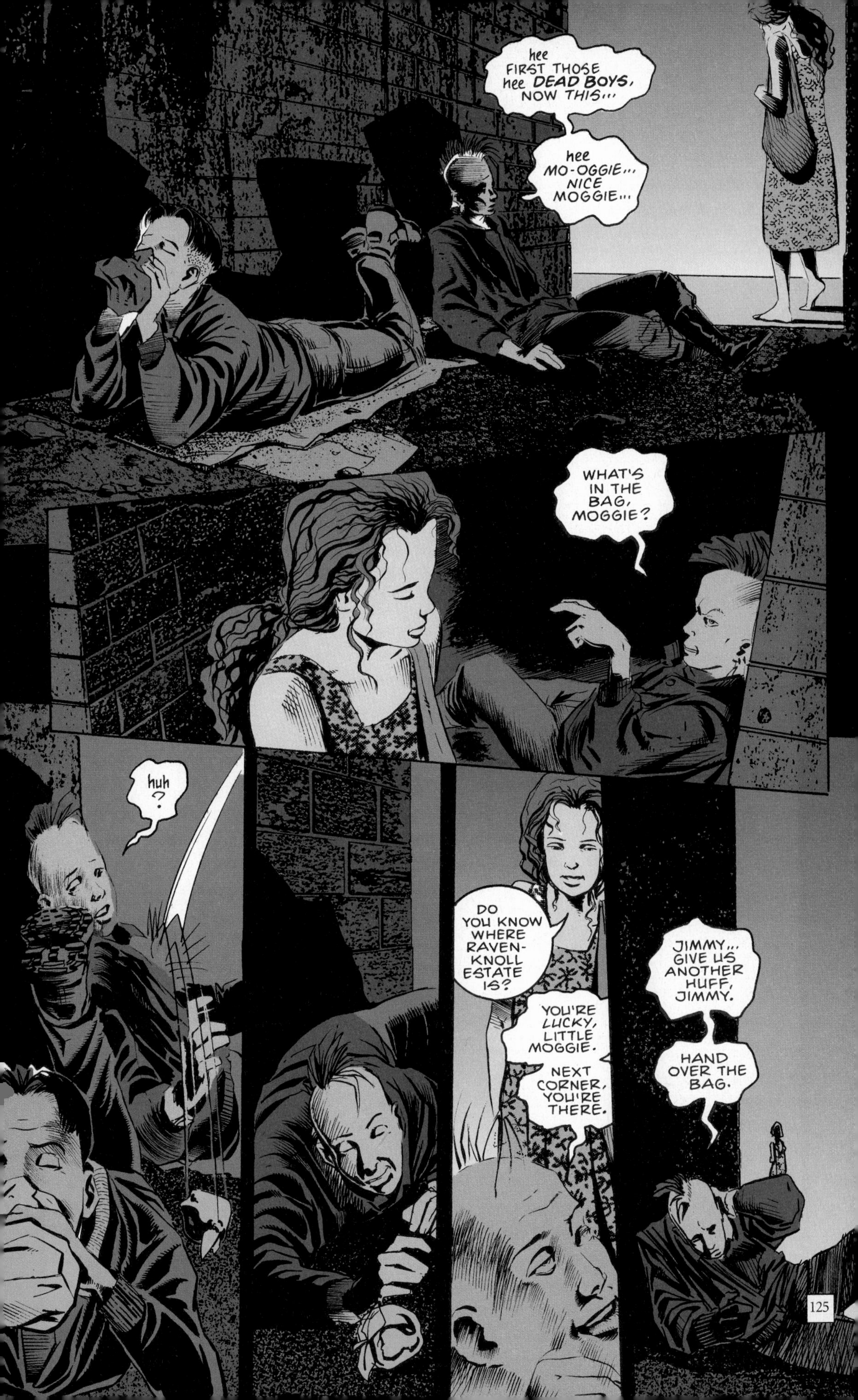
hee FIRST THOSE hee DEAD BOYS, NOW THIS...
hee MO-OGGIE... NICE MOGGIE...
WHAT'S IN THE BAG, MOGGIE?
huh?
DO YOU KNOW WHERE RAVEN-KNOLL ESTATE IS?
YOU'RE LUCKY, LITTLE MOGGIE.
NEXT CORNER, YOU'RE THERE.
JIMMY... GIVE US ANOTHER HUFF, JIMMY.
HAND OVER THE BAG.

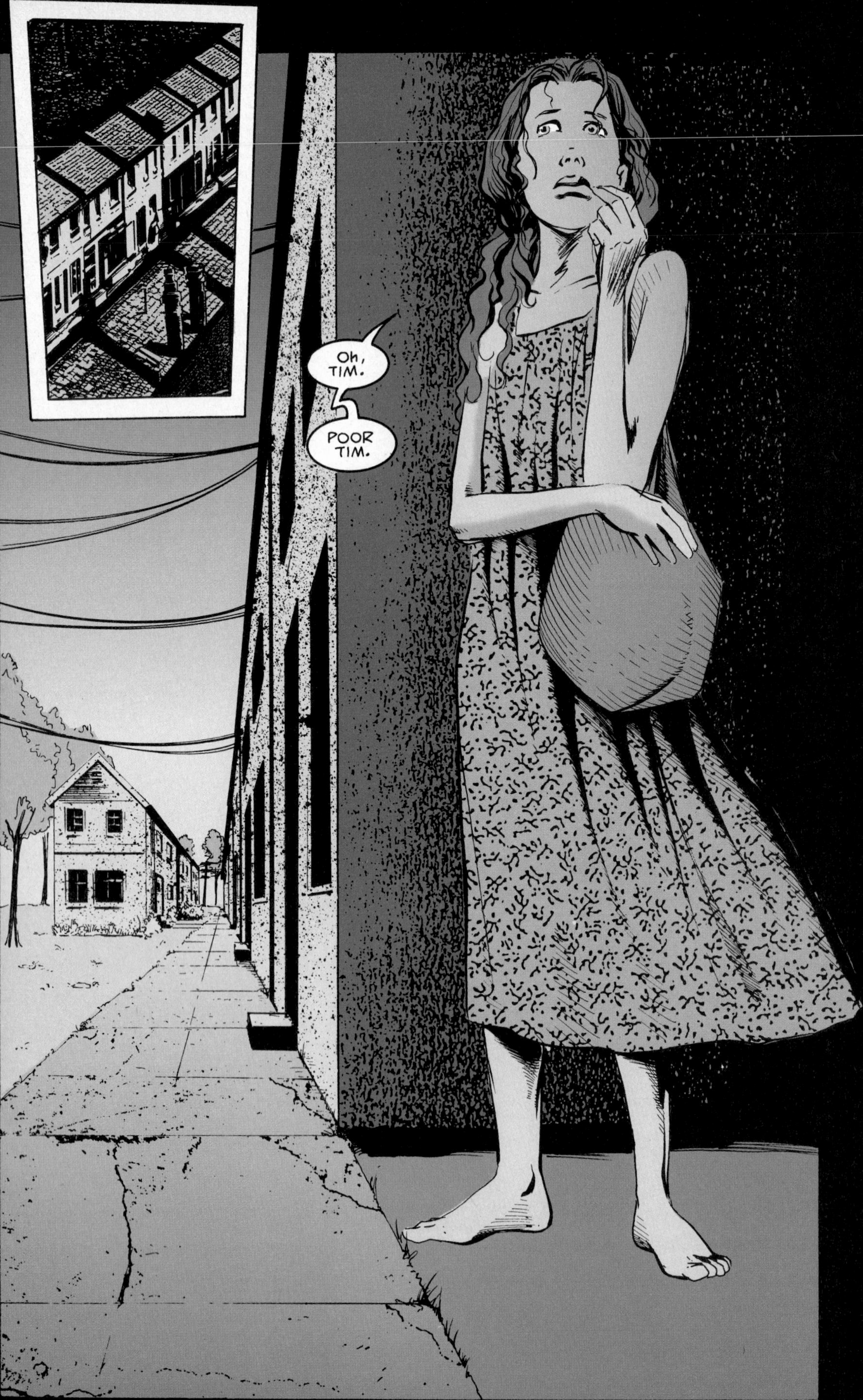
Oh, TIM.
POOR TIM.

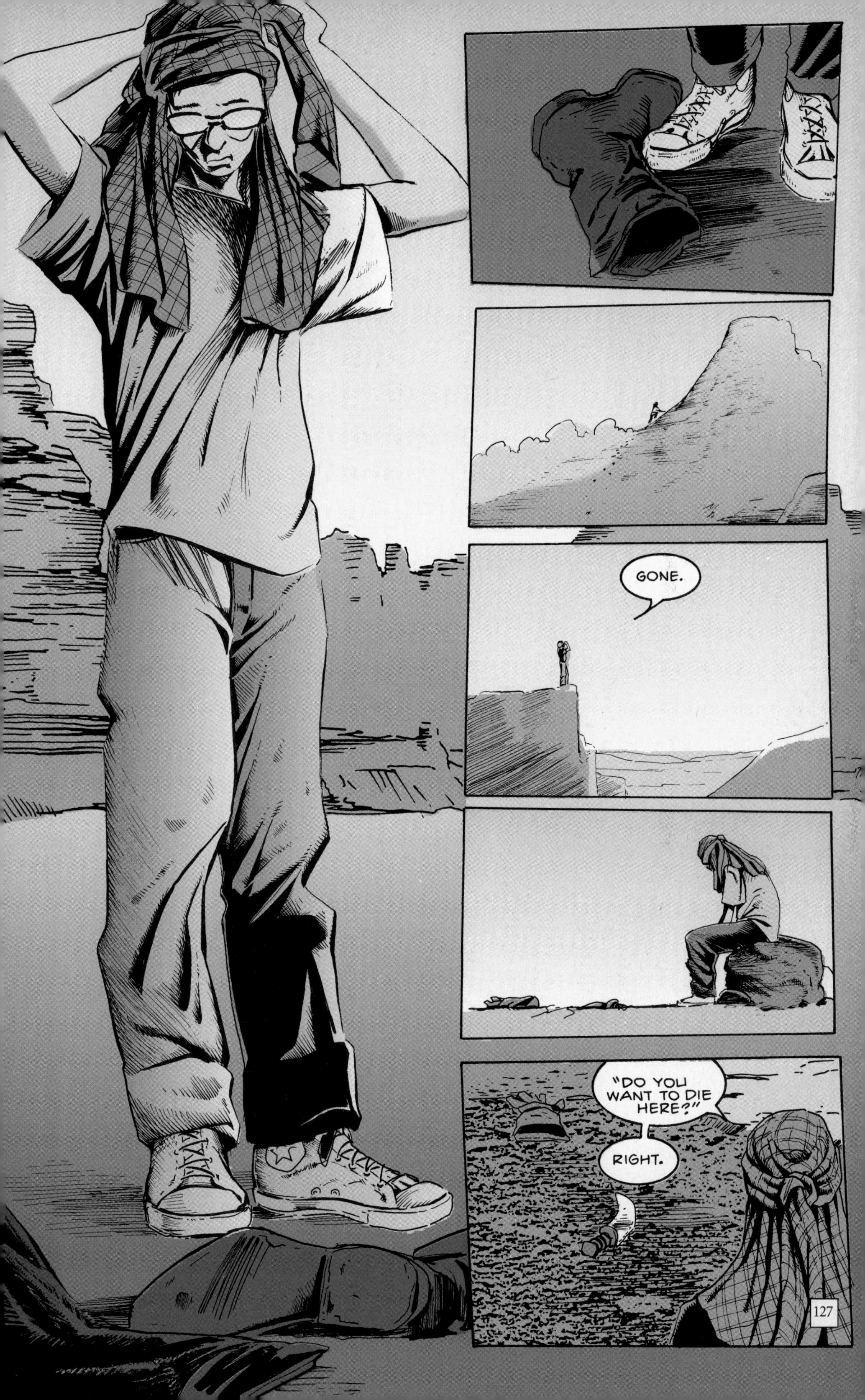
GONE.
"DO YOU WANT TO DIE HERE?"
RIGHT.

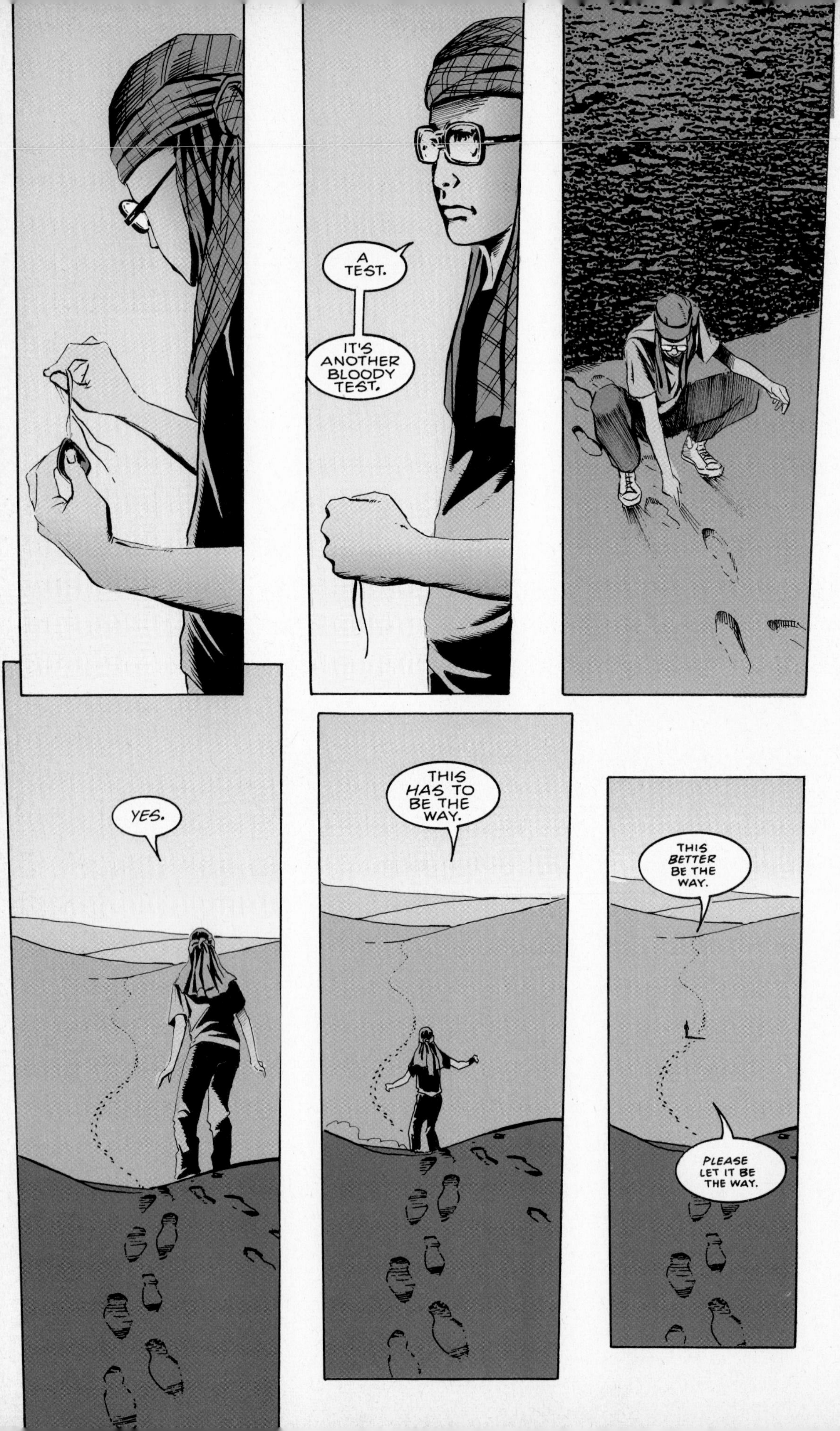
A TEST.
IT'S ANOTHER BLOODY TEST.
YES.
THIS HAS TO BE THE WAY.
THIS BETTER BE THE WAY.
PLEASE LET IT BE THE WAY.

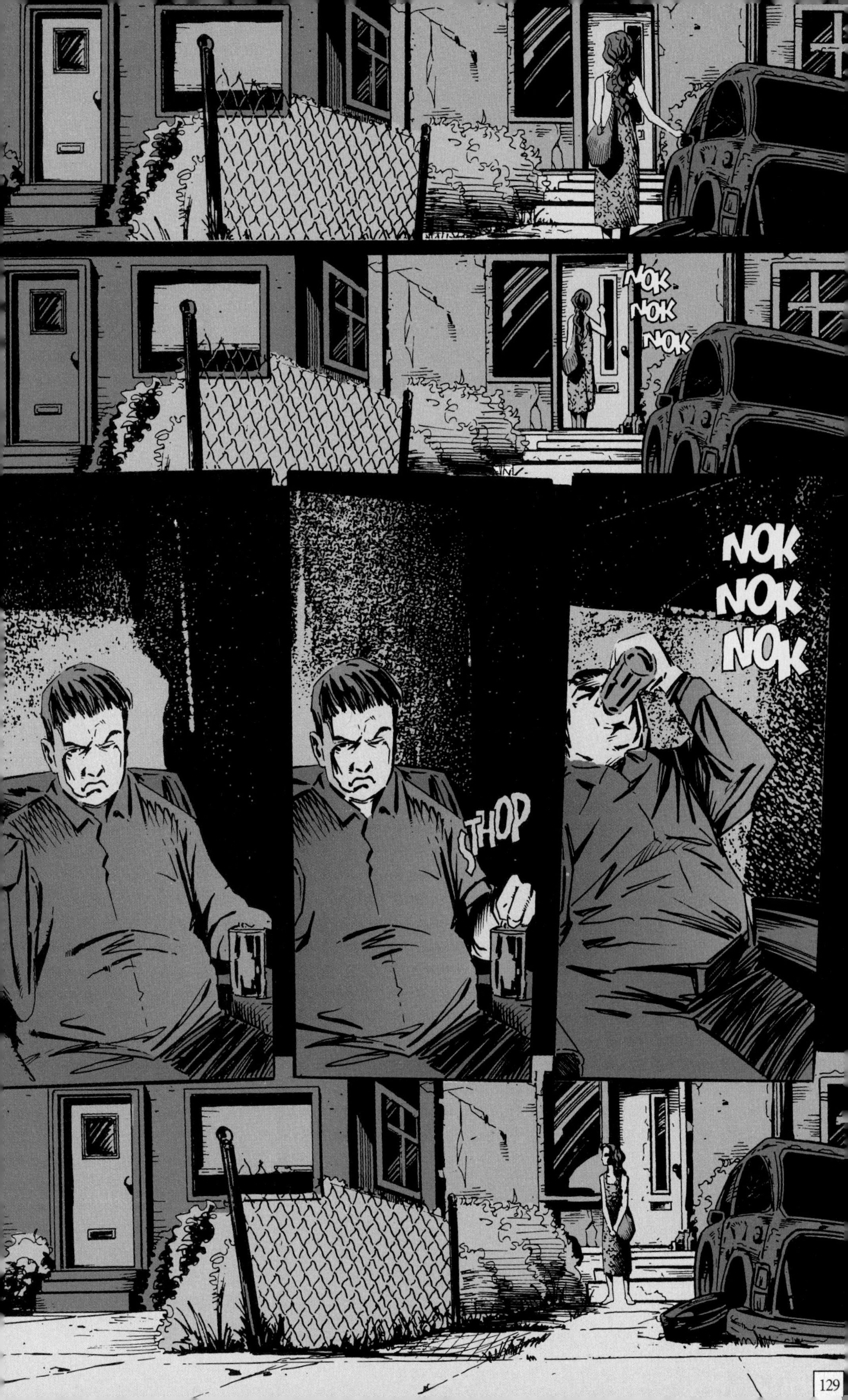
NOK
NOK
NOK
NOK
NOK
NOK
THOP

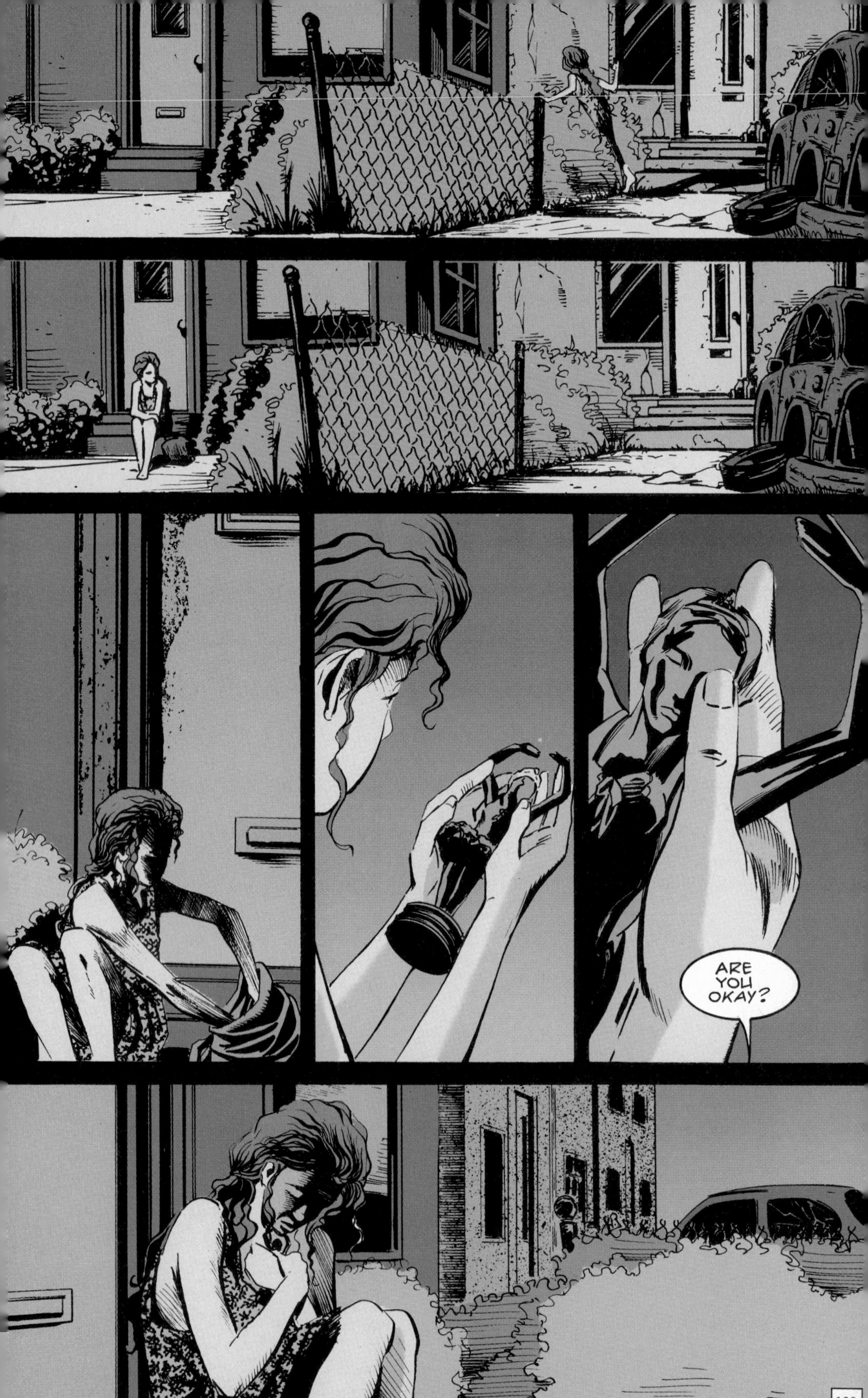
ARE YOU OKAY?

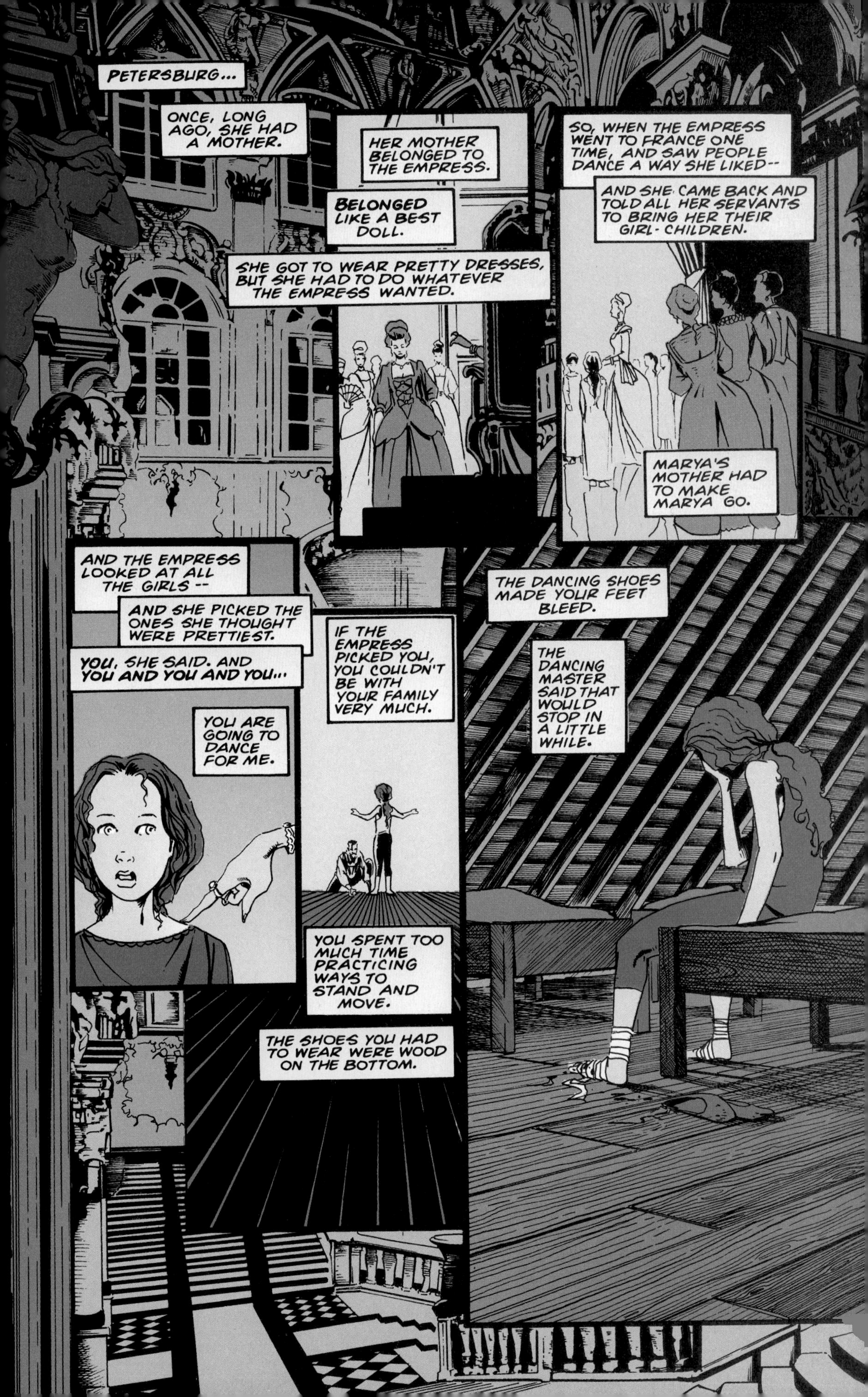
PETERSBURG...
ONCE, LONG AGO, SHE HAD A MOTHER.
HER MOTHER BELONGED TO THE EMPRESS.
BELONGED LIKE A BEST DOLL.
SHE GOT TO WEAR PRETTY DRESSES, BUT SHE HAD TO DO WHATEVER THE EMPRESS WANTED.
SO, WHEN THE EMPRESS WENT TO FRANCE ONE TIME, AND SAW PEOPLE DANCE A WAY SHE LIKED--
AND SHE CAME BACK AND TOLD ALL HER SERVANTS TO BRING HER THEIR GIRL-CHILDREN.
MARYA'S MOTHER HAD TO MAKE MARYA GO.
AND THE EMPRESS LOOKED AT ALL THE GIRLS --
AND SHE PICKED THE ONES SHE THOUGHT WERE PRETTIEST.
YOU, SHE SAID. AND YOU AND YOU AND YOU...
YOU ARE GOING TO DANCE FOR ME.
IF THE EMPRESS PICKED YOU, YOU COULDN'T BE WITH YOUR FAMILY VERY MUCH.
YOU SPENT TOO MUCH TIME PRACTICING WAYS TO STAND AND MOVE.
THE SHOES YOU HAD TO WEAR WERE WOOD ON THE BOTTOM.
THE DANCING SHOES MADE YOUR FEET BLEED.
THE DANCING MASTER SAID THAT WOULD STOP IN A LITTLE WHILE.

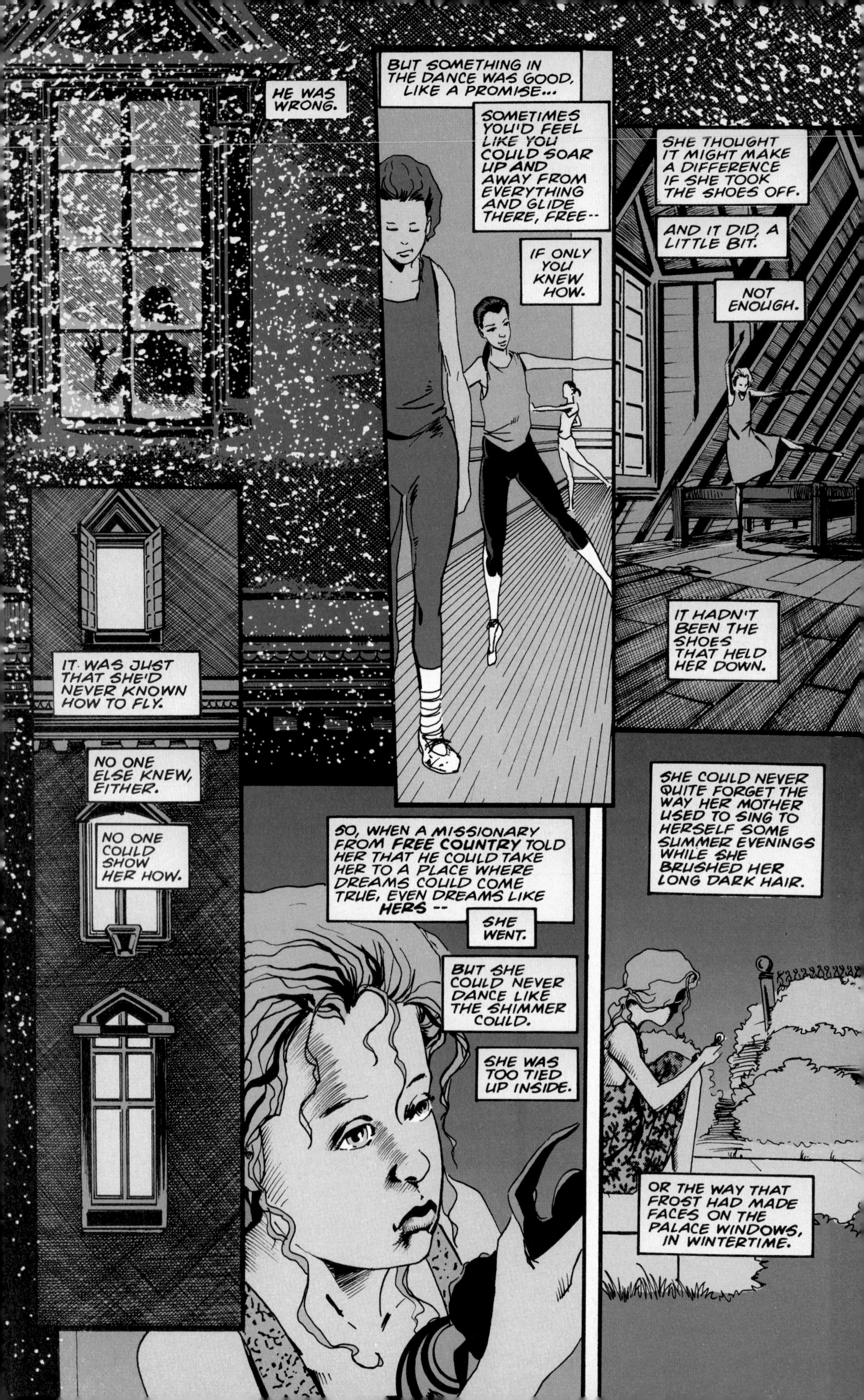
HE WAS WRONG.
BUT SOMETHING IN THE DANCE WAS GOOD, LIKE A PROMISE...
SOMETIMES YOU'D FEEL LIKE YOU COULD SOAR UP AND AWAY FROM EVERYTHING AND GLIDE THERE, FREE--
IF ONLY YOU KNEW HOW.
SHE THOUGHT IT MIGHT MAKE A DIFFERENCE IF SHE TOOK THE SHOES OFF.
AND IT DID, A LITTLE BIT.
NOT ENOUGH.
IT HADN'T BEEN THE SHOES THAT HELD HER DOWN.
IT WAS JUST THAT SHE'D NEVER KNOWN HOW TO FLY.
NO ONE ELSE KNEW, EITHER.
NO ONE COULD SHOW HER HOW.
SO, WHEN A MISSIONARY FROM FREE COUNTRY TOLD HER THAT HE COULD TAKE HER TO A PLACE WHERE DREAMS COULD COME TRUE, EVEN DREAMS LIKE HERS --
SHE WENT.
BUT SHE COULD NEVER DANCE LIKE THE SHIMMER COULD.
SHE WAS TOO TIED UP INSIDE.
SHE COULD NEVER QUITE FORGET THE WAY HER MOTHER USED TO SING TO HERSELF SOME SUMMER EVENINGS WHILE SHE BRUSHED HER LONG DARK HAIR.
OR THE WAY THAT FROST HAD MADE FACES ON THE PALACE WINDOWS, IN WINTERTIME.

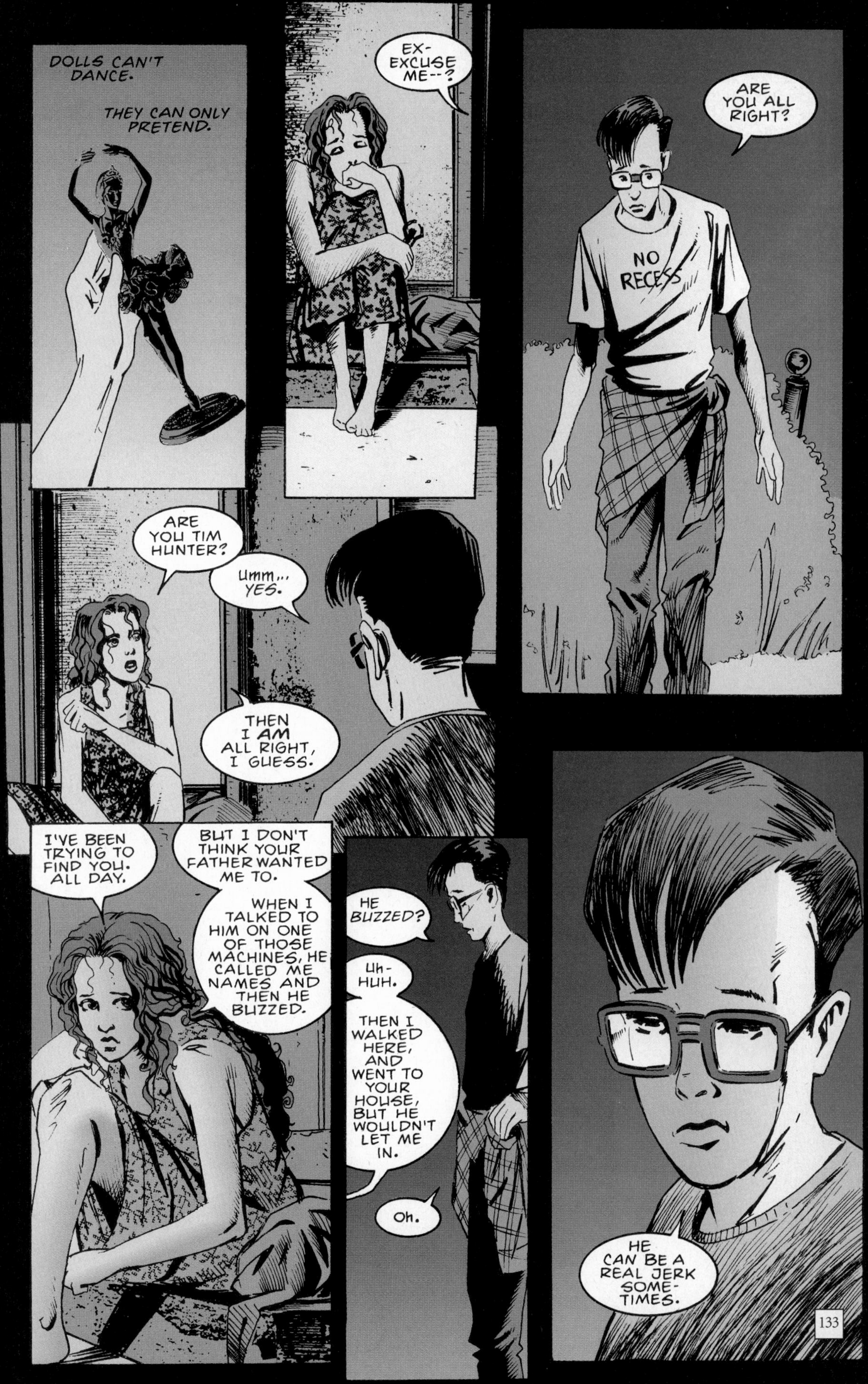
DOLLS CAN'T DANCE.
THEY CAN ONLY PRETEND.
EX- EXCUSE ME--?
ARE YOU ALL RIGHT?
NO RECESS
ARE YOU TIM HUNTER?
UMM... YES.
THEN I AM ALL RIGHT, I GUESS.
I'VE BEEN TRYING TO FIND YOU. ALL DAY.
BUT I DON'T THINK YOUR FATHER WANTED ME TO.
WHEN I TALKED TO HIM ON ONE OF THOSE MACHINES, HE CALLED ME NAMES AND THEN HE BUZZED.
HE BUZZED?
UH-HUH.
THEN I WALKED HERE, AND WENT TO YOUR HOUSE, BUT HE WOULDN'T LET ME IN.
OH.
HE CAN BE A REAL JERK SOME-TIMES.

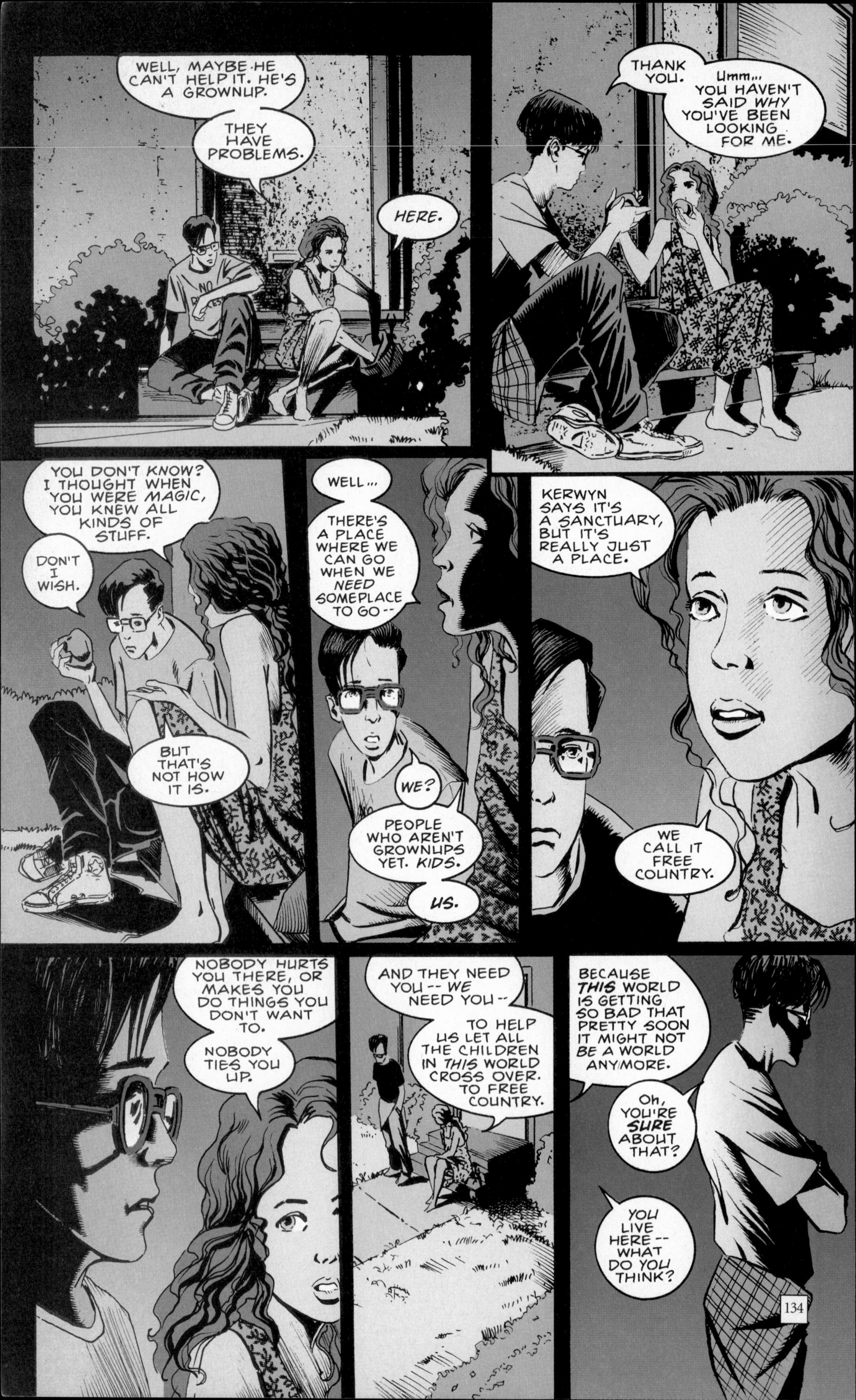
WELL, MAYBE HE CAN'T HELP IT. HE'S A GROWNUP.
THEY HAVE PROBLEMS.
HERE.
THANK YOU.
Umm... YOU HAVEN'T SAID WHY YOU'VE BEEN LOOKING FOR ME.
YOU DON'T KNOW? I THOUGHT WHEN YOU WERE MAGIC, YOU KNEW ALL KINDS OF STUFF.
DON'T I WISH.
BUT THAT'S NOT HOW IT IS.
WELL...
THERE'S A PLACE WHERE WE CAN GO WHEN WE NEED SOMEPLACE TO GO --
WE?
PEOPLE WHO AREN'T GROWNUPS YET. KIDS.
US.
KERWYN SAYS IT'S A SANCTUARY, BUT IT'S REALLY JUST A PLACE.
WE CALL IT FREE COUNTRY.
NOBODY HURTS YOU THERE, OR MAKES YOU DO THINGS YOU DON'T WANT TO.
NOBODY TIES YOU UP.
AND THEY NEED YOU -- WE NEED YOU --
TO HELP US LET ALL THE CHILDREN IN THIS WORLD CROSS OVER. TO FREE COUNTRY.
BECAUSE THIS WORLD IS GETTING SO BAD THAT PRETTY SOON IT MIGHT NOT BE A WORLD ANYMORE.
Oh, YOU'RE SURE ABOUT THAT?
YOU LIVE HERE -- WHAT DO YOU THINK?

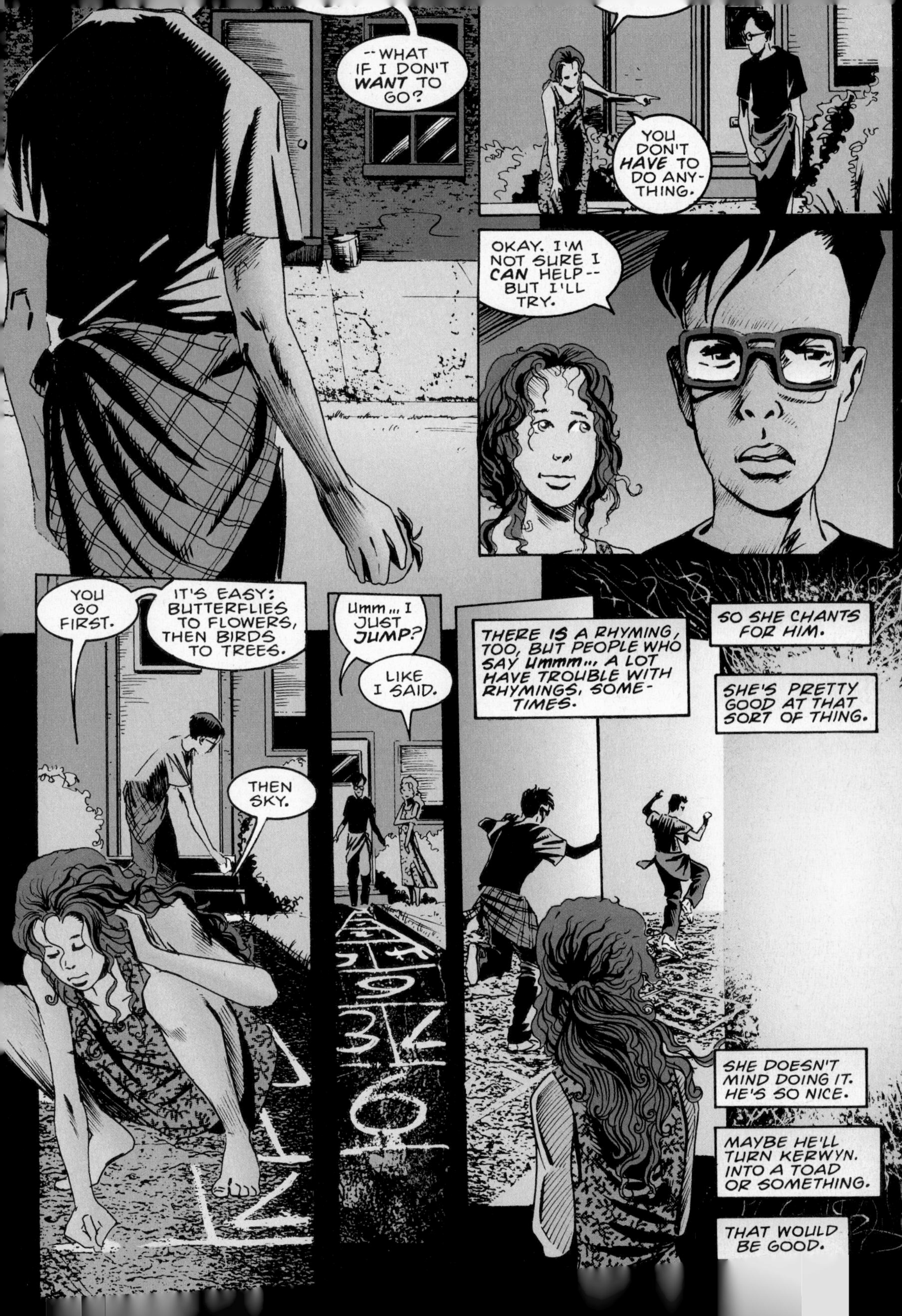
--WHAT IF I DON'T WANT TO GO?
YOU DON'T HAVE TO DO ANYTHING.
OKAY. I'M NOT SURE I CAN HELP--BUT I'LL TRY.
YOU GO FIRST.
IT'S EASY: BUTTERFLIES TO FLOWERS, THEN BIRDS TO TREES.
THEN SKY.
Umm... I JUST JUMP?
LIKE I SAID.
THERE IS A RHYMING, TOO, BUT PEOPLE WHO SAY Ummm... A LOT HAVE TROUBLE WITH RHYMINGS, SOMETIMES.
SO SHE CHANTS FOR HIM.
SHE'S PRETTY GOOD AT THAT SORT OF THING.
SHE DOESN'T MIND DOING IT. HE'S SO NICE.
MAYBE HE'LL TURN KERWYN INTO A TOAD OR SOMETHING.
THAT WOULD BE GOOD.

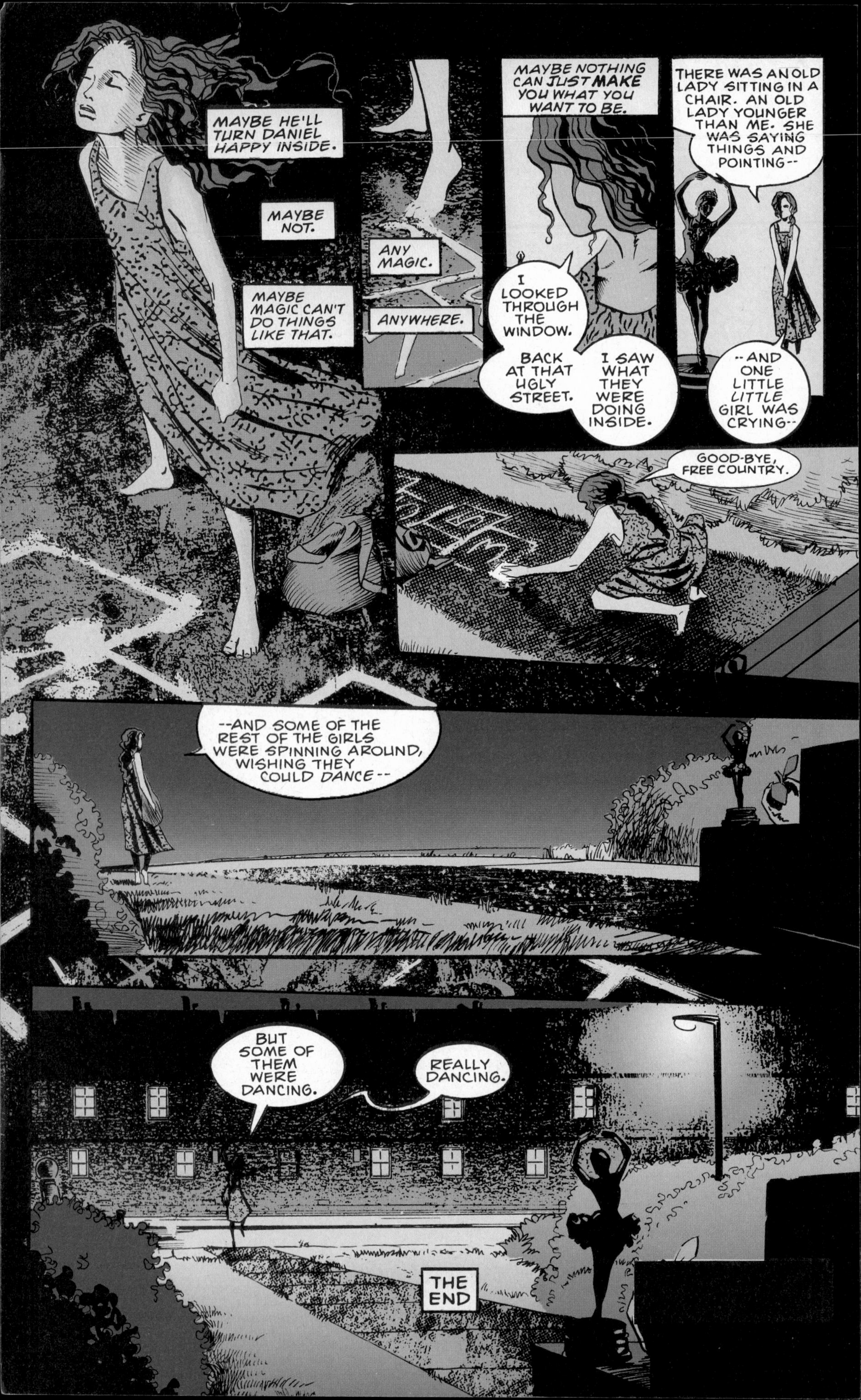
MAYBE HE'LL TURN DANIEL HAPPY INSIDE.
MAYBE NOT.
MAYBE MAGIC CAN'T DO THINGS LIKE THAT.
ANY MAGIC.
ANYWHERE.
MAYBE NOTHING CAN JUST MAKE YOU WHAT YOU WANT TO BE.
I LOOKED THROUGH THE WINDOW.
BACK AT THAT UGLY STREET.
I SAW WHAT THEY WERE DOING INSIDE.
THERE WAS AN OLD LADY SITTING IN A CHAIR. AN OLD LADY YOUNGER THAN ME. SHE WAS SAYING THINGS AND POINTING--
--AND ONE LITTLE LITTLE GIRL WAS CRYING--
GOOD-BYE, FREE COUNTRY.
--AND SOME OF THE REST OF THE GIRLS WERE SPINNING AROUND, WISHING THEY COULD DANCE--
BUT SOME OF THEM WERE DANCING.
REALLY DANCING.
THE END